AT LAST

AT LAST

VIVIAN MARR

Copyright © 2024 Vivian Marr

The moral right of the author has been asserted.

Apart from any fair dealing for the purposes of research or private study, or criticism or review, as permitted under the Copyright, Designs and Patents Act 1988, this publication may only be reproduced, stored or transmitted, in any form or by any means, with the prior permission in writing of the publishers, or in the case of reprographic reproduction in accordance with the terms of licences issued by the Copyright Licensing Agency. Enquiries concerning reproduction outside those terms should be sent to the publishers.

This is a work of fiction. Names, characters, businesses, places, events and incidents are either the products of the author's imagination or used in a fictitious manner. Any resemblance to actual persons, living or dead, or actual events is purely coincidental.

At Last
Music by Harry Warren Lyrics by Mack Gordon
© 1942 (Renewed) Twentieth Century Music Corporation
All Rights Controlled and Administered by Emi Feist Catalog Inc. (Publishing)
and Alfred Music (Print)
All Rights Reserved
Used by Permission of Alfred Music

Forever And Ever (And Ever)
Words and Music by Robert Costandinos and Stylianos Valvianos
Copyright © 1976 Allo Music Editions
Copyright Renewed
All Rights Administered by BMG Rights Management (US) LLC
All Rights Reserved Used by Permission
Reprinted by Permission of Hal Leonard LLC

Troubador Publishing Ltd
Unit E2, Airfield Business Park,
Harrison Road, Market Harborough,
Leicestershire, LE16 7UL
Tel: 0116 279 2299
Email: books@troubador.co.uk
Web: www.troubador.co.uk

ISBN 978-1-80514-203-4

British Library Cataloguing in Publication Data.
A catalogue record for this book is available from the British Library.

Printed and bound by CPI Group (UK) Ltd, Croydon, CR0 4YY
Typeset in 11pt Minion Pro by Troubador Publishing Ltd, Leicester, UK

Dedicated to my daughter, Elise, for her encouragement and belief.

Part 1

Chapter 1

She cried and she cried and she cried. The agony of leaving was hard to bear.

In the clear light of that quiet morning she had stepped out onto the terrace and looked down on the sea. A benign blue sea. A sea that would provide cool respite later that day. She would slip into it from the hot rocks. The awkwardness of stepping over them giving way in one surge to the exhilaration of free movement. Her nakedness feeling different, more sensual in the strong sea water.

Now, in the final hours of the day, she steadied herself in the buffeting breeze as she looked for the lights of his house on the dark island silhouetted against the dying light of the sky. That place which had affected her so profoundly, now receding from view and reduced to flickering lights on a black backdrop. She gripped the railing and looked down at the sea. The same sea but deep ink now and forbidding.

He would have already made his way up the hill. That wild breezy ride past small-holdings of olive groves, pistachio orchards, terraced clearings with hens and tethered goats, barking dogs. He would have driven the motorbike into the shelter; stopped, dismounted, pulled it back on to the stand. A rhythm of three movements, no more required. No need to remove the key from the ignition. He would have turned round and walked slowly up the stepped pathway through the garden. No colours under the clear, star-clustered sky but many smells. He may have crunched and scuffed along the dusty earth of a terrace carpeted patchily with old pine needles and dried-out grass. He may have weaved between the trees; olive, pine, fig, pomegranate, almond and laurel. He may have breathed in the night air and felt that frisson of connection with the earth below and all that he could see around him. He often made these meditative meanderings but tonight he may not have been in the mood. Tonight he may have headed straight to the house. He would definitely water the lemon tree later and she was sure he would now be standing on the top terrace watching the ferry leave the island, its lights becoming dimmer as it churned its way north.

The boat shuddered in the roughening sea. An unsettling vibration on top of the resolute rumble that was driving it away from the calm she had found in that bright existence. She could not relate that black shape to the enrichment and restoration she had experienced over these weeks. The sense of severance was visceral. Her throat felt clutched in a hot grip; wracking sobs issued from her aching chest. Her tears stung saltily in the warm wind. The lights were faint now and would soon disappear. She issued her silent plea across the glinting waves.

> 'You don't know how much you meant to me. How much you helped me. It was so much more than the passion, the sex. All of that was amazing, the best, but it went much deeper than that. You felt it too, didn't you? That connection. Life is going to be so much harder to bear without you. Please, please be there now, standing,

watching and please know that I am looking back and loving you. Yes, loving you even though we never talked about love. We couldn't go there, didn't dare to, but please don't forget me. I'll never forget you. Ever.'

She looked up into the infinite depth of the night sky, focusing her gaze on the brightest star.

'Are you there? Are you looking down on me? Please understand why I'm in this state. It was so emotional, so intense but you know you are the only one who really matters... It was so good to feel that you were with me. So far from home. That home I have to return to. Our home. It's going to be so difficult going back. Too difficult to think about. Living in a lifeless house.'

Her grief subsided. She felt tired and empty inside. Leaving had been inevitable but perhaps she would be able to return. Perhaps it would be possible to go back one day. Her mind was too exhausted to contemplate this. She turned away and walked towards the benches at the stern. There were people on the other side, a young couple making each other laugh, sharing a bottle of beer, casual, carefree. She would remain alone in this corner. She leaned back. The softly vibrating metal soothed her head as she closed her burning eyes. The warm airflow tugged at her hair. She would be home by mid-morning tomorrow. There were matters to deal with, to occupy her.

Returning to work and her life alone would be hard for a while. She knew though that the pain of separation would subside and that the wounds would heal. She was enduring a much greater loss and nothing else could hurt her as much.

She opened her eyes to the night sky. A wave of desperation passed through her. She closed them again. Oh to be pressed against him, naked together in the onshore breeze.

Chapter 2

The road rumble vibrated through the seat. Her body was relaxed, leaning against the side panel and window. Her mind was dazed, thoughts forming slowly for dreamy contemplation. She would remain relaxed until the bus passed the new hotel with its fashionable ground-floor bar. That was when she would focus her thoughts and pull herself onto her feet. She needn't worry about that for a while though. The cinema was only now coming into view. She had ten minutes until her stop would be reached.

She glanced at the film advertisements and thought of their male stars. Actors whose talent and worldwide fame had imbued them with powerful auras. Attractive men held in awe by many people. Men so different to her man, William. Her husband, so patient and understanding, so tall and thin, so much the antithesis of a film star's coolness and style. Yet the image of his careless, unkempt appearance made her heart glow warm and, remembering the sight of him naked this morning ignited a flame of desire deep within her.

She pressed her thighs together tightly and rocked discreetly from one buttock to the other. Butterflies of excitement fluttered in the pit of her belly as she recalled the urgent undressing, the desperate need to satiate their desire, the sensation of rolling around on the bed, the feel of their naked bodies, one moment pressed together, the next lightly touching. Suddenly feeling uncomfortable about her arousal she coughed lightly, shifted in her seat and tugged her skirt down while trying to think about other things.

Returning to her previous train of thought she began to think of female film stars. Should she feel pressure to be slim like them? She used to feel that to make the most of herself, to be as beautiful as she could, she should try.

She shook her head in regret as a mix of guilt and panic swirled inside her. She had stopped trying to lose weight soon after setting up home with William. Since then she had grown larger, more so in the last few years since turning thirty.

She loved that he continued to insist she was the most desirable woman he could imagine. Her heart glowed warmly as she thought of their lovemaking this morning. Of him telling her that she turned him on more than ever as she leaned over to look into his eyes, her belly squashing against his, tight as a drum, and her heavy breasts resting gently on his chest.

She was thankful that he was still so stimulated by her after seven years of marriage but was worried that the consequences of being overweight were becoming more apparent.

Her breathlessness and the ache of her heart straining as she rushed to catch the bus last week had alarmed her. Climbing the hill to the church had become more tiring. She had to arrive earlier now to give time for her energy and lung function to recover before choir practice started. Although fulfilling her husband's sexual desire was very important to her, he would have to make do with a reduced version of his wife. Looking after her own health was even more important. It was going to be difficult walking past Bertorelli's each morning without stopping to buy a latte and a pain au chocolat. Perhaps she would just buy a "skinny" latte. Was that made with fully skimmed milk? Would Giovanni have skimmed milk?

Was that Reverend Grandison coming out of the newsagent? No one else would wear that wide-brimmed hat. The jacket and trousers were ordinary but the hat was distinctive. It must have been him. Strange hat for a bland man. She could not believe that his services would be very inspiring. She needed the powerfully expressive worship her own church practised. Her certainty of this was now so secure that she no longer felt hurt when he seemed to disparage their ways of worship. She smiled as the prospect of choir practice filled her thoughts.

"*I'm going down to Jordan, I'm going down to the river to bathe.*"

The words and melody resonated inside her head. A thrill of anticipation fizzed through her heart. Singing with the choir was uplifting and a lot of fun. She was glad that she had been persuaded to audition.

The bus slowed down as it approached the stop. She grabbed hold of the handrail in readiness to pull herself onto her feet and disembark.

*

She slowed down to an amble as she passed El Paradiso. It looked like a pleasant place to have a drink. Fresh colours, light timber floors, comfortable modern chairs and sofas. It was not the sort of place they went to though. She and William went out rarely and never to such a fashionable bar. She tried to imagine them among so many smart people, many of them gay men. It could happen. They could go with Lionel and Stephen. She would laugh as she always did in their company, sometimes uncontrollably. They were like a double act with their effortless banter. Their humour had made her feel uncomfortable sometimes but she knew now that they would never take it too far. She had come to appreciate that they were both very kind and caring.

They were good people and it made no sense to her that her church should be so opposed to homosexuality. How could they justify their condemnation on the basis of strangely worded passages in obscure parts of the Bible? She felt her sense of wellbeing subside. Life could be so confusing with different parts of it at odds with each other. She should not need to think twice about going out with Lionel and Stephen.

She walked round the corner past the large plate glass windows of the bar towards Bertorelli's. She would ask Giovanni for a "skinny" latte. There would be hardly any fat in that.

She pushed the door open breathing in the mix of rich aromas and looking around at the salamis hanging on ceiling hooks, the cheeses on the marble slabs, the breads and pastries, the hams, the green olives, black olives and the tall shelves lined with packaged foodstuffs, bottles and tins. She breathed in again deeply through her nose. That was it, her favourite. The smell of fresh coffee. A smell that held the promise of stimulation, of mental clarity and feeling good.

'Morning, Maria. The usual?'

'Ah, I was wondering if you had skimmed milk.'

'Yes, I do but only the long-life stuff if that's all right?'

'Yes. I suppose that would be OK.'

'Just the one carton?'

'Well, no, I meant could you make my latte with it?'

'Oh. Are you sure? Might make it taste a bit funny.'

'Yes, I suppose it would. No, you're right, the usual's fine.'

'Are you sure, Maria? I didn't mean to be rude, my love, only...'

'No, Giovanni, you're right. It wouldn't taste right.'

'I use semi-skimmed anyway so it's not so bad... have you got your cup?'

'No, I forgot to bring it, I'm afraid.'

'Oh well, no problem.'

He moved off in a smooth glide, making the coffee on the gleaming Gaggia with the flourishes of a seasoned hand. He shouted over his shoulder as the steam hissed.

'Going to be another fine day by the looks of it.'

After placing the takeaway cup on the counter he grasped a pair of tongs and reached down to pick up a pain au chocolat from the pastry display and drop it into a paper bag.

'There we go. Your pain au chocolat.'

'Oh… right. Well, that's great. Thanks very much.'

After paying, Maria shoved her shoulder bag round before picking up the coffee and pain au chocolat and smiling at Giovanni as she moved away from the counter.

'Thanks, Gio. See you tomorrow.'

'*Ciao,* Maria. *A domani.*'

A woman in a smart suit held the door open as she entered. She watched impassively as Maria turned in response to Giovanni's shouted afterthought.

'Maria, Mrs Crawford's vine leaves are being delivered today.'

'Thanks, Giovanni. I'll pick them up tomorrow.'

Turning back towards the woman, Maria smiled guiltily.

'Oh, I am sorry. It's so kind of you. Thanks so much.'

The woman flashed a smile at her as she edged past.

Chapter 3

A sour smell filled her nasal passages and hit the back of her throat. She held her breath, tightening her nostrils and sealing her lips. She felt strange and less surefooted running down the stairs in smart shoes with a heel. The noise was different. They clattered loudly. Trainers and her other soft-soled shoes thudded and then squeaked when she turned round sharply on the concrete landings. She was uneasy about the loudness of her footsteps in these shoes, but continued rushing to reach the outside air as quickly as possible. The front door came into view as she rounded the last landing, wide open on its damaged hinges.

It was possible to close the door but the other residents rarely bothered to make the effort. They did not seem to care about opening the stair up to antisocial activity.

She kicked the takeaway food carton off the threshold as she raced out and down the short path onto the pavement.

She muttered angrily as she looked up and down the street with a sharp flick of her head.

Bastard. Where the fuck is he? And as for Dad, it's his own fucking sister he's letting down if I'm late, but he doesn't give a fuck. Lazy bastard.

Looking out for dog dirt she click-clacked along the pavement. She did not feel comfortable wearing Sharon's shoes and she was not convinced that she should be doing this. There were more obvious alternatives. Sharon could have set her up with something in her salon like hair washing and sweeping the floor or she could look for a job as a shop assistant or a waitress.

Sidestepping awkwardly between the parked cars, she glanced up and down before rushing across the road with staccato steps.

The fog of sleep now fast receding, she thought about her decision not to go for these more obvious jobs. She quickened her pace. She wanted to see how rich people lived and did not want to risk losing the opportunity by arriving late.

Sharon had described her as a classy old lady who suffered from arthritis and now required someone to help the woman who looked after her. She had been a scientist, Sharon said, and a successful businesswoman. She used to own the Pharmagen factory on the bypass. She had built the business up and then sold it when she retired. She must have made a lot of money because she was willing to pay a good wage. Certainly more than she could earn as a salon or shop assistant and probably as much as she would take home as a waitress.

She did not mind that it was a temporary contract to allow the carer more time off over the summer. Perhaps if she liked it they would extend it. She could tell them that she had changed her mind about going to college. She had never intended to go anyway and did not understand why Sharon was so determined that she should. Why was she so concerned about her future? Even her parents did not seem to care about what she did with her life. They warned her against doing anything that might harm her but had never given any advice about how to get on in life.

Her mother had said, "You can do better than this, you can do better than working in a bar and cleaning offices. It's up to you." But she never had the time or energy to talk about how she might achieve it. She was fully occupied with the early morning cleaning shift, afternoons and evenings working behind the bar and looking after Marlene, Kevin and Dad.

Her mother worked hard and rarely had time to relax. In contrast her father led an aimless, inactive life funded by invalidity benefit payments. Their very different attitudes to life and work were a cause of tension in the family. Thinking about this as she rushed down the hill filled her mind with hostile thoughts.

She despised her father's laziness and lack of consideration for anyone else's needs. It was difficult to understand why her mother had married him. What had she seen in him? She certainly did not seem to like him now although they still shared a bed. Charlene could not understand how they could bear to be so close to each other every night when they argued so much during the day, sometimes with seething aggression.

They never seemed to be happy together although she did recognise that she and Lee argued a lot too and that it was only when they were having sex that the irritations disappeared. In fact, she thought, the only possible way to avoid an angry confrontation today would be to repeat last night's performance.

She felt a surge of arousal as she replayed the experience in her mind. The constricted space had made it awkward and he had gripped her hips too tightly but she would do it again. All as before. From behind on the back seat of the car. Able to see out yet concealed from view by the dark windows.

It had all started with him leaning across to kiss her lips, his hand brushing across her exposed belly. That had been enough to get her going and although the idea of doing it again thrilled her, she resolved that she would not let it happen before he had apologised for this morning. Would he say sorry? She knew that he would not. It was not in his nature. He never showed humility. He would try and win her round with his usual swagger but she would resist and last night's performance would not be repeated, at least not anytime soon. Perhaps that was just as well; it would give time for the friction burns on her knees to heal.

The stream of rush hour traffic was visible now; moving slowly, stopping and moving slowly again along the road at the bottom of the hill. Only the buses passed freely on the inside lane. Although her father's refusal had annoyed her, hurt her even, it was as well he had not given in to her demands for a lift. She would not have arrived there on time crawling along in her father's old car, trying not to be seen behind that differently coloured replacement door. She resented having to travel by bus for the first time in five months since beginning her relationship with Lee, but it was the only way she would get there now. Even if Lee pulled up beside her with some excuse for being late, she would still have to go by bus to stand any chance of arriving there on time.

She increased her pace for a few steps breaking into a precarious jog and then slowing down to a fast walk. She checked her watch. Just over twenty minutes: that should be enough time.

The growling engine noise becoming louder behind her was unmistakable. It lowered to a threatening throb as the car drew alongside her. Being driven around in such an immaculate car was probably the biggest benefit of becoming his girlfriend. It gave her the freedom to escape from home and the neighbourhood she had hung out in for too long. It removed her from that group of girls who roamed around the streets and parks drinking cheap cider from plastic juice bottles. She could break away from all of that and she could do it in custom-built style. She had felt more special, more important, less of a girl when she first slid onto that white leather seat. She was more than ready to become the girlfriend of a car-owning painter and decorator, less ready to deal with Lee's macho need to drive to the limits. In time she had learned to manage her fear and seeing the car now filled her with an irresistible sense of satisfaction. She walked up to the passenger door, bending down to look through the open window.

'Hey, babe, I nearly didn't recognise you!'

'Don't "hey babe" me. You were supposed to pick me up at quarter past eight.'

She opened the door, manoeuvred into her seat and shut the door more sharply than she had been told a number of times was necessary.

'I slept in.'

'Yeah, well, you could have let me know. I tried phoning you but it kept going to voicemail. Was it switched off?'

He lifted his arm in and closed the window. A spliff remained lodged between his fingers as he drove off.

'Too right it was switched off. I didn't want any of your grief down the phone. I just came as quickly as I could.'

'What the fuck are you smoking that for at this time of day?'

'Keeping me chilled, babe. Keeping me chilled.'

'Chilled? I'm going to be late for my interview because of you and you don't give a fuck.'

'Yeah and I'm going to be late for work, man. I don't know why the fuck your lazy fat-arsed dad couldn't have made himself fucking useful and given you a lift.'

'You bastard, don't you dare talk about my dad like that. He's not well.'

'Come on, you bad mouth him all the time.'

They had reached the bottom of the road. Lee looked right as he drew the car to a halt. She opened the door.

'Fuck off, Lee.'

She ran along the pavement towards the bus stop. The sound of the roaring engine sent a shiver up her spine. She ran faster. He drove alongside her shouting through the passenger door window.

'Come on, you crazy cow, get inside.'

Looking back over her shoulder, she saw a bus approach. Ignoring Lee's fury she focused on the bus stop, preparing herself to ignore the frowns of disapproval from the people waiting.

The bus driver gave his horn a long blast. Lee revved the engine to make it roar in defiance before speeding off.

The people in the queue paid her little attention. Some watched Lee's car receding from view, others prepared themselves for boarding. Joining the end of the queue, Charlene raised her head to look at the number on the bus. It was not the one she needed. She snorted with frustration and turned round in annoyance to look up the road. Lee's car was already out of sight.

If she had known he was going to use the bus lane she would have stayed in the car. Her anger seethed before subsiding as she looked down the road and willed the quick arrival of her bus.

Chapter 4

A high male voice sang out from the back of the entrance lobby.

"*How do you solve a problem like Maria?*"

Maria stood still as the glass door swung closed behind her. She smiled warmly at the man as he turned around from the mailboxes while continuing to sing.

"*How do you catch a cloud and pin it down?*"

He walked slowly towards her, adding expression to the lyrics with dramatic gestures and facial contortions.

Maria held her free hand over her mouth as she tried to suppress the urge to laugh out loud. She relinquished her self-control when he himself emitted a spluttering laugh at the end of the line,

"*A flibbertigibbet! A will-o'-the-wisp! A clown!*"

He reached out to touch her arm as they gave full vent to their laughter, their eyes gleaming with delight.

'Oh, Stephen, that was great. You've got such a lovely voice. I'd no idea.'

He fiddled coyly with the gold necklace between the open collar of his floral shirt while dipping his head with faux self-effacement.

'Oh, you're too kind but I am a trained singer, you know. At drama college. That's where I did it and for a bit afterwards professionally. West End auditions as well but I got fed up with the knock-backs… you know, "don't phone us".'

She reached out to hold his hand consolingly.

'But, Stephen, that's such a shame. Not to be making more use of that talent.'

Clasping her hand between each of his, he smiled brightly.

'Oh, not really, Maria. It was all too much pressure. No, I'm quite happy leading a quiet life. Well mostly quiet. We can get noisy when we go out. Not always of course. We'll be well behaved at the concert. Very well behaved, you don't need to worry about that.'

'Oh Stephen, I'm not worried about that at all. I'm so glad you can make it and that, you know, you're OK about going to my church.'

'But of course I'm OK about going to your church. I don't have any problem with going to church. I'm quite spiritual, you know. I was in *Jesus Christ Superstar* many years ago and, I tell you what, if I'd been on the scene when Jesus was around, I'd have signed up to be one of the disciples, for sure. No sandals though, no way. I'd have preferred more of a Roman shoe type thing although the guys might not have been cool with that. Taking fashion tips from the enemy.'

Stephen glanced down at his sharply pointed polished shoes before continuing.

'Anyway. Of course we'll come and we can take Katherine. At least, that's what we were thinking of doing.'

Maria's face beamed with gratitude as he turned to walk beside her.

'Oh, Stephen. That would be perfect. I was worried about

how she'd get there. William was going to have to do it but it would be so much better if she goes with you and Lionel.'

'Well. We'd be delighted.'

Stephen waited as Maria unlocked Mrs Crawford's mailbox and withdrew the contents before continuing.

'You know what, Maria. It's not just Jesus and the disciples that fascinate me, I would have loved to have known Mary Magdalene. I've always been fascinated by her. She had such strength and you know how much I like strong women. Like you, Maria. And Katherine. I mean, what about her? Isn't she wonderful?'

Maria glanced up at him as they proceeded towards the lift.

'Isn't she just. She's amazing.'

'Yeah. It's just a shame she's had such bad luck with her health and it doesn't seem to be improving.'

She replied over her shoulder while walking into the lift.

'No. I'm afraid not. She's definitely getting less mobile. Less able to do things.'

'Well, don't forget that we're always ready to help. I think I did OK pushing the wheelchair.'

'You were wonderful, Stephen, you really were. Mrs Crawford was delighted although she hates the wheelchair, of course.'

'Of course she does, Maria. Of course she does but needs must.'

They fell silent as the lift doors wheezed shut and the lift lurched into its upward motion.

Maria tilted her head to look up at the floor numbers changing and cleared her throat quietly before breaking the silence.

'You know, Stephen, I was looking into El Paradiso on the way here and thinking that it would be fun if me and William went out sometime with you and Lionel.'

'Oh yes, we'd love that. It would be great fun and we'd love to meet William.'

Having vocalised her idea, it suddenly struck her that William would be very uncomfortable amongst such outgoing personalities in a fashionable bar.

'It would be fun, wouldn't it? Great fun. Only I'm not so sure William would be so keen when I think about it. He's not really one for going out. That's the only problem. He might take a bit of persuading. Oh well, I'll work on it but, well, I don't know.'

'Oh dear, that's a shame. But perhaps we can sort something out somehow. Come round to ours for drinks maybe.'

'Yes. That would be lovely. Maybe we could do that.'

The electronic chime sounded as the lift clunked to a halt at the seventh floor and the doors parted with a worn-out clatter. After preparing to set off in opposite directions, Stephen reached back to kiss Maria on the cheek.

'Let's arrange something soon, Maria. OK?'

'Yes, Stephen. Definitely. I'll see you soon.'

'Look forward to it, Maria. Byee!'

'Bye-bye, Stephen.'

A broad smile stretched across Maria's face and she fluttered a farewell wave before taking the final few steps to Mrs Crawford's door. She breathed in deeply before entering the apartment and singing out her usual greeting as she passed through the hall.

'Mrs Crawford, it's me!'

Sitting down in the kitchen armchair, she relaxed her body from her shoulders through the small of her back and down to her toes, now free to be stretched and lifted in her indoor sandals. The smooth classical music from the radio washed soothingly through her head. She leaned against the high back and took a slow sip of her latte to fully appreciate the smooth taste and texture of hot milk followed by the strength and richness of the coffee and that sense of stimulation spreading through her body. The numbness in her brain began to clear. These were moments to savour. Moments of comfort and pleasure in her own time, in her domain.

Everything in the kitchen was clean, tidy and where it should be whether visible or concealed in drawers and cupboards. It was all under her exclusive control.

The surfaces of the room emanated a heart-warming glow. Light oak, earthy red, luminescent ivory. A background palette against which the coloured kitchenware stood out vividly. The large blue and white ceramic bowl full of red apples, oranges and pears, the big mugs hanging on hooks, the round yellow teapot, the row of glass jars with their different contents, all parts of a reassuringly familiar scene. Maria felt more secure here than she did even in her own home. Fewer concerns invaded her thoughts while she was here. It was her domain and yet she had none of the responsibilities of ownership. The limits of her remit, of what she was required to do within these walls, were very clear. This room represented a very manageable part of her life.

Maria leaned forward to tear open the paper bag and remove the pain au chocolat. Her teeth crunched through the flaky exterior down to the soft chocolate core.

She drank the last mouthful of latte bringing her private time to an end by brushing the crumbs into the bag and crumpling it into the cup. The kettle had boiled. It was time to make the tea and start another pleasurable day of providing care and company.

Chapter 5

She looked into the bedroom. Soft textures and light colours, a soothing place to sleep and to wake gently. To Maria it seemed serenely unreal. No draped clothes, no pile of magazines, no books, no clutter on the dressing table. Everything in perfect order except for some rumples in the duvet.

Maria pushed the door open with her shoulder, both hands gripping the tray. 'Good morning, Mrs Crawford. How are you feeling?' she whispered, stepping carefully across the room, her footsteps which had clumped across the wooden hall floor now muffled by the deep carpet.

Catching each other's eyes in the muted light they exchanged quiet smiles. Maria placed the tray carefully on the bedside table. Without pausing she turned away with skirt-swishing briskness and walked to the window. The morning sunlight washed across the room as she pulled the curtains apart.

'I'm fine thanks, Maria. Pretty good today, I think.'

'Did you sleep well?'

'Yes, quite well, thank you.'

Maria slipped her arm under Mrs Crawford's back helping

her to lean forward while she plumped up the pillows behind her.

'There we go.'

She always voiced the morning ritual in a soothing sing-song tone, her heart warm with tender feelings. Maria felt fortunate to be caring for someone like Mrs Crawford. A person who commanded respect and inspired fondness at the same time. It gave her quiet satisfaction to recognise that their relationship had become so harmonious.

Maria had given much to Mrs Crawford, unstinting effort and dedication, all of which she did without expecting the extra rewards. Her gracious attempts to refuse Mrs Crawford's gifts were never successful and she greatly appreciated the theatre outings, the celebratory dinners in restaurants, the gift vouchers, the bottles of wine and champagne, but she was grateful above all for the reward of contentment. Contentment from knowing that she had become an integral and indispensable part of Mrs Crawford's life. The whole experience of being here had helped to make Maria's place in the world feel more secure. Having finally accepted her inability to conceive children, life seemed to have found a good balance with all other parts of it providing fulfilment. William was the utterly reliable anchor in her life, a source of strength and happiness. Her family and friends were also very supportive and, in recent years, the church, particularly the choir, had enriched her life in a way she would not have imagined possible. All in all, Maria had come to consider that her life was as perfect as it could be for a thirty-four-year-old childless woman. Having managed to come to terms with the tragedy of infertility, the full value of all of her relationships had become very apparent and she was determined never to take any of them for granted.

'Right now, back we go. How's that? Comfortable?'

'Ah yes, Maria, lovely.'

Maria transferred the cup of tea into Mrs Crawford's languid grasp and sat down on the bedside armchair.

'Of course we've got Sharon's niece coming this morning.'

'Yes, that's right, at nine thirty. Sharon's niece, now what's her name? Isn't that terrible? I can't remember.'

'Charlene.'

'Yes, that's right: Charlene. Unusual name. It would be rather awkward if we don't think she's suitable.'

'It would, I suppose.'

'Still, she'd only be here for three months and then we'll have to see how things go after that.'

'OK, but I'm sure I won't need any assistance after the summer.'

'Well, we'll see. It depends on the state I'm in by then, Maria. Who knows what I'll be like in three months but, in any event, the important thing is that you get more time off over the summer.'

'Well, I'm very grateful, Mrs Crawford. It's very kind but I really don't think I'll need any help.'

Mrs Crawford smiled fondly at Maria before sipping the last of the tea. She then lowered the cup and saucer onto her lap and, resting back against the pillows, gazed pensively at the ceiling.

'I had a lovely dream last night, Maria. About swimming. Just like I used to. In the sea. It was wonderful. I felt so free. I was much younger, of course, in the dream.'

Maria rose to remove the cup and saucer and return them to the tray.

Breathing in deeply and then emitting a sigh, Mrs Crawford slowly peeled back the bedclothes.

Returning quickly to the bedside, Maria watched Mrs Crawford as she pulled her legs up and swivelled her body round so that she was sitting on the edge of the bed.

She could imagine that Mrs Crawford would have been a good swimmer. All those years ago when she was fit and strong. Those stiff joints would have been supple then. She could imagine her swimming with long-limbed elegance.

She flexed her arm to support her as she rose weakly into an unsteady crouch.

'There we go. What would you like today, Mrs Crawford, shower or bath?'

'Oh, I think a shower would be fine, I don't feel quite so stiff today.'

Chapter 6

Charlene slowed down as she approached a man crouching down on the pavement. Her eyes narrowed as she saw that he was picking up dog dirt with a plastic poo bag.

Her face screwing up with revulsion she stepped out onto the road to give him a wide berth. Passing the man she flinched as he called after a little white dog trotting away from him along the grass verge.

'Mimi, darling. Wait. There's a good girl.'

Ignoring the man, the dog scampered alongside Charlene, yapping and jumping up and down as she increased her pace.

'Mimi, you bad girl! Stop that!'

Its attention arrested by the man's sharpened tone, the dog sat down on the pavement yapping excitedly.

Charlene stopped to look back as the man shouted his apology.

'I'm sorry, love. She's quite harmless.'

Turning away Charlene walked off as briskly as she dared. The bus had not reached the stop at El Paradiso until ten. She would be at least ten minutes late.

Her breath rasping from exertion, she scanned the list of names. Crawford, Floor Seven. A buzzing noise emitted from the speaker as she pressed the button.

She glanced anxiously at the man approaching with the dog, now panting eagerly as it pattered jauntily beside him, the red collar and lead standing out vividly against its rippling white coat. A sharp clunk sounded followed by an electronic crackle. She bent down to move her head closer to the speaker.

'Hello. Charlene?'

The clarity of the voice surprised her.

'Yes, yes it is. It's Charlene Pearson and I'm sorry I'm late.'

'Don't worry. You sound out of breath. Take your time, Charlene. There's no rush. Lionel will let you in, I'm sure.'

She turned sharply to look up at the man who was now directly behind her. Her eyes engaged fleetingly with his before taking in the rest of his face. A smile stretched the tanned skin across his cheeks and creased deep lines out from his eyes. His eyelashes seemed unusually long and curling and his eyebrows unnaturally neat. His hair was carefully styled and coloured brown from root to tip.

'Don't worry, Maria, I'll look after her.'

'Thanks, Lionel. See you in a few minutes, Charlene.'

She whipped her head back round to face the intercom panel.

'Thanks. Yes. See you.'

He held out his hand as she turned warily towards him, gripping her raised hand gently as he spoke.

'Well, we know each other's names now and you've already met Mimi. Pleased to meet you, Charlene. I'll let you in.'

'Thank you. Yes. Pleased…'

Releasing her hand he gestured with a flourish towards the entrance while pulling the dog back with his other arm. She glanced down to check that the dog was not in her way and moved forward, looking up at him with a half-smile as he addressed her brightly.

'By the way, you know that Maria could see us through the video camera?'

'No. No, I didn't.'

'Yes, that's how she knew it was you and that I was behind you.'

Twisting round tightly to look back at the small camera eye embedded into the top of the panel, she became unsteady on her heels and toppled back against him. The dog yapped and leapt backwards. Lionel gripped her arm as he braced his body to support her.

'Oops-a-daisy. Are you all right?'

His voice strained as he helped her stand up straight.

'Come on, my love, let's get you inside.'

She resisted his encouraging push on her back and remained defiantly rooted as she processed a flood of challenging anxieties.

This was an alien environment, a different world. Gay men with little dogs and rich people were never seen in her home territory. She should not be up at this end of town. What was she doing here? It wasn't right.

She looked up at the clean white facade rising high above. Dark-framed windows, deep balconies, floor to ceiling glass across the entrance lobby. More like a hotel than a block of flats. She would be like a fish out of water in this expensive world.

The dog reared against its lead, yapping as she wheeled away from the door and started walking off at a hurried pace. Lionel called after her.

'Charlene!'

The sound of her name being shouted stirred her distrust of authority and increased her resolve to flee. She walked as fast as she could until, after becoming increasingly unsteady, she stumbled, flailing to one side.

The searing sensation in her ankle eliminated all thought as a burst of pain flashed in her head. Her left leg immediately compensating as her right leg gave way, she hopped two steps before risking tentative support from her right foot. Finding it capable of taking some weight, she crossed the pavement with a jerky shuffle to the raised planter. She grimaced as she sat down on the wall and stretched out her injured leg. Her ankle throbbed and a sickening swirl spun round in her head.

'Good God, girl. Are you all right?'

'Leave me alone… please.'

Her hands gripped the edge of the wall as she closed her eyes and clenched her jaw. The wave of pain began to recede, leaving her mind in a calmer state. She breathed in deeply through her nose. Leaning forward she bowed her head and opened her eyes. Brown leather burnished to a gleaming glow. Her gaze lingered on his shoes before lifting slowly upwards. Chinos, crisp with a sharp crease disappearing below the hem line of a soft leather jacket buttoned up, except at the top, where his neck rose up from the open collar of a cream shirt to his tanned face still smiling, but this time tenderly undistracted by the dog yelping and whining as it strained against its lead tied to a lamppost.

'How are you feeling? Not too much pain when you wiggle your toes?'

'No. It's fine. Not so sore now.'

'That's good, Charlene. Well, I think you'd really better let Maria have a look at it, so as soon as you're ready I can help you, if you need any help walking, which I expect you will. It looked like a bad twist.'

She nodded before hunching over and closing her eyes. The pain had reduced to a warm ache in her ankle.

'Maria will look after you. I expect she'll put an ice pack on it, a bag of frozen peas perhaps.'

He sat down beside her.

'Do you want to give it a go?'

'Yes.'

The dog was whimpering now, its ears alert, its eyes fixed on the man.

'Come on then.'

His leather jacket creaked softly as he moved into position and helped her to stand up.

'You're Sharon's niece, aren't you?'

'Yes. Yes, I am, but how…'

She could feel the cackling laugh vibrate through his body.

'Oh, we're quite a tight circle, you know. She cuts my hair as well. She's very good, your aunt, the best I've had.'

Charlene grunted as they took their first laboured steps towards the apartment block. Ignoring the dog's anxious barking, Lionel focused his attention on providing support. Having leaned against him heavily over the first few steps, he was relieved to feel her reliance on him gradually reduce, so that by the time they had returned to the entrance, her grip had loosened and he was able to withdraw his arm.

'Are you OK to stand on your own?'

'Yes, I'm OK now.'

He pressed the entry code buttons and pushed the door open while looking back at the dog.

'Mimi love, calm down, I'll be with you in a minute!'

She walked past him.

'Do you think you'll manage from here, Charlene? I'm afraid I'll have to go and rescue Mimi before she does herself a mischief.'

'Yes, I'll be fine… Thanks.'

'OK, Charlene. Take it easy. The lift's over to the left. It's floor seven.'

He released his grip on the handle. The door started closing.

'See you later, my love.'

'See you.'

The door closed with a heavy clunk. The dog's barking became muted, the traffic noise was no longer audible. After watching Lionel walk away she turned round slowly, her eyes scanning the entrance lobby. A soft, silent space, carpeted, two sofas facing each other on the right, a vase of flowers placed on the low table between them. She sniffed the perfume of freshly cut blooms.

She felt trapped now, unable to escape. Still struggling to accept the situation, she reminded herself that this is what she had wanted, to see how rich people lived. She also looked forward to telling Lee about it. How smart it all was. She wouldn't tell him about Lionel. He would just start taking the piss and wouldn't listen to anything else.

Chapter 7

A still, quiet time, sitting motionless, her eyes fixed on the horizon, thoughts slowly forming, passing through and giving way to new thoughts. After the exertions of having a shower, this was the time to relish some moments of rest, feeling clean and fresh. The time to give way to the meditation of involuntary reflection.

The sea was a featureless, flat grey-blue band between the shoreline and sky, neither sun nor wind today to give it sparkle or spume. This was not the sea which had inspired her dream of swimming freely and strongly. This was not a sea to become intimate with. It was too inaccessible with a chalk cliff and many other barriers between her apartment and the shallow water lapping onto the shingle beach. Even at the water's edge there would be nothing to inspire making contact with that opaque expanse stretching far and wide. It was a sea best appreciated from a distance.

She spent many hours gazing at it and in those days, years ago, when she ached to return, she clung on to the faint reassurance that the sea visible from his home, the backdrop to his life, was part of the same continuous body of water.

Her time with him on the island, that intense experience, had not occupied her thoughts in this way for a long time. It was that vivid dream of diving deep, of rolling, twisting and kicking in that Aegean water which had revived these memories and brought them to the front of her mind.

It became a daily ritual, her descent to the sea. She would hear him make his high revving departure on the motorbike; gathering speed quickly until nearing the first corner when he would change down the gears, throttling the revs up at each gear change until, having banked round the bend, he would accelerate away moving quickly from the growling low gears up to the high-pitched roar of fifth. She would close her eyes and imagine the sensation of being behind him, her softness squashing against his broad back. Shivering with arousal, she would inhale a deep chest-shuddering sigh before rising to remove her towel from the back of the chair. She would then walk from below the canopy of the vine sprawling across the pergola into the warm morning sunshine. The sensation of that benign heat on her head and the back of her neck always gave her a soothing sense of wellbeing.

These were the meditative moments at the start of her days. Thoughts rolling through her mind as she made her loose-limbed way down the path, her sandals scuffing across the dusty paving. Her vision would be filled with the sky, the mountains on the mainland, the town and harbour on the other side of the bay, the sea, the pine woodland below, the trees and climbing plants, the stepped path descending through the terraces, but she would not focus on anything until reaching the road. Her familiarity with the descent through the garden allowed her mind to remain disengaged from the world around her. She was free to give dreamy consideration to thoughts as they floated through her mind.

Closing the gate behind her she would bring an end to her

meditative contemplation. Crossing the road safely at this point, downhill from a blind corner, required concentration. She would look up and down, listen, flex her foot muscles to grip her sandals to her soles and then run across the worn tarmac to the sweet-smelling sanctuary of the pines. The transparent blue-green sea was visible now below the scorched blonde rocks and between the trees. It was at this point that she always wished it was possible to get to her big flat-topped rock without having to descend the steep slopes by taking short-stepped rushes between grabbable trees. It made for an uncomfortable contrast to the easy, relaxed, hip-swinging meander through the garden.

Completing the awkward descent was rewarded with the pleasure of stepping out of the shade onto the heat-radiating rocks. Traversing the rocks was not easy but she enjoyed taking her sandals off and stretching from rock to rock, barefoot on the warm stone as she navigated the route to her resting place, her peaceful platform. Standing on it she would face out to sea, slip her fingers under the straps on her shoulders and pull her dress up and over her head, laying it to one side before peeling her black bikini briefs off her hips, pulling them down to her feet and kicking them onto her dress. She would then stand upright, her face tilted up towards the sun, her arms reaching high, every muscle stretching. With her eyes closed she would relish the feeling of being naked, of being as utterly natural as her surroundings. The sensation of her entire body being exposed to the morning sunshine gave her an exciting sense of being completely removed from the conventions of normal life. The feeling of liberation was enhanced when a breeze blew up and flowed warmly around her.

After relaxing her stretch, she would bend down to remove the coconut oil from her bag and massage it into every part of her body.

Her sensual delight reached it's height when he moored his boat alongside to take a break from fishing. It was when he sat nearby in his T shirt and shorts that her pleasure elevated to a state of contained excitement. He would face out to sea, regularly turning round to look at her, his eyes bright, his mouth stretching into a subtle smile. She would slowly change position on her towel, all the time engaging in inconsequential conversation while suppressing her growing desire.

The closest contact they made was when he leaned down to kiss her before leaving. After exchanging smiling goodbyes she would watch him yank the cord to fire up the outboard motor and putter off into the shimmering distance while her heart fizzed warmly. Her mornings by the sea were a much more mellow experience when he was unable to come by, although she did have that other highlight, the swim.

That moment of release when, after climbing down backwards onto her launching position, carefully avoiding the sea urchins, she was able to leave the awkward roughness of the rocks behind with one strong push of her legs. It was exhilarating to escape from the constraints of landbound movement, to have your body supported by the strong sea water, to be able to see the seabed so clearly and to surge away in any direction, to dive deep at any point, to roll, to twist, to kick, to revel in the liberation. She would always finish by breathing deeply and dropping her head to hang still, her long black hair swirling on the surface above. Immersed in the warm water she felt secure. She imagined that this was as close as she would ever get to the sensation of being in the womb.

Lifting her head above the surface to breathe again, the grief that she was trying to deal with would invariably invade her thoughts. Feeling vulnerable again, she would swim away returning to the point where the gently sloped rock shelf provided the most manageable route for clambering out of the water.

The sense of desperation would melt away as she stretched out on her towel, the sunlight diffusing brightly through her closed eyelids. She felt comforted by the recognition that, along with the sense of being at one with her natural surroundings, she also felt connected to the indefinable forces which transcend the physical world. This island had given her the space and time to feel these connections and, more than that, some kind of spiritual dimension which she had rarely experienced and never so strongly.

After resting for a few minutes she would rise slowly to her feet, pull on her bikini briefs, slip her dress on, roll up her towel and return to the house before the heat of the sun became unbearable.

She knew then that these days were forming a significant passage in her life and now, many decades later, she had long since become resigned to the truth that she would never be able to experience that way of living again.

She sighed deeply as she emerged from her state of reverie. It was a long time ago. She was old now. Not so much mentally but certainly physically. That future which she had envisaged would be difficult to live through was now largely in the past. She had survived it. So many years of suffering her loss. She had reached a stage where there was little future left and what did remain would be lived, for the most part, in passive reflection. She no longer had the energy or physical capability to fill her life with distracting activity. She had been stilled, unable to run away, to flee from the grief. It was more difficult now to avoid being consumed by thoughts and memories. But was it right to allow the remainder of her life to pass in this way? Had she not been waiting for something, for sense to be made of it all, for some form of reconciliation? Would it happen? When and how? Was it right to do nothing until the end? Would real reconciliation somehow be achieved beyond the end or were these memories the closest connection that could ever be made? Would there be anything beyond the end?

Her steady focus on the horizon wavered and blurred as her

chest heaved in panic and a swell of grief burned her throat and stung her eyes. She closed her eyes, dropped her head to the side and opened them again, her gaze settling on one framed photograph amongst the many on the table. The warm glow spread out from her heart as it always did when she saw that big smile, those bright eyes. An appearance of unassailable vitality.

She spoke to the face in the photograph silently.

Your spirit was so strong, so vigorous, it cannot have been extinguished. I still feel your existence somehow. You are with me, aren't you? We will be reunited. Won't we?

Trrrrring! The shrill ring of the doorbell jarred her aching soul and brought her back to the present. With the mists of emotion clearing from her mind, she brightened at the prospect of meeting Charlene. She was looking forward to having a young person around. Someone who had their journey through adulthood ahead of them.

She glanced back at the photograph.

I love you so much and always will. Always? Always, forever and ever. How long is forever? I must stop thinking about it. Must compose myself.

She lifted her arm off the chair and reached for a tissue. The tissue did not release with her first tug. The box jerked forward on her second tug. The tissue came away and her empty cup was knocked off the table.

Her chest rose and fell with a deep sigh. She could not retrieve the cup. It was out of reach from the chair. She remained seated hoping that Maria would pick it up discreetly so that Charlene would not notice.

Chapter 8

'Come in, Charlene. Now, how are you? Lionel says you went over on your ankle.'

'I'm fine. My ankle's a bit sore but I can walk, kind of.'

They looked at each other for a moment as Maria stepped back to open the door, smiling warmly while Charlene remained impassive.

'Let's have a look at you. Come through.'

Charlene's eyes widened as she stepped into the spacious hallway. It did not look like a normal home. It was more like the art gallery she and some other pupils had been taken to by the art teacher. Incomprehensible but beautifully colourful paintings hanging on white walls.

She breathed in deeply through her nose. It smelt so much fresher than her own home. First a floral fragrance then the clean smell of polished wood.

She turned around as Maria spoke.

'Right then, Charlene, let's head to the kitchen first.'

Feeling Maria's arm reach behind her, she allowed herself to be escorted across the dark oak floorboards, her high heels clacking in an uneven rhythm on the hard surface. At every limp on the injured ankle, her body pressed into Maria's bosom and belly. She tried to remain upright but could not avoid making cushioned contact with this large woman. Physical contact with another woman felt strange. Other than with her mother when she was much younger, she had only made bodily contact with another female in fights.

'It looks like you have sprained it. We'll need to get an ice pack on it.'

She felt Maria's hand clasp around her upper arm and pull her in close so that they could pass through the door side by side.

Having helped her to sit down, Maria pulled round another chair and, with a light touch and soothing reassurances, lifted Charlene's leg gently onto it so that her calf and ankle were supported.

'Now, I'll need to take your shoe off.'

Her mind became still and devoid of thoughts. She was only aware of the soft breathiness of Maria's voice and of the caressing touch of her fingers around her ankle and foot. She was overcome with the restful sense of being in a state of half hypnosis. She allowed her eyelids to droop.

'Now, Charlene, are these tights you're wearing?'

Instantly aroused, Charlene's eyes opened wide.

'They're not tights, just socks. Pop socks.'

'OK, so I can take them off for the ice pack?'

'I suppose so. Yes.'

Maria hummed quietly as she walked over to the fridge.

'Luckily I've got two ice packs in here. I need them for Mrs Crawford. Did Sharon explain that Mrs Crawford suffers from osteoarthritis?'

'No, she didn't.'

'Oh, well I'll explain about that later. Let's just concentrate on sorting you out, Charlene. I'm going to rub some arnica on first to keep the ankle from bruising too much. Have you ever used arnica before?'

'No.'

'Well, don't worry about it. It's a completely natural remedy. It works really well.'

Maria pulled the trouser leg back from Charlene's ankle carefully to avoid crumpling it until the top of her sock was revealed below the knee. She then peeled it off gently and placed it over the back of the chair.

Watching her, Charlene's eyes suddenly widened in fear that her skinned knees might be exposed. Her mind flooded with a surge of panic. How would she explain it? She could say that she had scraped them on the AstroTurf playing football. That used to happen a lot when she played football at school.

Satisfied that this explanation would be convincing, she shut out all troubling thoughts and succumbed again to the soothing sound of Maria's voice washing through her head and the intoxicating touch of her hands. She had never felt so relaxed and wished that she could remain in this state for as long as possible.

Maria finished applying the arnica and placed the ice pack on her ankle.

'Now, Charlene, I'm going to leave you here for a minute or two while I go and let Mrs Crawford know how we're getting on. OK?'

She opened her eyes slowly and looked up at Maria.

'Yes. Yes, that's fine.'

'I'll make you a tea or coffee or get you a cold drink when I come back. Won't be long.'

Maria swept past leaving a clean fragrance in her wake. Charlene breathed in deeply, exhaled and closed her eyes. She felt good and wished she could avoid having to exert herself or having to deal with any more difficult situations.

A repeated buzzing and vibration against her leg caused her to sit up sharply. The ice pack slid off her ankle.

She arched her back and raised her hip to remove the phone from her pocket. Seeing Lee's number on the screen, she pressed the "End Call" button and returned the phone to her pocket. Then, after reaching forward to replace the ice pack, she leaned back, closed her eyes and tried to restore her body and mind to their previous state of relaxation.

Beep! Beep!... Beep! Beep! Her eyes opened as she heard the sound of a text message being received.

She reached for her phone, frowning as she tried to avoid jarring her sore ankle.

Her frown intensified as she read the message.

I will b waitin 4 u luv lee

She leaned back, looked up at the ceiling momentarily, refocused on the screen and typed a reply.

Fuck off

The door opened. Charlene felt a draft as Maria breezed past to place the empty cup next to the sink.

'How are we doing, my love? Feeling a bit better?'

Charlene held the phone close to her chest while looking up at Maria. She took a moment to study Maria's features. Her shining eyes, her neat nose, her large smile which pushed her cheeks into a shapely plumpness.

'Yes, yes, I'm fine thanks.'

'Cup of tea? Coffee? A cold drink? We've got fifteen minutes before we go through and see Mrs Crawford.'

'Tea would be fine, thanks.'

'Okey doke. Milk in it?'

Maria turned round to switch the kettle on.

Charlene darted a glance at her phone and pressed the "Send" button.

'Sugar?'

'Ah, yes. Two, please.'

Maria turned back to face Charlene.

'Two? Well, perhaps a sweet tea is exactly what you need.'

Charlene pressed the button to lock her phone and returned it to her pocket.

Chapter 9

The immaculate decoration and furnishings reminded her of the celebrity homes she had seen on television. Snapping out of her awestruck gazing, she focused her attention on the woman sitting poised and smiling warmly next to a table half-covered in framed photographs.

She responded with an uncertain smile while taking in Mrs Crawford's appearance. The sophisticated cut of her white hair, the lustrous pearl earrings and necklace, the deep navy blue of her close-fitted top and tailored trousers, her kitten heeled shoes. Everything about Mrs Crawford and her surroundings seemed so well-ordered and stylish except for the cup lying on the carpet.

'Come in. Come in. Sit down and thanks so much for coming to see us. Excuse me for not getting up, I'm a little stiff this morning. Maria, have you explained to Charlene about the arthritis?'

Maria responded brightly while stooping down to retrieve the cup.

'Yes, Mrs Crawford, I've explained quite a few things to her already.'

'Oh, that's good, gets us off to a good start, although I believe we're both a bit incapacitated today, aren't we?... Is it very sore, my dear?'

'No, it's fine... getting better.'

'Good. Maria's worked her magic on it, has she?'

'Yes, yes, she has.'

She felt a tingling appreciation of comfort in the small of her back as she sank into the white linen cushions on the wide armchair. Maria pulled up a footstool and helped her to place her leg in a comfortable position before reversing to sit primly attentive on the chair between them.

Mrs Crawford waited until they had both settled before speaking.

'Well, Charlene, I think the first thing I'd like to establish is that you're OK about the hours. I appreciate that for someone of your age not getting home until shortly after eight, five evenings a week, might intrude too much on your social life.'

'Well, ah...'

Maria leaned forward to interject.

'Yes, Mrs Crawford, we did discuss this, and I think it's fair to say that you weren't sure about it, were you, Charlene? Sharon hadn't really made the hours thing very clear and so you felt you needed a little time to think about it, didn't you?'

'Yes, well, I think, I think it would be fine.'

'Are you sure, my dear, and Saturday morning as well?'

'Yes, well...'

'Well look, don't worry about it just now. Let's talk about other things first. Now you left school a few months ago and you're going to college in September, I believe.'

'Yes. Yes, that's right if I can get a place.'

'Yes, well it can be difficult sometimes getting in. What subjects are you hoping to study, Charlene?'

'Ah, I'm not sure yet. Maybe... no, I'm really not sure. I'll have to think about it.'

'Oh well, there's no great rush, I suppose, you have age on your side, lots of time. You're twenty, aren't you?'

'Yes, but I'll be twenty-one in August.'

'Ah, so you must have left school some time ago.'

'Yes. Two, well, nearly three years ago.'

'Yes, well, in fact Sharon did mention that. She told us that you had a little difficulty at school or rather that the school went through a difficult period which made it difficult for the pupils to do well. Is that right? You ended up leaving early because of it.'

'Yes. Yes, that's right. The school was put into "Special Measures" and its name was changed to give it a fresh start. That's what they called it, a "fresh start".'

'Yes, I see. We actually read about it in the paper. It must have made it very difficult to achieve very much. How did you cope? Was it very difficult?'

'Well, it was quite… um, the teachers had a hard time. Everyone on their case.'

'What, including some of the pupils, I suppose?'

'Yes, some of the pupils weren't very nice to them. You know, making their life a misery, I suppose.'

'That's a shame or did some of the teachers deserve to get a hard time, do you think?'

'No, no, I don't think they did. I think they were good. Not all of them but most of them were good.'

'I hope you don't mind me asking these questions, Charlene, it's just that I'm interested especially because I think it is so unfortunate that a school going downhill like this makes it so difficult for children to get an education.'

'It wasn't really the school's fault that I didn't finish though, Mrs Crawford. The teachers were really good to me. They tried and they wanted me to finish and to do well. It's just that it was too difficult. It was too difficult…'

'Too difficult. You mean the work was too difficult?'

'Not really. Well, yes, in a way. It was too difficult to study, to work away from school and I couldn't do it all at school. I needed to do so much work to keep up.'

'I see, so you found it difficult to work at home?'

'Yes, I tried but, well, it just didn't work, plus none of my friends stayed on, they were either working or… or not working. I didn't have any time to do it.'

'Oh dear, that's such a shame, Charlene, but, when you go to college, how are you going to manage? You'll need to study then, although you could use the library of course.'

'The library? Yes, I'll use the library.'

'Of course you might go away to college, so you wouldn't be staying at home, and you'd be away from your friends during the term.'

'Yes, I might do that. I've got another aunt who lives in London. I could go and stay with her. She said that I could.'

'Well, that might be a good idea, Charlene. You'll have to think about that but, anyway, it's great you're going to college. Really great. Sharon says that you're going to finish off your school courses, get your A levels and that maybe you'll go to university after that. Would you like to do that, do you think? Go to university?'

'Well… um. Maybe…'

'Good. Well, I can certainly recommend it but anyway, my dear, perhaps if you join us you'll learn some useful things in the meantime. Now Maria's probably explained most things. We do like to keep everything nice and clean as you can see and the food side of things should be straightforward I think.'

'Yes, Mrs Crawford, I explained that Charlene would just have to finish things off, heat it up or whatever. I'll make it nice and easy for her.'

'Yes and you wouldn't have to do too much nursemaiding, my dear. I can still get about well enough. Slowly, but I can still get about. I can get into bed easily enough, it's just getting out which can be difficult. Old age isn't nice, Charlene, it's not nice although I shouldn't complain. At least I've reached it.'

'You're not old, Mrs Crawford. You'd be fine if it wasn't for the arthritis.'

'Oh, I don't know, Maria, I don't know. Anyway, Charlene, you've got to think about the hours, haven't you? Four till eight each day so that you overlap with Maria for an hour and then ten until one on Saturdays although if that was a real problem we might be able to get round it some other way.'

'Or perhaps I could do every second Saturday, Mrs Crawford? That would be fine by me.'

'Maria, I really want you to have the weekends off. Anyway, Charlene, why don't you think about it overnight? Talk to your mum and dad and remember we would arrange for you to be taken home each day by taxi and today of course. We can't have you struggling home with your foot bandaged up like that. OK?'

*

She would have to make sure the taxi stopped as close to the front door as possible. Being seen with one foot in a canvas shoe and with the other bandaged up would not be cool.

Maria filled so much of the lift, Charlene had to strain her neck to avoid looking at her on their silent descent. At last the lift bumped to a stop at the ground floor. Understanding that she should exit first, Charlene side-stepped past Maria, carefully avoiding any physical contact.

She was struck again by the luxurious scent of flowers. Looking across at the large bouquet on the table she felt a frisson of pleasure at the prospect of this environment becoming part of her daily experience.

She glanced amenably at Maria as she bustled up alongside her.

'Now just watch the step here. You're doing well, Charlene.'

'Yeah, well it's not so sore now.'

Maria touched her hand lightly under Charlene's elbow as they made their way through the entrance lobby. The taxi was visible through the glazed frontage, waiting in the drop-off bay at the front door.

The parking zone a short way down the hill also came into view. The sight of Lee's car parked there filled her with alarm and an angry resolve to exit the building and bundle herself into the taxi as quickly as possible. She knew that everything about Lee would be perceived as alien and inappropriate to this part of town and she did not want her association with him to become evident.

'That'll be your taxi, Charlene.'

Charlene stopped and turned to face Maria.

'Thanks. Thank you very much. I'll be fine from here, thanks. You don't need to come out. I'll be fine.'

'It's no problem, Charlene. Mrs Crawford's good about taxis and we couldn't have you going home on a bus with that ankle. Now let me get the door, dear, it's very heavy. It doesn't look it but it's very heavy glass.'

Charlene felt the grip of irritation tighten in her head as her plan to make a rapid departure was thwarted by Maria standing in the door opening.

The tension in her rose as Maria looked at the taxi before stepping back to hold the door open for her.

'Yes, that's definitely your taxi, Charlene.'

Charlene walked forward trying to step lightly on her injured foot. This caused her to move with an ungainly hop and so she tensed her diaphragm and held her breath as she attempted to walk normally, turning sideways to pass Maria at the door. The bursts of pain in her ankle made her grunt slightly.

'Thank you, Maria. I'll get away now.'

Her voice sounded tight, strained.

'It was a pleasure, darling. Can you manage?'

Charlene did not stop or turn around.

'We'll hear from you tomorrow. Will we?'

Charlene fell back into the rear seat before reaching forward to grab the door handle, replying as loudly and clearly as she could before shutting the door.

'Yes, I'll phone you tomorrow.'

She smiled at Maria through the window of the closed door. Maria waved, still leaning against the open door, her mouth formed in a half smile.

'Stanley Osborne Way, is it?'

'Yes, that's right, number fourteen.'

The taxi driver accelerated out of the drop-off area. Charlene looked back over her shoulder. She saw Lee's arm chuck the unfinished joint onto the road. The smoke drifted out of the car window and then dissipated turbulently as he drove off with a high revving roar which echoed loudly around the courtyard. She turned around the other way to look back at the building entrance. The door was closed but she could see Maria behind it looking out.

Charlene resisted the temptation to look behind. She could hear from the loudness of the engine noise that Lee was driving close behind. Very close.

The taxi driver sat up straight in his seat, leaning slightly sideways to look in his rear-view mirror. Charlene noted the look of annoyance in his eyes becoming more pronounced with each glance.

'Stupid bastard. Excuse my language, miss, only that geezer behind is driving like a lunatic. He's far too close. I just wish he'd bleeding overtake if he's in such a hurry. Oh, oh, here he goes. Jeez, choose your moment, why don't you.'

Charlene looked to the side. Lee's car flashed past with a roar that made her shiver. She looked ahead. A car was heading towards them. It would be dangerously close but Charlene was used to Lee driving to the limits of safety. Driving was like a drug for him, a way to pursue the thrill of danger. An addiction that was compounded too often by being under the influence of drugs.

The car horn blared loudly. Lee cut in sharply. The taxi driver braked. The driver's furious face filled Charlene's vision in a flash as the car passed by.

'Fuck. Death wish or what. Excuse the French, miss, only that geezer's driving like a bleeding nutter.'

'Yeah, he's a nutter.'

'Sorry, love?'

'I said he's a nutter.'

'You're telling me! The thing is he'll not only kill himself, he'll kill other people. I mean, we could have had a nasty accident if I hadn't braked. Know what I mean?'

'Yes… he's a real nutter.'

She expected that Lee would be waiting for her when they arrived in her street but, resolving not to worry about how to deal with him, Charlene relaxed her neck and shoulders, moving her head round in a circular motion before resting back against the seat. She closed her eyes and slowed her thoughts down, soothed by the changing pitch and vibration of the engine and the comforting warmth of soft sunshine on the side of her face.

She reflected on the experience of meeting Mrs Crawford. It was not what she had expected. She was not the frail old lady she had imagined. Despite the arthritis and her age, the best word she could think of to describe her was "smart". Smart appearance and a smart mind. Smart but easy to talk to. Easier than she expected a wealthy woman to be.

Lonely was another word which came to mind. She gave the impression of living in a state of loneliness. Neither Maria nor Sharon had mentioned anything about other people in her life, about her having visitors or socialising in any way.

The photographs on the table seemed to be of an old-fashioned couple who she guessed might have been her parents and a young girl. Mrs Crawford did not seem motherly in any way so she presumed the girl was a niece or other relative. There were certainly no photographs of a man who might have been a husband or a father of any children.

Acknowledging that she would find out anything there was to know in due course, she opened her eyes and looked around for familiar landmarks. The traffic lights where they would turn off the main road to drive up the hill were visible ahead. She would be home in a few minutes. She sighed deeply. The whole process of going for the interview had been stressful, although some of it had been pleasant and she could see that working there would provide a break from the stresses of life with Lee and at home. A break from the frequent confrontations, from getting a hard time and from giving a hard time. She always gave at least as good as she got.

The taxi driver turned into Stanley Osborne Way.

'What number did you say it was, love, fourteen?'

'Yeah, that's right, fourteen.'

'I had an aunt who lived at number eighteen. Mrs Collins. Mary Collins. Ever come across her?'

'No. No, never.'

'Well, she moved away five or six years ago. She misses it, mind you. Liked it here.'

She resisted the impulse to challenge the possibility that anyone could enjoy living on this street.

'Right, here we go, number fourteen.'

Charlene sat forward to look at Lee's car parked further up the street. She could see it was empty but did not notice Lee sitting on a bench obscured from view on the other side of the road

He chucked his cigarette onto the ground and stood up, picking up the carrier bag by his side and turning towards the taxi.

'Hey, babe, what you done to your foot? What happened to

your shoes? I came to give you a lift home. Didn't you see me? I was waiting for you.'

Charlene shut the door and stood beside the taxi driver's open window while he filled out a receipt.

'All you need to do is sign this at the bottom, love.'

Charlene took the pen and signed her name.

'Thanks, love. See you again maybe.'

'Yes. Thanks.'

Charlene turned round to face Lee.

'I didn't need a lift, Lee. You didn't need to come. I sprained my ankle. It's fine.'

'I wanted to see you. I wanted to give you this.'

He held up the bag for her to take.

'What is it?'

'Have a look. Go on, take it.'

Charlene pulled the top of the bag apart revealing folded white cashmere. She lifted it out, passed the bag back to Lee and unfolded the garment.

'A coat. DKNY.'

'Yeah, funky, isn't it?'

'Sure is. Must have set you back, Lee.'

'Only a touch, babe, only a touch.'

'Where did you get it, Lee? Not many places you can buy DKNY in town.'

'That's for me to know and for you not to worry about, babe.'

'Lee, you shouldn't have. You can't afford it on your wages.'

'Listen, don't worry about it. It's no sweat.'

'No, Lee, it's too much. Take it back.'

Charlene thrust the jacket into Lee's arms.

'What're you on about? You know I can't take it back.'

'Yeah, I do know, Lee, and I'm not taking it.'

'What the fuck's got into you? You never bothered before. Look at it, babe. You'll look a million in it.'

'Yeah, it's cool, Lee, but I'm not taking any more of your dodgy gear.'

'Christ, you're in a fucking weird mood today. What's got into you?'

'Oh, just fuck off, Lee. Go back to work. I'm tired.'

Lee shoved the jacket into the carrier bag.

'Yeah, well I will fuck off but I'll be back later. Maybe you'll have chilled out by then.'

'Whatever, Lee, whatever.'

Lee started to walk backwards down the path swinging the bag by his side. Charlene turned her back on him and walked towards the door. He wheeled around and started jogging down the road before turning around and running backwards, bouncing from foot to foot as he shouted his parting message.

'Hey, sexy. Fucking chill, won't you? I'll be back later.'

Charlene walked straight through the open door and up the stairs, pinching her nose to keep out the smell.

Chapter 10

'She get off all right?'

'Yes, she did, although I think her boyfriend was waiting for her in his car. A young man went racing after the taxi anyway.'

'Oh, I guessed she must have a boyfriend. Attractive girl.'

'Yes, very.'

'And she seemed nice. Quiet. Did she say much to you?'

'No, not really, but she did seem nice.'

'And do you think she could do everything? Do you think she could do the job? Did she understand what's required?'

'Oh yes, I think so. It's not difficult really and she seemed smart enough and willing.'

'Good, yes, that's good. Well, it would be great if she wants to do it and it would be good to help her on her way too.'

'Yes, and Sharon would be pleased.'

'Yes, of course. Dear Sharon. Well, we'll see what she says tomorrow and in the meantime we've got George Grandison coming soon.'

'Yes, that's right, at half past three.'

'Well, I suppose we'd better feed him tea and biscuits at the very least.'

'I brought a fruit cake in. He could have some of that.'

'Oh Maria. Do you think he deserves some of your fruit cake? I suppose he does. Actually, I do enjoy his visits in a way. They're a diversion, although I do wish he'd give up hoping that I'll start going to church. You know, Maria, he just can't understand why I would pay for that window but not go to church. I never have gone and never will. Besides, I couldn't manage it now, it would be much too difficult.'

'You're going to make an exception for our performance though, aren't you?'

'Yes, my dear, of course I am, I'm not going to miss that. Certainly not.'

'Oh good. I'm so pleased and, oh, by the way, I was talking to Stephen earlier who said that he and Lionel are going and that they would love to go with you.'

'Oh, that would be wonderful. I'd love that. The Maria fan club. What fun!'

'Well, I hope so, Mrs Crawford. It should be good. We've practised enough.'

'It'll be great, Maria, I know it will. You sing beautifully and I can't wait to hear you in an actual performance.'

'Oh, Mrs Crawford, that's kind of you but I just hope my nerves don't get the better of me. I try not to think about it. Try and keep myself distracted. Talking of which, I'd better be getting on with things.'

'I suppose you better had, my dear. I suppose you better had.'

Mrs Crawford's expression softened as she turned to look at the photograph of the girl.

'"*Raindrops on roses*"... I loved singing to you, my darling, and you loved my singing. "Sing more, Mummy, sing more. Sing about the whiskers on kittens, Mummy, sing it, please".'

A smile twitched at the corners of her mouth as she gazed at the smiling face of her daughter.

'Oh, Amy, you filled me with so much joy. Completely and utterly. Never to be matched.'

Looking out at the blue sky, her mind began to fill with memories.

*

You would wriggle on the floor beneath me giggling and squealing with laughter.

'Mummy, stop it, stop it, stop tickling me.'

When I stopped, your wriggling would cease and your giggling would subside to bursts of laughter from a body tensed in anticipation of further delicious torture. You would look up, your eyes bright, your whole face lit with a big smile. I would usually tease with fingers poised for more tickling and then lift you up for a hug, holding you close, this growing body, this developing person who came from microscopic matter inside my body. I would hug you tighter as I felt that powerful sense of connection emanate from my womb.

Your birth felt miraculous in ways I could not have anticipated. Not the process of giving birth. That was unbearably painful but the agony was instantly erased by the ecstasy of holding you for the first time, by wonder and joy. I was lucky not to be too exhausted. I was fit and strong then.

I would carry you into the garden, run around with you in the sunshine. Push you on the swing, lift you to the top of the chute time and time again. It was tiring at times, stressful in a way but I was happy to be with you and surprisingly happy to keep the business at arm's length.

'Come on, baby, let's go inside, it's time you had your supper.'

'Don't want supper, Mummy. Want to slide on the chute.'

'Come on, Amy, it's spaghetti tonight.'

'Buscetti?'

'Yes, that's right, with tomato sauce and cheese.'

'Mmmm. I like buscetti, Mummy.'

'I know you do, cherub. Come on then, I'll chase you in. Hurry or I'll tickle you.'

You would run off in that funny quick-stepping way looking over your shoulder laughing wildly in anticipation of being caught. It was never very difficult persuading you to do things. There was very little sulking or bad temper.

After supper Daddy would come home. You did love him, your daddy. It's a shame I didn't, a great shame. You deserved to have a father and mother who loved each other, although I am not sure how much you noticed or sensed it. You always ran to him when he came home before bedtime; well, almost always. I would try to suppress that welling up of petty jealousy when you hugged each other. But then I would almost always have you to myself again at bath time and certainly at bedtime apart from him popping in for a goodnight kiss before returning to his papers, his preparation for court or whatever it was.

That was when I sang to you, at bedtime. "'Raindrops on roses…", "Chim-chimanee, chim-chimanee….", "You are my sunshine, my only sunshine….", "Rock a bye baby…". You wouldn't always be asleep by the time I had finished but you were almost always at the stage where you would be happy to roll over and let me leave the room.

I would come into your room later before going to bed to tuck you in and watch you for a while. David, Daddy, would also go in to see you before he went to bed. I have no doubt that he would also feel that warm tickle around his heart, that sense of joyous love for our precious little girl. Was he also scared by how much he loved you? I am not sure, we never talked about these things. We didn't talk about anything really.

The time at which you would pad into our room trailing big, floppy Annabel behind you would vary. Sometimes it was so early that I would have to carry you back to your own bed otherwise too much of our sleep would be disturbed by your squiggling.

But you know all this, don't you? I have told you this so many *times before and you know how wonderful it was to wake up with you in the morning.*

'Mummy, Daddy, look, it's the sunshine, it's time to get up. Come on, it's time to get up.'

And you know how utterly devastating it was to see you lying there. The light that had lit up my life extinguished. I couldn't accept that you would never wake up again. It couldn't be true but it was. The sun would never shine again. A dark veil had been drawn across my life. I felt as though a heavy, blunt instrument had cleaved my chest and then scraped everything out leaving me bruised and aching. I still feel like that whenever I think about you. I only ever felt any real relief from it when I was in Greece. I'm still not sure why I felt more at peace there. It was something to do with that strong sense of you being with me.

'Oh Amy, I miss you more than ever, my love. I really do.'

'I'm sorry, Mrs Crawford, I didn't catch that?'

'Oh, Maria, I didn't notice you. It was nothing. I was talking to myself.'

'I came in to let you know that Reverend Grandison, George Grandison is here.'

'Oh, I didn't hear the buzzer.'

'Oh, really? Well, it did sound. A short burst.'

'That's funny. Oh well, never mind. Maria, if you don't mind, would you pass me the tissues, please?'

Maria lifted the box of tissues and placed them on the table next to Mrs Crawford.

'Are you ready for him now?'

'Well, I never feel quite ready for him, Maria, but yes please, show him in.'

Maria released an involuntary laugh.

'Well, hopefully he won't stay too long. I'll bring the tea and cake in straight away.'

*

Oh Amy. I so want to believe in what he says but he's so unconvincing. I need him to be unequivocal about the existence of God and the state of heaven. I need him to help me reinforce my faith that we will be reunited. I need him to help me overcome my rational side. I need definitive responses from him. I am sure I was very direct with him today. I tried to elicit a strong, clear response. What was it I said? Yes, that was it.

'I completely rejected any notion of God, George, after Amy died. I was very, very angry with the church and with anyone who believed in a God who could allow such cruel things to happen. It was only after a long time that my views softened.'

Even that didn't startle him. Mealy-mouthed platitudes, that's what I got. Mealy-mouthed platitudes and a sympathetic smile.

'I'm not surprised, Katherine. That was an understandable way to respond. Entirely understandable. Life can seem so unfair but in the end God will look after us if we let him, he really will.'

'George, you know, I must be honest, I still have difficulty accepting it all. I want to but it's difficult.'

'Most of us have moments of wavering to some degree, Katherine, but I sense your faith. I just look at your window and I know it's there.'

I couldn't take it any further. I couldn't let him think that all of that magnificent stained glass was donated by a doubter. I didn't want to tarnish the pleasure he gets from looking at the window, the spiritual reassurance he gets from gazing at the Lord as his shepherd. I just desperately want to know that he is my shepherd, your shepherd looking after you and Mum and Dad. Dear Dad, it's as much a tribute to your deep faith as anything, that window.

Mum, Dad, Amy, you are there, aren't you? I need you all so much, so very much.

She sighed deeply, gripped the ends of the armrests and slowly rose to her feet. After standing still for a moment she walked stiffly across the room to the chair at the window. Bending her knees she lowered herself until she was able to grip each armrest. She then released her straining muscles and flopped back into the cushioned upholstery.

Oh Amy, my body feels so old. I am becoming decrepit. I know I should try and exercise more but I really can't be bothered. I am beginning to cease caring. Am I becoming resigned to a gradual decline? I suppose I must be, although I sometimes yearn for the strength and vitality of youth. Not just youth, middle age also. I have been having dreams about swimming. About how I used to swim in Greece. About feeling that sense of freedom. The sense of being an essential part of creation, of the perpetual cycle of life. It made me increasingly certain that all of this natural wonder was transcended by something unknowingly more wonderful. I felt it inside at the core of my being. An exhilarating sense of being connected to a powerful and benign energy. I had never experienced that before and have not recaptured it since.

I was connecting with God. I must have been. I knew then that you were safe. You were beyond my care but you were safe. Why can't I be so certain now? It's panic. I'm panicking. Time is running out. I'm not afraid of death, it's not that. Ever since you succumbed, Amy, I ceased to be afraid of the physical process of death. It's not that, it's the possibility that in dying I might be losing you again that I can't bear. You are with me now. You are the focus of all of my love. You inhabit my heart, my mind... my soul. I cannot allow the rational argument to invade my thinking. That it's ashes to ashes, dust to dust and no more. But how can it be more? We are entirely physical, insignificant in the vastness of the universe. Where is God amongst all of that? Why would there be a spiritual aspect to it all? We delude ourselves in believing that there is any truth other than the material evidence in front of our eyes.

Turning to stare searchingly at the horizon, she spoke as her sense of desperation rose and breached her silence.

'Amy, I'm sorry, so sorry. I get confused. We will be reunited. It will feel better and closer than even the biggest hug and we will never be parted again… It has to happen. I can't bear to think that it won't. I can't bear it. I need you so much. It has to happen.'

A molten heat welled up from her heart and clogged her throat. Her voice broke down, disabled by the sobs issuing from her constricted chest. The sky and sea became painfully bright as the stinging moistness covered her eyes. Her eyelids flickered against the glare. Tears trailed down her cheeks. She reached out for the tissues before realising that she had left them on the other side of the room.

She grabbed the ends of the armrests and pulled herself to her feet. After pausing to find her balance, she walked slowly, very slowly, back to the chair she had been sitting in before.

Chapter 11

'He's a... he's... he does interiors.'

As soon as she had spoken the words, Charlene recognised that she was trying to make her life seem more impressive than it was.

'Oh, that sounds interesting. Is it something to do with interior design?'

'Yes, well, yes, he paints them, the interiors, and decorates them.'

'Oh, I see. A painter and decorator. Very good.'

'Yes, that's right, he paints the walls and doors and things and he decorates, wallpaper mainly but not much.'

'Well, that must keep him busy. I'm sure there's always a demand for painters and decorators.'

'Yes, it's good. It's a good job for him.'

'Good. Well, I had the apartment redecorated last year. I like to keep it fresh. It was mostly paintwork actually. No wallpaper. I don't like patterns. I like to keep it simple and light. Maria wanted something warmer in the kitchen. It reflects her personality which is great but I prefer cool colours.'

Charlene flicked her eyes around to take in the whole room. She liked it. It was very stylish but she preferred the warmer, more comfortable environment of the kitchen.

Thinking that she probably did not need to say anything more, Charlene resumed setting the table. White linen mats on the polished mahogany. Modern steel cutlery. A crystal tumbler. All as Maria had shown her.

She handled everything with care, uneasy about its strangeness and also aware that it was expensive. She had been taken aback by Maria's instruction that the glasses could not be cleaned in the dishwasher. They had to be washed in hot soapy water and dried with a clean dish towel.

The sound of Mrs Crawford's voice penetrated the density of her thoughts.

'What's he like, Charlene?'

'I'm sorry?'

'Lee, what's he like? I'm sorry for being nosy. I hope you don't mind. You don't need…'

'No, I don't mind. He's, he's all right.'

'Handsome, I bet. I'm sure he must be good-looking.'

'Yes, he looks good.'

'Have you been together long?'

'Yes, since Christmas.'

'Six months. Well, that is quite a long time but short enough for it to be fresh and exciting still, if you know what I mean.'

Charlene nodded in agreement despite faltering on Mrs Crawford's suggestion that it must be fresh and exciting. The only exciting thing about their relationship she could think of was the sex. It seemed unlikely that Mrs Crawford had this in mind but she knew that she should respond positively anyway.

'Yes, I do. I mean, yes, it is.'

'How wonderful to be young and in love. I am envious!'

'Oh, I'm not in love, Mrs Crawford. Not with Lee. I wouldn't say that I… no, I'm not. I'm just going out with him and having a good time.'

'Oh, I see. I'm sorry, Charlene. I misunderstood. Well, you've plenty of time to find the right man, haven't you? There's no rush.'

'What? I mean, yes, well, I hadn't really thought about it but, yes, I suppose so. No rush.'

'Well, my dear, I wonder if supper will be ready now. Do you think so? In about five minutes?'

'Yes, it should be, Mrs Crawford. I'll just go and get it ready.'

*

Charlene reversed through the door pushing it open with her bottom while keeping the loaded tray steady and level. She lowered the tray onto the table and distributed everything in accordance with Maria's instructions.

Just as she finished she saw Mrs Crawford pull herself to her feet and start to make her way slowly across the room.

'Can you manage, Mrs Crawford? Can I help?'

She rushed to Mrs Crawford's side, her arms raised in readiness.

'I could manage but if you take my arm that would be a lovely help, Charlene.'

Charlene positioned her arm under Mrs Crawford's, unsure whether or not she was being a help or a hindrance.

'Thanks, Charlene. That's better.'

Arriving at the table Charlene carefully removed her supporting arm and pulled out a chair. Mrs Crawford then shuffled sideways waiting until Charlene had pushed the chair into position before dropping into it abruptly.

'Make the most of your mobility while you've got it, Charlene. You may always have it, of course, however it is awful when you go into decline as I am. Not the worst affliction but awful nevertheless. I was fit and active not so many years ago. It's important to stay fit and active, Charlene. Do you do any sports, any physical activity?'

Her face clouded as she considered how to respond. She had not played football since leaving school or taken part in any regular physical activity apart from dancing at the nightclub and sex.

'No, not really, Mrs Crawford.'

'Well, fitness seems like a given when you're young with a whole life in front of you but sooner or later you should think of ways to keep fit, my love. It keeps you young. Still, at least you don't smoke.'

'No, I can't stand smoking. The smell. It makes me sick.'

'I know what you mean. Now, Charlene, it looks like you are only catering for one here. Are you not joining me?'

Charlene removed the lid from the plate at Mrs Crawford's place setting.

'No, it's OK. I'll have a sandwich later.'

'Stuffed vine leaves. *Dolmades* in Greek. It's an acquired taste perhaps but you would have been very welcome to eat your sandwich with me. Have you ever tried them? Stuffed vine leaves? Not many people have.'

'No, I've never heard of them.'

'I'm not surprised, Charlene. It's a Greek dish. I like Greek food. I lived in Greece for a while and grew to really like it. It's tasty and very healthy. They use a lot of herbs, fresh herbs. You might like stifado. It's a beef stew with herbs and nutmeg, oh and orange zest and shallots, I think. Delicious. You eat meat, don't you, my dear?'

'Yes I do. I eat burgers mainly and Mum does a roast dinner sometimes.'

'Good. Well, I'll ask Maria to do a stifado although it's more of a winter dish, I suppose. She also does great meatballs which I'm sure you would like. We can't have you surviving on sandwiches. A good diet is so important but I'm not going to start preaching to you about diet so let's talk about something else.'

'OK, Mrs Crawford, but I was just going to go and put the kettle on. Would you like a cup of tea or something?'

'No thanks. Not just now. I'll have a cup of camomile tea later after I've finished supper but you go and make yourself something.'

She felt an exhilarating sense of relief as she spun away from the door and rushed across the hall.

She pushed back firmly against the door until the latch clicked shut. She then leaned back against it for a moment and looked around. The kitchen made her feel good. She had never seen that deep red colour on walls before. Everything looked better and much more colourful than her kitchen at home. She filled the kettle, switched it on and sat at the table.

Her mood mellowed as she thought through the process of getting ready for the nightclub so that they could go straight there when Lee came to collect her. She had to work out how to avoid Mrs Crawford seeing her in the dress. Its curve-clinging skimpy cut would give her a sense of empowerment in the nightclub but she would feel very uncomfortable revealing so much of her body to Mrs Crawford. She would have to go in and say goodbye at the last moment with her overcoat securely wrapped around her.

Hearing the kettle click as it switched off, Charlene rose and walked over to make the tea. She then danced across to the fridge, gyrating her hips in a slow rhythm and holding her arms high above her head. Singing softly she returned across the room with the milk carton, twirling a full circle in the middle of the floor with her arms stretched out to the side.

A frisson of anticipation fizzed inside her. She would have two or maybe three cocktails tonight, no more, and she would definitely not be taking any drugs. She needed to feel fresh tomorrow and, besides, she liked to stay in control and to be fully aware of the attention she attracted. She thrived on the empowerment of turning heads. It stirred the fire of her sexuality but she always deflected any further attention. She could not be bothered having to deal with Lee's anger when men flirted with her.

Turning her head to banish this negative thought, she caught sight of the kitchen clock.

She had to leave in just over an hour. It was time to return to Mrs Crawford.

*

'That was delicious, Charlene. I know it looks odd, rice and minced meat wrapped in leaves but it tastes really good. It also reminds me of Greece and my time there. Looking back. You do quite a lot of that at my stage in life.'

Charlene sat down at the opposite end of the table, placing her mug on a mat.

'I know most young people live for the moment but do you look forward, my dear? Do you think about what the future might hold? How to achieve things?'

Charlene looked down at the mug of tea nestled in the wrap of her hands. She felt a heavy melancholy sink within her. Thinking about the future was too difficult. She knew she would have to leave home. That was as far as her thinking went.

'Not really. It's difficult.'

'It must be difficult, my dear. I understand that or at least I think I do. You're just feeling your way forward now, I imagine.'

Surmising from her perplexed expression that Charlene was not going to respond, Mrs Crawford continued.

'It's a shame really that you can't look forward, Charlene. Won't it be great when you can get to the stage when you can look forward with excitement? When you can start working towards goals, to getting the most out of life, to falling in love and making a future together with someone else.'

Charlene lifted the mug to her lips with both hands, sipped some tea and lowered it back onto the mat. She associated falling in love with fairy tales, not with real life. Her own kind of life just happened in much the same way as it did for everyone else she knew. She did not do much about it other than try to stay out of trouble.

'I can't... I can't imagine it. That kind of life.'

Mrs Crawford looked at her warmly and smiled.

'Well, never mind, my dear. Enough chat. Could you help me back to my chair?'

'Yes, yes, of course.'

After helping Mrs Crawford to her feet, they crossed the room in an awkward coupling. Having manoeuvred into position at the armchair, Charlene was taken unawares when Mrs Crawford dropped onto the seat. Dragged down by her slumping body, Charlene's arm became stuck between her back and the chair and her face was pulled in close to the back of Mrs Crawford's perfumed neck. Groaning with effort, Mrs Crawford leaned forward to release her.

'Oh dear, I am sorry. I drop rather suddenly. My legs give way.'

'It's OK, Mrs Crawford. I'm fine. Are you all right?'

'Yes, my dear. My joints are aching a bit but I'm not bad. I always seem to feel a bit better when I resist the temptation to have a glass of wine. It seems to go to my joints somehow. I'll stick with the camomile tea tonight.'

'Oh yes, of course, I'll just go and get it.'

'No, don't worry, Charlene. No rush. You bring your tea over and sit for a while. You've got an hour, don't you?'

'Yes, yes, I do.'

Charlene picked up her tea from the dining room table and sat near to Mrs Crawford, placing the mug carefully on a coaster between the framed photographs on the side table between them.

'One of my shrines, you might say.'

'I'm sorry?'

'This table with the photographs.'

'Oh, I'm sorry.'

Charlene reached her hand out to remove the mug.

'Oh, I didn't mean that it was sacred in any way. I just meant that I like to look at the photographs and think about things, about life and remember. Remember Amy mainly. My daughter. I suppose that Maria has told you about her?'

'Yes, yes, that was sad. I'm... I'm sorry.'

'Thank you, Charlene. It was sad, very sad. It happened so quickly a very long time ago but I still think about her of course. I like to think about her. I love her as much now, if not more than ever. That's true love of course, a parent's love for a child. It doesn't go deeper than that, at least I can't imagine it does. I would have given up my life to save hers without question. Without hesitation.'

Not knowing how to respond, Charlene watched her in silence as she gazed lovingly at the photograph. She observed her eyes, her lashes accentuated with light mascara, her carefully pencilled eyebrows, her styled hair holding its shape around her face. An old face but elegant. The fine line of her nose, her pronounced cheekbones, the high forehead above the arching eyebrows and oval eyes, these were the features which dominated her appearance, not the sagging skin below her chin, the wrinkles and liver spots.

She tried to imagine her as a younger woman. It was difficult to form a clear picture. It was clear that she would have been strikingly beautiful, all of her, her face and her body. She would have had everything; looks, intelligence and wealth. As Charlene waited for Mrs Crawford to continue, she thought about the significance of someone so fortunate being willing to give it all up to save her child.

Could it be true that all parents would do that? She could

not imagine her own parents feeling so strongly about her even though they would be giving up far less. They might be more concerned about Marlene and she could imagine her mother doing it for Kevin. Not her father though. He did not seem to care enough about anything.

She softened her focus as Mrs Crawford turned towards her.

'Parents wish their children could be immortal. I certainly did. Of course that's not possible, at least not in a physical state but you certainly wish that they have a long, happy life and that you go long before them.'

Mrs Crawford's development of her theme sent Charlene's mind into a fretful spin. She queried her understanding of the word "immortal" but became certain it meant "never dying". She then wondered how she would react to the death of someone in her family. How would she feel if Marlene or Kevin contracted the same illness and died? She had heard of meningitis but did not know it could be so serious and become fatal so quickly. How would she feel? She would certainly feel sad. Yes, it would be very sad to lose them even though they annoyed her.

'It must be… it must be very sad for you not having her.'

'It has been and still is but she did give me a lot in her short life, Charlene, which has really given me a lot of strength. I understood or experienced deep love for the first time. Of course I loved my parents, my father, my mother but this was pure, unqualified love given back to me in equal measure.'

Mrs Crawford looked up and turned towards Charlene, her features lifting with the emergence of a smile, her eyes glistening.

'She still fills me full of joy, Charlene, even now. I hope you don't mind all of this, my dear, but I wanted to tell you about her. To tell you about the most important person in my life.'

'No, Mrs Crawford. I don't mind. I don't mind at all.'

'I'm glad about that, Charlene. I'm afraid you'll find I like to talk. I feel an increasing need to talk. I'm not sure exactly why but I do. Of course I talk to Maria but she's busy most of the time, bless her. Anyway, my love, I don't want to keep you. You had better tidy up and get off home.'

'Oh, I'm not going home. I'm going out.'

'Gosh, well of course, it's Friday. Well that's exciting, at least I hope it will be. Are you going clubbing?'

Taken aback that Mrs Crawford knew about clubbing, Charlene blurted her response.

'Yes, yes, I am. Lee's picking me up.'

'Good. Oh well, listen, we'd better cancel the taxi. If you could just pass me the phone.'

Charlene stood up abruptly.

'The taxi. I didn't think about that.'

'Doesn't matter, Charlene. I've set up an order so they come automatically. I can easily cancel it tonight.'

'Yes... yes.'

Charlene jerked her head around, agitatedly trying to locate the phone.

'It's over there on the credenza, the sideboard in the corner.'

'Oh.'

Charlene turned around sharply, knocking her knee on the arm of the chair and stumbling slightly. After regaining her balance she retrieved the phone and handed it to Mrs Crawford.

'Thank you. Now off you go and finish off.'

Charlene transferred everything from the table onto the tray while Mrs Crawford scrolled through the phone memory looking for the taxi number. Before phoning she looked up at Charlene.

'Charlene, my dear, use Maria's bathroom if you need to get ready. I know she won't mind as long as it's left clean and tidy.'

*

The lift whooshed softly to a stop at the ground floor. Charlene stepped out. She felt exhilaratingly underdressed beneath the wrap of her overcoat. She felt more exposed now than she would in the club with her coat off. Her tactic of telling Mrs Crawford that she had to rush because Lee was waiting had allowed her to say goodbye quickly without letting Mrs Crawford see her dress. The drawback of this manipulation of the truth was that she now had to wait in the entrance lobby for Lee to turn up. She would stay in the lobby until he arrived unless she heard the lift, in which case she would step outside and walk down the road. She would not risk her lingering presence being noticed by Lionel or another neighbour who might report it back to Mrs Crawford in passing conversation.

Charlene stood behind the full-height window, her hands thrust deep into the pockets of her coat. With everything outside remaining quiet, she withdrew her hands, untied the belt and opened the coat to reveal her dress. She looked in appreciation at her reflection. She was proud of her body, slim but shapely.

She looked down at her legs. Long limbed with fine ankles was how Mr Martin had described them. She thought that it was probably not right that he should have said that, but then he was an art teacher.

Charlene overlapped the coat flaps and retied the belt. Dispelling the exciting thought of what it would feel like to be completely naked under the coat, she resolved to keep it firmly wrapped until she was in the club. She did not want to have to deal with the consequences of arousing Lee's desire too early.

All of these considerations evaporated as the sound of someone descending the stairs with a dog caused her to stiffen. Her plan to exit before being seen would not work. It was too late to leave without being noticed and, even though she knew Lionel would recognise her from behind, she continued to look resolutely ahead.

A shiver ran up her spine as the dog's panting became louder.

'Rufus! Rufus! For goodness' sake, calm down!'

Hearing the unfamiliar female voice, her body relaxed and she released her withheld breath. She turned her head to get an oblique view of the woman reaching over the dog to open the door. At that same moment the woman looked back at Charlene and smiled weakly. Charlene's own face remained impassive as she turned away to carry on looking out for Lee.

She reflected on her conversations with Mrs Crawford. She thought in particular about telling her that she did not love Lee. She had said this without thinking about it and realised that it was not something that had entered her mind. She was glad to be going out with someone so popular. All of the cool people she knew wanted to associate with him and being his girlfriend had boosted her own status. Despite acknowledging this, the conversation with Mrs Crawford had made her realise that she did not actually love him. Why should she? She was certain he did not love her. Apart from giving her presents, he showed no real signs of having any great feeling for her and had certainly never said anything about love.

Shafting light from car headlights shone through the glass and washed brightly across the lobby. She knew it was Lee's car not just because of the twin headlights on each side but also because of the noise.

Hugging her coat around her, Charlene walked out, shoving the door open with her shoulder. Lee revved the car as he waited, each loud burst of engine noise momentarily drowning out the pulsating rhythm from his music system.

Lee turned down the volume and turned round to look at Charlene as she lowered into the seat while smoothing her coat under her thighs.

'How's it going, babe? I'm late, I know, but only a few minutes so let's not argue about it. OK?'

Lee turned the volume up again and accelerated off so rapidly that Charlene felt her back pressing into the seat. Relaxing her neck she allowed her head to tilt back against the headrest. He glanced at her, shouting to ensure she could hear him above the music.

'Quiet tonight. What's up? Is the old dear working you too hard?'

Charlene rolled her head round to look at him. He was smiling as he chewed gum, moving his head in time with the music. He turned to look at her again, his eyebrows raised enquiringly.

Charlene stretched out her arm and turned down the volume.

'How am I getting home tonight? If you're drinking or anything you won't be driving or at least you won't be driving me anywhere.'

'Christ, you aren't half getting a nag in your old age. Don't worry, I'll dump the car in the multistorey. We'll get a taxi.'

Charlene turned the volume up a couple of notches, tilted her head back again and closed her eyes. Lee reached across and increased the volume to its original level. Charlene frowned, her eyes remaining closed.

Chapter 12

Right arm raised then left arm, alternating in rhythm with the music, her face set in concentration as she became fully synchronised with the mesmeric beat. Her dress flicked up at the hem as her hip motion became more vigorous. She did not care that this might be revealing her thong strap and bare buttocks. In this situation, within the protected environment of the club, when she was in the groove, absorbed in the music, she found the exposure of her body thrilling. She did not consider the paradox that this was when she felt strongest, most secure about herself. She felt unassailably confident about being an object of attention while she herself was oblivious to everything except the rhythms and the beats.

Mega Mikeman mixed onto a new track. The urgent pulse of a different rhythm synchronised with lances of laser light darting in all directions stimulated a communal surge of adrenaline-fuelled excitement. All arms rose simultaneously in the air, all faces lifted up towards "The Mikeman" working the deck with one hand, the other held high in acknowledgement of this mass approval.

Charlene dropped her arm. She hadn't moved to the next level with everyone else. It was time to take a break. She turned around to head for the bar with her hand held out to palm people gently aside. She exchanged smiles with familiar people and friends. One man stood in front of her, dancing sinuously in drug-induced self-absorption. He reached out his hand, slipping it down her trailing arm as she moved past. Ignoring him, she surged forward until a man stepped in front of her. He was highly groomed with a tight T-shirt moulded to his gym-honed body.

'Hi, babe! You on your own tonight?'

'No, Lee's over there.'

Charlene turned to point at a group of young men shifting and shoving in a testosterone-charged dynamic. Lee stood in the focal position amongst them, the principal protagonist, alpha male.

'Oh right. With his mates. Well, he must be mental leaving you on your own. You're the best-looking babe here by a mile.'

'Thanks, Luke. You're not looking too bad yourself.'

A leering smile spread across his face as he moved closer to her. Placing his hand on her upper arm, he pressed his groin against her belly and whispered softly into her ear.

'Two good-looking people like you and me, we'd be hot together. Red hot. So how about it, babe?'

Pushing him away with a force which made him stagger backwards, Charlene's voice cut through the noise with searing clarity.

'Cut it out, Luke, if you know what's good for you. There's no way that's going to happen.'

She spun around and walked off with a dismissive wave.

Confounded between rage and humiliation, he shouted after her, the words dying away unheard as she weaved elegantly through the crowd.

'You know you want me… yeah… you just don't want to show it… yeah… well, you'd better make your mind up, or… or…'

Reaching the bar, Charlene walked to the end near Lee and his mates. She stood with her back towards them, one arm resting on the marble top. She sensed his arrival behind her before seeing his left hand appear alongside her's and feeling his right hand squeeze the upper part of her other arm.

'Hey, babe. That loser Luke was getting a bit fucking close.'

'Him? He's not worth worrying about. The guy's drunk, that's all.'

'Yeah, well he'll need to be drunk when I get to him cos he's gonna feel a lot of pain if he isn't.'

'Christ, let it go, Lee. He isn't worth it.'

'Yeah, well he's got a fucking nerve, messing about with my bird.'

'Look, just forget about it, would you? I'm going to get another Manhattan, do you want a beer?'

'No. Baz has just got a round in. I'll get you a drink. I've got a tab going.'

Lee beckoned to the barman.

'Hey, Carlos! Get the lady a Manhattan, would you? It's on the tab.'

Having received a nod of acknowledgment he moved in closer and whispered into her ear.

'I need it bad, babe, so bad. Just give me the nod and we'll get outta here. OK babe? Anytime. Just give me the nod.'

'I don't know Lee. We'll have to see how it goes. I'm tired. We might have to give it a miss tonight.'

'Oh, come on. You know you'll want it. You know you will.'

Lee stepped back to stand straight-backed with his legs apart as he nodded assertively at Charlene. Resisting the urge to turn around, she looked down the bar, wincing as he raised his voice to deliver his parting shot before retreating briskly beyond the reach of any final retort.

'You can't resist me, babe, like I can't resist you. Can you? You can't resist me.'

Charlene remained impassive, focusing her attention on Carlos as he shook her drink, the final flourish in his bottle-tossing, high-pouring performance before sliding his creation along the bar towards her.

'The best cocktail in town, specially made for a special lady.'

'Thanks, Carlos, you're a star.'

'It's the least I can do. I'd like to do more but Lee would probably punch my lights out.'

'Oh Carlos, he wouldn't dare!'

'I'm not going to put it to the test!'

Carlos grinned warmly and returned to the busy end of the bar. Charlene walked off slowly, sipping her drink through the straw. It was time to find company. It would be uncool to remain solo for much longer. She looked for the most appealing group to assimilate into. Her best mates were on the floor dancing. She wasn't ready to join them. Cynthia and Suzy were sitting at a table with an empty chair. Not the coolest company but an easy option. She moved across the room in a slow sashay. A seductive smile softened her face ready to acknowledge people as she passed. Without looking at the girls she drew alongside their table and swooped into the chair, her face brightening as she sat down.

'Hi, girls. How are you doing?'

'Hey, Charlene. Cool. We're cool, aren't we, Suze?'

'Yeah, cool. How're things with you?'

'Oh, not bad. Got a job.'

'Hey! What is it? Where are you working?'

'Oh it's, ah, it's what d'you call it, being an assistant carer.'

'What, like in a nursing home?'

'No. Well, it's like to an old lady, in her apartment. She's rich.'

'Oh, I see. Sounds cool.'

'Yes, it is. It's good. She lives up in Marine Heights. I've been doing it for a couple of weeks.'

Looking out across the dance floor, Charlene leaned forward

to pick up her drink. Staring at the light show flashing, pulsing and strobing, she reclined against the chair, flicking her hair back with a shake of her head.

They each became absorbed with watching the action on the dance floor until Suzy turned towards Cynthia.

'I'm just going to the toilet.'

'OK, Suze.'

Suzy squeezed out and walked off unsteady on her heels for the first few steps as she smoothed out the creases in her dress.

Charlene turned to look at Cynthia.

'All right, Cynth?'

'Yes, fine.'

'How's your work?'

'Oh, not bad. It gets a bit boring sometimes. Lots of typing. Threw a sickie today.'

'Cynth! Bad girl.'

'Well, I don't do it much. I'm trying to be good. Don't tell Mum.'

'Don't worry. I never see her anyway. Saw your dad though. In the pub.'

'Oh. I don't see him. Haven't seen him for over a year really.'

'Oh right. Sorry.'

'No. It's OK. How's your family?'

'Oh, same as usual. You know.'

'That's good. Seems like things are going well.'

'How d'you mean, Cynth? Going well?'

'Well, you know, you've got your family, a good job and Lee.'

'Yeah. I guess.'

Charlene placed her drink on the table and leaned back, resting her arms on the upholstered sides of the chair. She submitted again to the hypnotic allure of the dance floor, her head moving to the beat in miniscule movements until, breaking out of her trance on Suzy's return, she sat forward.

'My turn now. I might go back to the floor after but I'll see you later. OK?'

She turned around to look back at the bar as she passed the toilets before walking around the corner to the cloakroom. The attendant lowered her magazine onto the counter as Charlene drew near.

'Away early tonight?'

'Yes, I'm not feeling too good. Lee's staying though. I've given him permission.'

Charlene backed up her deceit with a wry smile.

'It's the long cream coat. Donna Karan. Lee's got the ticket. Sorry.'

'Don't worry. I remember you coming in with it. It's over here somewhere.'

Charlene glanced back in the direction of the bar area. She could hear the music, people talking loudly and laughing but she could see none of it from here. She turned back to watch the attendant walk towards her between the coat rails.

'This is it, isn't it?'

'That's the one. Thanks.'

'It's a nice one. I've noticed you in it before. Looks great on.'

'Thanks.'

Charlene pulled the coat on, flicking the collar up around her neck. She then reached into the pocket, extracted a pound and placed it amongst the other coins in the saucer before walking towards the entrance.

She felt calmer with each step towards her escape, until a voice shouting at her from behind filled her with a swirling mix of fear and fury.

'Hey, stop! Where the fuck are you going?'

Stiffening to a halt, she turned to face her aggressor as he walked up to her with a showy swagger. She held her hand up to convey the firm signal that she would be setting the boundaries in this exchange.

'Where I am going is none of your business and let me make it very clear, Luke, if Lee finds out that you are hassling me he will make it his business to batter you so just fuck off and leave me alone.'

She then swirled around and walked to the door ignoring Luke's riposte.

'Think I'm scared of Lee? Huh? No way could he batter me. No fucking way.'

Seeing one of the doormen open the glazed door from the outside as she approached, Charlene knew that Luke would not cause her any further trouble.

'Off early tonight?'

'Yeah, Trev, I'm not feeling one hundred per cent. Lee's staying but I just want to get home. Any chance you could phone me a cab?'

'Yeah. No problem, Charlie. For you, anytime. Just give me a sec.'

She flashed a smile at the other doorman as Trev walked off to the side. She pulled her coat tightly around her.

'That's it, Charlene. Be here in a couple of minutes.'

'You're a star, Trev. Thanks.'

Charlene shuffled from foot to foot to contain her fretful impatience as the doormen chatted about their workouts at the gym. She had anticipated it would take at least five minutes for a taxi to arrive and felt an exhilarating sense of relief when one pulled up much sooner.

After opening the car door, Trev ducked down to look at her as she settled into the seat.

'I'll make sure your man behaves himself. Don't you worry about that.'

Charlene smiled up at him as he closed the door.

'Where we off to then, love?'

She disguised her surprise as she looked at the familiar eyes in the rear-view mirror.

'Uh. Stanley Osborne Way. Number fourteen.'

The driver straining against the stiffness of his neck looked round at Charlene.

'Well I never. What are the chances of that? How many times is that now? I didn't recognise you in that coat and with your hair and all. Had a good night?'

'Yeah thanks. I'm tired though. I need to get home.'

'Don't worry, love. Just sit back and relax.'

Charlene looked back as the taxi drove off. Trev and the other doorman were laughing, their movements silhouetted against the blue-lit entrance foyer. This was a quiet period for them. The middle of the evening with no one arriving and no one leaving.

The thrill of having escaped began to subside. She expected that Lee would begin to wonder where she was and that he would soon be at the door asking Trev if he had seen her. She knew that he would be furious but that he would go back to his mates and play down her absence with some jokey remark.

Charlene leaned back and closed her eyes.

She reflected on her motivation for leaving. It surprised her that she had followed through in acting on the emerging realisation that she should end their relationship. She had been concerned about losing status but having escaped the nightclub, she recognised that it was not enough for her to be associated with such a popular guy and to be driven around in a flashy car. Neither Lee, her parents or anyone else would understand why that wasn't enough for her. They would not be able to understand her growing sense that she should be seeking more from a relationship than Lee could ever provide. That there was much more to life than finding a boyfriend who could become a husband and father to children. They would not understand but Mrs Crawford would.

She looked out of the window at the illuminated shop windows appearing and disappearing as they sped through the night-time streets. Turning her frowning gaze to the other side, she caught sight of the driver's eyes in the rear-view mirror as he glanced back.

'All right, love?'

'Yes, yes. I… I remembered something. It doesn't matter. Not important.'

'Sure, love? I can go back if…'

'No, no, it's fine. Honestly.'

She breathed in, releasing the tension in her body as she exhaled. Closing her eyes she breathed in again, this time deeply through her nose. She felt calmer after the second exhalation.

Becoming a single woman would be hard to deal with but she had to do it. To break away and see how life worked out without him. She had to get rid of at least one source of her nagging discontent.

Chapter 13

A wave of televised laughter followed by a ripple of applause burst the silence as she walked across the hallway. Her father was scratching the back of his head with his fat fingers. His other hand was holding a can of beer, his tattooed forearm lying heavily on the armrest.

'Hi, Dad.'

'Charlie, I didn't hear you. What you doing back so early?'

He heaved around to look at her as she walked into the room.

'What's up? Trouble with the boyfriend?'

'No, Dad. I'm just tired. I'm going to bed.'

'Blimey. Not like you. This work lark must be getting to you.'

'Whatever, Dad, whatever. I'm off.'

Breathing noisily with gargled rasps from the back of his throat, he shifted forward to grab a packet of cigarettes from the coffee table.

'Why don't you watch telly for a while? This is a right laugh.'

Charlene looked back on her way to the door.

'You must be joking. That guy's not funny.'

She watched her father suck in and then exhale a plume of smoke before wheeling away in disgust.

'Goodnight, Dad.'

*

Charlene chucked the make-up smeared pad into the bin, picked up the toothbrush and toothpaste and moved closer to the mirror.

She inspected her weary face and yearned as she did most nights for her own bedroom. She did not have the energy to deal with the questions which Marlene would fire at her about coming home early.

After cleaning her teeth she picked up her shoes and walked across the hall. Something on the bedroom floor made it difficult to open the door. Charlene shoved hard until the gap was wide enough to pass through into the dimly lit room, illuminated only by the soft glow of Marlene's computer screen. Marlene slipped her headphones onto her neck and swivelled around in the chair.

'Oh my god. It's you! I thought it must be Mum back early. I wasn't expecting you so soon.'

'Don't just sit there, you lazy cow. You might have picked up your bloody towel.'

Charlene walked across the room to switch on her bedside light.

'How come you're back so early?'

'I'm bloody knackered. I need to go to bed.'

'Oh c'mon. You've fallen out with Lee, haven't you?'

'No but even if I have it's none of your business.'

'You have. Haven't you?'

'No, I have not. I'm just tired and I'm going to bed. All right?'

'You've fallen out. I know you have.'

Marlene swivelled back to face the computer repositioning the headphones over her ears.

Charlene reached behind to unzip her dress before pulling it down and stepping out of it. After opening the wardrobe doors and hanging the dress up, she turned to look at herself in the mirror as she removed her bra. After flinging it into the laundry basket she looked at herself again, pulling her shoulders back and striking a pose.

She was proud of her body and that people admired it, but she needed to be more than an object of lustful attention, and certainly more than a trophy girlfriend and the outlet for Lee's sex drive.

Pivoting on the balls of her feet she turned towards the wardrobe shelves looking sideways at her profile, before removing a T-shirt. After slipping it on she pulled off her thong and dropped it in the laundry basket as she walked over to her bed. She bounced into position under the duvet and switched off the bedside light. Rocking her hips she worked her body into the comforting meld of the mattress. The sensation of heavily hugging cover and forgiving support sent a slow wave of relaxation through her body. The shiver of relief up her back induced a soft, stuttering moan. This was her refuge. This bed jammed into the corner of the bedroom. She felt unassailable here, secure. Marlene's presence reinforced her sense of safety. She watched her sister alternate between concentration and sitting back, her body occasionally responding to the music, sometimes with movement of her head and other times with her legs and feet also. Marlene had not taken to street life as Charlene had at her age. She preferred to stay at home in the evenings communicating with her friends through social media. She looked across at Charlene, flashed a smile and gave a brief finger-fluttering wave. After smiling back at her sister, Charlene looked up at the ceiling, thoughts rolling through her tired mind.

I guess I do love her really, and Mum and Kevin... and Dad. I would definitely hate anything bad to happen to her. At least we talk and look out for each other kind of, not like Mrs Crawford and her sister. All that talk about love and she doesn't talk to her sister. What was it Maria said... they were completely different, they fell out and she went to Canada. Started a new life in Canada. What was her name... strange name... Lily, yes, that's it, Lily... She doesn't talk about her husband either or any other men. Just her daughter. That must have been terrible. Losing her little girl, and she still hasn't got over it even though it happened so long ago, long before I was born. Imagine that. It's a shame.

Charlene rolled over and reached for the earplugs on the bedside table. After pushing them firmly into her ears she lay back and closed her eyes.

She sighed deeply and let her thoughts drift again. She was looking forward to the refuge of sleep and to heading back to Marine Heights in the morning.

Chapter 14

The dull glow from the electric lanterns hanging from the vine covered pergola provided a low level of illumination but it would be sufficient to read by. It was brighter around the bar where strong down-lighters made the bottles and glasses gleam and glint and the oranges, lemons and limes glow vividly. She would not sit there though. It would become busy later with carousing groups, their shrieking and joking fuelled by alcohol and holiday hysteria. She would sit in the corner to be as inconspicuous as possible.

She was glad that she had been tough with herself, that she had summoned the energy and courage to go out, this first night without Amanda. She knew that she would have felt lonelier at the villa and she now began to feel emboldened by the possibility that she might even enjoy the distraction of being in a public space.

Edging sideways between the tables and navigating a route which avoided coming close to the few early-evening diners, she made her way towards the corner.

She moved as quickly as she could without appearing hasty. She regretted her decision to wear a short black dress and wanted to conceal her legs under a table. A plain T-shirt and her baggy cotton trousers would have been much more comfortable for dining alone in a busy taverna.

Becoming aware of Spiros breezing across the floor to greet her, she stopped and turned towards him.

'Katherine. Good to see you. Amanda has gone already, yes? Never mind, I'll look after you. Now where you want to sit?'

'Thanks, Spiros. I'm going to sit in the corner and read a book.'

'Of course, of course.'

His belly like a rounded prow, Spiros surged past, his arm held high pointing towards the corner.

'Is it enough light to read here?'

'Yes, thanks. It will be enough.'

'You want a quiet time. Huh?'

'Yes, Spiros. Yes, I do.'

'That's OK. I will make sure you have quiet as much as possible.'

Katherine side-stepped between the table and the wall, pressing her bare legs against the table edge to avoid snagging her dress on the rough render. Having been distracted by the sight of three men approaching the bar, Spiros turned back towards Katherine.

'Oh, excuse me.'

He pulled the table back from the wall. After smoothing the dress down her hips, Katherine lowered herself into the seat. Spiros repositioned the table in front of her. He then flashed another look towards the bar while withdrawing an order pad and pen from the breast pocket on his shirt.

'Now. What to eat? Tonight we also have fresh little fishes and fresh calamari, fresh squid, really nice.'

'That sounds good. Can I have the calamari and a Greek salad, please? Oh, and a small flask of Retsina and a bottle of water.'

'Of course, of course. Large or small, the water?'

'Oh, small, I suppose. No, large. I'll take the bottle home if I don't finish it.'

'Of course. No problem.'

Shimmying between the tables with fluent, small-stepping grace, Spiros moved across the floor towards the three men at the bar.

'Giorgios! *Ti kanate!*'

Katherine looked across at the new arrivals, recognising with despair that it was the same Giorgios who had repaired the shower at the villa. He was a friendly man, perhaps more than friendly, and she was certain that if he noticed her, he would want to engage in conversation. She did not want to speak with anyone tonight, least of all with a man who might be motivated by sexual desire.

She shifted in her chair to present more of her back to the bar and, tilting the pages of her book towards the candlelight, started to read.

Losing concentration she shot a quick glance at the three men over her shoulder. They were good representations of Greek genetics. Not quite the apotheosis of classically sculptured physique, but close. Strong genetics and a Mediterranean diet seemed to make Greek men more attractive than their counterparts at home. Perhaps, she mused, if she was younger and in different circumstances she might invite attention from them, open herself to the possibility of taking things further than friendship.

She snorted in self-derision before looking up through the sprawling vine. She had never behaved in a liberated, carefree manner. She had never opened herself up to life's possibilities. Not that she wished her life had taken a different course. Despite everything, despite the almost unbearable grief, she would remain eternally grateful to have brought Amy into the world and for those six years of being together.

Her gaze fixing on the stars above, she felt her broken heart ache with a desperate sense of need. A need to have Amy with her here now. To see her brimming with vital energy, restless on the seat beside her. To be able to hug her and kiss her soft, cool cheek. To smell the scent of her daughter, to feel the warmth of her little girl.

Lowering her gaze, she focused on the candle flame. Her vision became blurred and her eyes burned as the stinging moistness washed across her eyes and trickled down her cheeks. Her throat felt constricted. She swallowed hard to relieve it. That aching sensation spread within her. That feeling as though her core was being twisted into a hot, heavy knot. She pulled her shoulder bag forward from the back of the chair and extracted some tissues.

Dabbing her cheeks discreetly and then blowing her nose quietly, she flashed a glance towards the bar. The men were laughing, their body movements relaxed and free.

She tried to refocus on the book but the words would not register. She read line after line without absorbing anything. Having reached the bottom of the page she returned to the top and set about re-reading with greater concentration. After briefly engaging with the story her mind drifted off again.

She could not bring Amy back but she knew that the love she felt for her would always be the most real and powerful emotion she would ever feel. That, at least, was something that could never be taken away from her.

She breathed deeply as the tension unwound. Her breath, catching against shivers of relief, exhaled as a sobbing sigh. Then the quiver in her jaw stilled as a tingling energy radiated from her burning heart and spread through her body in a wave. She shifted in her seat and straightened her back. A dawning smile lit up her face. She looked up through the vine leaves to the darkness of endless space and silently communicated the conviction which had come to her with unshakeable certainty.

You are with me, Amy. I know you are. I feel your presence so strongly here, in this place, on this island, in this taverna now. I feel the connection so clearly. I know that you are with me.

The speaking of her name disturbed her reverie. She lowered her head and looked towards the person addressing her.

'Katherine. It's Giorgios. Remember? I came to fix the shower.'

'Yes, Giorgios. I do remember. How are you?'

'Good, very good. I also have something good for you. My friend, you know, the one with the boat. He is here with me tonight. You can speak with him. His name is Nektarios.'

'Oh, Giorgios. How kind! But Amanda has gone home now and we were going to do it together.'

'But you will have too much time with nobody. You will be lonely.'

Katherine glanced away at the welcome sight of Spiros approaching with a laden tray balanced on his right hand and forearm.

'Giorgios, I'll be fine. I'm quite happy on my own. It's very kind of you though.'

Spiros glided in sideways and immediately unloaded the tray.

'OK. Retsina, bread, calamari, one Greek salad and one bottle of water.'

He then wedged the tray under his arm and spun round on the spot, raising himself up onto the balls of his feet to speak confidentially into Giorgios's ear in Greek.

'Giorgios, my friend, the lady wants to be left alone. Better leave it for now, eh?'

'OK, Spiros. I was just telling her that Nektarios has offered to take her in his *caique*.'

Giorgios smiled warmly at Katherine as Spiros dropped back onto his heels and weaved his way back to the kitchen.

'Think about it, Katherine. If you want you can come and speak to us later. We are at the bar. OK?'

He turned and walked off with languorous ease, lighting the cigarette withdrawn from the packet in his top pocket.

*

Katherine stood up and tugged her rumpled dress so that it hung smoothly. Although the neckline was high, it had a low backline and, once again, she became vexed about exposing so much of her body. The sensation of the fine linen abrading lightly against her skin made her feel nearly as self-conscious about the concealed parts of her body as her bare back and legs. Trying to dispel her insecurity, she lifted the bag, hoisting the strap over her head and allowing it to fall into position stretched across her chest. Immediately aware that the tightly pulled fabric was now moulded around her breasts, she expelled a puff of exasperation and lifted the strap back over her head to hang the bag off her shoulder. She then loosened off the dress, picked up the bottle of water and made her way across the restaurant.

Katherine knew that she should resist her desire to leave the restaurant discreetly. She knew that she had to speak to Giorgios and his companions but did not know what she was going to say and how she was going to turn down the offer of a boat trip. She could not think of a convincing excuse and hoped that, either, a reason to decline might somehow arise from the conversation or, she could get away with being vague and non-committal. At this stage of her journey across the floor she was focused only on holding her resolve.

Reaching a narrow gap between occupied chairs Katherine halted, momentarily uncertain of how to proceed. There was a temptingly clear route to the exit but, before she could justify fleeing, the female occupant of one chair turned round to look up at her blankly. Smiling at her gratefully, Katherine gestured her needs at the same time as using two of the basic Greek phrases she had learned.

'Excuse me. Thank you very much.'

The feet of the chair scraped with a sharp screech on the flagstones as the woman pulled it closer to the table allowing Katherine to edge past.

Giorgios, becoming aware of her approach, turned around. His two companions, one sitting on a stool, the other leaning on the bar, had been watching her awkward progress through the crowded restaurant. A bright beaming smile spread across Giorgios's face as Katherine reached them.

'Katherine! Come! Would you like a drink?'

'Oh, no thanks, Giorgios. I've had enough to drink already, thanks.'

'Not even a coke, a fruit cocktail maybe?'

'No thanks, Giorgios. It's kind of you but I'm tired. I must get home. I just came to say goodnight.'

'Ah goodnight, yes. But it is early, no? And we need to talk about the boat trip. This is my friend Nektarios. The man who has the boat.'

The man who had been seated was now standing. He extended his hand towards her.

'Very pleased to meet you. May I call you Katherine?'

The warmth of his voice resonating from deep within his chest and the firmness of his grip instantly captured her whole attention.

She absorbed his appearance. His strong square hand and neatly cut fingernails. The long-sleeved white linen shirt. Brown skin, healthy not sallow. Dark chest hair between the open-necked shirt. Head hair thick and well cut with a slight wave. Features well defined but softer than the classic angular Greek. Benign lines from the corner of each eye. No pronounced expression but subtle signals about the mouth and around the eyes and deep within them that a careful, sensitive response would be given. Brown eyes, easy to look into even at first connection.

'You may not want to accept the invitation now that your friend has gone, but I would recommend it as a really good way to see the island. We could also go across to Monastiri, to the far side of the island. There's a beautiful cove there. The best place for snorkelling if you like to snorkel. The only thing is it would be better for me if we went on a Wednesday afternoon. I can go other times but Wednesday suits me best. If there's someone else you want to bring along that would be fine.'

'No. There isn't anyone else but…'

'There's no rush, Katherine. I go out in the boat anyway. You'd be very welcome to join me. Phone me anytime.'

He removed his wallet from the back pocket of his trousers and extracted a business card. Reaching out to take the card, she became consumed again with insecurity, immediately deflecting her gaze onto the card.

'Oh thanks. Yes, I will. Thanks.'

She looked up at Giorgios, across to the other man and back to Giorgios.

'Thanks. Well, that's great. Thanks very much. I can call Nektarios if I can manage to go.'

Giorgios smiled.

'Yes, you can, Katherine. Don't worry, it's not a problem.'

'Good. Well, that's very kind. I do appreciate it but I'd better head off now.'

'Can I give you a lift?'

'No thanks, Giorgios. I've got a bicycle.'

She stepped back smiling at the other man, then at Giorgios and then, as she moved away, at Nektarios. She looked at his teeth, his good teeth, his mouth smiling in delight but she could not avoid his eyes. There it was in his eyes, even more clearly than around the mouth. An apparent desire to engage, to connect. Signals seeming to communicate pleasure at this encounter.

'Take care, Katherine. Watch out for those crazy boys on their motorbikes.'

'Yes… yes, I will… Nektarios… bye.'

Her heart fluttered, releasing a hot rush of confused emotions and causing her face to flush. A smile of embarrassment twitched at her mouth as she looked down at the floor and then at Nektarios before walking off, at first awkwardly and then with more composure as she was jolted by the possibility that they might be watching her.

Calming down as she approached the exit, she chastised herself for becoming flustered. Maintaining composure, particularly in business, had always been a matter of pride to her. It had been a long time since meeting a handsome man had affected her like that. Had it ever? Probably not. Could that be true? It could but then he was very handsome. He was also young. Younger than her anyway.

She stepped down through the opening in the wall onto the narrow street. Some girls were chatting and laughing at the street corner. An elderly woman in black walked away in the opposite direction. Katherine looked at the night sky between the old buildings, their facades articulated with balconies and shuttered windows. Her heart fluttered again and a shiver ran up her back as she appealed silently to her daughter.

Oh Amy. What's your mummy doing? Behaving like a silly girl, that's what. I should know better, shouldn't I? Well, don't worry. It won't happen again.

Katherine arrived at her bicycle propped against the wall behind the disorderly row of motorbikes and mopeds. Before moving it, Katherine looked at the business card, angling it towards the streetlight.

She read his name, Nektarios Alexandrou, and wondered about the significance of the letters after it. Did they relate to education or to professional or business organisations? He certainly gave the impression of being an educated man, although it then occurred to her that the familiar business name, Galeria Afia, was the very impressive art gallery and shop she had visited on the front. She raised her eyebrows appreciatively on making this connection.

Hearing voices of men leaving the restaurant, she dropped the card into her bag before shoving it into the old fishbox strapped to the rack behind the saddle. After wedging the water bottle in beside the bag, she quickly mounted the bike and cycled off without looking back. She rounded the corner and pedalled down the hill towards the front, freewheeling after she had reached a speed much faster than she usually travelled.

The breeze flowed freshly around her. Her dress tugged in the slipstream as her bike rattled down the road. She felt the hem fluttering at the top of her thighs and the cool airflow around her legs. Cycling in earlier, she had secured her dress by sitting on it. Now it was flapping freely and exposing all of her legs. She let go of her inhibitions and submitted her senses to the shakings and shudderings of her careering bicycle.

The squealing of the brakes sounded loud and shrill in the narrow street as she slowed the bike before passing between the busy awning-covered restaurants and stopping at the junction with the road along the front. She slid off the seat and planted her foot on the ground. A shiver of subsiding sensation ran up her back as she looked up and down the front and across at the boats berthed along the quayside. Passing from the quiet back streets of a town preparing to sleep, into this area where people were indulging in the pleasure of mellow end-of-day activities, required a moment of adjustment. Apart from children playing and racing around on foot, bicycles, roller skates and scooters, everyone was proceeding at a leisurely pace. Families on promenade after their evening meals, the adults walking, stopping and walking again, always engaged in conversation and with half an eye on their children.

The front was closed to traffic in the evening. With none of the daytime noise, all sounds were calmer, more relaxed; the hubbub of many conversations punctuated with laughter, the chatter and squealing of excited children and the creakings and slappings of the boats jostling gently in the night breeze. Katherine's heart tingled with wellbeing. She breathed in the smells of sun-warmed buildings, street restaurants and the Aegean harbourside before wheeling her bike across to the quieter side of the road.

She walked slowly alongside the walkway where the fishing boats, sleek yachts and luxury cruisers could be viewed at close quarters. The busiest part was where the most expensive boats were moored. The popular interest was in the large motor cruisers with their comfortably fitted-out rear decks where smart people lounged, apparently oblivious to surreptitious viewing by quayside amblers.

Relaxing as the people thinned out, Katherine lifted her head to look around. Now able to focus her thoughts, she reflected on her recent encounter and mused on her failure to find out what kind of boat Nektarios owned. She imagined it would be a smart boat, stylish, attractive. Not big otherwise he would not be able to sail it on his own. Sail it or drive it? She hoped it was not a speedboat. That would be too flash and showy. Although, why should she care? His boat was only of academic interest to her.

The cathedral entrance glowed brightly silhouetting the people gathered at the top of the steps waiting and watching. Katherine could hear the chanted liturgy broadcast tinnily on the public address system as she approached, and could see the activity of worship within the cavernous interior as she passed.

She thought that they must be preparing for a saint's day. She enjoyed the connection between everyday life and the church here and, although her religious practice had lapsed, she warmed to the idea of participating in their colourful ceremonies, so full of pageantry and yet so naturally ingrained in community life.

It all seemed to link somehow with that elusive sense she had begun to experience more strongly of spiritual states which transcend everyday human existence. She struggled to feel connected to such greater possibilities at home and was deeply and desperately grateful that it came to her so naturally on the island.

Once more she inclined her smiling face to look up into the night sky.

You're here, aren't you, Amy? You're with me? It's making me feel happiness again. I thought I'd feel lonely without Amanda but I don't. I feel closer to you, my love. I feel filled with your presence. It's a wonderful feeling.

Having passed between the bollards at the limit of the evening cordon, Katherine swung her leg over to stand astride her bike before tucking her dress under her bottom and cycling off.

Chapter 15

Katherine breathed in deeply, opening her eyes wide as she surfaced from the dream state of remembering significant times when life had presented possibilities now long since expired.

It had happened more than thirty years ago. That night when she met Nektarios for the first time. That night when she had worn her short black dress. She had regretted wearing it at the time but later she became glad that she had. Glad that she had made her first impression on him wearing that dress, the dress which she had previously worn only when she felt confident enough to attract attention.

She was fit and active then, possibly in her prime. She rarely wore dresses now and never short ones. It was not possible to look good in a dress at her age and in her physical condition when you had difficulty standing up straight and walking properly. Trousers seemed much more appropriate and practical especially when she had to use a wheelchair as she would tonight.

She resented needing to use the wheelchair but was determined not to let this detract from her enjoyment of the and prim positioning. He leaned back cupping his hands behind his head.

'She'll be fine. I agree with Lionel. She does have inner strength. It probably comes from her faith, her belief that God's looking after her. She's certainly got a God-given talent, that's for sure.'

Katherine smiled warmly at him.

'She certainly does, Stephen, and with all that hard work they've put into it I'm sure we're going to hear some great singing tonight.'

Stephen rolled his head round to reciprocate her smile.

'Ooh, aren't we just. It's going to be fabulous. I mean, Maria blows me away when she's singing, you know, casually, just imagine how good she's gonna be singing for real, you know, seriously!'

'I know. Perhaps it's just the anticipation that's making me feel nervous.'

Lionel leaned forward, his hands pressed together between his knees.

'Well, you don't look nervous, my darling. The picture of serenity and so smart.'

He cast a despairing glance at Stephen before continuing.

'It's good to see someone else has made an effort.'

'Well, that's very kind of you, Lionel, although I think Stephen looks great and, actually, I was just thinking that I don't really wear my lovely clothes these days, especially not when I have to use the wheelchair.'

'Darling, believe me, you look lovely and you have an elegance, yes, an eternal elegance that's always there no matter what.'

'Thanks, Lionel. You know how to make an old woman feel good about herself.'

'Hey! We're having none of that, are we, Stephen? None of that stuff about being old.'

'Absolutely not. Age is irrelevant. It has to be, otherwise I wouldn't be hitched to an old queen like him?'

Lionel spun round and slapped Stephen weakly across his knees.

'Stephen! That's enough. We don't want any of those mean comments especially when we're about to go to church.'

Stephen reached across to pat Lionel's back consolingly.

'Don't worry, Li, you know I don't mean it and don't worry, I'll be on my best behaviour. I'll have to be and so will you. It seems they're not too keen on people like us, the strict ones that is.'

Katherine raised her eyebrows apprehensively.

'Actually, that is a thought, isn't it? Some of them do have some rather unfortunate views on… on, well, sexuality so, well, let's just hope we don't meet the pastor. He sounds a bit grim.'

Lionel flicked his head defiantly.

'Oh, we don't care, do we, Stephen? Although we will keep it low key… or at least we'll try to, for Maria's sake.'

'Oh, don't worry about me, lovey. I'll be a model of restraint. It's you I'm worried about.'

'Oh, come on, Stephen. That's not fair. I'm not that bad.'

'Not that bad?'

Stephen rose to his feet and walked across the room winking conspiratorially at Katherine as he passed.

'You know what he's like when he gets going, Katherine. Outrageous and camp. My god, it's at another level. I mean, we're talking Everest base camp, we really are.'

Reaching the door he grasped the door handle and leaned back, waving his other arm in an extravagant gesture.

'I shall return shortly with your carriage, ma'am!'

The amusement on Lionel's face transformed into an expression of concern.

'Now, you know he was just winding us up, don't you, Katherine? I will be on my best behaviour tonight. We both will.'

'Oh, there's no need to worry, Lionel. I know he was just being funny. That's what he's like. You both are. You light up my life, you really do and I am really looking forward to going to the concert with you.'

'Well, Katherine, the feeling's mutual, it really is. We've loved getting to know you and Maria. And Charlene for that matter. By the way, where is she? Is she coming to the concert?'

'No. I'm afraid not. She wanted to but she's got an important match on tonight. A semi-final, I believe, and her captain said she had to play. It's a shame but it's great that she's playing football again and she seems to be doing very well.'

'Well, well, I didn't know that she plays football although she does look athletic when I think about it. Funny she didn't mention it, mind you. Playing in such an important game.'

'Well, Lionel, you know what she's like. Not very forthcoming. Doesn't like to talk about herself but, yes, she's very good at football apparently. A natural athlete as you say… Oh, talking about natural athletes, here comes the power behind my wheels. Well, I suppose we better go. The taxi will be here any minute.'

Chapter 16

Charlene felt a surging sense of determination as she ran forward, her legs suddenly charged with extra power and energy. The ball arced towards her, a spinning orb, swirling black and white and growing bigger and clearer in her unwavering focus. She shortened her stride from a run to a springy skip as the ball bounced in front of her, intercepting it at the right moment to cushion it on her instep and bring it under control. She then dragged it away from the approaching defender and, seeing Angy move into space ahead, pulled her leg back and swept her foot under the ball so that it rose steeply in an arching chip. The defender jumped attempting to clear it away with her head, but the ball reached its zenith just out of her reach.

She then sprinted past the unbalanced defender as Angy made a scything sideways connection with the ball on its first bounce, deflecting it into the space in front of her. Charlene accelerated and stretched out her leg to stop the ball from rocketing past. She then gathered it in and looked up quickly. The rapidly enlarging presence of the central defender flashed across her vision. She dipped her body to the right in a feint, also tapping the ball lightly in that direction before suddenly knocking it to the left. Bouncing from her bent right leg onto her left she swiftly followed the ball. Looking up and seeing a clear route to goal, she connected her foot with the ball so that it spun towards the top left corner of the posts in a bending trajectory. Having expected a right-foot shot to the near post, the goalkeeper twisted around, reaching out in vain as the ball curled beyond her fingertips and plunged into the back of the net.

Watching the ball bulge the netting, Charlene's incredulity was swept aside by a surge of triumph. Raising her arms in exultation, she jumped high, stretching her body in a full fingertip to toe extension. On landing she wheeled round and ran downfield, exhilarating in the freedom from formal play and filled with an ecstatic energy. She started to leap in a bouncing motion, her outstretched arms ready to receive the rapturous acclaim of her teammates. At the instant of reaching the highest point of a bouncing leap, Angy reached out and wrapped her arms around Charlene's waist. Their unsteady coupling was immediately stabilised as Wendy, Jen and Shana bunched around in a supportive scrum. Others gathered around as they moved back into their own, half carrying Charlene chaotically until she slipped through their entangled arms to regain contact with the ground.

'Charlie, that was fucking awesome!'

'What a beauty!'

'Sweet left foot!'

Charlene let the cacophony of praise and gratitude ring around her head. The group dissipated in midfield, spreading out into their positions. Her expression relaxed into a lingering smile and she continued to shine with excitement as Mandy the captain shouted exhortations from her position at centre back.

'Keep it tight. Stay focused. Five minutes to go. Charlie, Angy, hang deep. Defend. We don't need to go for it.'

Charlene tensed her muscles in readiness as the whistle blew. They stood their ground, closing in on the attacking players until Angy managed to tackle a player and knock the ball away. Charlene sped forward to intercept it and pass it back to Mandy who slowed the game down by acting as the pivot in a series of defensive passes.

After that Charlene spent most of the final minutes removed from the action. The opposition pressed forward in their increasingly impatient attempts to breach the defence. Galvanised by Mandy's bellowed encouragement, her team resisted the waves of attack, tackling, blocking and deflecting, sometimes desperately but always effectively. Charlene felt frustratingly ineffectual and agonisingly tense hovering on the edge of the action. Finally the ball skewed out from a messy passage of play and bounced erratically towards her. Charlene brought it under control as an opposing player bore down on her at speed.

Knowing that she should play safe she swivelled round and booted the ball upfield. It spun past the outstretched leg of the approaching defender and bounced out of play. Before the ball could be retrieved for a throw-in, the shrill blast of the referee's whistle penetrated the intense atmosphere, immediately releasing the stress of holding out against the opposition and filling Charlene and her teammates with the jubilation of victory. Charlene stretched her arms upwards and tilted her head back to look at the night sky above the floodlit arena. As she lowered her head Angy came into view, her arms raised and her eyes gleaming with excitement. A frisson of delight rippled up inside Charlene's chest turning to a burbling laugh as Angy collided with her. They hugged each other, laughing and jumping up and down triumphantly.

'Charlene, you beauty! That was a peach!'

'We did it, Ange! We finally beat them!'

The rest of the team gathered round in a dynamic cluster,

hugging, back-patting and high-fiving before moving off towards the changing block. Mandy turned round to face the group, walking backwards and clapping her hands above her head.

'Fantastic effort, girls. Absolutely brilliant. Beers on me at the Candy Bar. OK?'

'Cheers, Mand!'

'Oh yes! Bring on the beers!'

'Fuck the beers, we need prosecco after that?'

'Too right. It's time for bubbly!'

'Hey, don't push it, love. We'll do well to get a beer out of *El Capitan*!'

The team walked off the pitch into the shadows, their high-spirited chorus contrasting with the subdued demeanour of the opposition disappearing into the changing block ahead of them. They clattered into the building, their victorious banter reverberating loudly around the hard surfaces. Charlene sat down at her position on the bench, pulled her bag out from below and retrieved her phone. She pressed the button to activate it and turned sideways to look at Angy.

'Score a goal, hot shower, cold beer. That's me well sorted, I tell you, Ange. It doesn't get much better.'

'What? Better than sex?'

'A close call, Ange, a close call but, yeah, better than the sex I was getting anyway.'

'Still off, is it, Charlie? You and Lee?'

Distracted by her phone beeping sharply, Charlene focused her attention on the screen. The joy faded from her face as she opened up the message. After reading it she looked back up at Angy, waiting for her to pull off her jersey before providing her delayed response.

'Yeah, it is, Angy. Still off. Permanently.'

Angy dropped her jersey onto the bench.

'Oh right. Oh well. You're not too upset about it then?'

'No, I'm not.'

Charlene continued to look up at Angy.

'Ange, I've just got a weird message. I'm not sure what it's all about.'

'Oh, what's it say?'

'Well, it's from Stevy. Do y'know him? He's a mate of Lee's and it says: *Phone me quick. Lee doing bad stuff.*'

'Bad stuff. What the fuck's that?'

'Christ knows, Ange. Maybe bad drugs or something.'

'Are you going to phone him?'

'Could do. Only thing is, Stevy's hot on me. He's always coming on to me, so…'

Her explanation tailing off inconclusively, Charlene looked down at her phone again.

'Oh right, so you don't want to phone him?'

'Well, I don't know. I'm trying to give him the message that I'm not interested but it's difficult. He's not been full-on about it. He can't be, being Lee's mate n'all. He's just been sneaky, kinda sleazy about it.'

'Well, just leave it, Charlie. If you don't give a fuck about Lee and don't want to speak to this Stevy guy, then just leave it.'

'Yeah. I guess you're right, Ange, I'll just leave it. They're just a pair of wankers.'

After unclipping her bra strap, Angy leaned forward letting the bra slip down her arms and onto the bench. She then pulled down her knickers, kicking them off her foot and catching them with a flourish.

Charlene ranged her gaze over Angy's lithe body, entranced by her elegant muscularity.

She relished the special bond she felt with her teammates when they were unselfconsciously naked together sharing the hot showers and exchanging happy banter.

Charlene sat up as a wave of wellbeing washed through her, bubbling hotly through her heart. She looked up at Angy as she reached past to pull her towel off the hook. Their glistening eye contact communicated their deep sense of connection.

'C'mon, Charlie. Get your kit off, girl. We need to get a move on.'

'Too bloody right, Ange. I better make the most of scoring that goal.'

'It was a peach, my darling. A fucking peach. You'd have to pull me down from cloud nine if I'd scored it so c'mon, let's start celebrating.'

'Don't worry, Ange, I'll be right behind you.'

Charlene smiled at Angy before bending forward to untie her boot laces.

'Ooh, I can't wait, Charlie. Get as close as you want.'

Charlene looked up sharply.

'Ange!'

Angy stopped and shimmied her bottom in mocking response to Charlene's reproving tone before walking round the corner.

Now on her own in the changing room, Charlene continued to undress until hearing the sound of another message being received. She sat still staring straight ahead before dipping down to retrieve the phone and look at the message.

Fone me. Lee sd sumthin weerd. Cd be bad. Stevy

After trying to convince herself that she did not care about Lee and should not respond, she selected the option to dial the sender's number. It was answered after the second ring.

'Stevy?'

'Charlene.'

'Got your message. What the fuck's going on?'

'I'm not sure, Charlie, it's just that you know we normally play pool at the Prince of Wales on a Thursday, Lee and me? Well, he said he couldn't make it tonight because he had some business to do, also he was off his fucking head on I don't know what but he was fucking flying, Charlie. Know what I mean?'

'Yeah, and… by the way, Stevy, would you mind your language, all right?'

'Oh yeah. Sorry, Charlene. Anyway, he said something about this cat's got some playing to do while the mice are away… away at a concert, he said. Anyway, I wouldn't have thought much about it only he said I'm going to turn her world upside fucking down, the bitch, he said, and I said who, you mean Charlie, and he wouldn't say, y'know, only I thought I better phone. I mean, y'know, I wouldn't grass on Lee, he'd fucking kill me only I thought he might be out to get you and…'

'Yeah, Stevy. That's cool. Cool.'

'Anyway, are you at a concert or something?'

'No. I've been playing football.'

'Oh well. It can't be you then, Charlie, can it, cos he definitely said something about a concert. I'm sorry then, only I thought it might be you cos he's so sore about it.'

'Yeah, Stevy, I know why you thought that but it can't be me.'

'Oh well, that's cool then, only I thought I better phone, know what I mean? No need to say anything to Lee, is there, Charlie? You won't say anything to him, will you, Charlie, only….?'

'No, Stevy. I won't say anything.'

'Cool. Well, see you around then, Charlie. All right?'

'Yeah. See you around, Stevy.'

'Maybe we could go out for a drink. Y'know, when Lee's over it. That is if you don't get back together.'

'Yeah, whatever, Stevy, whatever. Gotta go, Stevy. All right?'

'Yeah, Charlie. Cheers. Good to speak to you.'

'Yeah. Cheers, Stevy.'

After ending the call, Charlene sat still, looking ahead unseeingly, thoughts rushing through her head.

The revelation of Lee's malevolence sickened her. It had not occurred to her that he would be so vengeful. That was certainly the message she had taken from Stevy's phone call. That Lee was intent on carrying out some form of vindictive disruption. The possibility that he would target Mrs Crawford's home in some way and that he might be there right now filled her with alarm. Would he really do anything though or was it all just big talk? It was too risky to leave to chance and she knew that she would have to phone him, to overcome her revulsion at having to communicate with him. Either that or she could go round to the apartment but that would take so much time and she might find no sign of him only for him to strike later. She shook her head in resignation. She knew that the first thing she should do is try to contact him.

She looked down at her phone, hunching her shoulders as she made the call. She then rose to her feet and walked towards the entrance holding the phone against her ear. Her eyebrows flexed in apprehension causing deep lines of concern to stretch across her forehead. She leaned against the door, her hand ready to turn the lock and step outside as soon as the call was answered. Hearing the ring tone stop she shoved the door open. The tension in her face eased as the automated answering message started. Promptly ending the call, she let the door close behind her and walked back to the bench.

She quickly completed the process of undressing, spraying on deodorant and putting on her clean clothes. Then, after packing her bag, she swung it onto her shoulder, wheeled round and walked off. Casting a nervous glance at the opening into the shower room she quickened her pace. After stepping outside she looked back at the steam drifting into the changing room before releasing the door. The happy cacophony of her teammates faded to a muted clamour as the heavy door closed shut with a thud and the simultaneous clunk of the latch. Charlene looked momentarily at the locked steel door gleaming dully under the security light before turning away and walking towards the bus stop on the main road. She hitched her bag into a more comfortable position on the back of her hip and lengthened her stride. She needed to get to Marine Heights as quickly as possible.

evening. She knew that above all she should be grateful for the mobility it provided and that she was very fortunate to have such willing escorts.

She glanced at the clock. Lionel and Stephen would arrive soon. Very soon. They were never late.

Clasping her hands around the ends of the armrests, she shifted herself into a straighter position. She then lifted her handbag from the side table onto her lap, extracted a compact mirror and examined her face and hair.

Her head twitched as the doorbell rang sharply. Snapping the mirror shut, she dropped it into her handbag and looked around inside to check that it contained everything she might need. She then zipped it up, her frown easing into an expression of calm contentment.

She listened to the metallic clunks of the door being unlocked and smiled in anticipation of seeing Lionel and Stephen. The rich tone of Lionel's voice singing her name filled the room and warmed her heart. She turned stiffly towards them, her smile stretching widely across her face.

'Hi, boys. Come in, come in. Take a seat. We've got about ten minutes before we need to leave. How are you, anyway?'

Lionel swept into the middle of the room with Stephen following brightly in his wake.

'Oh, we're great, thanks. Really looking forward to tonight. Have been for ages.'

'Oh, I know. It's going to be great, although I am feeling a bit nervous for Maria. It's her big night, isn't it? She's put so much into it.'

Lionel lowered himself onto the front edge of the sofa, smoothing down his silver-buttoned blazer as he replied.

'She has indeed but she'll be great. She's got so much inner strength, or seems to have, anyway.'

Stephen flopped down next to Lionel, his casual clothes and relaxed posture contrasting with his partner's smart appearance

'Well, I'm fine, Stephen. You're doing all the hard work.'

'This is nothing. It's easy. No effort. Believe me. Right, here we go.'

Stephen pushed the wheelchair onto the landing and turned it round alongside Lionel who beamed brightly at the man holding the door.

'In we go, darlings.'

Lionel pushed Stephen lightly on the back as he wheeled Katherine towards the door. Undeterred by the man's inscrutable expression, Katherine looked into his blank eyes and smiled warmly.

'Thank you.'

'It's a pleasure, madam. Welcome to St Mungo's.'

Keen to move beyond the forbidding formality of their welcome, they hurried past and halted on the edge of the starkly illuminated foyer. Katherine scanned the scene of people, most standing stiffly in groups sipping tea or coffee from plastic cups.

Apart from a group of kids in street fashion, they appeared to be a conservative crowd not greatly concerned with fashion or style. It was the situation she had feared, one in which she and her colourful companions would appear incongruous. She hoped that they would not attract too much attention and, most of all, that they could avoid meeting the pastor.

Lionel's voice distracted her thoughts and brought her fleeting contemplation to an end.

'Well, it looks like a G & T is out of the question so would anyone like to join me in a plastic cup of tea?'

He stepped forward and looked down at Katherine.

'Katherine? Join me in a cup of tea?'

'Yes. Why not?'

'Biscuit?'

'No, no, not for me.'

'Stephen?'

'No, darling, I'll wait until the interval.'

'Not even an orange squash? I'm sure they'll have some.'
'What! Diluting orange juice! I don't think so, Lionel.'
'Oh, yes, I should have known. You're my big boy now.'
'Lionel!'

Smiling innocently in response to Stephen enunciating his name in a reproachful hiss, Lionel moved off, gliding between the clusters of people, his right arm held out with elegant poise.

Katherine addressed Stephen over her shoulder.

'Stephen, my love?'

Stephen ducked down to speak softly into her ear.

'Yes… I know… we need to be on our best behaviour. Sorry.'

'Well, you know, they do look a bit serious, don't they? Like they might be easily offended.'

Stephen's face registered momentary discomfort as he surveyed the scene.

'Yeees.'

Katherine looked around also until she spotted Maria's husband standing on the edge of a large group. She wagged her finger in his direction as she spoke.

'I think that's William over there, Stephen. You know, Maria's husband. In fact, I'm sure it is. D'you see? The thin man in the brownish jumper… dark hair and specs.'

'Oooh yes, Well, well, well. Not really what I would have expected, although I suppose he does look like a teacher, doesn't he? It's English he teaches, isn't it?'

'Yes, that's right. He's head of the department.'

'Oh well, he must be good and… and tall. Tall and thin. Very thin. A case of opposites attract perhaps… oh dear, that wasn't very kind… sorry, again.'

'Oh, Stephen, but there is a bit of a contrast, isn't there? Anyway, we should say hello. Shall we go over?'

'Oh, y'know. I think he's just spotted you. Yes, he has.'

Having caught sight of Katherine, William turned towards her, smiling and raising his cup of tea in a gesture of greeting.

Then, after nodding his head eagerly and excusing himself, he disengaged from the group, placed the cup on a side table and walked over to them.

'William. How nice to see you.'

'And you, Mrs Crawford. I'm really glad you could make it.'

'Oh, we wouldn't have missed it, would we, Stephen? Now, William, I don't think you've met Stephen although Maria's probably told you about him and Lionel. Lionel's just gone to fetch some tea.'

Stephen stepped forward to shake William's hand, clasping it with both of his.

'Delighted to meet you, William, Maria has spoken about you, often.'

'Oh… oh, has she? Yes, yes, I'm very pleased to meet you too. Maria has told me about you and Lionel… nice things. Yes.'

Stephen loosened his grip allowing William to tug his hand away.

'We all love Maria. She's fab. Truly fabulous.'

'Yes. Yes, she is. Wonderful.'

His demeanour now becoming agitated, William transferred his attention to Katherine.

'It's good to see you, Mrs Crawford. How are you keeping? I mean, you're obviously…'

'I'm not too bad, William, all things considered. Obviously not so mobile but that's OK when I've got such lovely people looking after me. But anyway, how are you?'

'Oh, I'm fine, thanks. A bit nervous, that's all, you know, for Maria's sake.'

'Of course, of course, that's understandable although she's sung here before, hasn't she? And, well, she's amongst friends.'

'That's true, Mrs Crawford. She's always been great and they are very supportive. In fact… in fact…'

William raised his hand to his mouth as a spasm of laughter convulsed his body. Katherine and Stephen watched him benignly as his amusement abated and he pulled a handkerchief from his pocket to wipe his mouth.

'Sorry. Sorry about that. It's just that, well, even the pastor came up to me after the last concert and said...'

Before William could finish, a tall figure emerged from the swelling crowd and stood at his shoulder. Katherine's face clouded as she looked up at the looming presence of the man who had opened the door for them.

She was struck by the strength and dignity of his features and by the richness of his voice which rolled out from deep within his chest.

'Hello, William, how are you and how is your wonderful wife?'

William seemed to crumple in awestruck surprise. Transferring his attention from William, the man looked down at Katherine and then up at Stephen before continuing.

'I'm Maria's biggest fan, you know. What a wonderful voice and a great spirit. We are blessed to have her in our congregation and, of course, in our choir.'

Regaining his poise, William pulled himself up to his full height, lifting his shoulders and opening his arms out, as his face lit up in delight.

'That's incredible. I was just about to say that you told me you were her number one fan when, well, suddenly, there you were saying it yourself!'

Realising that this impressive but formidable figure must be the pastor, Katherine gazed at him with both wonder and concern as he placed his large hand on William's shoulder and released a sonorous guffaw of laughter.

'Ah well. The Lord works in mysterious ways, doesn't he, William? He rewards our faith with many surprises, even small ones to delight us every now and then. Eh, William?'

William nodded eagerly.

'Yes, Mr Johns, absolutely. Yes, yes, many surprises, indeed.'

With his hand remaining on William's shoulder, the man ceased smiling as he gazed neutrally into the distance while leaning into William.

'Who knows, William? Perhaps God will surprise me one day by inspiring you to join us in church. Eh?'

A booming laugh exploded out of him as he removed his hand and straightened his stance.

'Eh, William?'

Hunching his shoulders, William's face wilted as he stumbled through his response.

'Well... ah... I suppose... ah... I won't lie to you... but, well... ah... ah... I should... I should introduce you to Mrs Crawford, Mr Johns. Yes, this is Mrs Crawford. Maria works for her. She may have told you about her and, Mrs Crawford, this is Mr Johns, the pastor here at St Mungo's.'

Smoothly assuming an expression of pastoral compassion, Mr Johns smiled gently at Katherine and reached out to shake her hand.

'Oh yes. Indeed she has. Delighted to meet you, Mrs Crawford. Delighted to meet you. Maria told me you have done many great things for your church. Marvellous. It all sounded marvellous.'

Maria looked up at him as he enveloped her hand in his.

'It's very good to meet you, Mr Johns. Maria has told us about you so it's a great honour for us... By the way, I should introduce you to our good friend, Stephen....'

Suddenly distracted by the triumphant tones of Lionel announcing his return, Mr Johns released Katherine's hand to look at him as he appeared holding a cup of tea in each hand.

'... and I'm Lionel!'

After leaning down to hand Katherine her cup of tea, Lionel cocked sidelong looks at Mr Johns and William while gesturing towards Stephen.

'We're Katherine's neighbours, Stephen and I. The odd

couple next door, you might say. Odd but very happy, I should add. A case of opposites attract perhaps...'

Lionel looked around his unresponsive audience before continuing.

'... Oh dear. Was that too much information?...Oh well, never mind. Sorry!'

Katherine and Stephen exchanged glances of apprehension before turning their gazes towards Mr Johns as he spoke in a measured rumble.

'Have no fear, Lionel. I would never presume to judge the domestic arrangements of other men. After all, we are all God's children, are we not, Lionel? God's children.'

Seeing that Lionel had been taken aback by this unexpected response, Katherine interjected to stop the awkward silence from extending further.

'Lionel, this is Mr Johns, the pastor in this church and... and Maria's biggest fan and this is William, Maria's husband.'

Now appearing eagerly earnest, Lionel raised his cup of tea and nodded respectfully to each man as he acknowledged Katherine's introduction.

'Ah... it is an honour to meet you, Mr Johns, and you, William, at last. A real pleasure.'

Lionel flinched as Mr Johns started to speak.

'Well. You are all welcome here in our church, all of you, and I am sure you are going to have a wonderful evening. Now, if you'll excuse me, I need to circulate a bit more before the concert begins but, if I were you, I'd make my way into the hall now before it gets too busy. We've only got about ten minutes before it starts.'

He then smiled graciously at each of them in turn, before walking off to join another cluster in the crowd. After watching him leave, Katherine and Stephen turned their attention to Lionel who had raised his hand to cover his mouth as it opened in an exaggerated expression of shock. Dropping his hand, he launched into an appeal for forgiveness.

'Ooops! I think I put my size tens right in it that time… sorry folks… sorry, William… not the best introduction but perhaps funny in hindsight… possibly…?'

Katherine looked up at him shaking her head in despairing admonishment.

'Lionel, you are incorrigible. Honestly! What are you like!… Anyway, come on. Let's drink up our tea and go and get a seat… William, you are welcome to join us unless…'

William dipped his head diffidently while responding.

'Well, no. Thanks all the same but I'm with friends so I'd better, you know, I'd better go with them.'

'Of course, William. Of course you should but we'll see you after the concert. With Maria. We'll look forward to seeing you then.'

Nodding manically and murmuring his barely intelligible farewells, William reversed away, his hunched posture causing his fringe to flop over his eyes.

Having extricated himself, he turned round and lurched off, weaving an erratic route across the crowded floor.

Chapter 18

Charlene heard the beep of a message being received as a pothole rocked the bus from side to side. She steadied herself by jamming the bag against the support pole with her hip. She then glanced out of the window before reading the text.

Mad cow! Fone me later. Ange

The changing streetscape flashed across her vision as she pondered the possibility that she might be mad for following a hunch. She shook her head, slipped the phone into her pocket and turned to look out for the bus stop. She had to check the apartment. Lee was unpredictable at the best of times and could become wild and dangerous when he was high on drugs. She had felt a sharp stab of anxiety when it became clear that Lee had remembered about the concert. She had told him they were all going to the concert as a reason for turning down his offer to take her to the opening of the new cocktail bar. He had asked her casually as if it was of no consequence, but she knew he would be furious that she had thwarted another attempt at reconciliation. Drug-inflamed fury combined with knowledge that the apartment would be empty could have ugly consequences.

Charlene pushed the bag onto her back before stepping off the bus and walking off. She leaned forward and accelerated to her fastest walking pace.

She began to think more about how he would get into the apartment. Surely the only way would be to break and enter with a crowbar. Would he really do that? She slowed down and shook her head. The door had a heavy-duty lock. It would be very difficult to break in by force. Unless there was another way to do it. He knew enough criminals to find out how to burgle a seventh-floor apartment. She quickened her pace driven by an angry determination that Mrs Crawford should not be a victim of burglary or vengeful vandalism.

The buzz of the lock-release mechanism provided a jagged underscore to her fury and she shoved the door open. Momentarily unnerved by the stillness of the interior, she stood with her body buttressing against the weight of the door and looked round towards the lift lobby.

Then, after refocusing her resolve, she stepped forward and rushed across to the lift as the front door closed slowly behind her. She winced and looked back across the lobby as the lift jolted into action and descended to the ground floor with a mechanical wheeze and clatter. She stepped in, pressed the seventh-floor button and stood looking straight ahead at her reflection in the mirrored wall.

After turning her head from side to side to examine her reflection, she dropped her bag onto the floor and ran her fingers through her hair, forming it into a neater and fuller shape. The lift slowed as it approached the seventh floor. Charlene turned around abruptly and reached down to grab the bag and hoist it over her shoulder. The doors opened with a clank and a hydraulic sigh which burst through her ears and filled her head so loudly she stiffened into temporary paralysis before stepping out with slow apprehension. Encouraged by the sight of the entrance door appearing intact, she darted a glance to the other end of the landing before walking up to the apartment.

She spread her fingers against the door and pushed. Her hand flattened as it resisted her pressure and remained shut tight. She then pressed her ear to the door until she was satisfied that there were no noises to be heard inside the apartment. Letting her hand drop away, she closed her eyes and breathed in deeply, exhaling with a shiver as her anxiety subsided.

She then turned around and walked back to the lift, stepping in wearily and letting the bag slip off her shoulder and drop to the floor.

Remaining still as the doors shut behind her, she looked into her reflected eyes and tried to focus her tired mind on assessing her options.

She knew that the locked door did not demonstrate conclusively that her fears were misplaced, but she was concerned that her hunch might be too flimsy to justify making an irregular entrance into the apartment. She had been given keys so that she could let herself in without disturbing Mrs Crawford. They were for work-related uses and nothing else. This understanding stood out clearly enough in the fog of her confusion that she could think of no other option than to give in to her exhaustion and go home.

She pressed the button for the ground floor and looked up at the ceiling as the lift lurched downwards. Lowering her head she glanced fleetingly at herself in the mirror before turning around in readiness to exit. She hoisted the bag onto her shoulder and looked left and right before walking swiftly across the lobby. Stepping outside, her spine tingled with the thrill of release and she relished the sensation of the cool night air flowing around her as she walked quickly down the hill.

Her mind began to relax, soothed by the prospect of sleep, until her attention was alerted by the muffled ring of the phone in her pocket. She braced herself to resist a barrage of demands from Angy to join her teammates in their celebrations.

Reducing her pace to a slow walk, she pulled the phone out and stopped abruptly on seeing the single syllable of Lee's name stand out sharply and insistently in capitals.

The glowing screen illuminated her face as she concentrated her mind before answering the call. Then in a quick flash of movement, she accepted the call and flicked her arm up to press the phone against her ear.

Her body stiffened as she heard the voice.

'Charlene.'

He spoke in a croaky, drug-hoarsened drawl.

Her lips pressed together tightly as she clenched her jaw.

'Charlene. I thought you were going to a concert tonight.'

Containing her anger, she responded with a steely stiffness.

'How do you know I'm not at a concert?'

'I know. I fucking know you're not at a concert.'

'How? Who told you? Stevy?'

'Why the fuck would Stevy tell me? How the fuck would he know? What's this about Stevy? What the fuck's going on? Are you...'

'There's nothing going on. He just... he just knew I was playing football. Anyway, never mind about me. Why the fuck are you phoning me?'

'Why the fuck shouldn't I phone you? Maybe I need to keep fucking tabs on you. Maybe I've got lots of fucking reasons. Like you've been telling me lies. Like you're getting too fucking close to my mates...'

'I'm not getting close to any of your mates. I couldn't give a fuck about any of your mates. I don't want anything to do with you!'

'You might find it difficult to fucking avoid me, darling.'

'What do you mean? Where the fuck are you?'

'Never mind where I am, babe. Never mind where I am.'

She turned around slowly to look up at Marine Heights. Screwing up her eyes she scanned the building until locating the seventh floor. The windows were dark. She twitched her head to look back at the balcony alerted by the movement of a dark shape disappearing behind the parapet.

'Lee. Where the fuck are you?'

After a short silence, she snatched the phone away from her ear and looked at the screen. It had deactivated. She shoved it in her pocket and, continuing to look up at the balcony, started to walk up the hill, slowly at first and then with increasing urgency.

Chapter 17

'I'll go and open the door.'
Lionel climbed the steps with a spritely spring. Halfway up he stopped to look down at Stephen pushing Katherine up the dog-legged ramp.

'How are you getting on? Are you sure you don't need any help?'

'Don't worry. We're fine. Just taking it easy.'

'OK, I'll wait for you at the top.'

Just before Lionel reached the glazed entrance door, it was opened from the inside by a tall middle-aged black man wearing a dark blue suit, shirt and tie.

'Good evening, sir. Welcome to St Mungo's.'

'Oh I say, thank you but I'm just waiting for my friends. Hang on a sec, would you?'

Lionel rushed back to the other side of the concrete landing and called out to Stephen and Katherine.

'How are you getting on, my loves? A nice man is holding the door open for us.'

'We're fine, aren't we, Katherine? Nearly there.'

Chapter 19

With the whole choir coming into view under the floodlights as they prepared for the next song, Katherine studied each row. About two thirds of them were women, one third men. From short to tall, from slim to fat. Mostly black, a few white and some with an Asian appearance. A disparate group unified partly by their white shirts or blouses and dark skirts or trousers, and unified completely when they sang with what sounded like harmonic perfection, whether singing a quiet passage or projecting with full power.

A thrill of excitement and wonder fizzed up inside her. Katherine had not expected to come to an ordinary church building in such a remote corner of town and be enthralled by one of the most engaging performances she had ever experienced. She was perplexed by their excellence. How could they be so good? Perhaps with very little exposure to musical performance in recent years her critical faculties had become dulled. Maybe, but did that matter? She could not remember being so moved by a concert. It was pushing and pulling her emotions from one extreme to another. Much of it inspired bubbling, smile-stretching happiness, other parts induced a mellow sadness.

For some songs an individual moved out of the group to stand in front and sing the solo lead. Knowing that at some stage it would be Maria's turn to do this, Katherine felt a flutter of anxiety arise at each changeover and then subside when it became clear that Maria was remaining in the body of the choir. It was just as the final notes of "Amazing Grace" faded to silence and the choirmaster relaxed his posture that Katherine noticed Maria look down prior to side-stepping out of the choir and walking around to stand in the soloist's position. Katherine inhaled deeply to quell her nervous excitement as she watched Maria exchange a flickering smile with the choirmaster before composing herself behind the microphone stand.

The choirmaster lifted his arms. The choristers looked at him brightly, their eyebrows rising in unison as they emitted the first softly sung note. Maria looked down at the floor in front of her. She tugged discreetly at the sides of her tightly fitting skirt to smooth down the rumples. She continued to look at the floor as the choir sang with increasing power.

Katherine became conscious of her chest heaving as she watched Maria. She had been moved by the choir's rendition of "Amazing Grace" and now, watching Maria prepare to sing, the intensity of her emotions increased. She blinked to clear the moisture in her eyes and gulped as a hot, hard lump seemed to swell up in her throat. Despite a sensation of heat spreading through her, she shivered and her chest ached with love for Maria.

Maria raised her head so that her mouth was close to the microphone. Having appeared calm prior to casting her head downwards, she was now looking troubled, creases tracing faintly on her brow. The choir, having graduated smoothly to a crescendo, suddenly stopped singing. At that same instant the floodlighting on the choir was dimmed and the spotlight on Maria turned up to its starkest intensity, the creases now appearing as etched lines across her forehead. She started to sing strongly and slowly, the soulful emotion becoming more intense with each line.

> "If I walk in the pathway of duty
> If I work till the close of the day
> I shall see the great king in his beauty
> When I go the last mile of the way."

A shiver ran up Katherine's spine. She sat forward, her whole being compelled to focus on Maria. Maria, this woman she knew so well and yet not well enough to anticipate that she had the self-belief to sing so powerfully and with such resolve. She seemed not to be performing but to be actually in the song, the words and her voice, the message and her emotions inextricably integrated. She seemed oblivious to the audience and yet was commanding their whole attention. Katherine felt uplifted by the electrifying experience of a phenomenon being revealed from something so familiar. Her rapt wonderment then gave way to rolling waves of emotion as the choir began to build a soft wall of sound to support the next verse.

> "When I go the last mile of the way
> I will rest at the close of the day
> And I know that God will await me
> When I go the last mile of the way."

Katherine listened intently to the words, absorbing their significance. The last mile of the way. Was she on the last mile of the way? Not yet perhaps.

She swallowed around the hot, hard lump in her throat. Her eyes stung.

The choir stopped singing. Maria's voice filled the hall

accompanied only by the sparse support of softly played chords.

> "If I live life with love and sweet charity
> If I forgive them their sins when I pray
> I shall be with those gone before me
> When I go the last mile of the way."

The incredible possibility expressed so simply, that we can be with those gone before us, gripped Katherine's heart. She cast a desperate glance into the shadowed depths of the ceiling and offered up an intense prayer.

Oh dear God. Will we, God? Will we?... We will, Amy. We will be reunited. We will.

Looking back at Maria, her chest shuddered as she drew in a deep breath. The choir began to increase the intensity of their backing, as Maria drew on all of her vocal and emotional resources to lift her voice to an even higher level.

> "When I go the last mile of the way
> I will rest at the close of the day
> And I know that God will await me
> When I go the last mile of the way."

With the last note of the verse fading to silence, the floodlight on the choir was instantly extinguished leaving only Maria visible in her spotlight. She moved her mouth closer to the microphone, closed her eyes and started to sing the last line again, this time in a breathily delicate rendering, her brow furrowing more deeply and her chin quivering. Just as she began to sing the final word, the choir burst into harmonic support under their faded-up floodlights. A smile dawned on Maria's face, clearing away the emotional intensity as the choir brought the song to its powerful conclusion.

Still enraptured, Katherine was startled as loud applause cracked across the hall. In that same instant her impulse to join in was confused by Lionel and Stephen rising up to each side of her. She looked up at them. Stephen had already turned round and was bending down to help her on to her feet. His tear-streaked face filled her vision. She leant against him feeling secure in his strong embrace. Neither could clap now. Lionel had also stopped clapping. His hands were cupped around his mouth as he shouted out loudly.

'Bravo, Maria! Bravo!'

Maria shone with pleasure as she faced this emphatic appreciation happily but with a diffidence which seemed to belie the supreme talent she had just revealed. Katherine was crying now, gripped by feelings too complex to rationalise and too powerful to resist.

A single thought emerged from her emotional turmoil.

Maria, you are an angel. You don't seem to know it but you are definitely an angel. My god, you're an angel.

Chapter 20

Charlene emerged from the lift, her face taut with apprehension. Her expression easing at the sight of the front door remaining quietly closed, she glanced in the other direction before walking briskly to the apartment.

After pushing against the door to check that it was still locked she shunted her bag round and pulled out the keys. She raised the key but stopped short of inserting it as her mind filled with uncertainty.

Should she implicate herself in anything that Lee might do? If Lee did do anything and she stayed clear, they might never make the connection. He would never leave a trail. He was too smart to do that… surely? But what if that shadowy figure had not been Lee? What if it had been someone else? Some maniac? Some madman?

Charlene dropped her hand and slipped the keys back into the front pocket. She then stepped back, continuing to look at the door before turning round and walking back to the lift.

The clanking of a lock being turned instantly commandeered every part of her consciousness. She whipped round to glance behind her before turning away again, her quickening pace driven by the instinct to flee from the threat of danger. The creak of the apartment door opening induced a heart-fluttering surge of adrenaline. Her panic soared to breath-constricting heights as the command, 'Stop you stupid cow!' was hurled aggressively at her retreating back. Then, with each word penetrating the fog of her fear, her rising hysteria stalled and faded away as she recognised that this was the voice she should have expected. Breathing in deeply, she stopped and turned round to face Lee as he spoke.

'What the fuck you doing, babe? Are you coming or going?'

'What the fuck am I doing?'

'Yeah. Why the fuck are you here at this time of night?'

'Why the fuck shouldn't I be here? I fucking work here!'

'Not at this time of night, you don't, and what's all this weird stuff about coming to the door twice and not coming in? That's fucking mental stuff, man. Fucking mental!'

Lee straddled the doorway so that only half of his body was visible. Pressing his hand against the frame, he pushed back against the door and skewed his neck to look at Charlene.

'Mental! I'll tell you what's fucking mental! You standing there in your fucking overalls telling me I shouldn't be here!'

'Oh yeah? Well, why are you here?'

'I'm here because… Listen, never mind why I'm fucking here. What the fuck are you doing here?'

'Doing a job, babe, aren't I? Just doing a quick estimate.'

'Listen, dickhead, if it's the kind of job I think it is, I'm calling the cops right now.'

'Just you fucking dare, bitch. Just you fucking dare. I've got you stitched up, babe, good and proper, so I'd keep the fucking cops out of it if I were you.'

Lee shoved against the door with his backside and side-stepped into the apartment. Charlene shrugged the bag off her shoulder and ran to the door, reaching it as it swung closed with a click of the lock.

'Fuck, fuck, fuck, fuck.'

She dashed back to grab the bag and, after slinging the strap over her shoulder, pulled out the keys, unlocked the door and shoved it wide open. Taking one step into the apartment she held the door open to let the illumination from the lobby lights wash across the unlit hallway. Lee was immediately visible leaning back against a side table, his buttocks resting on the edge. He rocked the top half of his body backwards and forwards in rhythmic agitation. On the reverse movement his back pushed against flowers arranged in a glass vase behind him. The antique table joints squeaked under the strain. All the time he stared at Charlene with a blank expression devoid of emotion. A surge of fury burst through Charlene's confusion lodging a single imperative in her mind. Her face taut with determination, she spoke with tight-lipped resolve.

'Right, get the fuck out of here. Now!'

Continuing to rock, Lee responded with sneering defiance.

'Fuck off. What makes you think you can call the shots?'

'Get out! Now!'

'No. Why should I?'

'Out!'

'No. You go. Just fuck off out of my life, you scumbag whore!'

'Right!'

Charlene spun round to slap the light switches on. Lee instantly stopped rocking and ducked his head, screwing his eyes shut as the hallway transformed from shades of grey into stark illumination. After dropping her bag onto the floor and kicking it to one side Charlene pulled her phone out of her jacket pocket. Pushing his hand into the trouser pocket of his white overalls, Lee slowly raised his head to look at her, his eyes half open below his flinching eyebrows.

'What the fucking cops gonna get me for? I haven't done nothing illegal.'

'Yeah. You're so fucking wired you wouldn't know what day it is. Breaking and entering will do for a start.'

'Why would I break in when I've got keys?'

Lee withdrew his hand from the pocket and held up two keys, dangling them from their connecting ring. Charlene began to move towards him, her eyes fixed on the keys.

'How the fuck did you get those?'

'Well, let me see. I seem to remember you gave them to me.'

'Like fuck I did!'

'Oh yeah? Your memory must be fucked or are you just telling lies?'

Charlene lunged forward thrusting her hand at the keys.

'Give me them!'

Lee jerked his arm back, smashing his hand against the painting on the wall behind. The glass in the frame cracked and the vase and flowers toppled over, the water spilling across the table onto the floor. Having regained her balance, Charlene stood shocked into stillness as she assimilated the damage. Her determination to take possession of the keys and eject Lee from the apartment was momentarily superseded by an impulse to sort out the mess and think of a way to deal with the cracked glass. Shaking her head to banish these concerns, her mind filled with a flare of anger. She turned towards Lee, his hunched body rocking again as he tried to suppress the aching pain in his blood-smeared knuckles.

'What the fuck you do that for, you shit-brained dickhead?'

Lee screwed his neck round to look at her, his narrowed eyes glistening with pain-sharpened anger.

'Fuck off, bitch!'

'No, Lee. You fuck off. Just give me those keys and fuck off out of here.'

Lee sat back on the edge of the table resting the injured hand on his thighs while shoving the keys back into his trouser pocket. He continued to look up at Charlene, his face set in a malevolent glare. The adrenaline-charged anger which had been driving her actions with an unflinching focus, suddenly drained away. She felt weak and lacking the energy to impose her will on Lee. She shrugged in exhaustion.

'Look, Lee, I don't know what you're trying to do but can you just give me the keys and leave me alone to clear up this mess.'

Lee stood up and turned towards her, jutting his head forward and moving in on her face as he spoke. She pulled her head back to keep as far away from his enraged approach as she could without retreating. She twisted her head to one side as she felt the wetness of spittle showering from his shouting mouth.

'I'm not trying to do fuck all. It's you who's doing everything, fucking everything up and I've had enough. All right? I've had enough! If you want a mess to clear up I'll give you a fucking mess!'

After glaring at her wildly, he spun round, stretched his arm out and swooped down to sweep all the ornaments, framed photographs and the toppled vase and flowers off the table. Charlene watched everything fall to the floor through the blur of Lee's body as he barged past. She winced as fragile objects broke in a crashing cacophony. The train of wreckage having reached its end, she looked round to see Lee grab his workbag from a chair in the corner. Seeing that her attention had turned to him he stopped running and started walking with strutting arrogance towards the front door, swinging his bag defiantly. Her eyes focusing on the bag, Charlene walked across the hall. His pace quickened as she closed in on his path to the door. She looked up at his face now set in a menacing sneer.

'What have got in that bag? You bastard.'

She lunged forward to grab the bag. He stretched his arm out to stop her and, with the palm of his hand pressed against her chest, shoved her away. He watched her stagger back, his eyes glaring and his nostrils flaring. Unable to withstand the momentum of this assault, Charlene lost her balance and collapsed onto the floor. Before she could regain her balance and gather the strength to rise up, Lee had swivelled round and opened the door. He looked down at her, his expression now coldly neutral as he stepped out and disappeared from view. Just before the door closed, Charlene reached out to grab the handle and heave it open enough for her to stumble into the lobby. Immediately looking to the right she glimpsed the white flash of Lee's back and trailing leg as he entered the lift. Twisting her body, she sprang into a desperate dash for the lift. Then, suddenly halting her forward motion, she pivoted and ran headlong back to the apartment.

'Fuuuuck! The door! Oh Jesus, the fucking door!'

Stretching out both arms she slapped her hands against the door, stopping its slow closure just as the lock was about to engage. Leaning against the door she fell onto her knees as it opened. She then sat back, her head hanging between her arms for a few seconds before pushing against the door until it had opened wide enough for her to collapse forward into the apartment. Immediately rolling over onto her back she lay clear of the door as it swung closed. She stretched out on the floor, her chest heaving.

A hardening resolve began to emerge from her despair. Leaving the wreckage behind and acting innocently ignorant seemed the obvious thing to do. It would be a shock but Mrs Crawford would get over it and she would be able to claim the costs of repair and replacement on her insurance. They would never trace Lee from the evidence and, like so many petty crimes, it would not be worth pursuing. Surely.

She wailed in frustration as she realised the flaws in her thought process. He had not been wearing gloves so his fingerprints would be all over the place. If the police had samples of his DNA, they would be able to trace him from even the slightest smear of blood. And, he had keys. He could come back at any time, tonight, tomorrow, whenever. She would need to tell Mrs Crawford something which persuaded her to change the lock.

Charlene clenched her hands and, emitting a rasping scream, thumped her fists on the floor. With the scream dying away she sucked in a replenishing breath and, emitting an anguished groan, rolled over onto her side drawing her knees up and beating the floor weakly with the palm of her hand.

'But I can't stay here! I have to go home. I have to take my chances and get out of here. Now. Before they get back. I need to sleep… in my bed. Fall asleep and forget it ever happened.'

and I'm afraid champagne seems to aggravate my arthritis. It's worse than wine which is bad enough.'

'Oh no, does it really? What a terrible shame.'

'Yes and anyway if Maria gives me just a little help getting to bed then she can relax properly and really unwind and enjoy herself. Heaven knows she deserves it, the angel.'

'Doesn't she just! She deserves a drink or two and to have some fun… and William of course.'

The lift bumped gently as it came to a halt. The doors parted with a rattling wheeze. Stephen gripped the wheelchair's handles in preparation to push.

'Right. Here we go, Katherine. Shall I take you straight to the apartment or should we wait for Maria? They weren't far behind.'

'I suppose we might as well wait and then Maria could take me, and William could go with you.'

'Sounds good. We'll look after William. Keep him entertained, won't we, Lionel?'

'Yes, of course, although I'm not sure how happy he'll be going off with us. Especially after my blunder with the pastor. My god, such a faux pas. I'm so sorry… so embarrassing.'

Stephen swung the wheelchair round to face the lift. Continuing to look straight ahead, Katherine remained still as she spoke, softly but firmly.

'Oh for goodness' sake, Lionel. Stop worrying about it. I'm sure it was very good for Pastor Johns to be confronted with such an unapologetic declaration of… of same-sex co-habitation and don't worry about William. Just be nice to him and he'll be fine.'

Lionel replied while continuing to look up at the floor numbers ticking down to zero.

'Thanks, Katherine, for being so positive about it and don't worry, we'll be nice to William, of course we will… oh, here they come.'

None of them choosing to continue the conversation above the clanking and clattering of the ascending lift, Katherine stared blankly at the doors while Lionel and Stephen watched the floor numbers change, their transfixed gazes shifting onto the doors as the lift arrived.

Stepping out first, Maria's face radiated with excitement.

'A welcome committee! How nice!'

Lionel and Stephen, animated with delight at the sight of Maria shadowed by the stooping figure of William, exchanged grinning glances and started a patter of applause. Remaining still, Katherine communicated her pleasure silently by exchanging eye-glistening contact with Maria. Ceasing to clap, Lionel pressed his hands together as if in prayer and then flipped them over to point downwards while addressing Maria and William in a chirruping lilt.

'OK, guys, Katherine thought it would be best if you went with her, Maria, to get her nicely tucked up and we'll go ahead with William and get the bubbly cracked open. How does that sound?'

Maria smiled fondly at Katherine before replying.

'Sounds fine. You must be tired, Mrs Crawford. I'm not surprised you want to get to bed and bubbly's just going to make your joints sore, isn't it?'

'It would do, wouldn't it? In fact, I was just saying that to the boys.'

'Yes. Better avoid it, I suppose. Well, let's head off, shall we?'

Stephen stepped back allowing Maria to manoeuvre the wheelchair away from the lift. William started to follow, reaching out towards her retreating shoulder.

'Ah. Are you sure I shouldn't come with you, love?'

'No, dear. It's OK. There's really nothing for you to do. You go ahead with the boys.'

William's thin frame curled slightly as Lionel stepped forward to reach around his shoulders and usher him away from Maria. Hunching in apprehension, he looked back at his wife heading off in the opposite direction.

'Come this way, William. We're down here, at the other end.'

Lionel dropped his arm as they walked around the corner. Released from the embrace, William swung away from Lionel, his lunging leg tripping over Stephen's as he walked forward from behind.

'Oops-a-daisy. Are you all right?'

Stephen swooped forward to steady William, helping him to regain his balance and resume a forward momentum by wrapping his arm behind his back. With a twist of his torso William extricated himself from Stephen's grasp, looking sideways at him as he replied.

'Yes, I'm fine, thanks. Yes and I am sorry. That was clumsy. Sorry. Are you all right?'

'Yes. Yes. Don't worry about it, William. It's usually me who's tripping up. Isn't it, Lionel? I can be a right clumsy clogs. Can't I?'

'You can be, my love. You certainly can be. Right, here we go.'

Arriving at their apartment, Lionel unlocked the door and opened it wide.

'In you come. Welcome chez nous.'

Chapter 22

Charlene breathed in deeply until her lungs filled. Releasing her breath slowly she opened her eyes. Her head felt heavy resting against the wall, her neck muscles tired. The featureless ceiling offered nothing for her flickering eyes to focus on. Her mind became slowly permeated with the weary certainty that confrontation was inevitable. In the fog of her exhaustion she had not been able to grasp onto any alternative course of action. She could not think through the rights and wrongs, the consequences of acting against her gut instinct that it would be wrong to slip away unnoticed. Pressing the palms of her hands against the wall, she pushed herself upright and walked around the corner.

Instantly noticing Charlene in her peripheral vision, Maria stopped pushing the wheelchair and turned towards her, staring with wide-eyed surprise.

'Charlene! What on earth are you doing here?'

Turning to look at Charlene, Katherine echoed Maria's surprise.

'My goodness! Charlene.'

Charlene stepped towards them, her face twisting in anxiety.

'Ah. Something happened. I had to come back. I left my purse in the kitchen and I needed it because… anyway, I had an accident and the glass in the picture broke. I fell over and knocked the stuff off the table. I'll pay for it. I'm sorry, Mrs Crawford. I'm really sorry. It was an accident.'

Having expelled her explanation in a breathless babble, Charlene stood beside Katherine, her body wilting, her face cast downwards.

Maria stood still, staring incredulously at Charlene, unsure how to respond. Breaking out of her incomprehension, Katherine reached out to hold Charlene's hand in a gesture of reassurance.

'Come on, let's go inside. Charlene, could you open the door, please?'

Charlene moved towards the door looking alternately at Katherine and Maria as she spoke, her demeanour transforming from listlessness to agitated urgency.

'I was looking at my phone. A message had come through. I was walking backwards and I tripped. You know. And when I fell the phone flew out of my hand at the picture which was behind me and I fell back onto the table. It was a mess. I'm sorry. I've tidied up but things got broke. The glass in the picture and ornaments and stuff. I'm sorry. I… I will pay for it. I'm sorry. It was an accident.'

Maria nodded in disbelief as she prepared to push the wheelchair.

'Charlene, I'm finding it hard to take in. Couldn't you have phoned me? Oh, I don't know. Couldn't you have managed without your purse? You shouldn't have come back, shouldn't have let yourself in and then none of this would have happened. This accident. It will be very upsetting for you, Mrs Crawford, won't it? These were precious things.'

Katherine looked down, sighing softly before lifting her head slowly as she responded.

'They are, yes, but let's see what the damage is. Come on, Charlene, my dear, why don't you open the door and let us in?'

After removing the keys from her bag, Charlene unlocked the door and pushed it wide open, holding it back while bowing her head and fixing her gaze fearfully on the floor. Maria pushed Katherine past and then turned round to switch the lights on. Katherine and Maria looked straight ahead at the picture with its broken glass and at the side table, the ornaments on it now reduced to two framed photographs.

Charlene released the door allowing it to swing to a close. The silence after it had clunked shut was broken by Katherine's voice sounding barely louder than a whisper.

'Oh well. At least the actual painting hasn't been damaged and Mummy and Daddy are still in one piece.'

Suddenly becoming animated, Charlene wheeled round, opening her arms wide in a gesture of appeal.

'Yes, they're fine, your... your mummy and daddy. There's nothing wrong with them.'

Katherine responded with quiet resignation.

'Well, I'm pleased to know they're fine. Bless them. But what about the rest of it? The porcelain and the vase. I take it they're broken.'

Charlene dropped her arms, looking down again as Maria stepped back from the wheelchair.

'Yes, they are a bit. Mostly broken. Maybe some could be fixed.'

Maria reached forward to pull the wheelchair round so that Katherine could look at Charlene as she responded.

'Well, perhaps, but the porcelain will have lost its antique value even if we could glue it together. The vase, well, I can buy another one but it is a regrettable situation I'm afraid, Charlene. A regrettable situation although I do appreciate it was an accident.'

With Charlene continuing to gaze disconsolately at the floor,

Maria dipped her head in an attempt to capture her attention as she spoke.

'Oh, Charlene! Do you realise what you've done? You've come back here when you really shouldn't have and caused a lot of damage. It's turned out to be a very expensive accident.'

'I know. I'll try and pay for it. I am sorry. I shouldn't have come back only… well… I had to… I'm sorry but I will pay for it.'

Charlene's head jolted up in surprise at the strength and sharpness of Katherine's voice.

'No you won't, Charlene. You won't pay for it. The porcelain figures were very rare, very valuable. Probably irreplaceable. I'll probably make an insurance claim. In fact, I will definitely so don't worry about it. It was an accident. An extraordinary accident. I don't quite understand how it happened, however we've had a wonderful evening. I'm very tired and I don't want to spoil it by having to think any more about it, this accident. We can deal with it all tomorrow morning.'

Maria stopped staring at Charlene and shook her head in vexation as she turned to focus on Katherine.

'OK, Mrs Crawford. Let's help get you safely into bed. Perhaps you could help too, Charlene, unless you want to head off?'

'No, it's too late. I mean it's too late for me to go out now, so I can help.'

'Good, well, perhaps you could turn back Mrs Crawford's duvet and lay out her pyjamas on the chair next to the bed. You know, in the way which makes it all handy.'

'Yes. Yes, I know what you mean.'

'Come on then, let's go.'

Maria's face strained as she shoved the wheelchair towards the bedroom. Charlene rotated her head to relieve the tension in her neck and breathed in deeply as she summoned the energy to move past them to hold the door open. An aftershock of anxiety shook her as they passed. Her brow twisted as she called out after them.

'I'm sorry, Mrs Crawford. I really am. It's all so... stupid and... and bad. I'm sorry.'

Maria stopped pushing as Katherine spoke over her shoulder.

'Don't worry, dear. We'll sort it out tomorrow. We've had a wonderful evening. Maria was brilliant. I wish you could have seen her and heard her. She was incredible. Really moving.'

Maria's blushing cheeks bulged as she smiled. Her voice purred soft and warm.

'Oh, Mrs Crawford. You're very kind but it's not Charlene's thing, gospel music.'

Charlene's eyes widened and her voice strained, the words rushing out.

'I wish I could have. I wish I could have come. I really do... only... only... I had to play. I couldn't miss the game, well, maybe... well... things happened and...'

Maria's shining delight softened to a benign glow.

'Don't worry about it, Charlene. I'll be singing in other concerts if you really want to come along. But let's help Mrs Crawford get settled, shall we? Her pyjamas are folded under the pillow. OK?'

'OK. Yes.'

Weighed down with weariness, Charlene walked weakly towards the bed.

Now that she had given an explanation of events which they seemed to accept, she wanted desperately to go home but struggled to focus her tired mind on how to make it happen. Perhaps she could share a taxi with Maria. Maria must be tired as well. She would want to get home soon. There was no reason she could think of for them to stay after Mrs Crawford had settled in her bed. She would be fine. She was not aware that she had been burgled. She may not have been burgled. There was no sign of anything having been taken. Everything really valuable was in the safe. There was no reason for him to come back. He had dealt his blow against her. He hadn't trashed the place but had caused her enough grief. That part of his mission had been accomplished and he would now be too stoned to inflict further damage. As for the keys, she would find a way of getting them off him. There had to be a way. She would think about it tomorrow. In the meantime she would get home as quickly as possible, get into bed and forget about it.

The prospect of going home stimulated a resurgence of energy. She pulled back the duvet and arranged the pyjamas, before pushing the wheelchair out of the bedroom and into the large cupboard on the other side of the hall.

Maria was supporting Katherine in her stiff-stepped progress to the feather-cushioned respite of her bed, when Charlene re-entered the room. Maria looked round at her.

'Thanks for dealing with the wheelchair, Charlene. I wonder if you'd mind also fetching a glass of water from the kitchen.'

'Yes, no problem. Do you want it from the tap or the fizzy stuff from the bottle?'

Maria helped Katherine lower herself into a sitting position on the edge of the bed.

'You usually just have tap water for your pills, don't you, Mrs Crawford?'

'Yes, dear, I do. But you know what, I really fancy a brandy but don't you worry about it, Maria, you could get that for me, couldn't you, Charlene?'

'Yes, yes. I've done it before. I know how.'

'Good. I really shouldn't, although it's not as bad as champagne, and I really fancy just lying back and reflecting on the evening with a nice drink. Then if Charlene sorts that out you could head along and join the boys, Maria. You don't mind, do you, Charlene? It won't take long and then we could get you a taxi. Couldn't we?'

'Yes, Mrs Crawford. That would be fine. So, Maria, you're not going home, you're...'

'No, not yet. William's waiting for me with the boys. We're going to have a drink. A glass of champagne.'

'Oh. OK.'

Katherine looked up at Charlene, her eyebrows raised in concern.

'Are you sure that's OK for you, dear. It's not getting too late?'

'No, Mrs Crawford. It's fine, honestly.'

'Good girl.'

'I'll just go and get it then.'

'Yes, that would be great. Actually, Charlene, you know what you could do is stay here tonight if you want. It's getting so late and we'd probably have to wait quite a long time for a taxi and then we could give Maria a lie-in tomorrow morning. You could deal with breakfast, couldn't you? You were coming in early tomorrow anyway.'

'Yes, but...'

'Listen, don't worry about it, Charlene. If it doesn't suit, it's not a problem. It was just a thought. You can order yourself a taxi. It'll probably come in half an hour or so. Don't worry about it.'

'No, Mrs Crawford. I will stay. I've got my stuff. It's not a problem. I can just text my mum. It'll be fine. No problem.'

Chapter 23

Katherine placed the unfinished glass of brandy on the bedside table and closed her eyes to reflect on the evening.

She had not expected to be so moved by Maria's singing. By her emotional expression and by the words of the song. She had embraced their meaning with a desperate need. A need to believe that we will pass on to a heavenly state where we will be reunited with our loved ones.

Faint creases of concentration appeared on her forehead as she recalled lines from the song:

*"I shall be with those gone before me
When I go the last mile of the way."*

She ached for that to be true. That she could be with Amy again, and her mother and father. She needed to believe that it would come about, to believe it with an absolute faith now that she was in the final stages of her life.

Was she on "the last mile of the way"? She felt increasingly as though she was. She was beginning to run out of energy and the will to keep going. She was certainly feeling exhausted right now, deeply exhausted.

Katherine opened her eyes and raised the glass to her lips, lifting her head off the pillow to drink the last of the brandy. She then placed the glass on the bedside table and switched off the light.

The cool blue light of the moon washed across the room so strongly it cast each object into stark definition. She had asked Maria to keep the curtains open so that she could enjoy the ethereal moonlight radiating through the clear sky.

Katherine looked across the room as a new stream of thoughts began to flow.

Thoughts of moonlight. Of how it illuminates the earth with reflected sunshine. Thoughts of the contrast between her current physical condition, left weak and exhausted by an evening out, and the strength and sensuality she possessed on those hot moonlit nights three decades ago. Those nights when she felt an essential connection to life on earth, this planet in its eternally reliable orbit. Night turning to day, to night. Summer to autumn to winter to spring, year after year, until that time comes when we depart from the eternal cycle.

She recalled that strong sense she had felt, amidst the passion; the stripped back simplicity of that life lived in partnership with nature, that all of the astonishing vastness of space and the implausible infinity of planets, moons and stars was somehow transcended. Since then she had difficulty in feeling so certain about it. She struggled to progress beyond the fundamental questions. Why was it that people, so insignificant amongst all of it, so frail and transitory, why should they be able to pass from the physical experience of life to an eternal existence beyond comprehension? How could there be more than the evident pattern of growth, blossom, decay and absolute death? Was it not just a conceit humanity was able to indulge in because of people's power to imagine? She hoped not. Was

Chapter 21

Stephen pulled the wheelchair backwards into the lift, cocking his head to avoid Lionel's arm as he stretched out to reach the buttons. He pressed himself against the rear wall, pulling the wheelchair against his body.

'Oh my! What a squeeze! I'm well and truly wedged in.'

Lionel looked back at him with raised eyebrows as he pressed the button for the seventh floor.

'No funny comments, please, Stephen. Not after tonight.'

'Don't worry, my love. I had no intention. I'm still feeling emotional.'

Katherine looked up at Lionel, smiling as she spoke.

'It was sublime, wasn't it? Hearing her sing like that. Absolutely sublime.'

Lionel leaned back against the mirrored wall, his features softening in wistful recollection.

'She was wonderful. Spellbinding. Amazing and I'm so excited that she's coming. Are you sure we can't tempt you to join us, Katherine?'

'It is tempting, my dear. Very tempting but I am very tired

it not just as rational, maybe more so, to recognise that there were possibilities which went beyond imagination, beyond our limited ability to comprehend the concept of God and heaven and all the rest of it? She hoped so. Desperately.

*"And I know that God will await me
When I go the last mile of the way."*

She closed her eyes.
I wish I did know that. With a certain faith. I wish I did. All I know now is that I'm very tired and it's time to try and clear my mind and fall asleep.

*

A soft tickling sensation traced from her hairline down the middle of her forehead, between her eyebrows and along the ridge of her nose. Her nostrils twitched and she sniffed sharply. A sweet aroma evocative of a cherished time consumed her senses. Katherine opened her eyes with a start as her mind switched from reverie to consciousness. Seeing a small hand being withdrawn, she rolled her head over on the pillow and flinched with shock as a child came into view.

A charge of emotion burst out from her chest and spread in a tingling rush along her limbs. She sat up abruptly, her vision focusing on the radiant, smiling face looking up at her.

'Amy! My love! Is it… It is. Isn't it? It is you! Amy!'

'Of course it's me, Mummy. I'm sorry. I didn't mean to frighten you. I was only stroking your face.'

'Don't worry, darling. It's just that… that…'

Katherine's voice shuddered as her mind tumbled in a turmoil of confusion and her emotions welled up in a wild and uncontrollable whirl. Her eyes burned and her vision blurred as tears ran hotly down her face. Resting her weight on her elbow, she reached across half blindly with her other arm to take hold of Amy's upheld hand. Feeling its warmth and smallness within the wrap of her own, Katherine emitted a straining wail from deep within her aching soul.

'I'm sorry, my love... it's just... just I can't believe it... I've missed you so much.'

'I've missed you too, Mummy. I love you.'

Katherine's eyes glistened as Amy's face came into focus and her mouth flexed into a quivering smile. Releasing her gentle grip of Amy's hand she combed her shaking fingers into Amy's hair before withdrawing them slowly to stroke a soft caress down her cheek and under her chin. She then rested her hand on Amy's shoulder, still gazing in wonderment at her daughter's face now grinning brightly.

'Amy, my beautiful girl, I need to hold you close. I need to hug you, my love. I need to feel my baby close to me.'

'I'm not a baby, Mummy! I'm a big girl!'

Katherine's burst of laughter resonated with maternal joy.

'Of course you're a big girl but you'll always be my baby, Amy. My precious baby. Come here, come close.'

She reached out her arm, a quizzical frown creasing her forehead as she looked at her own skin, smooth and brown as it used to be. Quickly reverting her attention to Amy she leaned down and kissed her lips offered up in a moist pucker. She then swept the duvet off her legs.

'I need to hold you, my love. Come to me, Amy. Come here, my love.'

Amy stepped back, a giggle of excitement gurgling up from her chest as she braced her body for running away.

'You'll have to catch me first!'

She ran a few steps and turned round to look back at Katherine, laughing in anticipation of the chase. Swinging her legs round in a fluent motion, Katherine sat on the edge of the bed and stretched out her arms.

'Amy! Stop! Come back!'

Amy looked over her shoulder as she skipped off.

'Catch me if you can, Mummy. Catch me if you can!'

Katherine stood up as she watched Amy disappear into the shadowed corner beyond the window.

'Amy!'

Feeling suddenly weakened, she sat back down on the bed, her shoulders hunching age-worn and aching. Agony etched across her face, she continued to look into the dark depths of the corner.

'Amy! Come back! Where are you? Come back! Please!'

She reached across with a stiff, slow sweep of her arm to switch on the bedside light. Seeing the room empty, she cried out in a wavering wail of desperation, her shoulders rolling over and her head dropping as her shuddering midriff crumpled. Sitting up as the shaking eased to a tremble, Katherine edged up the bed and leaned back carefully against the pillows, using the backward motion to lift her legs onto the mattress. Exhausted by the effort, she lay motionless, her mind racing behind her blank stare.

It defied comprehension. She appeared to be in full possession of her senses and yet she had just experienced something which seemed impossible. She had been awake and remained awake so it could not have been a dream. Anyway, she had actually talked to her, touched her, kissed her, smelled her. Could it have been a trick of the mind? A powerful hallucination? It all seemed so real and yet how can it have been?

Feeling a giddying resurgence of desperate emotion, Katherine flexed her back and rolled over to switch off the bedside light. The warmth of the artificial light immediately gave way to the blue wash of cool moonlight. Her voice quavered, tentative and sorrowful.

'Amy? My love. Amy. Please?'

Her head twitched as she strained to hear in the silence and then stilled as she discerned a faint voice calling from above.

'Come soon, Mummy. Come soon.'

Katherine gasped with a sing-song flutter as she collapsed back against the pillows.

'I will, my love. I will… I love you, Amy… so much. I love you so much.'

Katherine's inner ears hissed in the silence.

'Amy?'

The hissing continued until, accepting that there would be no response, she whispered softly and finally.

'Bye, bye, my love.'

A warm wave of relaxation rolled through her body clearing her mind and leaving her utterly tranquil and ready to slip into the depths of unconsciousness.

Chapter 24

She grabbed the frame and pulled the painting off the wall. It crashed to the floor behind her as she ran off, weaving her way between impassive bystanders. Passing through the entrance foyer, she pushed over a sculpture before running out of the gallery onto the busy street. She did not know where to go or what to do. The only thing she did know was that she had to flee as fast as she could despite knowing amidst her panic that she would never be able to escape the consequences of the wreckage she had created.

She rocked her head on the pillow, her body writhing in a burst of agitated motion and her eyelids flickering as consciousness took hold behind her closed eyes.

Realising that it had all been a dream, powerfully vivid, but only a dream, she relished the sensation of her anxiety being washed away by a wave of relief.

She rolled onto her side and pulled her knees up, her warm back muscles stretching pleasurably as she tucked into the foetal position. The receding anxiety dissipated completely as she sighed deeply and submitted all her senses to the reassuring comfort of the softly hugging duvet and the body-moulding give of the mattress. A sleepy smile stretched slowly across her face. She compressed her eyelids tightly, the daylight filtering through as she relaxed them. Pointing her feet and pulling her arms above her head, she moved into an elongated stretch. Luxuriating in the relaxed state of her body, she sighed with contentment and opened her eyes. Instantly recognising where she was and why, her eyes widened with alarm and then narrowed in annoyance at forgetting.

She pushed herself up onto the pillows at the same time as glancing at the alarm clock. Seeing, with relief, that she had thirty-five minutes before she was supposed to wake Mrs Crawford, she tugged the duvet up to cover her nakedness and looked around the room.

She relapsed briefly into the calm space between sleep and wakefulness before an invasion of recollections from the night before crowded into her mind.

How should she play it? What exactly had she said? She had left her purse and… Did that work? Was it believable? She would have to go with it. She could not change it now. They had accepted it anyway so all she needed to do was get the keys from Lee and everything would be fine. She was so grateful that the door had a chain on it. If he had returned he would not have been able to get in, although he could have shouted through the gap. Caused a disturbance.

A burst of fury flared in her head. Why had she not thought of that? Perhaps he had come back when she was too deeply asleep to hear anything. Perhaps he had left the door open, restrained by the chain.

In fluid, fleet movements Charlene swept back the duvet, slipped her legs out and ran across the thick, springy carpet. Pulling the door half-open she looked into the hall, first at the front door closed shut and then at the photograph of Mrs Crawford's smiling parents on the side table and the picture with its broken glass above.

Her fretful apprehension began to subside as she became increasingly convinced that the situation could be dealt with and then forgotten.

Fitting new glass in the picture frame would not be expensive and, as Mrs Crawford had said, she would be able to make an insurance claim for the broken ornaments. She began to feel optimistic that it might not be necessary for any further questions to be asked about her version of events and she felt certain now that there could be no reason for the police to be involved.

Charlene stepped backwards into the bedroom, closing the door slowly and quietly. She stood still for a moment before turning and rushing to the bathroom.

She had to get ready. Mrs Crawford would need her cup of tea in twenty-five minutes. She could get her head around things properly when she had got herself together.

*

Charlene tilted her head back, shaking out her drying hair as she walked briskly across the hall, her socks slipping on the polished floorboards. Pushing her hand through her loosened hair she darted a glance at the broken picture glass before sliding to a stop at the kitchen door.

Recalling that Maria had told her to make sure Mrs Crawford was awake before making the tea, Charlene spun round and walked across to her bedroom.

Her heartbeat quickening, Charlene gripped the handle with her moistening hand and turned it carefully until she felt the latch disengage from the keeper. Clearing her throat with a nervous gulp she prepared to say "Good morning" in an imitation of Maria's breezy brightness. She took in a deep breath and peered around the half-opened door.

Seeing Mrs Crawford lying asleep, serenely still on her

back, Charlene stepped back slowly and pulled the door back. After closing it quietly, she turned round and started walking pensively towards the kitchen.

Something about the sight of Mrs Crawford disturbed her. Her stillness. The position of her prostrate body, unnaturally straight. An image of Mrs Crawford in an open coffin loomed in her mind.

Charlene pressed her eyes shut and shook her head despairingly before turning to walk in heavy-legged apprehension back to the bedroom. Her face tightened and the fullness of her mouth compressed to a flat line as she pushed the door open far enough for her to look round, her eyes narrowing, fearful at what she would see.

She stared intently at Mrs Crawford, noting that she was in exactly the same position. There was no sign of any movement, not even from breathing.

Her focus wavering as she became consumed by panic, she stepped back and pulled the door closed. Continuing to face the door, she closed her eyes as a flood of fear welled up, burning her throat with the acid heat of nausea.

She looked up at the ceiling giving voice to her thoughts in a muttered whisper.

'Oh my god. She's dead. She died in the night. Oh my god, she died while I was asleep in her apartment. She can't have. It can't be true. Christ, how bad can things get? What the hell have I got myself into? It's a fucking nightmare.'

Her shoulders sagged as she turned and ran in a slack shuffle to the kitchen, her arms held out to shove the door open. Bursting into the room she stumbled towards Maria's chair, twisting her body and slumping into it with a groan.

The awfulness of the consequences defeated her. For her, as the person who had been responsible for looking after Mrs Crawford overnight. For Maria, whose job depended on Mrs Crawford remaining alive. For Sharon, whose faith in her to look after one of her trusted clients had been betrayed. For all of them losing someone they liked so much, loved even.

It was all too difficult for her to reconcile. It seemed that everything had turned into an even greater disaster. She struggled to resist the impulse to flee until her powers of reason asserted themselves sufficiently to convince her that running away would make everything much worse.

She gripped the armrests, hauled herself upright and walked with a weary sway across to the kettle. Placing each hand wide apart on the edge of the worktop, she bowed her head, slumping her body against the support of her outstretched arms. She frowned and sought to bring order to her thoughts by vocalising them quietly and deliberately.

'There's no point making the tea. I'm not going back in there. I can't go back in. No way, so I can't make the tea. That would look stupid. I'll have to wait for Maria to turn up and then say that she's still asleep. I'll have to let Maria go in. She'll know what to do. I'll have to say that I looked and thought she was still asleep... Oh my god. This is bad.'

She pushed back and spun round to face into the room, her face twisting in anguish and her voice rising to a higher pitch.

'But... but they can't blame me. She was fine last night. Maria saw she was OK. Besides, it wasn't that bad. What happened. What they thought happened. It wasn't that bad... Oh my god.'

Charlene sniffed sharply and held her breath to suppress a sudden churning swell of nausea. She gulped as the sour scorch of sickness gagged her throat and, after releasing her breath, walked across to the sink to fill a glass with cold water. As she raised the glass to her mouth she heard the muffled buzz of her phone vibrating in the back pocket of her trousers. Hastily placing the glass on the worktop she withdrew the phone and looked at the screen.

Seeing that the call was from Maria, her heart froze as the

possibility that she might not be coming flashed alarmingly in her mind. Panic struck, she continued to stare at the screen until telling herself that she would have to answer the call and reminding herself of what she had resolved to say.

'Hello.'

'Hi, Charlene. It's me. Maria. How are you getting on? How's Mrs C?'

'Asleep. She's still asleep.'

'My goodness. That's unusual. But it's good. I phoned your mobile just in case she was. She'll have needed a good rest after last night. Have you been checking on her, love? You know...'

'Yes, yes. I looked a minute ago. She wasn't moving. Asleep. She was still asleep.'

'Yes. She is quite a still sleeper, isn't she, although she never sleeps very deeply. She'll wake up immediately if you go in unless you want to wait till I get there.'

'Well. I don't know. Um...'

'Well, never mind. Why don't you wait for me? I won't be long. I'm at Bertorelli's, you know, the deli. That's really why I'm phoning. I'm just getting myself a latte, a skinny latte. Would you like a hot chocolate?'

'No thanks. I'm fine, thanks.'

'Are you sure? I'm having a croissant. A plain croissant. Do you fancy a nice pastry? A chocolate croissant?'

'No thanks, Maria. I couldn't. I'm not hungry right now.'

'Oh well, we'll get you something later. Mrs C will probably have a boiled egg. You could have one or we've got some bacon. Anyway, I won't be long, Charlene. OK? See you in about five minutes. OK?'

'Yes. See you soon. Bye.'

Charlene ended the call and continued to stare at the screen unseeingly, as she tried to convince herself that Mrs Crawford might not be dead, just deeply asleep.

She lowered her arm slowly before turning around with a faint cry that fluttered up from her rapidly beating heart and shuffling across the room to find some solace in the soft-cushioned comfort of Maria's chair.

Hearing the clattering zip of Maria's key engaging in the lock, Charlene rose and turned around to tidy the cushions with agitated speed. She then stepped into the middle of the room and stood looking at the door, her face rendered blank by the panic of not knowing how to respond to Maria's arrival and the events it might trigger.

Charlene felt a sudden freshness fill the air as Maria's overcoated figure appeared from behind the door, holding a lidded cup of coffee in front of her.

'Well, it's cold out there. Clear. It's going to be a lovely day but it's been a cold night.'

Maria swooshed past leaving Charlene in her refreshing wake of cool, clean air. After placing her cup on the table she pulled off her overcoat, shimmying her shoulders to accelerate the process. She started to speak while hanging the coat on the door hook.

'How's Mrs C? I take it she's still asleep?'

'Yes. Yes, I looked in and she was just lying there, not moving.'

'That's amazing. Amazing but good. She'll have needed the rest after last night.'

Maria pirouetted with firmly grounded grace and pitter-pattered back to the table. Pulling the chair in behind her she sat down and removed the lid from the coffee cup.

'Better drink this now before it gets cold. Besides, Mrs C can always ring the bell if she needs us although she never does… ring the bell that is. I could probably count the times she's used it on one hand. She's lovely that way. Not demanding. Very giving, in fact. You know I couldn't ask for someone better to work for, to look after. I look after her and she looks after me, if you know what I mean, Charlene.'

Charlene remained in the middle of the floor standing slackly lopsided, her eyes cast downwards.

'Yes… yes, I know what you mean.'

Maria darted a backward glance at her.

'I still can't believe how your accident happened, you know. Falling on to the table. Very strange and very unlucky. We'll have to see what Mrs C wants to do about it. Talking of which, would you be a love and put the kettle on for her tea?'

'Yes, OK. Of course.'

Turning away from her, Charlene heard the hollow sound of Maria's empty cup being placed on the table with an emphasis that signalled the start of her working day.

'Right, here we go then. Won't be long.'

Looking over her shoulder Charlene saw Maria shove her chair back and bustle out of the kitchen with gathering resolve. She felt weakened by Maria's strength and energy and seized by a gut-wrenching swell of anxiety. Once again she placed her hands wide apart on the edge of the worktop and leaned forward, dropping her head until her chin pressed against the searing ache in her throat.

Her mind churned in a turmoil of guilt and fear until a surge of anger cut through to take charge of her emotions. Anger directed at herself for feeling guilty when she had done nothing wrong and visceral anger at Lee for having invaded this part of her life so destructively.

Energised by her rising fury she pushed back from the worktop.

She blamed Lee entirely. The destruction he caused would have been extremely stressful for Mrs Crawford. So stressful that it may have caused heart failure. Mrs Crawford had enjoyed a wonderful evening and Lee had spoiled it all.

She shook her head despairingly. Making tea for her seemed futile but she had to act as though she was still alive. She must not give any sign of knowing that Mrs Crawford had died.

In sharp, angry movements Charlene made the tea and set the tray. She then pulled a chair away from the table, lowering herself onto it but rising before making contact with the seat. After pushing it back under the table she moved around the kitchen randomly in agitated activity, adjusting the towels on the cooker rail and shifting the position of objects on the worktops and shelves. Then, suddenly halting, she stood still, angling her head to listen for sounds through the door. Her face straining, she remained motionless until hearing the urgent slap of Maria's sandals as she crossed the hall. She swivelled on her stockinged feet to face the door, physically poised but mentally paralyzed by the growing terror of irreconcilable circumstances.

The door swung open sharply as Maria swept in, her face taut with concern. Charlene rocked back on her heels, shocked by the contrast between Maria's brightness when she arrived and the darkly clouded atmosphere which shrouded her now. She turned as if pulled round by the magnetic force of Maria sweeping past towards the phone on the wall.

'Dr Miller. I need to phone Dr Miller.'

'Dr Miller? Why Dr Miller? Is there something…? Is she, is she, she's not…'

'What? No, no, she's fine. Well, maybe not fine. Anyway, I need to get more painkillers. We've lost… actually, Charlene, you haven't seen them, have you? They were in her bathroom. A cardboard pack. A small one. She was down to her last one. Her last pack.'

Maria paused before lifting the phone to her ear, her face now bright with hope.

'No. No, I haven't seen them. I haven't been in her bathroom.'

Maria pressed the phone to her ear, her voice now flat with resignation.

'OK. Give me a minute, will you? I need to get to him before he goes out. I don't want Mrs C to go the whole weekend without them.'

Charlene felt a rush of dizzying relief burst through her as she watched Maria press the buttons and wait for a reply. She walked across to the table and sat down softly, sighing deeply as her elation subsided to warm contentment. Leaning back, she listened as Maria communicated her enquiry with a hesitant, hopeful lilt followed by strongly voiced gratitude. She watched Maria place the phone on its mount with deliberate care, noticing a frown appear as she turned round.

'Charlene, you didn't hear anything last night, did you? It's just that I think Mrs C had a disturbed night. She says that, well, how can I put it… she… well, I think she must have had a strange dream. Very strange… very vivid. You didn't hear anything, did you?'

Charlene straightened into an upright position placing her hands on her lap.

'No. Nothing. I didn't hear anything. I slept until… until about seven and then I went in to see her at eight and well… and well… she was quiet. Asleep. She was asleep.'

'I see. OK. Well, she seems OK. It's just that… she never usually tells me about what's happened in the night… about what she saw… in her dreams or whatever. Anyway, she'll need her tea and we'd better make a fresh pot. It's been so long.'

Charlene leaned forward placing her hand on the table in preparation to rise.

'No, you stay there, love. I'll make it and then you can take it in.'

Chapter 25

'Hang on a sec, Charlene. Let me open the door for you.' Maria moved in front of Charlene and pushed the door open. Reversing against it to allow Charlene past, she sang out a greeting.

'Here we are, Mrs Crawford. Here's your tea. I've phoned Dr Miller and he said it would be no problem to pop in with a prescription. OK? I'll just get on with things in the kitchen. Charlene will give you your tea. Won't be long, OK?'

Charlene spoke without diverting her focus from crossing the floor with the laden tray.

'Morning, Mrs Crawford.'

'Morning, dear.'

She placed the tray carefully on top of the sideboard and after pouring the tea, lifted the cup and saucer with both hands. Breathing in deeply to quell her rising anxiety, she walked slowly over to the bed.

'Here we go, Mrs Crawford. Here's your tea. Uh… shall I put it on the table or do you want it?'

'I'll take it, Charlene. I'll manage fine. That's right, just hand it over.'

Katherine turned stiffly, holding up her hands to take the cup and saucer. She then settled back and, releasing her right hand, motioned towards the bedside chair.

'Please sit down, my love. Let's talk for a bit until Maria brings breakfast in. I'm not quite ready to eat even though it's so late. It's been a very long time since I slept so late. My goodness.'

Charlene lowered herself hesitantly to sit obliquely on the front edge of the armchair. Katherine rested her head against the pillows and looked ahead as she spoke.

'A very long time, but then it was a late night and an eventful night… wonderfully eventful apart from your unfortunate accident, of course. That was very unfortunate and, I have to be honest, I am very upset about my china getting smashed. It was cherished stuff, you know. Highly valuable both financially and emotionally, if you know what I mean. Yes, I can make an insurance claim but really they're irreplaceable. Family heirlooms, you might say. Anyway, I'm sure you understand and I don't want to go on about it but I just had to mention it, Charlene, to let you know that… that these things meant a lot to me… oh dear, never mind…'

Katherine rolled her head round to look at Charlene, her eyes glistening with regret. Charlene leaned towards her.

'I know, Mrs Crawford. I know that they were… that they were precious. I'm sorry. I'm very sorry.'

'Don't worry, dear. They were precious but… but in the end they were only things. It's people that are important. Yes, they were reminders of people. Family heirlooms but let's face it, I've no one to leave them to anyway. No family that I'm close to. They've all passed on. My loved ones. All gone before me.'

Katherine sighed and settled back against the pillows.

'It was wonderful last night, Charlene. Those were words from the song she sang, "*I shall be with those gone before me, when I go the last mile of the way*". Beautiful. It brought tears to my eyes. It really did. I cried. It was so moving. The words and the way she sang. It was all so beautiful. So emotional.'

Charlene sat rigidly on the edge of the chair, her face impassive while her mind was puzzling about why Maria's singing had made Mrs Crawford cry. She had screamed and cried when she had gone to see boy bands with her friends but she recognised that this was different. The love she and her friends had felt for those boys was intense, at a different level. Mrs Crawford became emotional in different ways, about different things, including ornaments.

Katherine strained forward to sip some tea. After replacing the cup on the saucer, she turned to look at Charlene.

'You must go and hear her sing sometime. You really should.'

'Ah? Oh yes, I will go. I wanted to go. It was just... you know... it was just...'

'Charlene! I'm sorry, I completely forgot to ask. How was the football? Did you win?'

'Yes. Yes, we did. Two-nil.'

'Wonderful. Wonderful. And did you play well?'

'Yes. It was good. I did play well. I think. Yes, I did. I... I scored.'

'Oh, that's great, Charlene. It must have felt great. Imagine that. Scoring a goal.'

'Yes, it was good... Thanks.'

'I'm so pleased you're playing football. Keeping fit. It's so important and team games are excellent. You must feel a great bond with the other girls.'

'Yes, they're great. I really like them.'

'Oh, that's good. I must say you really seem to be sorting your life out since... since, you know... you ended your relationship. Are you still OK about it, Charlene? Are you OK?'

'Yes. Fine. I'm fine about it.'

'Good. I'm very pleased about that. Anyway, you deserve a good relationship with someone you can love. Don't you? I mean I got the impression that you didn't really love Lee. Not really. In fact, I remember you telling me that.'

'Yes I did. I did tell you that. I didn't really like him. We were never going to get on very well. Not really.'

'Yes, well, it's important to find someone you can love.'

Turning away, Katherine's voice softened.

'I'm afraid I didn't manage to do that. That's the sad truth as I may have told you already. Amy's dad. David. He seemed the right kind of person. Educated. Articulate. A successful lawyer but we never really got off first base. We never really developed a relationship. We led busy, independent lives and just ended up irritating each other.'

Flopping her head to the side, Katherine looked at Charlene, her face drawn in sadness.

'I hope, I really hope that you find someone really good, Charlene. That's the important thing. Not that they're rich and successful but that they've got a good heart and that you can understand each other. Love each other.'

Breaking eye contact with Charlene, Katherine dipped her head.

'Actually, David had a good heart. He loved Amy and she adored him, of course. He was devastated at losing her. Never recovered. That's really what killed him. He drank more and more after we separated. Didn't look after himself and then… well… heart attack, I'm afraid, as Maria may have told you. Bad heart in that sense. Poor David, I feel for him now more than ever but… ah well… it's complicated…'

Looking up, she gazed wistfully ahead.

'Actually, I did find someone wonderful. Someone who I did fall in love with but, well, some relationships aren't meant to last. They can't, although they can still be significant and very precious. But, well, that's another story.'

Katherine sighed deeply before continuing, her voice now brisker and brighter.

'I'm sorry if it feels like I'm lecturing you, Charlene. I used to be worse when I was a hard-headed businesswoman. David hated it. I changed after Amy. Realised the error of my ways. It was too late for our relationship though. Much too late. Anyway, the point of this… this rambling is to pass on some of the lessons I've learned in the hope that it helps you in some way, Charlene. It's difficult for each of us to realise our potential and perhaps passing on some wisdom and experience might help.'

Charlene shifted her bottom which was now beginning to ache from the discomfort of her perched position. Feeling the urge to swallow and clear her throat, she emitted a gulping cough as delicately and quietly as she could. Although it made her feel slightly uncomfortable, she was happy to be told about Mrs Crawford's relationships rather than to be asked questions about last night. She began to hope that last night might be forgotten about, until Katherine started to speak in a more authoritative tone.

'Now, Charlene, there is something I do want to talk to you about, but before I do, I wonder if you would mind moving the chair along a bit so that I can see you without having to turn my head all the time.'

Charlene stood up with a rush of nervous anxiety and, after stumbling around to the back of the chair, shoved it forward on its castors through the thick pile.

'Yes, I… I mean no. No, I don't mind.'

After pushing the chair round to face Katherine, she coughed to clear the sour wave of nausea gagging at her throat. Then, feeling unsteady as thoughts crammed in her head, she sat down heavily, full square in the chair.

She was losing confidence in her ability to restate her version of events and felt a growing dread that she would falter and lack conviction.

Then, determined to get a grip of herself, she breathed in sharply and dispelled her self-doubt with the defiant recognition that she could refuse to respond if Katherine started asking her difficult questions. She could say nothing and leave. It had worked for her before. Walking away from difficult situations. She could do that and never see them again.

Her mind clearing, Charlene leaned back, ready to deal with whatever came her way. Her face remained blankly defiant until a quizzical frown began to form as she saw Katherine's cheeks flex and her mouth flicker into the beginnings of a smile.

'That's better, dear. Now I can see you without straining. Right, well, what I want to talk about is your future. When you started here the idea was that you stay three months until you go to college and, well, you've been with us for three months and so I was wondering how your plans are going? You hadn't managed to sort anything out when we last spoke. Have you managed to make any progress since then?'

Stunned at her reprieve, Charlene glanced away before facing Katherine who was now beaming gently.

'Ah well, I've, I've… not really done much about it… yet.'

'OK, well, my love, I wonder if there's anything I could do to help. It's just that I think education is so important. It's the foundation for a better life as I'm sure you know and I don't want it to sound like I'm nagging but you are a bright girl, very bright, more so than you realise, I think. Also, if you don't mind me saying, I think it would do you good to get away from here for a bit. To spread your wings. Don't you think?'

Charlene stared vacantly at Katherine as she considered the unimaginable possibility of moving away to go to college.

'Yes. Yes, it would be good but, but I don't see it working. That's the problem. It's just… it's just too difficult.'

'I know what you mean, dear. It can all seem too much sometimes but that's when you need to make a plan and I can help you with that. I'm used to that. That's what I used to do when I ran the business. Made plans to achieve things. Shall we do that, Charlene? Make a plan?'

'But, but I need to earn. I don't have any money. I need to earn money.'

'Well, I'm sure you must be able to get a grant and you could get a part-time job. But let's not worry about it. I'd help out anyway. I've got funds and no real need to leave an inheritance, so I might as well spend some money helping good causes and, believe me, I would regard your education as a very good cause. So shall we make a plan? It would be fun. Don't you think?'

Charlene leaned forward, her voice rising in agitation.

'But, but, Mrs Crawford, I couldn't take your money. I just couldn't. I don't… I don't deserve it and besides I don't know what I could study.'

'Well, we can think about what you could study and, Charlene, you mustn't think you don't deserve my help. You do. You're a great person. A good person. You've helped me a lot and you've shown a lot of courage and determination in trying to turn your life around. Ending the relationship and joining the football team. It's all admirable and you're hard-working and honest. You have many very good qualities and you do deserve more out of life so please let me help you make a plan and then we can work out the finances. Would that be OK, Charlene? It's not that we want rid of you. Far from it and anyway you'll be around a bit longer while we work things out. OK? Shall we do that?'

Charlene hunched her shoulders, staring down at the white linen valance. Her eyes hurt and her head ached. After closing her eyes for a moment and sighing deeply she looked up at Katherine.

'Yes. Thanks, Mrs Crawford. I'll make a plan. You're right, I need to make a plan.'

A smile burst across Katherine's face. Her eyes shone brightly as she reached out towards Charlene with her quivering hand.

'Oh, that's great, Charlene. It'll be fun. Give me your hand, my love… let's… let's shake on it and then I'll let you go and get on with your Saturday.'

Charlene wrapped her hands around Katherine's, holding it softly. She then lowered Katherine's arm gently onto the bed before sliding her hands away and standing up. She gazed tenderly at Katherine before walking off, confused by the unfamiliar intimacy and the warm sensation fizzing deep within her.

'Charlene, be a dear, would you, and take my cup away? I've had enough for now, thanks.'

Without looking at her, Charlene reached back to remove the cup and saucer. Katherine spoke over her shoulder as Charlene walked over to the sideboard.

'You know, you have so much more potential than I think you realise, Charlene. You have your whole future in front of you. So much opportunity. It's exciting and I would love to help you in whatever way I can to make the most of it.'

She twisted around on the pillows, her voice tightening as she strained her body.

'Please don't think I'm being an interfering busybody, Charlene. It's not that, I promise. It's just that I want to help. I feel kind of stuck, I suppose. I have no future to plan for, not mine or anyone else's and, well, I suppose it's about legacy, about trying to make a difference to a young life. Oh dear, it's difficult to explain. Anyway, I hope you understand, Charlene. I think I can help you and you deserve a better chance than… than your circumstances can… can give you. Oh, I don't know. I'm not explaining myself well. Sorry, Charlene, sorry.'

Charlene heard Katherine sigh deeply followed by the soft crumpling of pillows as she slumped back into a resting position. She placed the cup and saucer on the tray and stood still, besieged by incomprehension.

It should be the other way round. She should be the person apologising. She could not think of any reason why Katherine would feel the need to say sorry to her. Neither could she understand why she was so determined to help her. To plan for her future. What future? It was not something she bothered to think about. It would all just happen. Especially if she didn't go to college. There were not many options to think about. It was all about getting some kind of job. Earning some money. Meeting a better man. Thinking about much else wasn't worth the effort. She wasn't worth it. She could not understand why Katherine thought she was. Why she seemed to care so much when she herself didn't.

She felt the irritating grip of frustration tighten round her head. It was all wrong. Katherine was wrong to care and she certainly wouldn't if she knew that she had told her so many lies about last night. Charlene's desperate recognition that it had all got out of hand overwhelmed her.

She wheeled around and propelled herself back to the chair driven by an instinctual need to force the truth through her confusion.

'No, you don't understand. I'm not worth it, Mrs Crawford. I'm really not worth it.'

Katherine stiffened against the pillows, startled by Charlene sweeping past and swinging round to sit on the front edge of the chair. She remained pressed back as Charlene leaned forward, her whole being now infused with an urgent energy.

'I don't deserve this, Mrs Crawford. It's not how you think it is. I'm not good enough. I don't need help anyway because… because I don't want to go to college. It's too much for me, the whole thing, it's too difficult. Besides… besides…'

The energy suddenly dissipating, her body slackened and she bowed her head in despair.

'… I don't think Auntie Liz would want me. You know. To live with her in London. It's not big enough. Her flat. It's too small.'

Katherine lifted her head off the pillows and slid her hand across the duvet towards Charlene, her expression transforming from alarm to gentle concern.

'Oh, sweetheart, you mustn't worry about these things and you are worth it. Of course you are. You don't think you are. I know that. But… but that's just about self-esteem. Let me help you understand how much you've got to offer. How much you can do in life. How much you can achieve. How much you deserve to achieve. Let me help you. Please. Let me help you to believe in yourself.'

Charlene shook her head and clamped her clasped hands between her knees.

'Charlene. I know you're confident in many ways. Strong. But you can do so much more and the truth is… the truth is…'

Katherine leaned back and looked up at the ceiling before lowering her head and continuing in a flatter, confessional tone.

'The truth is you can help me as much as I can help you. You see, I am being selfish in a way. I need to give. I need to pass on something to someone with a future in a way, in a way that I've never had the opportunity to do. And, well, you know, time… time's… well, let's just say that I'm not getting any younger.'

Charlene sensed from the increased strength of Katherine's voice that she had turned to look at her.

'And Charlene, it's not just anyone. It's you. I really like you. I've grown very fond of you as… as our relationship has developed. As we've got to know each other better. I admire you and I really like you.'

Charlene breathed in deeply as the warm fizzing sensation around her heart returned more strongly than before. As she exhaled it seemed to transfuse through her whole body releasing an emotional wave which burst into effervescence in her head. She looked up at Katherine, her face flinching in fear of the force of this unfamiliar feeling. Her eyes felt dry and prickly and, when she started to speak, her vision became blurred as a wet film formed. Blinking the wetness away, the tears began to cascade down her cheeks. Her voice trembled as her chest heaved and her throat became clogged.

'Oh, I'm sorry. I'm so sorry, Mrs Crawford.'

Katherine flinched in surprise at the force of Charlene's apology before reaching forward in a desperate desire to console.

'Don't worry, dear. There's nothing to be sorry about. Really there isn't.'

Charlene twisted away, ducking her head and hunching her shoulders as she tried to subdue her sobbing before responding.

'Yes, there is. There is. I haven't told you the truth about last night. It didn't happen like that. Like I told you.'

'What do you mean, Charlene? What are you saying? What did happen? I don't understand.'

'Well, it's just that… well, it wasn't just me. It was Lee. He was here and we had a fight.'

Charlene swivelled round to back up her revelation face-to-face as Katherine collapsed back into the pillows, her voice rising in incredulity.

'Lee? But I thought you'd… you'd broken up. Are you still with him? Have you got back together?'

'No. No, we haven't. Never. We would never… I… I hate him!'

'Then why… how come he was here?'

Charlene stuttered before releasing her confession in a torrent of words.

'He… he was here already. Oh, Mrs Crawford, I'm so sorry. He took my keys and copied them. He must have done. I lost them for a while and he must have taken them and, well, he knew you were out and he… he wanted to get back at me. To ruin everything and he was gone. Gone on drugs. Totally gone so he came here. He's evil. Evil. He wanted to mess things up for me, only a friend told me he was up to no good and I thought… I thought… I just knew he would be up here so I came round and found him. I was afraid he'd broken in but he showed me the keys and we had a fight and he… he smashed the picture and then with his arm he just… just took everything off the table and… and… I'm so sorry, Mrs Crawford. I'm so sorry.'

'My goodness, Charlene, but… but, well, it wasn't your fault, was it, dear?'

'Yes. Yes, it was. You see it's just like that with me. It's difficult. Some people are not good. They're bad. Evil and they do stuff. I should never have come here. I should never have started working here and it would never have happened. This would never have happened.'

Katherine shifted on her pillows angling her body to face Charlene.

'Now, Charlene, that's not true. You mustn't think that. It's good that you came here. It's just as well that you did because I can help you. I can help you spread your wings and get away from all these things. All these things that are making your life difficult, that are dragging you down, preventing you from fulfilling your potential. So you mustn't worry about it, Charlene. Really you mustn't. OK, my love? Please don't worry about it.'

'But he came into your house and… and…'

'Yes, I know, dear. It's a horrible thought and he did cause a lot of damage but it could have been worse.'

Charlene sucked in a shuddering intake of breath, her eyes wide with incomprehension. Wailing wildly on her outward breath she leaned over, crossing her arms tightly to contain the emotional storm battering her bedrock of resilience.

Katherine strained forward reaching out to place her quivering hand gently on Charlene's heaving shoulder.

'Don't worry, Charlene. We'll change the lock today and arrange for the security numbers to be changed as soon as possible. It's not a problem.'

She rubbed Charlene's shoulder lightly and looked over to the corner of the room, a wistful smile illuminating her face.

'After all, they're just things. Material things. They're not important. It's you and me who are important. And Maria. And our loved ones whether near or far and whether they're with us now or whether they've gone before us. Gone before us and waiting for us. That's what's important. That's all that's important. So don't worry, dear. There's nothing to worry about.'

The tingling touch of Katherine's hand on her shoulder released a molten flow of feeling from her heart. Her whole being became filled with an unprecedented and overpowering sense of love. Pressing her head into the side of the bed she cried and she cried and she cried.

Part 2

Chapter 26

I'm coming. I'm coming for you at last.

I am being freed from physical confinement. I wish I could have come sooner now that the truth of transcendence is clearer to me than anything has ever been. The shell of my temporal existence is spent. Too weak, too worn to serve any further purpose. It's time to exhaust the final breath. To be released from this redundant state.

I'm coming. I'm leaving. Leaving it all behind. The husk of my being, the domain I inhabited. All of this which I had perceived as reality I can now see in its totality and understand that it has been an imperfect transition to our true existence.

I'm coming. Succumbing to the irresistible pull towards that infinite harmony radiating with the brilliant light of revelation.

I'm coming to join you, Amy. The agonising ache of loss is soon to be soothed forever. Mum, Dad, I'm coming. How futile to have been vexed about moving on from this strange and awkward life where we are so constrained in our understanding, except when illuminated by glimmerings of the greater truth.

To those who helped me make those fleeting connections,

be reassured. The struggle is necessary for it all to make sense in the end. Let my passing make you stronger in your sense that the essence of life transcends the evident. Be receptive to those moments when you open yourselves to being filled with a glowing burst of revelation.

I'm coming now. I'm ready to take the final step of the last mile. Coming to be perfectly unified in love so profound it could never have been imagined.

The time has come at last.

Chapter 27

Maria stepped forward from the front row of the choir into the pool of white light at the front of the stage. The feeling of her energy being sucked into a swirling black hole of nervous turmoil suddenly transformed into a gushing fount of conviction which filled her with an unfamiliar and powerful sense of self-belief.

She glanced sideways and smiled as the choirmaster moved alongside to introduce her.

'Ladies and gentlemen. We're in for a great treat. Maria, singing one of her all-time favourites, "At Last". It was of course a great hit for Etta James and was sung as you may remember by Beyoncé at President Obama's inauguration.'

Responding to the ripple of excited applause and murmurs of approval, he paused and smiled at Maria before continuing.

'It's a great song and like many chosen tonight, although not directly spiritual, it's full of heart and soul. And so without further ado I give you our wonderful Maria!'

The patter of clapping welled up again as the choirmaster adjusted the microphone stand to a lower height and stepped out of the spotlight. A wash of low floodlighting brought the choir into muted definition as he resumed his position in front of them, the applause ceasing as he raised his hands. Maria lifted her head, opening her eyes to the blinding intensity of the lights. She inhaled a chest-expanding breath and became filled with an energising sense of empowerment.

She knew in that moment that this would be the best she had ever sung. She was singing it for William in the audience and for Mrs Crawford even though she had been confined to her bed for days now, weakened by her declining health. She recognised with absolute clarity that her performance would be a wholehearted expression of the intense love and compassion she was feeling for them, the people she most cherished at this time in her life.

Maria bowed her head as she listened to the organ, each note of the introduction resonating deep within her soul. At the beginning of the final bar, she lifted her head to look straight ahead, the white spotlight rendering dark lines of concentration on her brow. She positioned her mouth behind the microphone, breathed in deeply and allowed her singing to emanate freely from her soul.

"At last
My love has come along
My lonely days are over
And life is like a song."

In the interlude before the second verse, Maria was struck by her sense of being utterly at one with the music and emotions of this, her favourite song. She knew that she would now be able to release the emotion behind the words at the same time as exercising absolute control of her voice. She knew as she prepared to sing the next verse that she had elevated into a rare state beyond the spoiling reach of nervousness and psychological frailty.

"At last
The skies above are blue
My heart was wrapped up in clover
The night I looked at you."

Maria looked up again, closing her eyes to protect them from the burning intensity of the spotlights as she projected her silent message of intent.

This is for you, Mrs Crawford. It's for you and Amy. Yes, it's for you, you and your little girl.

"I found a dream
That I could speak to
A dream that I
Can call my own
I found a thrill
To press my cheek to
A thrill that I have never known."

Her head swayed from side to side and a smile spread across her face, transforming her expression from sweet agony to wistful awe. Slow tears trailed hotly down her face as she became consumed by a desperate sense of compassion. Removing the microphone from its sheath, she stepped to the side of the stand and leaned forward, her eyes closing as she gave expression to the full meaning of each phrase.

"You smile
You smile
And then the spell was cast
Now here we are in heaven
For you are mine at last."

With the last note sung and the organ playing the final bars, she became overwhelmed by a confusion of feelings. She cast her face down and her shoulders shivered as she tried to control her sobbing.

Hearing the intense applause and the noise of people rising to their feet, she lifted her face and felt her spirit rise from the depths of her anguish. A bright smile dawned across her face as the spotlights faded and the standing audience came into view. She bowed hesitantly before turning to fix the microphone into its holder. She then stepped back and bowed again.

The choirmaster moved into the spotlight, gesturing his acclamation as he spoke.

'What about that! I told you we were in for a treat. Ladies and gentlemen, the wonderful Maria!'

The audience increased the intensity of their clapping in a final show of appreciation, before allowing it to die away as Maria resumed her position in the choir, her face still radiating with wonder.

She reflected on her sense of having been elevated to a higher level where she had been gifted the ability to deliver the most perfect performance possible, as if she had been conferred with an extraordinary power, as if God had been with her.

Maria closed her eyes and felt her cheeks stretch as a beatific afterglow of fulfilment lit up her face. Opening her eyes, she drew in a deep breath and prepared herself to blend in with the background harmonies.

Chapter 28

The headlight illuminated the rough stone wall and the wooden shelter as he turned off the road onto the lay-by. Dropping his head to avoid the overhanging bougainvillea, he advanced slowly into the shelter. After pulling the bike back onto the stand with a sharp gasp of exertion, he dismounted, lifted the bag of shopping out of the pannier box and walked to the gate.

After removing letters from the post box, he passed through the gate and, reaching down, pressed the button to turn on the bollard lights ranged alongside the path leading up through the terraces to the house. Under illumination from the nearest light, he scanned the envelopes before dropping them into the bag and making his way up the path.

He climbed the stepped platforms in long strides until reaching the terrace where the path changed direction. Standing tall he inhaled deeply, slowing down his breathing before turning to rest his forearms on the railing, the bag dangling from his clasped hands. His gaze became transfixed on the distant splash of lights around the harbour on the other side of the bay.

Becoming aware that he was in a rare moment when everything around him had stilled as if life was being held in suspension, he remained motionless apart from the gentle rhythm of his breathing. Feeling as if he was the sole life force, he drew in a deep draught of night air, pushed back from the railing and resumed his progress up to the house.

Just before reaching the front door, he stopped abruptly and twitched his head towards the bay. A whispering rustle of agitated leaves spread up from the sea, as a sudden breeze seemed to breathe new life into the world. It eddied around him inducing a frisson of exhilaration which shivered through his body. He turned round to view the activated landscape, a rapt smile stretching across his face. His slow sweep of the panorama came to rest on the trembling foliage of the lemon tree behind him, the yellow of its fruit radiating softly in the dying light.

He sighed deeply before speaking softly.

'Katherine? Ah, Katherine. Look how your tree has grown. How it flourishes after all these years. I have looked after it and always will. It's my living connection with you isn't it?... Is that it? All that's left? This tree, my memories, the photographs and... and your dress, your clothes, the necklace, bracelet...you should have worn them again. Should have allowed them to rediscover their... their dynamic form. You should have re-animated them after their years of lifelessness. But that will never happen now, will it? It's too late now to warm them with your lifeblood. That possibility has gone... gone forever, hasn't it?'

He remained rooted by this strange but powerful sense of connection before breaking it with a heavy, shuddering sigh and turning to walk the final few steps to his house.

He looked up at the stars before unlocking the door.

'Katherine, you were special. You should know that. So special.'

Chapter 29

She shifted in her seat until, finding a comfortable position, she relaxed and submitted to the rolling and lurching of the bus.

The sunlight filtered in a flickering glow through her closed eyelids and warmed her face. She sighed deeply as a slow stream of unsolicited thoughts meandered through her mind.

The last time she had taken this journey her life had been settled, as perfectly as it ever had been. She had been concerned about Mrs Crawford's illness but had not considered she might not recover. She had not felt even the faintest flicker of fear that the harmony she had found in her life with Mrs Crawford would be shattered. It was still difficult for her to believe that she would never see her again. That she was gone. Dead.

Neither could she accept fully that she would lose all the other parts of that life. She could not process the consequences of Mrs Crawford's death. She was too overwhelmed by the emotions of loss and by the recognition that she had loved Mrs Crawford. The truth of this struck her now with a force and clarity she had not felt before.

The knot of despair tightened and seemed to grind against her heart. A flash of anguish burst into her head, heightening her grief and releasing tears from her eyes.

She pulled the bag from the empty seat beside her onto her lap to extract a tissue. Dabbing the wetness from her face, she drew a deep breath into her aching chest, holding it tightly for as long as she could to contain the swell of sorrow which threatened to engulf her.

The memory of their last chat before the concert, their final chat, and the reality that their companionable existence had come to an end, filled her with a desperate yearning to rewind time and find a way to change that fateful outcome.

Sniffing sharply, she inhaled another deep breath as she sought distraction by looking outside. The view of the glistening grey-blue sea stretching to the hazy horizon brought her thoughts straight back to Mrs Crawford.

She had often talked about the sea. About how she had loved swimming in it when she was younger. When she was strong. Before her ability to live life to the full had been taken away.

Maria felt a spike of anger that the passage of time should have such cruel consequences. She frowned at the seeming unfairness of life passing so quickly and sometimes ending so suddenly, that one minute you are significantly present and the next you are gone. Gone and never again able to feel the warmth of the sun on your face, to see the start of a new day shining in the morning light. To smell mown grass and the sea. All of these simple but profound pleasures denied by death. It seemed so bleakly tragic it was difficult to look beyond it and try to imagine the glory of heaven.

Vexed by the imponderable nature of her troubled musings she looked around in agitation until, settling her gaze on the blurred division between sea and sky, thoughts resumed their ebb and flow across her mind.

She recalled how she had sung for Mrs Crawford at the

concert. Within hours of her passing away, possibly at the same time. Singing better than she ever had. Singing as if empowered by God. She shivered in awe as her contemplation of this possibility grew into a firm conviction. It was such a big thing, so profound that she did not want to dwell on it. Breaking out of her trance she diverted her gaze from the far-reaching view to the everyday routine of people rising from their seats as they prepared to disembark.

As the bus drew into the stop, Maria pulled her jacket across her and pressed closer to the window to leave the full width of the adjacent seat free for another passenger. Straining her neck, she looked out over the bus queue into the garden of the house behind. Her instinctive compulsion to be accommodating belied her dread of someone sitting beside her while she was in a state of emotional instability.

Hearing the hydraulic doors whoosh and clunk closed, she turned to look forward as the bus moved off. All the boarded passengers having sat down in other seats, she released the tension in her body, resting her head back and flopping her arm onto the empty seat.

Alternating shafts of sunlight and shade flashed across the bus as it rumbled down the treelined avenue alongside the park. Turning to look out the window she saw a young woman and a small girl dressed for school making their way hand in hand along a path through the freshly cut grass. The girl skipped and bounced, swinging arms with the woman in joyful interplay.

Imagining this to be the sight of a mother and child in the early hope-filled years of their life together, Maria turned her thoughts to Mrs Crawford and Amy and of how images of them together had filled her mind when she had sung that song. The words had taken on a new meaning. They seemed to be about them. About the poignancy of their separation and the joy of their reunion.

"And here we are in heaven
For you are mine at last."

It seemed incredible to her that she had been singing those words in those moments, their relevance suddenly becoming clear in a way that would not have occurred to her before. Words which told of the truth that Mrs Crawford and Amy would now be together in heaven. She tried to capture an image of their heavenly state but, finding this elusive, satisfied herself with the sure belief that Mrs Crawford's suffering was now at an end and that finally she was at peace, eternally reunited with her daughter.

Her mind calmed by this reassuring conviction, Maria closed her eyes, giving in to her tired state and allowing a radiant light to fill her head. She expelled a long, slow sigh, gratified that she had found some respite after so much turmoil and knowing that she would remain this way for the rest of the journey.

Chapter 30

The bells jangled as she opened the door. The dissonant clatter filled her head as if she had never heard it before.

Pushing the door closed she glanced across at Giovanni as he prepared coffee for a young man in a suit. She raised her arm and fanned a brief wave at him as he looked up, his face softening with concern.

'Morning, Maria. I'll be with you in a minute.'

He pressed the lid down on the cardboard cup and slid it across the counter.

'There we go, sir. One flat white.'

Maria's gaze ranged around the shelves as Giovanni processed the payment.

She viewed it all as a cornucopia of colour and delight which had provided enrichment in Mrs Crawford's life and hers in turn. It had always been an important part of their life together. Now it all began to look irrelevant, pointless. All of the pleasure it had provided seemed out of reach now. Disappearing irretrievably into the past.

Slumping into despondency, she waited impassively for the distraction of engaging with Giovanni.

Turning towards her, Giovanni's face radiated with delight before clouding with anxious concern.

'Maria, I'm so pleased to see you. Are you OK? I was so sorry to hear about Mrs Crawford.'

'Oh, I'm OK, thanks. Yes, I'm OK. You know.'

'Oh good. I'm glad you're OK. I've been worried about you. I haven't seen you since, when was it, Monday I think, and then I heard the news. I was so sorry to hear about it.'

Maria cast her eyes downwards, focusing on her hand as she traced her fingers softly along the edge of the counter.

'Yes, I've been taking time off to… you know… to…'

Incapable in her exhaustion of offering an explanation, Maria looked up at Giovanni, her face straining as she tried to control her emotional turmoil. His features softening, Giovanni reached out to take hold of Maria's hand.

'I know, Maria. It must have been a terrible shock. Was it actually on Monday that she… that she passed away?'

'No. Well, they think it was on Sunday evening. I don't know, I just discovered her when… you know, on Monday morning when… when I…'

Maria withdrew her hand as another surge of grief welled up inside her. Gasping and gulping in her effort to control the tremble in her chest and throat, she ceased trying to speak and resorted to patting her chest and dabbing her tears with a tissue, as Giovanni walked round the end of the counter to stand beside her and rest his arm gently across her shoulder.

'There we go, Maria. Take it easy. It must have been a terrible shock and you were so fond of her, I know. She was such a nice lady and you were so close to her. I know. There, there.'

Hearing the bells jangle as the door opened, Giovanni looked over his shoulder at the elegantly dressed woman entering.

'Morning, Mrs Aitken, I'm cuddling all my customers today. It's your turn next.'

Ignoring her bray of nervous laughter, Giovanni bent down to speak softly into Maria's ear.

'Tell you what, Maria, why don't you have a seat by the window while I serve Mrs Aitken and then we can have a nice chat. OK? Would that be OK? You got time to do that? Yes?'

He straightened to his full height, looking down at Maria as she nodded affirmatively before moving away.

Maria lowered herself onto the chair, relieved to feel the wave of emotion recede and the heaving of her chest subside. She looked up at the strip of sky above the terraced houses on the other side of the street, its fresh, early-day blueness hazing in the building heat of a late summer's day.

Seeking in this moment of calm to find a more balanced view of her situation, she reminded herself yet again that dealing with the death of clients was part of what she had to do as a professional carer. Realising that she was still not ready to assuage her grief with reason and, no longer able to withstand the brightness, she closed her eyes and bowed her head as she followed another train of thought.

I loved Mrs Crawford. It was so much more than a professional relationship and, anyway, you can't be a good carer without developing a relationship, without getting close.

You can never become hardened to it, especially not when you've been with someone like Mrs Crawford for so long.

It's a bit like someone from your family dying although nothing like it must be for a parent when a child dies. Poor, poor Mrs Crawford having to live with that. I couldn't bear it. That's one good thing about not being able to have children. I've just got to worry about William. Bless him. Pray God that we can grow old together. Pray God.

Chapter 31

Maria placed her coffee and the croissant on top of the unit and unlocked the mailboxes, taking out the mail and shuffling it into bundles before inserting them into her bag. She then reached for her coffee and walked towards the lift until a sudden thought occurred to her.

She was following normal procedures and yet this was not a normal morning. There was no one up there. Mrs Crawford had gone and the boys were on holiday. Feeling her energy drain away at the prospect of being alone on the seventh floor, she decided to drink her coffee in the reception area and go up when the caffeine had revived her.

She walked with weary resignation over to the seating area and lowered herself slowly onto the sofa.

She was thankful that the boys were returning at the weekend. At least they were coming back. Unlike Mrs Crawford. She had made her final departure from the building and yet, only two weeks before, they had come down to sit in the sun.

She felt her mood lift as she drank the coffee and relaxed into the yielding comfort of the cushions.

It was another sunny day. The kind of day that made you glad to be alive. It was always good to feel the warmth of the sun. She recalled that Mrs Crawford had said that; how it makes you feel so much better. How it made her want to be in a hot country again.

Becalmed in the unlit interior, she gazed at the unremitting brightness outside.

That was when their conversation had become uncomfortable. It had been her terse response to Maria asking her about Greece which had been so unsettling. Her sharp assertion that Greece was the one hot country she would not go back to had taken Maria aback. Greece was the only hot country she had ever mentioned and she loved the food.

Mrs Crawford's contrition and hasty explanation of why she would not go back had left Maria feeling more uncomfortable and confused. She could just about understand why she felt the need to focus on her business, but had struggled to understand why it would have been too confusing emotionally. It made more sense now. About not wanting to betray Amy. About how she wanted to love her and nobody else.

Mrs Crawford had not referred to him explicitly, but Maria understood the inference that her feelings for the Greek man had become a distraction from her need to be solely devoted to her daughter. That must have been why she left him, her "lover" as she had once described him. Mrs Crawford with a lover. It was hard to imagine Mrs Crawford in a passionate relationship.

Tipping her head back, Maria drank until the final dregs had dribbled into her mouth. She then placed the empty cup in her bag, steeled herself for the tasks ahead and walked to the lift. The worry at the back of her mind transformed into panic as the lift rose. The prospect of entering the empty apartment was unsettling and she began to regret having volunteered to save Mrs Crawford's cousin from the inconvenience of coming from London to sort everything out. It was not just the stress of undertaking the various tasks which was upsetting her, it was also her concern that it was not appropriate for her to be carrying out such personal duties.

Drawing in a deep breath and gulping to suppress her churning anxiety, Maria stepped out of the lift and turned towards Mrs Crawford's apartment, her mind racing as she walked.

Grasping at the justifications from her whirling thoughts, she reassembled the argument which had persuaded her to take on the tasks. Firstly, it was clear that Mrs Evans wanted her to do them. It was not just that it would be difficult for her to arrange everything from London, but it was also because Maria was familiar with all the people and providers who would play a part. Secondly, Mrs Evans had felt certain that Katherine would have wished Maria to do it. It had become very clear to her from their telephone conversations that the relationship between Katherine and Maria had been very special. Full of the kind of love and respect which made it absolutely appropriate that she should take the lead role in fulfilling her cousin's wishes.

Maria sighed nervously as she inserted the key into the lock. After pausing with her head bowed and eyes closed, she turned the key, pushed the door open and stepped into the void between a cherished history and an unpredictable future.

Shivering as a chill ran up her spine, she stood still allowing the door to close behind her. The latch engaged with a clunk and she walked quickly to the kitchen, looking back over her shoulder at Mrs Crawford's bedroom door before stumbling clumsily into her beloved place of refuge. She closed the door, leaned back against it and looked around.

It all appeared strange somehow, almost as if she was seeing it for the first time and yet everything remained unchanged. She scanned the objects on the surfaces and hanging from hooks and thought about the contents of the cupboards. These things which had made up her world, this beautiful existence which had now come to an end and would need to be dismantled.

Filling up with a churning mixture of fear and despair, she dropped her bag on the end of the worktop, pulled out a notebook and pen and walked to the table. She dragged the chair back and collapsed into it, propping her arms on the table and resting her head in her hands. Sitting motionless, she waited until the dark shadows in her head gave way to the luminance of new thoughts.

She never did have any rights to protect this part of her life. It had been a wonderful life, so precious, but she should not feel sorry for herself. She was still alive and able to open a new chapter in her life. She would do that. It is what Mrs Crawford would want her to do and she would do it with the unfailing support of her beloved William. Before then, however, she had to complete her remaining duties to Mrs Crawford. To complete them to the very best of her ability. To express her love and respect for Mrs Crawford by applying herself to everything with the utmost care and dedication.

Galvanised by defiant determination she shoved the chair back and hurried over to the phone. She sat down, opened the notebook on her lap and dialled the number. Her head twitched as a bright voice rang in her ear.

'Good morning, Wilkins and Pettigrew.'

'Ah, good morning. Can I speak to Mr Wilkins, please?'

'Mr Wilkins? Yes, I'll see if he's available. Who may I say is calling?'

'Ah, Maria. Maria Maitland. It's about Mrs Crawford…'

'Thank you. Please hold, thank you.'

Maria pressed the notebook flat and straightened her posture as she prepared to record a list of actions.

'Hello. Maria?'

'Yes, Mr Wilkins. How are you?'

'Well, I'm fine, thanks. Sad of course about Mrs Crawford, or Katherine should I say, because of course she was a friend, a dear friend. But I'm more concerned about you, Maria. How are you?'

'Well… you know…'

Maria paused, swallowing as a sudden accretion of fluid clogged her throat. Closing her eyes, she tried desperately to subdue the wave of emotion. Her brow twisted with anxiety as her thickened voice wavered tremulously.

'… I'm OK… most of the time, but it's all been a bit of a shock, you know.'

'Yes, I can imagine, Maria. It must have been a terrible shock. The way you coped with it was great. Mrs Crawford would have been so proud and grateful for the way you dealt with it. I know that might seem a strange thing to say but she… she thought you were wonderful, Maria. She was so grateful for everything you did for her… she told me so on a number of occasions, and you certainly didn't let her down when you found her. As I say, you did her proud with the way you dealt with it. I know it must have been difficult so all I can say is thank you, Maria.'

Maria breathed in deeply, feeling stronger as her voice cleared.

'Well, it was the least I could do, Mr Wilkins. She was wonderful to me. I can't imagine… well, I can't imagine a better… a better person to work for. She was just… just great.'

'Yes. You had a special relationship, didn't you?'

'Yes. Yes, we did.'

'Well, Maria, we need to continue to do our best for her, for Mrs Crawford. We need to do the things I was talking about the other day. Now, as I was saying, I am Mrs Crawford's executor as well as her lawyer so I can deal with most of the arrangements, but are you still OK to do things like the catering and the flowers?'

'Yes, I've already lined them up. I'm just adding the flowers to the usual weekly delivery, and I was going to speak to Giovanni at the deli about the catering, if that's OK?'

'Yes, of course. That would be ideal. As soon as possible, because I've reserved Monday at eleven thirty for the funeral. Is that OK for you? I've spoken to Mrs Evans and it's fine for her.'

'Yes. Yes, that's fine. In fact, it's good because Lionel and Stephen will be back by then. They're back from holiday on Saturday.'

'Yes, I was aware they were on holiday so that's great that they're back. Now that makes numbers a bit clearer but it's still a bit difficult to be exactly sure about how many we need to allow for. Unfortunately, Lily, Mrs Crawford's sister, can't come over. She's just had an eye operation and can't fly. She's very distressed about it, of course, but anyway, that leaves us with sixteen people to be notified and I've notified nearly all of them. However, I'll need your help with one of them, Charlene Pearson.'

'Oh yes, Charlene. I can't believe I forgot about her. Isn't that awful?'

'No, it's not. It's understandable. It's only been three days. Now I do have a contact number for her, however I thought it might be better if you break the sad news to her first, if that's OK with you, Maria?'

'Yes, of course I'll do that or at least I'll try. She wasn't answering her phone you see, but that was some time ago so I'll certainly try again. I'll do it straight away. As soon as we're finished.'

'OK. Good. Now, Maria, I should explain about her will. Mrs Crawford was very well organised about her affairs and very clear about them. There are a number of beneficiaries. Not very many because as you know she didn't have many relatives but, anyway, Maria, I am pleased to say that you are one of the beneficiaries so, ideally, we should meet very soon so that we can go through the details. Would you be able to come to my office in the next day or so?'

'Oh gosh, well, that's nice, very nice to be in the will. I didn't expect… but yes, yes, of course I can come and see you. That would be fine. When would you like to do it?'

'Well, would Friday afternoon at three suit?'

'Yes. That should be fine. Friday. Yes. No problem.'

'Excellent. That's ideal. Now I wonder if you could help me with something else. You see, the thing is, Maria, that Miss Pearson is also a beneficiary so I was wondering whether she could also come to my office. I mean, it's not strictly necessary. I could do it by letter, however I would like to go through it personally with her if that can be arranged, so I wonder if you could ask her to give me a phone at her convenience.'

'Yes… yes, of course I will, if she answers her phone that is which hopefully she will. I mean, even if she doesn't I can always send her a text. Hopefully she'll get back to me if I say it's urgent or something.'

'Well, let's hope so, Maria. See how you get on. It's not that there's a great rush to do it. I'm not proposing a formal reading of the will but it would be nice to get it done and it would certainly be better if she could come before the funeral.'

'Of course, of course. I'll see if I can arrange it.'

'Great, and in the meantime, I look forward to seeing you on Friday.'

'Yes, that's right. I'll come on Friday. Oh and shall I just bring Mrs Crawford's mail with me?'

'Yes, I'm sure that would be fine. Yes, I'm sure there's nothing that can't wait a day or two. Now, before we finish, there is something else I need to discuss with you. It's about the music for the funeral. Mrs Crawford specified music however she did express a wish for you, Maria, to sing something. I'm not sure… I mean, I don't know if she mentioned this to you?'

'No. No, we never… we never talked about it. I mean we never talked about her… you know, not being here. I wouldn't have wanted to… wanted to think about that so no… we never…'

'No, of course. That's understandable. Of course not. Well, she mentioned to me that if it ever came to it she would love you to sing at her funeral. One song in particular. I believe you sang it at a concert she went to. She said it was very moving. It's called "The Last Mile Of The Way", I believe.'

'Yes, "The Last Mile Of The Way". She did seem to like it. Yes.'

'So, would that be OK? Is that something you think you could do? She did also mention that it would be nice if some of your friends could support you. You know, your friends from the choir. She said they're lovely girls. She was very fond of them. She mentioned Orricene and Mahalia.'

'Yes, well, I'm not sure if I could. I… I suppose that I could. There's not much time but… but I'll speak to them and see if we can do it.'

'Oh Maria. It would be wonderful if you could. The organist from church, Mr Allan, is going to play the music so perhaps you could rehearse with him beforehand. I would be happy to speak to him.'

'OK. Yes. Yes, I'll have a word with the girls.'

'Excellent, well, if they can make it then I think we should cater for about twenty at about one thirty for a buffet lunch in the apartment. How does that sound?'

'That sounds fine. Yes, I'll speak to Giovanni. I'm sure that'll be fine for him. Monday's not so busy for him so that's good. I'll give him a phone.'

'Perfect. Thanks, Maria. Incidentally, before you go, does the name Nektarios Alexandrou mean anything to you?'

'Nek… Nekta… No, I can't say I've ever heard that name.'

'Oh. I was hoping it might mean something to you. He was a friend of Mrs Crawford's, albeit she hadn't seen him for a long time. She met him in Greece. You know how she spent time living in Greece?'

An electric rush of sensation fizzed up from her heart and burst through her body, transforming her tangled anxiety into excitement.

'Yes. Yes, I knew about that. Certainly. She loved Greece and she mentioned a man she knew there so maybe that's his name. She never mentioned his name.'

'Ah. Well. That'll be him. He was very close to her apparently. Well, at least he was when she lived there. Meant a lot to her and he's also a beneficiary. I'm going to send him a notification, however I thought I'd check to see if you'd had any contact with him ever.'

'No, never. I don't even remember Mrs Crawford having any contact with him. Not even a letter. She did talk about him a bit. A little bit but she never mentioned his name.'

'Well, she was an extraordinary woman, Katherine. Utterly resolute in her principles and beliefs. I'm not sure of the history between them but, although she obviously decided not to maintain contact, she must have had a soft spot for him. Anyway, I've sent him a notification. He certainly appears to be alive from the Greek records and also still living at the same address. We tried phoning but without success so I don't expect he'll turn up for the funeral. It would seem very unlikely if they've not had any contact, don't you think?'

Dwelling on the coincidence of her earlier thoughts about the legend of Mrs Crawford's lover with these matter-of-fact references to him, Maria did not immediately register Mr Wilkins's question.

'Maria?'

'Yes. Sorry, Mr Wilkins. Yes, it is unlikely that he'll come, like you say.'

'I suppose that's right. Very unlikely, which is a shame in a way. It would be fascinating to meet him. He himself must be an old man by now so, well, anyway let's not count him in.'

'No. No, I won't.'

'Twenty should give us a bit of spare capacity anyway. Better to over provide a bit, isn't it?'

'Yes. Yes, that's right.'

'Good. Well, just get Giovanni to send the invoice to me when you've sorted out the menu. Like I said on Monday, she was happy to leave that to you and Giovanni.'

'Yes. That's fine although, well, Mr Wilkins, it just… it just seems so strange that she was thinking about this while she was well or at least before she became very ill. I mean, I know people do but it's hard to imagine her actually doing it.'

'Yes, Maria. I can see why you might feel like that but Mrs Crawford was businesslike if you know what I mean. She was always very well organised. That's partly why she'd been so successful. That and her vision and determination. You knew her in the later stages of her life so it may not have been so obvious, although these qualities were always there and… and in the last few months she actually became very determined to make sure everything was properly in place. I did notice that, I must say. A sense of urgency and, well, who knows, Maria, who knows? We just have to do our best to make sure everything happens as she would have liked, and it looks like everything is in hand, so if you would let me know how you get on with Miss Pearson that would be great.'

'Yes, I'll do that. I'll hopefully be able to speak to her today and let you know straight away.'

'That would be great, Maria. That would be great. And remember, give me a phone any time if you want to talk about anything. Remember we were both very fond of her. OK?'

'Yes, Mr Wilkins. Thanks. Thanks very much.'

'I should be thanking you, Maria. I should be thanking you. So I'll see you on Friday and we'll speak before then.'

'Yes, I'll be in touch.'

'OK. Bye, Maria.'

'Bye, Mr Wilkins.'

'Bye.'

Remaining seated with her knees pressed together, Maria stretched round to place the phone on the hook. Turning back, the pensive frown cleared from her face as she gave voice to her emotions.

'Oh my god! Oh dear Lord!'

She rose to her feet and walked round the kitchen, trailing

her hand along the worktop and pondering on the sense of unease fluttering wildly within her. It was not just to do with the pressure of having to organise so much of the funeral; of the need to contact Charlene; of the commitment she had made to perform, of having to ask Mahalia and Orricene if they would sing with her. These were all daunting tasks which unsettled her; but she knew that it was also something to do with the revelation that she had been left something in Mrs Crawford's will. She admitted to herself that she had expected Mrs Crawford would leave her something and scolded herself for having been so presumptuous. It would have served her right if she had not been remembered. But then it was undeniable that their relationship had been special and, anyway, it might not be money. It might just be a small memento. Also, if Charlene had been left something then she should certainly not feel so guilty about it. No, she should just feel blessed to be a beneficiary of Mrs Crawford's unfailing generosity.

Thinking about it with complete honesty, she was slightly surprised that Mrs Crawford's generosity had extended to Charlene, although, when she thought further about it, she guessed that Mrs Crawford would probably have felt the need to leave her something so that she could complete her course. Yes, that was the most likely reason for Charlene to be included in the will.

Reaching the end of the worktop she wheeled around and crossed briskly to the table, her mind clearing as she sat down to process Mr Wilkins' surprising references to the man in Greece.

They provided proof of his existence and of his significance to Mrs Crawford. Her brow furrowed as she recalled his name… Nektarios. Nektarios Alexandrou. A good name for a legend brought to life.

She smiled at the thought of him finding out about the will. He was bound to be amazed and, she conceded, her smile fading, greatly saddened by the news as any good man would be.

And of course he must be a very good man to be worthy of Mrs Crawford's lasting love.

Her image of the man brightened and then began to fade under an encroaching cloud of concern that after so much time his feelings for Mrs Crawford may have diminished, maybe to nothing. Determined that this negative possibility should not take root, she dispelled it with the exciting prospect of telling Charlene about him.

At first excited at the thought of Charlene's amazement she then began to wonder about how the course of her life might be progressing. Would it all be going as planned? Would she be fulfilling Mrs Crawford's expectations? It had been months since Maria had heard from her. She feared that life may have led her astray and that she may not be living up to Mrs Crawford's faith in her. But then, she reasoned, even if that did turn out to be the case, Charlene was an honourable person at heart and she would surely respond positively if she had been left money to complete her education.

She was also sensitive under that shield of toughness and would find the news upsetting. Maria filled with dread as she considered how to tell her.

She knew that receiving an unexpected phone call would put Charlene on guard, and so she decided that she would come to the point quickly but not too bluntly. It would be important to stress that Mrs Crawford's illness had been brief and that she had passed away peacefully. She thought that she might also need to persuade her against feeling guilty about not keeping in touch. She was not quite sure how to do this convincingly, when in other circumstances she would have wanted Charlene to feel regret about it. She would just have to gloss over it and move on as quickly as she could to telling her about the will and Nektarios Alexandrou.

Deciding that she should just get on with it, Maria heaved herself up and walked over to the phone. After pressing the number she sat down anxiously alert with the phone pressed against her ear. Her posture softened as the voicemail message began to play and she closed her eyes while waiting to speak.

'Hi Charlene. It's Maria. Hope you're well. Listen, love, I do need to speak to you about… about something that's happened… that's happened with Mrs Crawford… it's nothing to worry about, it's just that… well, I need to speak to you. OK, Charlene, my love. Give me a phone. Byeee.'

Maria looked straight ahead while reaching back to replace the phone. She replayed the message in her mind, worrying that she had not put it very well, but unable to decide how it might have been improved and so, satisfied that it would serve its purpose, she rose to her feet and walked out of the kitchen into the hall.

She looked around with keen eyes, observing the few items of furniture and the paintings on the walls as she never had before. She felt wryly bemused that she was so unfamiliar with the paintings after crossing the hall countless times over the past seven years.

She had appreciated the colours but had been dismissive about their modern style. They were too abstract for her taste. She preferred the beautifully realistic representations of classical art and, despite trying to view them positively as she walked over to the half-moon side table, they remained as inaccessible to her now as then.

Focusing her attention on the painting above the table, she recalled the eventful night when its glass had been shattered. She was still astonished that Mrs Crawford had been so understanding. Her heart glowed warmly in appreciation of her forgiving nature.

Lifting the photographs of Mrs Crawford's parents, her brow furrowed as she examined their faces, so alive in that moment, so happy but now so dead like their daughter and their granddaughter. All gone, passed on but now reunited. All together in heaven at last.

Sighing deeply, she replaced the photograph on the table, continuing to look at their smiling faces as she withdrew her hands.

She stepped back and scanned the hall with a nervous swivel of her head, until fixing her gaze on the door to Mrs Crawford's bedroom.

Feeling another chill run up her spine, she swirled round and bustled into the front room, reversing her body against the door to close it. She leaned against the door blinking, as her eyes adjusted to the strong sunlight slanting into the front half of the room. Suddenly bursting into anxious activity she rushed to the windows and, with the lowering of each blind, moderated the glare to a suffused glow. Her head throbbed from the blood rush of movement and exposure to the intense sunlight. After pausing briefly to gather thoughts between her pulsating temples, she moved swiftly away from the windows into the shaded half of the room and lowered herself heavily into her favourite chair, the one she had sat in while having all those cherished conversations with Mrs Crawford. Resting back until feeling some relief from her discomfort, she sat forward addressing words quietly at Mrs Crawford's chair.

'Sorry about that. I should have come in earlier. Shouldn't have allowed the room to heat up like this. It'll cool down now and of course I would have brought the fan in if you'd been here. I suppose there's no point bringing it in now, is there? No, there's no point really.'

Her face flinching in sorrowful regret, she transferred her gaze from the empty chair to the framed photographs on the adjacent table, a gallery of portraits which would now evoke only faint memories and meaning to a very few people.

She leaned forward and carefully lifted the photograph of Amy. Propping it on her lap she looked down at the image of the young girl smiling, the brightness of her eyes captured in a moment of excitement.

She had admired the photo many times but now, for the first time, she thought about the situation surrounding it. She imagined that Amy would have been smiling at her mother. She must have been and Mrs Crawford would have been smiling at her. So much love being communicated between them and so much happiness in that moment all those years ago. A moment when Mrs Crawford could never have imagined losing her beautiful daughter. One of many joyful moments before those empty years when she had been left with nothing more than some photographs and many memories.

The agony of Mrs Crawford's loss struck her now more powerfully than it ever had, and she wished that she had shown more empathy and told her how sorry she was. She could not think of anyone else who might have offered much sympathy or support. The truth was that she had been in the best position to provide this, but had failed to realise it with any clarity until now when it was too late.

A pernicious mix of guilt and regret invaded her mind and whipped up into a whirl of panic. Sitting transfixed, the photograph blurred out of focus as her eyes moistened. Blinking to clear her vision, a slow stream of tears began to trail down her cheeks. She grasped the frame blindly in her left hand and, half rising from the chair, she reached across to the table on the other side of Mrs Crawford's chair and ripped a tissue clumsily from the box. After collapsing back she dabbed her face dry and blew her nose vigorously. Feeling more composed she looked down again at the photograph, resolving to keep it and the others safe if neither Lily or Mrs Evans wanted them.

She rose from the chair, tenderly repositioned the photograph and walked out of the room and across the hall to Mrs Crawford's bedroom.

She turned the knob and pushed the door open slowly against the deep pile of the carpet. Feeling as if the rapid rate of her heartbeat was pumping her up into a high-pressured state of sharpened perception, she stepped forward to look around the door. Her eyes opened wide and, fearful of the eerie silence, she became acutely conscious of the hissing in her ears. She stared at the empty bed, noting that the end of the duvet had been laid neatly on top of the pillows rather than tucked underneath as she would have done. Looking around the room and seeing that everything else remained in the right order, she moved forward leaving the door open. Standing still in the middle of the room she continued to look down at the bed, her face becoming drawn in anguish.

She had appeared to be asleep. Peaceful and still as she often was, until being awoken with Maria's cheerful greeting and the curtains being opened. She would always waken then, not just lie there without moving. Horror tugged at her heart as she recalled the feel of her arm, so cold and lifeless. She had pressed her fingertips into Mrs Crawford's wrist in the futile search for a pulse. After pulling her hand away from under the limp weight of her arm, she had sat back feeling her rising panic transform into a spiralling sense of loss. She could not have imagined she would feel so bereft. It showed how much she had meant to her, how much she had loved her, how much she needed her. She had been frail but she had always been strong. The truth of how much support Mrs Crawford had given Maria was only now becoming fully apparent to her. Now that it had been taken away so suddenly.

She stared hard at the empty bed, wishing desperately that it was still occupied by the loveliest woman she had ever known. That she could at least have the opportunity of one final bedside chat. Not to chat about the day ahead as they had always done but, this time, to tell her all of those things that should not have remained unsaid. To tell her that she loved their relationship, that she meant so much to her, that she sympathised deeply with the loss she had borne for so long.

But none of that would be possible because she had gone.

Her body had lain there, stilled by the release of that final breath, but she had not been looking at Mrs Crawford. It was so obvious that she had departed. Moved on to be with her loved ones. With Amy and her mother and father. She had departed, leaving those few people behind who had been part of her everyday existence. All of us and, she mused with a shiver of excitement, her lover, Nektarios Alexandrou.

She wondered what her death would mean to him. Would he come to the funeral? Would they see him, a sad old man filled with memories of Mrs Crawford as a beautiful young woman? She hoped so. She imagined speaking to him gently. Telling him how Mrs Crawford had continued to cherish her memories of Greece. How much the experience and her relationship with him had meant to her. Yes, it would be good if he came, very good.

Soothed by these thoughts, Maria moved forward to lift the pillows and smooth the duvet underneath them.

She then lowered herself onto the front edge of the bedside chair leaning forward and continuing to look at the pillows, her hands pressed together between her knees as she confronted the truth that this order she wished desperately to maintain would soon cease to be relevant. She resolved though that, until it became clear that her services were no longer required, she would keep everything as Mrs Crawford liked it to be.

Releasing her hands, Maria relaxed into the chair, shifting her body into a comfortable position. She closed her eyes in the hope of finding respite but, instead, she felt besieged by the anxieties which had fluttered inside her over the last three days. Anxieties about the life changes which faced her. She was unnerved by the prospect of having to move on. Everything had been satisfyingly settled and now she would have to summon the energy and courage to find a new position.

She rocked her head from side to side as she tried to banish these troubling thoughts. She should leave all of that until after the funeral. It was not right or necessary to address her future now. Feeling her anxiety subside, she gave her shoulders a little jiggle to release the tension and slumped back against the soft upholstery. After sighing deeply, she became aware of a soothing pressure on her temples. Succumbing to this hypnotic sensation, she sighed submissively, as her mind filled with the brightness of hope and restoration.

Maria's head twitched as she awoke to the sound of her mobile phone ringing from the hall table.

It ceased ringing just as she reached full consciousness. Hearing the sound notification of a text message she pulled herself up and looked around the room. A sleepy smile pulled at the corners of her mouth, as she relished the sensation of having been soothed, her body rested and her mind cleansed.

Her gaze lingered on the far corner of the room where the shadow seemed to fade and then strengthen, as her vision adjusted to full clarity. She stood up and, after casting a backward glance at the corner, walked into the hall feeling a renewed sense of inner strength.

She retrieved her phone and read the text.

Phoned you back. Will try later. Hope you & Mrs C OK. C

Turning around she walked to the kitchen while scrolling through her contacts list. She dialled Charlene's number on the kitchen phone and sat down on the chair, her body tensing in anticipation. Hearing Charlene's voice, she raised her hand to press the tips of her fingers against her forehead.

'Hi. Maria?'

'Charlene. Yes, it's me. How are you?'

'OK. Yes, I'm OK. Did you get my message? I phoned you on the mobile just in case, you know, just in case Mrs Crawford was asleep or resting.'

'No, of course, that's fine. That was sensible but, well, anyway, listen, thanks for phoning back, Charlene. I need to speak to you because I've got something to tell you. Some sad news. Some sad news about Mrs Crawford.'

Maria paused, taking a moment to prepare herself but then, unnerved by the silence, her mind blanked and she started to panic.

'Charlene? Charlene, are you still there…?'

After a further silence, Charlene responded with soft intensity.

'Yes. I'm still here, Maria. What is it, Maria? What's wrong with Mrs Crawford? Is she not well? I hope she's not ill.'

Her earnest expression easing, Maria's eyes opened wide.

'No, she's not ill, Charlene. She was ill, I'm afraid. She was ill and she became very weak. Weaker and weaker, Charlene, until I'm afraid she…well, she passed away, Charlene. Peacefully, very peacefully.'

Maria paused before continuing in a rush of regret.

'I'm sorry, Charlene. This must be a shock for you. I shouldn't have told you on the phone. I should have told you face to face, it's just I wasn't sure where you were and I thought you should know… Charlene? Are you still there?'

'Yes, Maria. I'm still here. It's a shock. I don't know… I don't know what to say. I…'

'Listen, Charlene. Don't worry. There's no need to say anything. You'll need time for it to sink in.'

Maria stretched her back to release the tension. Her voice sounded brighter as she continued.

'Look, Charlene. Could we meet up? Would that be possible? I think it would be good if we could as soon as possible. It's much better than talking on the phone and I need to explain things to you. Things like the will. She's remembered you in her will, Charlene. I don't know what she's done exactly but she has left you something. Her lawyer told me. Mr Wilkins, if you remember him. Anyway, I'm not sure but I don't think you'll need to worry about your studies you know, the arrangements Mrs Crawford made. At least I don't imagine you will. So would it be possible to get together, do you think?… Charlene?'

'Yes. Yes, that would be fine. I'm not doing anything just now, at least not until later.'

'Oh OK. You mean you're back home? You mean you could come round?'

'Yes. Yes, I could come round.'

'Oh right. It's just that, well, I thought you might be at college.'

'No. Not today I'm not at college. No.'

'Oh right. Well, that would be great if you could pop round. If you could do it sometime soon that would be great. It's just that, well, I've got to go out for an hour or so after lunch so...'

'No. That's OK. I can come round now.'

'Oh great, so let's see, it's eleven twenty now so if you're taking the bus you could be here, what, around midday?'

'Yes. I suppose, except I've got to get ready so it might be a bit later than that.'

'OK, well, don't worry, Charlene. I don't have to leave here until about half past one, so just come as soon as you can. OK?'

'Yes, OK.'

'Right. Well, see you later, my love. I'm glad you can come round. It'll be good to see you and, well, Charlene, I know it's very sad but I keep reminding myself that she passed away peacefully, very peacefully, and that she'll be with her loved ones now, so try and keep those thoughts in your head. OK, Charlene?'

'Um... yes. Yes, OK. Yes, I'll do that.'

Maria pulled her legs in and dipped her head as she modified her voice to a more intimate tone.

'OK, my love, we'll see you very soon then.'

'Yes, OK. See you.'

'Ok, Charlene. Bye then.'

'Bye.'

'Byeee!'

Chapter 32

Maria closed the cupboard door sharply and returned to her chair. She was frustrated by her inability to decide between throwing everything in the bin, keeping it for her own use or offering it to Lionel and Stephen. It would be wrong to waste it, but eating Mrs Crawford's food did not seem right.

She glanced at the clock on the wall, transferring her frustration to Charlene's lateness. Waiting was making her irritable and anxious about getting to the printers in time. With the consequences of missing the appointment pressing on her mind, she dialled Charlene's number and stood up, pushing the chair back with her legs. The screech of the chair scraping across the tiles chimed discordantly with the abrupt ring of the doorbell.

Leaving her phone on the table Maria strode out of the kitchen and across the hall to the entry-phone. She lifted the handset and watched the screen as it flickered into definition. Charlene's face appeared and behind her she saw the flash of a car driving off with a loud growl. The screen then became filled with Charlene's hair as she dipped down to speak into the microphone. Unable to hear her above the roaring engine, Maria pressed the button to unlock the door and replaced the handset.

The car had sounded exactly like Lee's. She frowned at the thought that they may have got back together.

After snibbing the lock and wedging the door open, Maria walked slowly to the lift. Watching the floor numbers change as it made its way up the building, she lifted and lowered her heels nervously as a mixture of anxiety and excitement swirled inside her. She remained rested on her heels as the number seven illuminated, her face settling into an expression of sympathy.

The lift clunked to a halt and Charlene stepped out as the doors parted. Screwing her body round to avoid the unexpected presence of Maria, Charlene fell awkwardly into her embrace.

'Oops, did I surprise you, love? Sorry. Are you all right?'

Holding Charlene against her, Maria leaned forward and kissed her temple before releasing her.

'Oh my goodness, Charlene. You've changed your hair! You look different.'

'Yes. I let it grow and Sharon put highlights in it and waves.'

'Well, it ah… it looks great. Quite a change of image especially with the…'

Maria cocked her head knowingly while tapping the side of her nose.

'Yes, it's a stud. Diamonique. You know, like diamond. Fake diamond.'

'Well, it certainly glitters. Anyway, it's good to see you although I'm sorry, you know, about the circumstances. Very sorry.'

Maria reached behind Charlene to hug her as they walked to the front door.

'Yes. It's a shock. A real shock. I can't believe it. She was special. I really liked her and I feel bad. Bad that I haven't phoned for, well, for a long time. It's bad. I should have phoned. I feel so bad.'

'Listen, you mustn't worry about that. Really. Mrs Crawford didn't mind and anyway she was ill and didn't really want to speak to anyone. Not really.'

'Oh, Maria. But it must have been terrible for you. To be here when she, when she… and you must miss her so much. Oh, Maria. What's going to happen? It's terrible.'

'Well, yes, it is terrible. It was… awful. So awful. I still can't quite believe it and I will miss her so much. She was so special to me. Very special. She wasn't like any client you know, Charlene. I loved her. She meant a lot to me.'

'I know. I could tell. I could see that you were close. Very close. Both of you.'

Reaching the open door, Charlene stopped abruptly and turned to face Maria.

'Maria. She's not… she's not in there, is she?'

'Oh no. Don't worry, she's been, well, she's been taken away. Oh and she didn't, you know, pass away while I was here. I came in on Monday morning and found her and, you know, Charlene, she looked so peaceful. So peaceful I thought she was asleep. You know how still she was when she slept.'

The uncomprehending blankness of Charlene's face became etched with despair as she stared into Maria's eyes. Her lower lip began to quiver and her moistening eyes widened as if surprised by the gulps of grief which prevented her from speaking. Succumbing to this loss of control, she looked away despairingly. Engulfed by a swell of compassion, Maria embraced Charlene's sobbing body and held her tight. They stood clasped together sharing their distress, until Maria released her embrace and began to stroke Charlene's head consolingly.

'There, there, my love. It's good to cry. I've been doing a lot of it. It comes over you sometimes when you least expect it but, well, it's natural and it's good. It's all part of grieving.'

Pressing her hand gently against Charlene's back, Maria ushered her into the apartment.

'Well. It's some time since you were last here, isn't it, my love? Those were happier days, well, they were for me at least. Happy days. I've no doubt lots of good things have happened for you since then, or at least I hope they have.'

Charlene stood limply while Maria closed the door, her complexion washed out and streaked with tear stains. She was perplexed by her emotional state, by once again being consumed by uncontrollable feelings connected in ways she could not fully comprehend to her relationship with Mrs Crawford.

Her face creasing with compassion, Maria swivelled away from the door and swept across the floor to guide Charlene towards the kitchen.

'Come on. We'll have plenty of time to catch up later. Let's just get you a cup of tea or hot chocolate, whatever you prefer. I guess you won't want a coffee, at least not the real stuff.'

Maria opened the kitchen door for Charlene, continuing to talk to her as she passed.

'Now, Charlene, my love, I'll make you a cup of something and then I'll have to dash off for an hour or so to sort out the order of service at the printers, or at least I've got to choose the paper and the style of it. I'll have to sort out the running order with Reverend Grandison tomorrow. Mrs Crawford wants me to sing at it. Would you believe it? With the girls, if they're willing. She told Mr Wilkins, the lawyer, that's what she wanted. Oh dear, it makes me a bit nervous but I'll do it if that's what she wanted. Now you have a seat down here. OK?'

She pulled back the chair and waited for Charlene to sit down before switching the kettle on.

'Is tea OK, love?'

She stopped to look back and catch Charlene's affirmative nod before carrying on.

'Now I hope you are OK to stay here for a while. Hopefully it won't take too long and I'll be back in an hour. Now is that OK, Charlene? When do you have to get home?'

Maria turned round to wait for Charlene's response. Having started to reply with a moisture-clogged throat, Charlene coughed lightly until she was able to begin again with a clearer voice.

'Five o'clock. Around then. I've got to be somewhere at half six.'

'OK. Well, if I'm back by three, will that be OK? That would give us more than an hour. Will you be getting the bus back?'

'No. Uh. No, I'll get a lift. I can phone and I'll get picked up so it's no problem.'

'Oh I see, so did you get a lift here?'

'Yes. Yes, I did.'

'Oh, so that was the car? The noisy car.'

'Ah well. Maybe. It might have been.'

'Oh well, it doesn't matter, it's just that… that it sounded a bit like, you know, your ex-boyfriend's car.'

'Oh yes, Lee. Yes, well, I know what you mean, well… well…'

'Anyhow, it's good that you can get a lift. That should give us a bit longer.'

Maria placed the mug of tea in front of Charlene and bustled over to lift her jacket off the hook on the door. Pulling it on she looked across at Charlene.

'Now do make yourself at home, Charlene. You know where everything is and do have a comfy seat in the sitting room if you want after you've finished your tea. OK?'

She waited a couple of seconds until, accepting that Charlene was not going to respond, she turned to leave, chirruping her parting message through the narrowing gap as she closed the door.

'Take it easy, love. OK? I won't be long.'

Just before closing the door, Maria re-opened it to look back at Charlene, expressing her afterthought with breathless excitement.

'Oh, by the way. I can't think why I forgot to tell you, but you know the Greek man Mrs Crawford mentioned occasionally?

You know, the one she spent time with when she lived in Greece on the island. Well, apparently she remembered him in her will. You know, she's left him something. So she must have, you know, well, he must have really meant something to her. Isn't that amazing after all these years!'

Charlene's jaw slackened and her eyes widened as she looked up at Maria.

'Oh my god. I didn't realise, I mean I thought it was all in the past. I didn't realise that they were still in touch.'

'They weren't! Not since I knew her and before that but, well, she must have loved him all this time.'

'Wow, that is amazing.'

'Isn't it! Well, we can chat about it later. Sorry to leave you on that note. OK. Byee!'

Stepping back, Maria flashed a smile at Charlene before closing the door and leaving the apartment.

Chapter 33

Charlene sashayed slowly across the sitting room looking down at her bare feet sinking into the carpet.

Reaching the window she pulled the cord to raise the blind and shivered with delight as the sunshine warmed her body. Anticipating that the strong sunlight would be uncomfortable on her face, she left the blind partially closed. Turning around, she luxuriated in the warmth before stretching her neck muscles with circular movements of her head, breathing in deeply and walking into the middle of the room.

Noticing a CD case lying on the sideboard next to the music player, she languidly changed direction to pick it up.

She knew the name Demis Roussos and recognised the photograph of the large man in a voluminous kaftan from one of her mother's old CDs. She could also recall his high voice and the extravagant orchestration of the music. It was not cool music and she would never have admitted that she quite liked it except perhaps to Mrs Crawford. It would have been good to listen to it with her, although it was difficult to imagine her enjoying Demis Roussos, until her recollection that he was Greek made it slightly more believable.

Opening the case and finding it empty, Charlene turned on the CD player and ejected the disk tray. Seeing the missing CD in position, she pushed the tray in and pressed the play button.

"*Ever and ever, forever and ever*
You'll be the one
That shines on me
Like the morning sun"

The soaring melody and high-reaching vocal, echoing with vibrato, filled the room. Charlene peeled away from the sideboard and, wafting her arms up and down in rhythm with the music, swirled across the room with balletic grace.

"*Ever and ever, forever and ever*
You'll be my spring
My rainbow's end
And the song I sing
Take me far beyond imagination
You're my dream come true
My consolation"

Increasingly absorbed in the music, she lifted her arms higher, twisting her waist and rotating her hips in sensual response to its lush extravagance. Half closing her eyes she changed direction, traversing in slow spins until coming to an abrupt halt as she crunched her hip against the side of a chair. Jolted back to the reality of her situation, she rushed across to the CD player and, pressing the standby button, restored the room to silence. With her mind becoming consumed again by troubled thoughts, she walked weakly to the chair opposite Mrs Crawford's and dropped onto it, pressing her hands together between her thighs as she leaned forward to vocalise her concerns.

'I'm so sorry, Mrs Crawford. I've let you down but it's just that I'm not used to it. To people trusting me. It's too much pressure and college, well, it just doesn't feel right. Nobody else is at college, at least nobody I know. I did most of it. I just wasn't ready for the exams. I got scared. I've never bothered with exams and it was too scary. It's just not me and I'm sorry. I would have paid the money back but I don't know what to do now. What do I do?'

Charlene released her hands and, propping her elbows on her knees, rested her head on her palms before collapsing against the back of the chair.

'Also, I got lonely. I mean, don't get me wrong, there were some nice people at college. I went out with them sometimes but it felt a bit strange and now that I'm back at home this feels strange and I'm getting to hate it again. Oh Christ, it's so fucking difficult! It really is.'

Suddenly tensing, she gripped the chair arms and pulled herself into an upright position, casting a sidelong glance at Mrs Crawford's chair, her brow creasing in anxiety.

'Oh my god, I'm so sorry about the language.'

Then, shaking her head, she rose to her feet and walked around the edge of the room, gesturing her exasperation as she spoke.

'Oh my god, she's not here. She's dead. Why the… why the hell are you talking to her? Why the hell are you talking to yourself?! Get a frigging grip.'

Crossing the room, she stopped halfway to look down at the framed photographs on the table. She studied each one in turn before picking up the photograph of Amy and stepping back to drop into the chair.

Her smile, as she absorbed Amy's beauty and her radiance in that moment, faded under her furrowing brow as she began to consider how all that happiness had come to an end. She strained to imagine Mrs Crawford's agony on losing her only daughter and shook her head in incredulity at how she had shown such generosity and patience while suffering such inconsolable loss. Reflecting on this she became consumed with shame that she should be feeling so troubled about her own life.

Placing the photo flat on her lap she gazed across the room at the blinds glowing with diffused light. Stiffening her posture she spoke again but louder than before.

'And what the fuck am I doing?'

Turning round she frowned briefly in the direction of Mrs Crawford's chair before continuing.

'I'm sorry, Mrs Crawford, but it's wrong what I've done. I should have tried harder. For you. For me. For… for… for the future, my future. I mean, at least I've got a future, not like you. You and Amy.'

After casting a forlorn glance at Amy's portrait, she stood up and carefully replaced it on the table. She then sighed and walked out of the room, her mind filling with fretful thoughts.

'Oh fuck. What am I going to do? I'm going to have to tell Maria. I will, Mrs Crawford, I'll tell Maria everything, even about Lee. Fuck him. I'm going to tell him it's over. I should have never let him back in. Oh shit. This is going to be a nightmare. I'll let him take me home but after that I'll ditch him… again. Oh Christ, what a mess, but I'm going to have to sort it out. I really am.'

Chapter 34

'Nice day.'
'Yes, although I feel strange.'
'Nervous?'
'Yes, I suppose so. Apprehensive and also like I've forgotten to do something.'
'Ah right. Yes, well, I know that feeling, but don't worry, love, I'm sure you haven't actually forgotten anything. I mean, Mr Wilkins or the vicar, what's his name, Grandison, Reverend Grandison, would have mentioned it if you had or if anything wasn't, you know, in place.'

Maria looked up, blinking at William in the glare of the sunlight and narrowing her eyes to focus on his face. Unable to see anything clearly other than the silhouetted mess of his hair, she turned away and squeezed his hand. She then checked her watch and looked out for people descending the path through the trees from the car park. She spoke to him over her shoulder.

'No, you're right. I know everything is organised but I've still got a knot in my stomach and it's not just about the singing.'

William stretched his arm out and gave her a reassuring

squeeze. Momentarily unbalanced, she leaned into him and pressed her head against his shoulder before revealing a further cause of her concern.

'Oh William, I hope everyone turns up. I mean, I know the girls will. I just hope everyone else does, especially Charlene.'

'I'm sure they will, love, including Charlene. I mean, why wouldn't she?'

'Well, I don't know, she's sometimes not very reliable. I should have insisted that she came with us but, oh, I don't know, and it's not just her. I suppose I'm also wondering if, you know, Nektarios Alexandrou will turn up.'

'Aha, yes. Well, did Mr Wilkins say if he'd replied?'

'No, I mean yes, he said that he hadn't, at least he hadn't by the time he left the office last night. That's one of the things he's doing now. Checking to see if they've received anything this morning.'

'Oh right, I wondered where he'd gone.'

'Well, he hasn't *gone* gone. He's only gone to his car to make some phone calls.'

'Ah right, well, you should find out soon then.'

'I suppose so, if I get the chance to speak to him before the service. Actually I'm not really that bothered about him. About Nektarios Alexandrou. It's really Charlene I'm worried about. I really hope she turns up on time. I hope she understands the importance of showing respect, especially after Mrs Crawford's been so kind to her.'

Having relaxed his embrace, William tightened it again, pulling Maria close against him, a gratified smile breaking out below the blank lenses of his large, light-sensitive glasses.

'Yes, she was generous. A very good woman and you certainly deserve all of her kindness. You really do.'

Pushing against him with her trapped arm to signal that it was time for him to release her, Maria stepped sideways, tugging the rumples out of her coat before smoothing it down.

'Oh, I don't know, William. I've been thinking more about it and I'm even less sure that we should just accept it. That I deserve it. It's the money really. I mean the paintings are fine although they're not my cup of tea but, well, it's such a lot of money. I mean, I know she was quite definite about it and that we should respect her wishes. It's just that I think we need to think about it. What we do with it. Do you know what I mean, William?… William?'

'Yes, Maria. OK. Let's talk about it but not right now. There's people coming. Two people. It must be Orricene and Mahalia. Yes, in fact it's definitely them.'

Maria spun round and focused her gaze on the approaching women.

'Yes, that's them. Good girls. Nice and early.'

An effervescence of affection welled up inside her. It thrilled her that she had become so close to Orricene and Mahalia. They had seemed so different from the people in other parts of her life. Women with a West Indian heritage. Devout women who, despite the prescriptive doctrine of their church, always remained so light-hearted and open. They had not even seemed to mind about Lionel and Stephen. Her pang of guilt at telling them that they were Mrs Crawford's friends, and not hers as well, receded as they drew near.

'Hi, girls!'

After hitching the strap of her bag further up her shoulder, Maria opened her arms and stepped forward to embrace and kiss each of them in turn.

'I'm so glad you're here. We've just arrived ourselves. Everything's ready. I've spoken to Reverend Grandison and Mr Wilkins. Oh, and Mr Allan is on his way.'

'Oh, we always like to arrive in plenty of time. Don't we, Mahalia?'

'Oh, for sure. We've got to support our sister. That right, William? We gotta support your good woman!'

Mahalia's face stretched into a broad smile and her body shook as a sonorous laugh rumbled up from deep within her, transforming into a raucous cackle as it reached her throat.

William danced in awkward delight from foot to foot, his head dipping diffidently and his hands shoved into his trouser pockets. His eyes, peering over the top of his spectacles, shone excitedly through his wispy fringe.

'Yes. That's right, Mahalia. She… she deserves it. We've ah… we're all… ah… we're all here for her.'

'We sure are and for Mrs Crawford. To remember that fine woman.'

'Sure. Yes. Of course. She was a good woman. Very generous.'

Mahalia turned her attention to Maria who had resumed her position beside William.

'Well, it's turning into a fine day. God is shining his light on us which is very nice.'

'Yes, it's lovely. I thought we were all going to get wet but actually it's getting warm again.'

Having surveyed the setting, Orricene looked down the path towards the shelter set back from the chapel entrance.

'I suppose we could have stood in there although it's so nice to stand in the sunshine.'

Turning back towards Maria, her cheeks plumped as she smiled.

'We're looking forward to seeing Charlene. Find out how she's getting on.'

Maria's face flinched with concern.

'Yes. Well, I'm really hoping she turns up on time. She's not always so reliable.'

Orricene's eyebrows arched reproachfully.

'Oh, surely she won't be late! After Mrs Crawford has been so kind. Surely!'

'Oh no. I'm sure she won't be. At least, she won't mean to be. Her heart's in the right place. I'm… I'm sure about that. She'll try to get here on time. Yes, she'll certainly try to get here. I hope.'

'Well. Never mind. Let's not worry about that. Everyone else will get here.'

'Yes, that's right. There's Mrs Crawford's niece, Mrs Evans and her daughters, Melanie and Kate. They're really nice and there will be some of the people she used to work with. Her business partners. Lovely people. Quite old and… and quite… quite posh, I suppose, but very nice.'

Holding her bag in front of her with both hands gripping the strap, Mahalia leaned sideways towards Orricene, nudging her gently with her elbow.

'Never mind her business partners, we want to meet Mrs Crawford's old flame. Eh, Orricene?'

'Absolutely. I hope he's going to show up, Maria. You heard from him?'

'No, 'fraid not, Orricene. At least, not yet. Mr Wilkins is phoning the office to check but we really don't think he'll make it. It's a long way, isn't it? All the way from Greece.'

'Well, sure, but then she did leave him something, didn't she, so you'd think he'd make the effort?'

Pulling her head back Mahalia turned to look at Orricene.

'Give him a break, sister. Imagine how old he must be. Travelling all the way here at his age and at short notice too.'

Turning to look at her friends, Maria smiled warmly.

'You're right, Mahalia, he will be quite old and who knows, he might not be strong enough to make the journey. I'm not really expecting him to turn up, but I'm sure he'll contact Mr Wilkins at some stage. I'm sure he'll write or something and, oh, listen, something I didn't tell you, you know how Mrs Crawford wrote us a letter – to both of us, Charlene and me – well, what I didn't tell you is that in Charlene's letter she asked her to go to Greece. To visit the island she stayed on. She wanted Charlene to do what she had never managed to do, to go back to the island…'

Mahalia leaned forward, her eyes widening with intrigue.

'Well I never, you mean… you mean…'

'Yes, she wanted to know that… that although she couldn't go, someone would go after she… after she had gone. After she had passed away. I suppose she was hoping that Charlene would go and visit Nektarios Alexandrou and, well, see the place which was so special to her.'

'Well, how amazing. What an amazing thing to do. Well I never!'

After coughing sharply to command attention, William twitched his head to flick his fringe back from his eyes and pushed his spectacles back up his nose.

'Connection. I think she wanted to know that some sort of connection would be made with the place which had apparently meant so much to her. She needed the reassurance of knowing that someone else would experience it perhaps in the same way she had. The same special way, with any luck. I think that would have given her some satisfaction. To know that someone was going in her place.'

Having looked straight ahead while making his pronouncement, William tucked his chin back against his neck and looked down at Maria's upturned face.

'That's my take on it, anyway. What do you think, love? Do you think that's the gist of what she intended? The inference of what she wrote?'

'Yes, I think so, William. Yes, I think you're right.'

After glancing wide-eyed at Orricene, Mahalia tilted her head to one side as Maria turned towards her.

'Well I never. Goodness me, and do you think she'll go? Well, I suppose she'll have to. Won't she?'

'Oh yes, I'm sure she'll go. Yes. I expect so although she did seem puzzled by it and, well, I suppose it is a bit puzzling. Just a bit and, well, it'll probably be quite different now. You know how places change and, of course, he'll be a lot older although she didn't mention him in her letter which is a bit strange. Don't you think?'

Mahalia nodded emphatically.

'Yes. It is a bit strange especially because…well… they're such different people, Mrs Crawford and Charlene. Different generations of course but also, well, just very different. You know, Mrs Crawford was so… so sophisticated and educated.'

Maria chuckled warmly.

'Mahalia, you're so right but then she was full of surprises, Mrs Crawford, she really was.'

Clearing his throat again in staccato coughs, William jerked his head towards the chapel.

'Oh, oh. Here we go. That's that service finished. Here they come.'

Shifting in nervous agitation, his attention was caught by activity in the opposite direction.

'Oh blimey, it's all happening now. Look, here's a crowd coming to our service as well. It's Mrs Evans with her family and, oh crikey, it's ah, it's Lionel and Stephen behind them. Oh well, here we go. Let battle commence! Well, not really but it's going to get busy!'

Maria flashed a glance up the path as Mahalia and Orricene stepped back onto the verge to allow the people leaving to pass.

'Yes. It's them all right. In good time, although it's a shame that we're going to get a bit mixed up.'

She turned her head to mutter discreetly at William.

'I thought they were supposed to go out a different way.'

William ceased nodding at the passers-by to look down at Maria, his fixed grin of sympathy transforming to an expression of loving concern.

'I think it's us that's in the wrong place, dear. We're neither up nor down. We should probably be down there by the shelter.'

'Oh dear, I think you're right. Well, never mind. We can go down now with the others.'

Smiling eagerly, Maria looked towards Mrs Evans while fluttering a wave. Seeing Mrs Evans beam back at her, Maria stretched up onto the balls of her feet to wave at Lionel and Stephen following behind. With each of them responding enthusiastically, Maria stood back to await their arrival. Looking straight ahead, her posture relaxed as she began to feel less apprehensive until the roar of an approaching car caused her to stiffen. Concerned by what this familiar noise might signify, she looked up at William, her eyes widening in alarm. Understanding the cause of her concern, William flexed his eyebrows knowingly before twitching his head to direct Maria's attention towards Mrs Evans. Following his cue, Maria raised her hands, allowing Mrs Evans to grasp them in a compassionate clutch as she spoke.

'Maria, my dear... oh my goodness, what a noisy car!'

Maria cast a fearful glance up the path before refocusing on Mrs Evans.

'Yes, it is... ah... noisy. Very loud but... oh... that's better.'

'Ah yes. Thank goodness for that. Anyway, it's great to see you and, look, I am so grateful for everything you've done.'

'Oh well, that's kind of you to say so, but it was the least I could do.'

Still clasping her hands, Mrs Evans pressed closer to Maria to make more room for the upward procession of people. After a swift glance back at Lionel and Stephen, she smiled at Mahalia and Orricene before returning to face Maria.

'Oh dear me, I think we're making things difficult here. We'd better keep going but we'll see you down there, shall we?'

'Yes. Yes. Absolutely. We were thinking of coming down now anyway. We've just realised we're not in a great place here so I guess we'll follow you.'

'OK, right, well, I'll just keep going then.'

With Mrs Evans edging away, Maria turned her attention to Melanie and Kate who pressed against each other while smiling shyly.

'Hello, girls. How lovely to see you again. We're not in a great place here, are we, so we'll just follow you down and I can introduce you to everyone when we're settled in a better place if that's OK with you?'

Murmuring their assent, Maria squeezed their hands supportively as they moved off to follow their mother. Then, suddenly distracted by William sidling behind her, Maria swivelled round, her brow puckering in puzzlement.

'William?'

'Yes, dear. Don't worry, I'm just getting ready to follow you.'

'Yes but… oh well. Never mind.'

Turning back, her face brightened as she clasped hands with Stephen.

'Maria, so good to see you… and William.'

Stephen looked up at William now standing directly behind Maria, his head turned away as he stared at the last of the passers-by walking up the path. Jolted out of his affected distraction by Maria jabbing her elbow into his side, he jerked his head round to face Stephen.

'Ah yes. Oh, hello, Stephen. Yes, I wasn't paying attention. It's… ah… it's good to see you.'

Then at the same time as pushing his spectacles back up onto the bridge of his nose, he switched his attention to Lionel.

'And you, Lionel, how are you? It's nice to… nice to see you again.'

A wide smile flashed on Lionel's face.

'It's good to see you, William, my dear, although I do wish we were all meeting in different circumstances. Really, this shouldn't be happening. Should it? I mean, it was such a shock. Such a shock to lose her. I still can't quite believe it.'

With William nodding in agreement while covering his mouth with his hand and clearing his throat nervously with hacking grunts, Lionel moved in towards Maria.

'Oh, Maria, my dear, how are you? It's all too awful, isn't it?'

'Yes, it's awful. Truly awful for all of us, however I guess we'll have to do our best to… you know. Well…'

'Yes. You're right. Let's do our best to give her a good send-off. That's what she would want. It's the least we can do and we're all really looking forward to hearing you sing. You and the girls.'

Lionel turned towards Mahalia and Orricene.

'Hello, I'm Lionel and this is Stephen. Pleased to meet you.'

'Oh yes, I should have introduced everyone properly. I was going to do it once we'd got down but anyway, Lionel, Stephen this is Mahalia and Orricene.'

Maria stood back against William, allowing hands to be shaken and pleasantries to be exchanged, before speaking brightly to focus their attention.

'Right. Well, we'd better get going. They'll be ready for us in the chapel I expect, so, well, shall we go?'

Beaming benevolently she allowed them all to proceed. Then, as she stepped forward, William started coughing in a way she knew was intended to attract her attention. Maria swung her head round to view the upward stretch of path where she sensed the reason for William's warning would be revealed. She could not see their faces clearly but knew from their slow and irregular progress that it must be Mrs Crawford's elderly former business colleagues.

'Oh dear. Right, we'd better get going. It could take forever if we wait for them and I couldn't bear it if we got held up now, so come on, my love, let's go.'

'Oh right. I hope they haven't seen us.'

'Let's not worry too much about that. Just don't look back. Come on. Let's go.'

Looking down the path with focused determination, Maria stepped out and bustled after the others making no concession to William's ungainly stumblings as he tried to keep up. After a few strides she suddenly stopped and twitched her head to the side. She braced herself as William, unable to adjust his pace quickly enough, crumpled against her.

'Oh sorry, dear, I… I didn't notice.'

'Never mind. I'm fine, but listen. What's that noise?'

'What noise?'

'Sshh. Listen. That shouting. It's getting louder.'

'Oh. So it is. It's somebody shouting. Two people shouting.'

'Wait. Listen.'

William straightened up and, removing his hands from Maria's shoulder, turned round with her to look up the path. Maria shook her head despairingly as the person came into view.

'Oh my god. I might have known. It's Charlene. Oh for goodness' sake. Listen to her! Now everyone's looking at her. Come on, William. Let's go. Quick.'

Maria whirled round and recommenced her descent until the sound of William's voice brought her progress to an abrupt halt.

'Maria. Who's that with her? The man she's arguing with. I think it could be… you know…'

She stretched round to look back.

'Oh, that's all we need! She can't bring him. Not that… that… that hooligan.'

'No, she's not. That's what she's doing. She's telling him to go away, well, to eff off actually. My goodness. What language! At a funeral!'

'It's disgraceful. I thought she'd finished with him. She said she had. Ages ago. She's impossible. She really is. What would Mrs C have thought! Come on, William. Let's go. Quickly.'

Chapter 35

Reverend Grandison rested his forearm on the bottom edge of the lectern and stooped down to speak discreetly.

'OK. That sounds great. Well done, Maria. We're not due to start for a few minutes but perhaps we can kick off. It looks like most people are here already.'

Maria glanced over her shoulder at the small congregation of people seated in the front rows.

'Well, there's at least one person still to come or at least to come inside. She is here. I saw her outside.'

'OK. Well, we can wait for her. I take it you're talking about… about…'

'Charlene? Yes, that's right.'

'Ah yes. Well, that's fine. Perhaps you could ask Mr Allan to keep on playing until she arrives and then we'll get going.'

'Yes, OK. Actually, perhaps I'd better pop outside and find her. What do you… do you…?'

Accepting that Reverend Grandison had resumed his demeanour of professional piety and become oblivious to her, Maria walked over to Mr Allan, bowing her head as she passed the flower-adorned coffin in the middle of the nave. Then, after her whispered exchange with Mr Allan, she dipped her head and returned across the dais to descend the steps to the chapel floor. She looked up on reaching the central aisle and paused as she noticed the front door begin to open. Seeing Charlene appear unaccompanied, she rushed up to her.

'Goodness me. You've arrived just in time.'

Maria moved alongside Charlene, pressing her hand gently against the base of Charlene's back as they started to walk side by side down the aisle.

'Oh… yes. Hi. I've been here for a… for about ten minutes. It's just that I… I…'

'I know, we heard you arrive. Heard you arguing with… with Lee.'

'Ah yes, ah, he gave me a lift.'

Halting, Maria removed her hand and waited for Charlene to look back at her before leaning forward to whisper her vexation.

'Charlene, I thought you had split up? You and Lee.'

Charlene's posture wilted and her face strained in anxiety. She raised her arms in a gesture of entreaty.

'I have, Maria. Honestly I have, but he tries to be nice and I can't get away from him. He drove past and I took a lift. I shouldn't have. It was crazy. I told him I would never go back. He went mad. Scary. Anyway, he's gone now. I told him just to… just to go.'

Her demeanour softening, Maria swept forward to link arms with Charlene and escort her towards the small congregation.

'Well, that's a relief, Charlene, I can tell you. You are much too good for him, and by the way, you are looking beautiful. So elegant! Much better without that stud in your nose.'

'Oh thanks, Maria. I got fed up with it and, anyway, I wanted to make an effort for Mrs Crawford. I wanted her to be proud, if you know what I mean.'

'I do, Charlene. I do and she would be. Very proud and by the way, you can come back to Marine Heights with us. OK?'

'Yes. That would be great. Thanks.'

'Right. Well, I need to be on the front row with the girls but why don't you go in here next to William and the boys?'

Moving closer, Maria whispered confidentially into Charlene's ear.

'He will appreciate the moral support, if you know what I mean.'

Charlene cast a wild-eyed glance at Maria before manoeuvring her way along the row towards William.

Continuing to sweep forward, her face now solemn, Maria raised her thumb at Mr Allan as he looked up from the sheet music. Bringing the prolonged piece to a conclusion, Mr Allan raised the volume on the final emphatic chords as Maria settled into her seat beside Mahalia and Orricene.

A benign beam spreading across his face, Reverend Grandison raised his head and cleared his throat with a peremptory rasp. He opened his mouth but, just as he prepared to enunciate the first word, the heavy entrance door opened with a slow swoosh. The evangelical gleam in his eyes faded as he focused on the figure appearing from behind the door.

The sounds of rustling, cloth rumpling and shoe shuffling amplified sharply in the high-reaching space, as everyone turned to witness the reason for this interruption.

Restoring his clerical composure, Reverend Grandison smiled graciously, raising his arms in a symbolic embrace of the new arrival.

'Welcome. I take it you have come to join us in remembering our dear friend Katherine Crawford. Come. Please sit down. You are most welcome.'

Maria turned around to look conferringly at Mahalia, her wide eyes shining brightly. Mahalia leaned in, speaking in an urgent whisper as she placed her hand on Maria's arm.

'Is that him? Do you think that's him?'

Maria twisted round to watch the man sit down at the end of

the vacant row behind. She looked for anything revealing about his face but it remained blankly inscrutable.

Mahalia stretched over to whisper into Maria's ear.

'What do you think? Is that the man?'

Settling back into a comfortable position, Maria projected her murmured response from the side of her mouth.

'I don't know. It could be. It must be. He looks Greek, doesn't he?'

Hearing Mahalia's deep throaty laugh stutter jaggedly as she tried to contain it, Maria hunched forward into a conspiratorial coupling with her and waited to hear the reason for her amusement.

'They all look the same to me, sister. Looks good though… give you that… for an old guy…'

Maria gave her an affectionate shove, fond smile lines creasing around her glowing cheeks.

'He's not bad, is he? Very handsome.'

After casting another swift glance at the man, she and Mahalia looked up at Reverend Grandison, excitement radiating from their faces.

Reverend Grandison surveyed the congregation as they settled down, cleared his throat and commenced his eulogy.

Maria observed his expressions with absent-minded attention. She watched his mouth as he spoke but only heard the occasional phrase.

'… Katherine was more than a parishioner and benefactor, she was also a friend, a great friend…'

Ceasing again to listen, Maria followed her own train of thought.

Reverend Grandison may have thought he was a friend but the truth was that she did not have any great, long-standing friendships. Her own relationship with Mrs Crawford was definitely a friendship, a loving friendship. Respectful of professional boundaries but nevertheless a genuine and meaningful relationship. As for true love, there had only been one man she had ever admitted to loving and he was here. He had finally come to see her, now, when it was too late, although perhaps Mrs Crawford would not have wanted him to see her when she had become so weak. This way at least he would remember her only as the vibrant, beautiful woman who had ignited flames of love and passion within him. How sad and difficult it must be for him, she thought, to be filled with these feelings and memories and to be looking at her coffin. The coffin which contained her body but nothing more because the real Mrs Crawford, her soul, had gone to be with her loved ones.

Maria looked up at the stained-glass window depicting the ascension of Jesus to heaven accompanied by a host of angels. Her thoughts continued to drift until the sound of her name captured her attention.

'... Maria was, as you know, more than a carer. She was a cherished friend to Katherine who relied on her greatly and who would be so proud of the very important part she has played in organising proceedings today. Of course amongst Maria's many talents, one that Katherine loved, was her great talent for singing. As you will all know, Maria has been blessed with a beautiful voice and I am delighted to say that she is going to sing to us now along with Mahalia and Orricene from her choir. They are going to sing a song especially requested by Katherine. A song which moved Katherine greatly when she heard Maria and her choir sing it at a concert last year. It's an old gospel song called "The Last Mile of the Way".'

Her mind now sharply focused, Maria raised her eyebrows as she made eye contact with Mahalia and Orricene, and twitched her head to indicate that they should make their way onto the dais.

With the opening chords floating plaintively around the chapel, they took position with Maria in the middle. She tugged discreetly at her skirt to smooth out the creases, while looking across at Mr Allan to signal that they were ready.

Resisting the desire to glance at the man, Maria looked fixedly at the edge of the dais while Mahalia and Orricene sang the introductory refrain, their bodies swaying in rhythmic unison.

Maria shivered as a frisson of exhilaration filled her with courage. She looked up to the back of the chapel, her face lighting up as she felt empowered to sing to the very best of her ability. She wanted everyone to appreciate the song as Mrs Crawford had. To understand why she had been so moved by it. Most of all she wanted him to like it, this man who had come so far. This man who was here because of a love which had endured so many years. She would sing it for him.

Having built up the introduction to its climax, Mahalia and Orricene stopped to open up two beats of silence, before Maria's voice filled the chapel with an emotional resonance which seemed to lift up from the depths of her soul.

"*If I walk in the pathway of duty*
If I work to the close of the day
I shall see the great king in his beauty
When I go the last mile of the way."

She looked down again as Mahalia and Orricene blended in their backing to the final line before continuing with the refrain.

She felt a soothing warmth on her neck as the clouds cleared and the sun radiated through the stained-glass window, casting a multi-hued light on the chapel floor. Maria closed her eyes and waited for her cue into the second verse.

"*When I go the last mile of the way*
I will rest at the close of the day
And I know that God will await me
When I go the last mile of the way."

Raising her arms in an emotional impulse, Maria ranged her view across the small gathering. Seeing the audience would have unnerved her previously but today she absorbed their rapt attention as a fuelling energy. Her sweep across the congregation settled on Reverend Grandison as she sang the final phrase of the verse. Feeling her soul sink at the sight of him half smiling with his head bowed as he read surreptitiously from his notebook, she immediately looked away and opened herself to the inspirational strength of her friends' singing. She then looked up into the chapel and sang the next verse with replenished conviction.

> *"If I live life with love and sweet charity*
> *If I forgive them their sins when I pray*
> *I shall be with those gone before me*
> *When I go the last mile of the way."*

Maria ventured to look at the man as she waited to sing the final verse. Seeing him looking straight back at her, she dipped her head before lifting it again to reconnect eye to eye as he bent forward, his hands pressed together as if praying.

Filled with an exhilarating sense that he was understanding the message of the song, the message which Mrs Crawford had wished to communicate, Maria straightened her posture and prepared to sing the final verse.

> *"When I go the last mile of the way*
> *I will rest at the close of the day*
> *And I know that God will await me*
> *When I go the last mile of the way."*

Taking a moment for emotional recovery, she relaxed her body and deflected her gaze downwards, before looking up in response to the spatter of applause and smiling at the enraptured faces, all familiar except for one. Venturing to look at him again, she saw him rise to his feet and stride purposefully down the aisle and onto the dais. Feeling a sudden flutter of alarm, she pressed her hand against her chest, as she watched him reach under the flap of his leather jerkin to withdraw a short branch with a splash of yellow amidst the leaves. Focusing on this verdant offering as he laid it on the end of the coffin, Maria recognised that the yellow object was a lemon. Fully formed and glisteningly ripe.

After genuflecting, the man swung around and, as part of a fluent sequence of movement, bowed to Maria before walking off, followed by the gaze of the congregation as they all turned to watch his rapid exit through the chapel and out the door.

Stunned by this unorthodox turn of events, Maria continued to stare at the door after it had closed slowly and heavily behind him. Then, shaking her head, she broke out of her inertia and looked back at the coffin, the flowers now vividly bright in the strong sunlight shafting through the stained-glass window, but all of them outshone by the lemon radiating vibrantly at its end.

Chapter 36

'That's it. In we go, love.'

Charlene looked around as she stepped tentatively into the apartment with Maria following her, and William stretching out from behind to hold the door open.

'It's looking good, isn't it? See how we've set that table for drinks and, look, those flowers on the side table, they're from Sharon. Lovely, aren't they?'

Giving way to Maria's urgent energy, Charlene sidestepped to stand uncertainly on the edge of the hall. Her face strained with apprehension as she watched Maria survey the room while removing her coat.

'Sharon was sorry she couldn't come. Did she mention that, Charlene?'

'Yes. She was very sorry. In two minds about going, she said.'

'Well, it was a difficult decision but she was absolutely right to go. Mrs C wouldn't have wanted to spoil her holiday. I'm sure about that.'

Charlene responded while glancing anxiously at William as he moved alongside her.

'Yes. That's what she said. She said Mrs C always wanted to hear about her holidays.'

Maria smiled warmly at her before continuing in a brisker tone.

'OK. Let's get ready. We can leave our coats in the kitchen but, Charlene, my love, would you mind asking people to leave their coats and stuff in the main guest bedroom? You know, the one with the ensuite bathroom.'

'Ah… right… no…'

'It's OK, my love. You just have to stand at the door asking them and, you know, pointing to where the bedroom is until they've all arrived and then you're done. Free.'

'Yes. No. Yes, that's no problem.'

Having turned towards William, Maria then looked back at Charlene, grinning in delight as she spoke.

'Oh, and if "you know who" arrives then forget about everything else, just come and let me know straight away. OK? We don't want him to do his disappearing trick again, do we?'

The worry lifted from Charlene's face as she became animated with excitement but, before she could respond, Maria had started talking to William while he struggled to take off his anorak.

'And please, William, make sure he's made to feel welcome if he does arrive. I mean, I know Stephen and Lionel will probably do most of the meeting and greeting, but do keep an eye out and make sure he's looked after. OK?'

Jerking his arm wildly in an attempt to shake the sleeve off, William grunted in frustration. After watching his efforts with affectionate despair, Maria hurried over to tug the sleeve off.

'There we go. Now, were you listening, William?'

'What? Oh yes. If Nektarios Alexandrou turns up, I've to make sure he stays and doesn't run off.'

Maria responded patiently as she removed the anorak.

'Yes, but you've got to do it nicely. Make him feel welcome or make sure one of the boys does it. That might be better. OK?'

'Yes, darling. OK. I understand.'

'Good. Well, let's dump our coats in the kitchen and get the drinks ready before they arrive.'

After hanging her coat on the back of the kitchen door, Charlene left Maria and William removing chilled champagne from the fridge, and wandered listlessly around the hall, pausing at each painting to view it distractedly.

She wondered why Mrs Crawford had left the paintings to Maria. She and Maria had talked about them and neither of them understood why Mrs Crawford liked them so much. They could appreciate the colours, but the way they were painted seemed primitive and weird. What was the point of distorting forms and objects in that way? It mystified them but seemed to inspire and excite Mrs Crawford. An example of how her tastes and appreciation of life often went beyond their understanding. A reflection of her intellect, her personality. All that was left of her. These paintings along with her photographs and a few precious possessions.

Spinning round to escape her thoughts before they brought on that unnerving sadness again, Charlene's flailing arm brushed against Sharon's flowers. Her stomach lurched sickeningly as she watched the vase wobble on the half-moon table. Immediately crouching she stretched out below the expansive bouquet and placed her hands firmly around the vase. After stabilising it, she removed her arms slowly and looked anxiously at the painting above, its glass intact and newly polished.

She stood transfixed by the agonising memory of the night that Lee had caused so much disruption and damage, and became filled with that recurring guilt that she had not done enough to make up for it. Her unsettling sense of regret transformed to anger with herself that, after banishing Lee from her life, she had allowed him back in. Giving way to his insistence that he drive her to the funeral had been an inexcusable mistake. She would leave no room for doubt or any comeback when she told him that she wanted nothing more to do with him.

'You all right, love?'

Charlene turned to face Maria as she emerged from the kitchen.

'Yes. Yes, I'm fine thanks, Maria. Fine.'

'Good girl. Well, I'm just going to check the buffet in the sitting room. Have you had a look?'

'No. No, not yet.'

'Oh, well, you must come and have a look. Giovanni has excelled himself. It's a fantastic spread.'

'Gio… Giovanni?'

'Yes, Giovanni. The guy who owns Bertorelli's. You know, the deli.'

'Oh yes, the deli. Of course.'

Submitting to her irresistible enthusiasm, Charlene allowed Maria to propel her towards the sitting room until the sound of the doorbell halted their progress.

'Ah, someone's arrived. Bang on time, bless them. Well, my love, do you mind letting them in while I do a final check on the buffet? I'll come straight back. OK?'

Charlene made her way to the front door with a show of haste which belied her reluctance to engage in social interaction. She breathed in deeply as she pulled the door open, the weight of dread lifting as Mahalia and Orricene were revealed.

'Charlene! Good to see you! You're looking great, by the way. How are you getting on?'

'Fine, Mahalia. Fine. Yes. Come in. Maria's checking the food.'

'Oh. Are we the first to arrive?'

'Yes. Yes. But it's fine.'

'Well. We do like to be on time. Don't we, Orricene?'

Orricene looked around her as she stepped into the hall.

'We sure do, girl. We sure do. Well, this is a fine place. Isn't it? Really nice.'

Charlene pushed the door shut and turned round to respond.

'Yes. It is. She did it very nice, Mrs Crawford. She knew what she liked. All these paintings and everything.'

After a cursory scan of the room, Mahalia reached forward to place her hand on Charlene's arm and draw her into a conspiratorial huddle with Orricene.

'Yes, very nice, very tasteful although I'm not sure what Maria's going to do with the paintings. Maybe she'll just have to sell them like Mr Wilkins says but, anyway, wasn't that a bit of excitement? The man turning up. You know… Mrs Crawford's man from Greece.'

'Mrs Crawford's man from Greece? Well, I guess… I guess it must have been him…'

Orricene leaned in, her low voice earnestly emphatic.

'Of course it was him. I mean, he was definitely Greek, wasn't he, and who else would do something like that?'

'That's right! Leaving a lemon must have meant something. Something special. Or, or it's a Greek tradition. It could be, couldn't it?'

Charlene looked from one to the other as they exchanged their dialogue.

'I don't think it would be a tradition, Mahalia. I mean, why a lemon? Why not olives or, ah, figs, know what I mean? I think it would be a special thing and, anyway, what about him? He didn't look that old. I mean, he wasn't an old man. Was he?'

'Well, he was no spring chicken, was he, and maybe he looked younger than he was? I mean, Mrs Crawford probably looked a bit older with her arthritis anyway. Poor love.'

'Poor dear. She had it bad that's for sure but imagine her without it? What a fine woman. She must have been a real beauty when she was younger. A real beauty.'

'Well, he was quite handsome, I suppose. Although it all happened so quickly I didn't get a good look. Did you, Charlene? Did you think he was handsome, you know, for an older man?'

Caught out by suddenly becoming the focus of their

attention, a silence opened up before Charlene tried to fill it with a stuttering reply.

'Well… well… I guess…'

The frantic whirl in her head was suddenly cut through by Maria's joyous greeting as she re-entered the hall.

'Girls, girls! You're here! How wonderful. Dump your coats. Charlene will show you where. Come in!'

Crossing the hall as the doorbell rang out, she addressed Charlene over her shoulder.

'You show the girls where to leave the coats, I'll get the door and, oh, would you give William a shout? Thanks, love.'

*

Charlene pulled the door shut and listened to the dampened cacophony. It had become too loud. The more champagne was drunk, the more raucous it became. Turning away, she moved across the hall in a loose-limbed, desultory sway.

She shoved the bathroom door open and, after locking it, viewed her image at different angles in the mirror. She then sat down on the closed lid of the toilet and, propping her arms on her lap, slouched forward to rest her head in her hands.

After expelling a despairing sigh, she stood up to wash her hands, raising them to her nose to smell the perfumed lather before rinsing it off. She then leaned towards the mirror and addressed her reflection quietly but firmly.

'Come on, girl. What are you getting so bothered about? It's no big deal, you can do it. It's what Mrs Crawford would want. You've got to do it for her. You've got to remember her even though no one else seems to care that she's not here. Christ's sake!'

Walking back to the sitting room, her stride slowed to a reluctant scuff as she approached the door. She turned away and weaved disconsolately around the hall until halting at the door to Mrs Crawford's bedroom. In its closed position, this door had always signified the need to respect Mrs Crawford's privacy. The significance of this seemed to have increased even now when it was vacant. She looked at it hesitantly until bringing her gaze to rest on the handle. After staring at it she slowly reached out to grasp it. Gripping it strongly she remained motionless before turning it and pushing the door open against the deep-pile carpet. She looked tentatively into the immaculate interior, before stepping into the profound stillness and reversing against the door to close it.

The bedroom would not now and never again would be Mrs Crawford's domain, and yet she felt that she was invading her personal space. Annoyed that this irrational feeling was making her hesitate from finding solace in this, the scene of her most significant engagements with Mrs Crawford, she pushed off against the door and crossed over to the bedside chair. Sitting down, she pressed her hands between her knees and looked around apprehensively, as she recalled the morning after Lee's invasion of Mrs Crawford's civilised existence. That morning when she had seen Mrs Crawford serenely lifeless in her bed. That morning when Mrs Crawford had expressed compassion rather than condemnation. That morning when Mrs Crawford's response had moved her to feel new emotions.

The truth that she could never again experience Mrs Crawford's wisdom and love weighed heavily on her heart, and made the hilarity in the sitting room even harder for her to accept. Surely it wasn't right that they should be laughing so much? It had started quietly but the mood had become more light-hearted and the laughter louder the more champagne they drank. That couldn't be right. It should be an occasion of respectful remembrance, of suffering the loss of an amazing person. A person she wished could be here right now. A person that she needed to speak to just as she had that morning.

She reached out to rest her arm on the duvet before slumping forward. Tensing her diaphragm, she tried to suppress the waves of grief as they welled up from her aching chest, clogging her throat with an acid heat and stinging her eyes. She sniffed sharply and pulled her hand back to remove the tissues from her pocket.

After blowing her nose and dabbing a tissue below each eye to absorb the moisture without spoiling her make-up, she reclined wearily against the backrest. She then inhaled deeply, her breath catching against the spasmodic tremble in her chest, and exhaled a calming sigh. The anguish which had twisted into knots inside her head suddenly unravelled, allowing a soothing glow to fill her empty mind. Submitting to this unexpected release of tension, she closed her eyes and, feeling almost as though someone was applying a soothing pressure on her temples, she sank into a state of deep relaxation.

Becoming aware of a hand gripping her shoulder softly, she opened her eyes and looked into Stephen's face as he leaned towards her.

'Are you all right, Charlene? Have you been asleep?'

'Me? No. I just closed my eyes. Why? What time is it?'

'It's OK. It's not late. It's just we noticed you had gone and I came to look for you on my way to the kitchen. It's no problem.'

Charlene sat up running her fingers through her hair and shaking her head.

'Oh dear. I must have been here longer than I thought. I… I just came in here for a moment to… to check… to see if… ah… well, to just see it, Mrs Crawford's room, you know, before, one last time, before, you know…'

Stephen dipped down towards her, the compassion on his face intensifying.

'Don't worry, darling. I know exactly what you mean. But why don't you come back and join us when you're ready, eh? How about that? Yes?'

Charlene returned his gaze, her eyes filled with apprehension.

'Oh, I don't know, Stephen. I don't feel right in there. It doesn't, well, it doesn't seem right, everyone having a good time laughing and not, well, not kind of remembering Mrs C.'

'Oh, Charlene. You mustn't think of it like that, love. We are remembering her. We all loved her and we're doing exactly what she wanted. Having a good time and drinking the champagne she ordered specially for this occasion. She didn't drink champagne herself because of the arthritis, but she wanted to know that everyone else would drink it and have the kind of party she would have enjoyed so much. In fact, that's what I was doing right now, going back to the kitchen to get some more.'

She looked away, the frown fading from her forehead.

'Oh right. I didn't know people did that. You know, say what people needed to do after they died. I didn't know that.'

Stephen knelt down on the floor and placed his hand on her arm.

'Well, not everybody does it, Charlene. In fact, not many people do it but Katherine, Mrs Crawford, was, well, she was very organised and forward thinking, if you know what I mean. She wanted to be sure that she had done as much as she could and, well, you know, put things in place.'

Charlene turned to look at him.

'Yeah. I know what you're saying, Stephen. That's what she did with me. You know. Putting money aside for college and for going to Greece. That's the bit I don't get though. Going to Greece.'

'Well, you know how much it meant to her, and I guess she wanted someone like you to experience it. To see how special it was. To go instead of her. That's the way I see it. She couldn't go back herself but knowing you would go instead is the next best thing.'

'But… but I'm not her and… and it'll be different, won't it? Me going?'

'Well, yes, I suppose it will but you never know. You might

love it like she did and I guess it doesn't matter if you don't. You'll just have to see.'

'I suppose but, well, she fell in love with the man, that man and that's not going to happen to me, is it?'

'Well, perhaps not but that's the other thing, you could visit him and tell him all about Katherine. It doesn't look like he's going to join us today so, you know, you could speak to him like she always wanted to, well, not exactly like that but you would at least be communicating with him and that must have been a nice thought for Katherine, that someone was going to make a connection with him.'

'Yes, but she doesn't say I have to visit him. In her letter. She doesn't say that.'

'Oh, well, in that case perhaps you don't have to, but it would be a shame don't you think, to go all that way and not see him.'

'Oh, I don't know, Stephen. I'm getting all confused again. I was all calm and now I'm getting confused again.'

'Well, listen, sweetheart, don't worry about it right now. There's nothing to worry about. Going to Greece will be fun and you just need to enjoy yourself, so don't worry about it. OK?'

'OK, but I've never been there before. I've only been to Ibiza and that was with friends.'

'Well, you can take a friend with you, can't you? She said that in her letter, didn't she?'

'Yes. She did. A girlfriend or maybe two girlfriends if there's enough money. Except I don't know who would want to come with me. It's not like, well, it's not like Ibiza or Magaluf. The kind of place my mates go to.'

'No, maybe not but you might love it. A quieter place and beautiful. I'm sure you'd have a great time. But anyway, come on, let's get some more champagne and go back to the party. Eh? Come on. My knees are killing me.'

Stephen pushed up onto his feet and, reaching out to hold Charlene's hands, helped her to stand up.

'Come on, you lovely girl. You are looking lovely today, you know, Charlene. Katherine would be proud.'

Exchanging warm smiles, Stephen interlocked his arm with Charlene's, and they walked out through the open door into the hall. After decoupling briefly so that Stephen could pull the door shut, they continued arm in arm to the kitchen.

After returning across the hall, Charlene opened the door to the sitting room for Stephen to pass through with a bottle of champagne in each hand. Just as she was about to follow, the intercom buzzer cut through the convivial cacophony. She called after Stephen as he became reabsorbed in the party.

'I'll get it!'

Turning around she walked back towards the front door sighing with relief as the closing door subdued the noise to a dull clamour. After exhaling, she drew in her next breath sharply, as her pulse quickened at the possibility that this unexpected latecomer could be Mrs Crawford's Greek lover.

She gazed uncertainly at the distorted image of the man on the intercom screen peering into the camera. A frown of concentration formed on her face as he spoke.

'Allo. Is this the right place? Is this the party for Mrs Crawford? Have I pressed the right...'

Without daring to offer a reply, Charlene pressed the button to open the door, terminating the man's enquiry with the buzzing of the lock release. She then shoved the receiver roughly back on its rest and ran across the hall into the sitting room. She walked quickly round to Maria, trying not to attract attention. Seeing Charlene approach, Maria's face lit up and she started to trill a joyful greeting.

'Charlene, darling, I wondered where you'd...'

Silenced by the firmness of Charlene's grip as she pulled her away, Maria listened intently as Charlene spoke with quiet urgency.

'He's here. He's just buzzed the intercom. It's him. You know who.'

Maria's expression transformed to incredulous wonder as she absorbed Charlene's message.

'Oh my goodness. Are you sure?'

Charlene walked sideways in front of Maria, looking back at her as they walked around the room and into the hall.

'Yes. I saw him on the screen. The intercom screen and he spoke, you know, like he was foreign. Honestly, Maria. I let him in. He'll be here any second.'

'Well, well. He's left it very late. I mean, it must be, what, well I'm not sure, but we've been here at least a couple of hours already. He took his time, didn't he? Well, well.'

On hearing the doorbell ring, Charlene halted letting Maria overtake her as she hurried to welcome this stranger. This man who had been part of the life which filled their hearts and minds, the life they were commemorating and remembering. This man who had been central to a momentous chapter in the story of Mrs Crawford's life. A chapter which Maria knew had been very meaningful, but which remained unknown to them apart from a few tantalising snippets.

Charlene stood still in the middle of the hall. The door would shield the man from view, but she would be able to watch Maria confront him, this mysterious arrival from a foreign place she found hard to imagine.

Maria grasped the handle and pulled the door wide open with a welcoming smile.

Charlene's face flinched in confusion when, instead of following with a generous greeting, she saw Maria's posture relax and heard her speak with low-key warmth.

'... Giovanni! It's... it's... my goodness, is it that time already? My, how time flies. Do come in. The buffet was wonderful. Perfect. Everyone loved it. But anyway, come in. Have a glass of champagne. It's great to see you.'

Chapter 37

Maria stepped over the threshold of the sliding doors onto the patio. Exposed to the autumn chill, she shivered and tightened the wrap of her dressing gown, retying the sash. Seeing William picking apples from the tree at the far end of the garden, she walked across the grass towards him, ignoring the discomfort of the cold dew seeping into her sheepskin slippers.

William looked round as she approached, lowering the half-filled basket onto the ground. His face clouded with concern as Maria walked up to him without speaking.

'What's up, love? Are you all right?'

Maria shivered as if breaking out of a trance.

'Yes… yes, I'm fine. No, it's just that, well, Mr Wilkins has just phoned about the paintings.'

'The paintings? What's happened to them? I thought he was going to sell them for you.'

'Yes, that's just it, William. They have been sold. All of them. At Sotheby's.'

'Sotheby's, oh my goodness. That's posh. I didn't think they'd be that valuable.'

'Well, that's it, William. Oh, William, I don't know what to think, they were sold for nearly half a million! He says I'll get almost four hundred thousand pounds after tax and commission!'

William slumped into a bent position, gripping his legs above the knee and looking up at Maria aghast.

'Oh my god! Four hundred thousand pounds!'

Standing up straight he reached out to take hold of Maria's hands, his face now shining with delight.

'Four hundred thousand pounds, Maria! For those paintings. Who would have thought!'

A wan smile stretched weakly below her worried eyes.

'I know. I had no idea. Mr Wilkins said they were quite valuable but, four hundred thousand pounds, for goodness' sake, William, I can't take it in.'

'It's amazing and, well, it just goes to show that she knew what she was doing.'

Maria's smile faded.

'But did she, William? I mean, this is crazy. The fifty thousand pounds was more than enough but this, well, it's so much money.'

William moved in to embrace her in a reassuring hug.

'I wouldn't worry, love, honestly, I am sure she knew exactly what she was doing. She'll have known that you'd put it to good use and it's still quite a bit less than Mrs Evans and her daughters are getting… and her sister.'

'But, William, they're her relatives. I was only her carer.'

William pulled back to kiss her cheek and look into her eyes.

'Maria. You were much more than her carer. No one spent more time with her, no one was closer to her than you were for all those years, so you have no reason to feel guilty. You deserve it. She'll have wanted to change your life. It's her legacy. To give you the opportunity to make your life better… and to make other people's lives better. Like you did for her.'

'Well, I do want to do that, William. I want to make other people's lives better.'

A fond smile spread across his face.

'Well, you'll certainly be able to do that. You'll just have to figure out how. I mean, you'll be able to take your time about things. In fact, you shouldn't need to get a job, not if you don't want to. You could invest it and then with my salary and so on, well, we'd be fine. More than fine.'

She buried her face in his jumper, her shoulders heaving as she emitted muffled sobs. William patted her back comfortingly.

'There, there, love. It's all good. You don't need to get upset.'

Maria lifted her head from his chest with a shuddering sigh.

'Oh, William. I'm not really upset. I'm just so grateful and… and, if I'm really honest, I feel like a big weight has been lifted. Do you know what I'm saying? I was already feeling like that, a sense of relief but this, well, it really takes the pressure off, doesn't it?'

'It certainly does, my love. It certainly does.'

He stepped back, holding her shoulders and looking into her eyes while shaking his head in incomprehension. His voice trembled with restrained excitement.

'I mean, four hundred thousand pounds! That's transformational. She's really looked after you, my love, she really has.'

She shrugged her shoulders and nodded meekly.

'I guess she has. Bless her. She was always so generous but this, well, I just can't get my head around it.'

Smiling warmly he placed one arm over her shoulder, turned her round and started walking her back to the house.

'Come on. I'm going to make you a nice cup of tea.'

*

William opened the back door and stood aside to allow Maria

past. She kicked off her slippers, placing them on the shoe rack before squeezing past the cardboard boxes stacked high on the other side of the vestibule. William grinned and called after her as he wiped his feet on the doormat.

'Perhaps we should build an extension!'

Maria released a burst of laughter before shouting her reply from the kitchen.

'Don't worry, I'll find a space for it all… after I've taken our old stuff to the charity shop.'

Still grinning, William walked into the kitchen.

'Still, at least we don't have to find room to hang the paintings.'

Maria smiled wryly as she sat down at the small table.

'Yes, well, that is a blessing although, to be fair, Mr Wilkins never gave us the option; he never asked if we'd like to keep them. I thought it was because he knew I wasn't keen on them but now I can see why.'

Maria pulled the flaps of her dressing gown across her thighs before continuing.

'I mean, he did say they were valuable but I was thinking hundreds of pounds, not hundreds of thousands. My god!'

She leaned back against the wall, rolling her head from side to side in disbelief.

William turned to look at her, sweeping his fringe away from his eyes as he spoke.

'It's like winning the lottery, isn't it? It'll take time to sink in, the enormity of it.'

'Yes. I guess it will, William, although I was wondering, even with the fifty thousand pounds, I was thinking we should spend some money on the house. I mean, we've talked about a conservatory before and we could do up the spare room, make it nice for Mum and Dad.'

Alerted by the boiling kettle switching off, William replied as he spun round.

'That would be great, my love, a conservatory… oh and the

spare room. Your parents could come down more often now that you'll have more free time.'

'Yes. I'd like that. To see more of them.'

They remained pensively silent as the clattering of William's tea preparation filled the room. Maria looked up as he placed the steaming mug in front of her.

'Thanks, sweetheart… William, do you think they'll ever need help, Mum and Dad? With money?'

William shook his head as he sat down opposite her.

'No, love. I can't see it. Not on your dad's pension. They don't dish out pensions like that these days. It's much better than the one I'll get and, besides, Chris will always help out if it comes to it like he did with their building works. I know it's his own company but even so he seems to have plenty of cash, even after paying the school fees!'

'He does, doesn't he? But he's generous. Supporting all those charities and everything.'

'Oh, there's no doubt about it. Like I always say, he's a very good man, your Chris. No wonder your parents are proud of you. What more could they hope for?'

Maria focused frowningly on the mug held between her hands, before looking up at William.

'More grandchildren.'

William stretched across to hold her hands.

'Oh, my love. They couldn't want more than to have a daughter like you. They really couldn't.'

She leaned towards him, her earnest eyes shining with gratitude.

'I don't know about that, my darling man, but I do know I couldn't want more than to have a husband like you. You're my rock and I know life will always be fine so long as I have you.'

William bent forward to kiss her on the lips.

'You can rely on that, my love. I'll always be here for you. I couldn't love you more and I know life will be fine. More than fine.'

Gazing into each other's eyes, Maria pulled her hand free and stroked his forearm.

'We are lucky to have each other, aren't we, love, and so lucky with Mrs Crawford's generosity. So unbelievably lucky.'

She sat back pulling her dressing gown tightly across her chest.

'You know, William, I was thinking that I could volunteer to help with that musical outreach thing I was telling you about, helping young people to form choirs, young people from deprived areas. I'd really love to do that and, well, I think Mrs Crawford would think it was a great thing to do.'

Sitting up straight, William nodded vigorously.

'She certainly would. It's a great idea, a great way to make the most of this opportunity and you'd be great at it.'

'Oh, William, I'm glad you think so. I would love to do it and you know how much Mrs C loved to help people herself, you know, like Charlene.'

'Of course, of course, Charlene. Absolutely. Anyway, you should go for it. They'll be delighted to have a volunteer like you. Absolutely delighted.'

'Do you think so, William? Do you really think so?'

William emitted a guffaw of mock incredulity.

'Are you kidding? Of course they will! Someone with your talent!… They'll welcome you with open arms.'

'Well, I don't know about that, William, but they certainly need volunteers and I'd give it my best, I really would.'

'Yes and your best is going to be better than they could have hoped for. Really.'

William folded his arms as he leaned back.

'Talking about Charlene, my love, how's she getting on? I mean, is she going to Greece or not?'

'Oh yes. I mean, I hope she is. She's going to complete this year in college and then go in the summer, with a couple of friends.'

'Oh, that's good. I suppose she had to go, really.'

'Oh yes, she knows she has to go, although she still doesn't really understand why. She doesn't understand why it has to be her.'

'Well, I suppose she's got a point, darling, I mean, she could have asked you.'

'No, William. Mrs Crawford wouldn't have asked me. She wanted Charlene to go so that she could broaden her horizons while she's young and, you know, not tied down. Besides, she knew that hot sunshine and beaches aren't our thing.'

'Hmph. True, but you could have met the mysterious man.'

Maria chuckled.

'Wouldn't that be great! I'd love to meet him and I really hope that Charlene visits him.'

'Well, she surely can't go all that way without going to see him, can she?'

'Well, we'll see William. I hope not. We know where he lives or at least Mr Wilkins does so it should be easy enough. It's such a shame we didn't get to meet him. To find out about him and his time with Mrs C.'

William responded while swinging his legs round and standing up.

'Well, it would have been good but he clearly didn't want to meet anyone, did he? Rushing away like that. Very strange.'

He picked up the mugs from the table, speaking as he walked over to the sink.

'Anyway, I suppose we'd better think about going to the supermarket soon, before lunchtime, anyway.'

Maria swivelled round on her chair to look at him.

'Yes and let's get some champagne, William. For a special treat. So we can make a toast to Mrs C.'

'Oh, yes. We should definitely do that. Definitely.'

Maria looked ahead, her face lit by a dreamy smile, oblivious to the clatterings and splashings of William tidying up. After closing the door of the dishwasher with an emphatic clank, William turned round to face Maria.

'Actually, my love, I've been thinking. You know what Mrs Crawford would really like?'

Maria swung round her face now bright with surprise.

'What? What do you mean? What would she like?'

William walked across to the window before turning towards her.

'She'd like us to give it a go, Maria. She suggested it often enough. She'd like us to give IVF a go. Now that we'll have the money and you've got the time. Don't you think? Maria?'

She bowed her head while responding in a flattened tone.

'Oh, William. Do you think so? I've become so reconciled to life being just the two of us. Do you think we should, you know, go through with all that… all that intervention? I mean, we decided not to do it and I'm even older now.'

'I know, love, but you're still young enough and it feels different now. It's not just about having the money and the time, the freedom, it somehow feels like it would be right for other reasons. I don't know… I can't really explain.'

Maria looked up at him, her face twisted in anguish but her eyes shining with hope.

'I know. I know what you mean and, if I'm honest, it's been at the back of my mind… thinking that maybe we should try it, before it's too late.'

He walked over and, after pulling her to her feet, held her in a tight embrace.

'I'm right, aren't I, about Mrs Crawford? Like she used to tell you, she takes a scientist's view of these things. That they're good and that you could look at them as God's way of performing miracles through mankind. Isn't that what she used to say? Something along those lines?'

She sighed before replying, her voice soft with the warmth of fondness.

'She certainly did. That's exactly what she said. Mind you, she got much more spiritual towards the end. She wasn't so much of the scientist then. It was nice. Her asking for "The Last Mile of the Way" clinched it for me, that she really did believe. That she knew she was going to be with Amy again… and her parents… in heaven.'

William gave her an affectionate squeeze before leaning back to look down at her, a hint of mischief in his smile and a wildness in his eyes. He gulped before speaking.

'Well, my gorgeous woman, my sexy woman, all I can say is, I hope she's not looking down on us now. Not right now.'

Taking a half step back, he pulled the flaps of her dressing gown apart. He gulped and his breathing became heavier, as he looked down at her naked body, soft and fulsome.

'William!…You naughty boy!'

His voice wavered weakly as he placed his hands on her hips.

'Oh my god. You're so sexy. Sexier than ever.'

Maria's laugh rang out with delight as she looked up at him while pressing her body against his.

'Come on then, we can go to the supermarket later.'

Swirling around, she let the loosened sash untie and fall away, as she grabbed William's hand to lead him out of the kitchen and up the stairs to the bedroom.

Part 3

Chapter 38

Her mind drifted dreamily between involuntary thoughts soothingly in tune with the early-day noises echoing softly around the awakening harbour. She sat motionless, her body relaxing as she submitted to the weight of drowsiness. Expelling a deeply drawn breath with a heart-fluttering sigh, Charlene sank further into this pleasurable state of suspended animation as the low sun, washing warmly across the seafront, radiated hypnotically on the back of her head.

Her gaze rested on the old ferry boat rocking gently on the glistening water. The same ferry boat which had taken them yesterday to the tranquil bay on the far side of the neighbouring island. They had enjoyed that trip, but today they were going to walk to the beach on the other side of the town. With only two full days remaining, this was a day for the activity of a busier beach. A beach where they could fulfil the promises made the night before, to meet the young Greek men who had insinuated themselves charmingly into their fleeting existence, in this foreign place. This island which had become familiar within the parameters of their limited needs. Their brightly whitewashed apartment accessed through a pleasant pot-planted courtyard off a quiet side street; the busy cafes and restaurants on the front with their tables and chairs arranged on the deep, awning-covered pavement; the backstreet shops and mini supermarkets which provided for their miscellaneous requirements; the quayside which provided spectacle ranging from the charmingly practical fishing boats to the sleek yachts and luxurious motor cruisers; the open-roofed nightclubs on the edge of town where, stimulated by cocktails and adrenaline-pumping music, they pursued their elusive dreams of holiday romance.

Movement in the periphery of Charlene's vision interrupted her reverie, and she turned languidly to face the approaching waiter, a gentle smile stretching weakly across her face.

'Morning, ladies! You very early today!'

Charlene shifted into an upright position while responding.

'Hi, Petros! Yes, we want to get as much sunshine as we can. We go home on Saturday.'

'So soon? You should not go so soon.'

Charlene turned to exchange eye contact with her friends in silent communication of their shared fondness for this young waiter, the provider of their sustenance at the start of each day. She then turned back to reply.

'We've got to go back, Petros. We can't stay here.'

Stirring themselves out of their torpor, Cynthia and Suzy backed up Charlene with a chorus of support.

'Yeah, we've got jobs to go back to, me and Suzy. We've got to go home.'

'That's right, we've got to make some money. Not like you, Charlie. You lucky… you lucky girl.'

Charlene leaned back, smiling brightly at her friends.

'Hey! I've got work to do as well. It's not an easy ride, you know. Studying for exams. It's bloody hard work.'

'Ooooh! College girl! Who would have thought it!'

'Yeah, college girl with a big bank account!'

'Listen, I never thought I'd end up in college but that's the deal, isn't it? No college, no money. Besides, I've got to do it. You know I have. Anyway, c'mon. What we going to have, girls? Same as usual?'

Charlene turned back towards Petros who stood waiting to take their order, a warm smile concealing his incomprehension.

'It looks like it's French toast all round, Petros, with the full works and cappuccinos. Same as usual. Thanks very much.'

Petros raised his pad and poised his pen.

'French toast with bacon and maple syrup and large cappuccinos. One, two three. That right?'

'That's it, Petros. That right, girls?'

'That's fine for me.'

'Yep, that should do the business.'

After scribbling down the order, Petros tapped the pad with his pen and looked from Charlene to each of the girls.

'OK, ladies, that all for now?'

'Yes, thanks, Petros. That's all for now.'

Charlene watched him spin round and cross the paved area, swinging his hips smoothly to one side and the other to avoid the tables and chairs. She continued to gaze at the entrance of the cafe after he had disappeared into its shadowed interior, before summoning the energy to turn and face her friends across the table.

'How are you feeling, girls? A bit better now?'

'I'll feel better after breakfast. I'm still tired and hungover. Mainly tired.'

'Yeah, we didn't drink that much last night. Did we?'

Charlene placed her elbows on the table and, propping her head in her hands, looked down as she spoke.

'Oh, I don't know. We had quite a bit. You know what Dimitri's like with his measures. Mum would get the fucking sack if she sloshed it in the way he does… Oops! Excuse my language. Sorry.'

'Yeah, well, at least we didn't pour it down each other's throats like those guys. That was weird. Pouring it down their throats while they were dancing, on their own, to that plunky-plunk music.'

'Oh my god. You're not joking. It was going everywhere. What was that all about? Weird!'

'Yeah and then they want to dance with, you know, with beer and stuff all down their shirts, yeah, and in their hair some of them. I don't think so!'

Charlene lowered her arms onto the table and interjected into her friends' scandalised commentary.

'That's what they do here, girls. Isn't it? Greek dancing and stuff. It's a different culture.'

'Yeah, well, it's still weird. We never saw anything like that at Ayia Napa. Did we, Suze?'

'No. That was like going out at home, except better. More... more exotic.'

'Yeah, that was like mega. Like really crazy. Way more action than here.'

'That's right but it's not like we're saying it's not good here, Charlie. We're not saying that. Are we, Suze? It is good here. Cool. Quiet but cool and the Greek guys are sweet.'

'Yeah, sweet and sexy, some of them. Like Costa, eh, Cynth? Like Costa. You and Costa were getting hot last night. Weren't you? Red hot!'

Cynthia flapped her hand at Suzy and then, holding up her arms, fanned her hands rapidly under her chin.

'Shut up, Suze! It wasn't like that. We were just dancing!'

'Yeah, snogging as well! And all that bump and grind!'

'Stop it, Suze! You're just jealous!'

Suzy reached across to squeeze Cynthia's upper arm reassuringly.

'Listen, don't worry about it. It's cool. I wouldn't have minded some action like that. You lucky tart! He's OK, Costa. You've done well.'

Cynthia dropped her arms onto the table and dipped her head in diffident denial.

'Well, anyway, I don't actually fancy him. Well, not that much. I mean, I couldn't actually go out with him. It wouldn't feel right. They're too different these Greek guys. Aren't they?'

Suzy leaned back, shaking her head witheringly.

'They're different all right and they say you'll never be good enough for their mums. Too close to their mums, they say. It's not right. Not healthy.'

Charlene spread her hands out on the table, palms downward and, after inspecting them briefly, looked up at her.

'It's not that bad. Is it? Families being close.'

'Maybe not, but you don't fancy any of them, anyway. Do you? It's not like there's anything stopping you. You're like Cynthia, free and single. Free to play the field. Have some fun. No need to hold back on my account. I might join you, anyway. Have some fun while I'm away.'

'Well, I could certainly do with some action. I need a shag, badly. It's been ages. It's just, well, it's just I can't be bothered.'

Suzy leaned forward to place her hand over Charlene's and look into her eyes.

'Well, you've not got much time left, and you've still got to see that man, unless you're not going to bother with that either.'

Pulling her hand away, she broke eye contact with Suzy to watch a small fishing boat putter into the harbour. Her face twisted in vexation as she turned back.

'I guess I do but it's not that easy. I can't find his... you know, his details.'

With Suzy now distracted by a cafe cat rubbing against her chair, Cynthia continued the dialogue.

'But when did you have them? Can you remember?'

'Well, I did have them on a piece of paper from the, you know, from the solicitor, and then I put them on my phone or, well, I thought I did but they're not there.'

'So couldn't you phone the solicitor? Have you got his number?'

Flopping back, Charlene sighed despairingly before replying, her eyes squinting as she looked up at the morning sky.

'I suppose I could. I suppose. It's just I'd feel such a twat and I don't know, well, she didn't say I should go and see him. In her letter. She didn't say that I had to visit him.'

'Well, that's OK then. Why are you bothered about it?'

Charlene reached for the sunglasses gripped onto the top of her head, and slid them onto her nose.

'Because, well, because everyone else wants me to. They think I should. They think Mrs Crawford would have wanted me to. Oh, I don't know. It's too difficult.'

'Who is everyone else? You mean Maria?'

'Yes and the boys, you know, Lionel and Stephen.'

'OK, well, why don't you phone Maria? Won't she have the details?'

'No, she doesn't have them. Why would she?'

'Well, maybe she could get them for you.'

Lodging her sunglasses back on her head, Charlene looked directly at Cynthia.

'I couldn't do that, Cynth. I don't want to put her to any trouble.'

'She wouldn't mind. Would she?'

'No, it's not that. It's just I don't want to stress her. She's… she's, well, it's been a secret but, well, she's pregnant.'

Instantly distracted from stroking the cat, Suzy looked up open-mouthed as Cynthia expressed her surprise.

'Pregnant. Oh my god. I didn't know that. Did you, Suze?'

'No way. Oh my god. I wouldn't have expected that. I mean, I thought, you know, she's a bit old to be having a baby.'

'Yeah. I can't believe it. I mean she must be, what, about… I don't know.'

Charlene looked from one to the other, fond amusement playing on her face.

'She's thirty-six which is old, but anyway she's nearly four months pregnant.'

'Wow! That's amazing! Did she... did she... was it an accident or...?'

'No. Oh my god, no. They had been trying and then they gave up but then, when Mrs Crawford left Maria the money, they decided, you know, to try IVF.'

Cynthia looked at Suzy with bright-eyed excitement as she absorbed Charlene's revelation.

'So it worked. That's brilliant!'

'No. No, it didn't work. They were just about to start when she suddenly got pregnant after, well, after years of trying. How about that? Lionel reckons it was because she'd lost a lot of weight and wasn't having to work, but Maria reckons it was the will of God. She'd never wanted to do it, you know, artificially and then she didn't have to. Pretty fucking... sorry, pretty amazing story, isn't it?'

Leaving Cynthia to ask her questions, Suzy sat in slack-jawed silence, her stunned gaze remaining fixed on Charlene.

'My god, you're not joking. They should put it in a paper or a magazine. It's a miracle. Maybe she's right about the God bit. Don't you think?'

'Oh, I don't know. Maybe.'

'I mean, is she big on God? Is she, like, religious?'

'Well, she's in a choir. A church choir. That's mainly why she went to church. For the singing but she said when Mrs Crawford died that was when she, like, really knew that she believed in God.'

'Why? What happened?'

'Oh, I don't know. She felt something. She felt God was telling her that... that she'd died and gone to heaven. She couldn't really explain it. She just knew.'

Charlene lifted her arms high above her head and closed her eyes, as she stretched her upper body. Relaxing with a shake of her shoulders, she swivelled in her seat, turning away from Cynthia and looking towards the cafe. Cynthia's brow creased as she continued.

'I don't get it. Do you?'

Resting her forearms on her thighs, Charlene leaned forward to stare unseeingly at the dusty paving as she replied.

'Get what?'

'You know, God. People believing in God.'

'No. Well, I never really thought about it. Not until Mrs Crawford died, anyway. I thought about it then. About her and about her daughter. Amy. About her and Amy meeting in heaven. It's sad. Sad and happy. Sad that she died and happy that they're together after so long.'

'Do you believe that?'

Charlene twisted back sharply to look at Cynthia.

'What?'

'Do you believe that they're in heaven?'

Turning away again Charlene sat up, a tinge of impatience straining faintly on her face as she refocused her view on the cafe entrance.

'Oh, I don't know, Cynthia. Who knows?'

Seeing Petros appear from the dark interior with a laden tray, Charlene wound round on her chair to face her friends across the table.

'Anyway, girls. Here comes Petros. Breakfast time at last!'

Chapter 39

The whispering whoosh of the sea as it washed up the sand, and the soft gargling of its retreat, hypnotised her drowsy mind. Gradually returning to wakefulness, Charlene opened her eyes and, after drawing in a reviving breath, rolled over from her front onto her side. Propping her arm, she rested her head against her hand and looked across at Cynthia and Suzy beatifically asleep in the shade of beach umbrellas.

Rolling back she pushed up, sweeping her legs off the sunbed and rising into a seated position in one sinuous movement. She then reached back for her bikini top, putting it on while scanning the row of quietly occupied sunbeds and umbrellas stretching hazily along the beach, and the activity of people at the water's edge and in the sea. Returning her gaze to the sleeping forms of her friends, she reached below her sunbed to grasp the bottle of water. After pulling out the nozzle, she raised it to her lips and took a long draft into her dry mouth. The sides of the bottle sucked in with the crackle of crumpling plastic, returning to their original form when she stopped drinking. Stretching her arm under the sunbed, she repositioned the bottle before rising up into a stooped position below the umbrella. Shuffling into her flip flops she moved onto the hot sand and into the intensity of the midday sun. After dragging her sunglasses from the top of her head onto her nose, she walked off in a slow hip-swinging motion, relishing the sensation of hot sunshine on her body. With a clear way in front of her, she walked towards the shimmering sea, kicking off her flip flops before stepping onto the margin of damp sand and into the cool caress of the clear water lapping up and down the shallow shoreline. With the soles of her feet tickling as they sank into the granular seabed, she stopped to look down at the billowing suspension of fine sand clouding around her feet before moving forward with surging strides. Reaching a depth where the rippling surface lapped around the top of her thighs, Charlene breathed in sharply and immersed her sunbaked body into the refreshing water. She thrust forward with a kick of her legs stretching her body into a glide, as she revelled in finding respite from the heat of the sun. After a few strong strokes Charlene allowed her body to sink through the water into a vertical position. Locating the seabed with her feet, she sculled round to stand at shoulder depth looking back towards the shore. Then, raising her hand to shield her eyes against the glare, she turned her head slowly to survey the full sweep of the bay. Her gaze ranged from the pine-covered promontory with glimpses of elegant houses among the trees; to the long stretch of restaurants, bars and accommodation behind the beach; to the more rugged spit on the right, where jagged ruins and decapitated columns, having once provided graceful support to pediments and temple roofs, now stood in eroding remembrance against the azure sky. Continuing to view her surroundings, Charlene pushed back, flapping her arms slowly to maintain a floating position.

Taking in the glistening beauty of her surroundings, pristine under the blue sky, she smiled with pleasure. This scene, along with others she had experienced in and around the town and harbour, left her awestruck in a way she had never felt before. She imagined that it all remained very much as Mrs Crawford would have seen it all those years ago. It was all so beautiful and yet she could not completely comprehend why it had inspired such a deep and enduring passion. Then, recalling that there was another aspect to her passion for this place, she felt a sickening surge of guilt over her failure to seek out Nektarios Alexandrou, a failure which she knew would disappoint Maria and the boys. Her only consolation was that the full extent of their disappointment would never be expressed. They might mention it mildly but would then move on allowing the lost opportunity to become forgotten with the passage of time.

Determined to banish these troubling thoughts from her mind, she flipped her body beneath her and kicked out towards the shore in a steady breaststroke, stretching her neck to keep her head above the rippling surface.

Reaching shallow water, Charlene ceased swimming and brought her legs forward. She planted her feet on the soft seabed, bent her knees and pushed herself upright, the water bubbling turbulently around her and streaming off her body as she rose into the dry air. Pulling her sunglasses onto her nose, she stood thigh deep as she regained her bearings.

She spotted her friends and squinted to focus on the man sitting on her sunbed. It looked like Manos, the postman. Postmanos Patos as they called him. She became sure it must be him. He would have finished his round early and come straight to the beach. She suspected that the main motivation for his arrival was to see her. It had become obvious that he found her attractive and, while she recognised that he was a good-looking man, she did not have reciprocal feelings for him. She was quite relaxed about this imbalance. It was a familiar situation. She would not make the lack of mutual attraction explicit unless he came on too strong at Island Nights tonight.

Heading for the area where she had entered the water, Charlene pushed through the shallow depths, her fingers tracing a trail of disturbed water until the surface dropped out of reach. Succumbing again to the mind-stilling effect of the sun's radiance, she walked out of the sea, wiggled her feet into her flip flops and scuffed slowly across the beach to the freshwater shower.

After rinsing her hair under the gushing torrent of warm water, Charlene twisted and turned her body to wash away the prickling residue of salt. She then reached up to stretch her muscles before turning the shower off, retrieving her sunglasses and walking off.

Charlene raised her hand in response to Cynthia's limp wave, and raised it again to acknowledge Manos as he turned round to watch her approach. Grinning eagerly, Manos moved out from under the umbrella as Charlene dipped into its shade.

'Hi, Charlene. You look like a goddess rising from the sea. Aphrodite, you know.'

'Oh, Manos. I bet you say that to all the girls. Anyway, look, you can sit down on the end here. Come on.'

After flopping onto the sunbed, Charlene drew her legs up to leave space for Manos.

'Come on, Manos. Sit down.'

'No. It's OK, Charlene. You take the bed. I am OK just here. Anyway, I go to the bar to get a drink. I'm getting cokes for Cynth and Suze. What you like?'

Charlene pulled off her sunglasses and squinted up at Manos standing splay-legged with each hand pushed into the back pockets of his knee-length shorts.

'Oh, that would be really nice, Manos. A coke would be great, thanks. It's a bit early for anything stronger, isn't it?'

Manos's hair flicked back from his forehead as a deep laugh gurgled up from his chest.

'I think so, especially after last night! Eh, girls!'

Charlene exchanged wide-eyed glances with Cynthia before

looking up at Manos, raising her arms in a gesture of innocent incomprehension.

'What do you mean, Manos? We were just saying earlier that we didn't think we had that much to drink last night.'

Returning her gaze with a good-humoured twinkle and a lip-sealed smile, Manos withdrew his hands from his pockets and opened his arms with a shrug of his shoulders. Accepting his silence, Charlene carried on.

'Well. Maybe compared to you, Manos, but we are on holiday. We don't have to get up at six o'clock. Thank God.'

Maintaining his silence, Manos's smile widened, his narrowing eyes glinting brightly as he turned away.

Sliding her feet down the sunbed, Charlene flattened her legs and leaned forward to call after him.

'Ah, Manos!'

Stopping instantly, he pivoted round and stepped back, grasping the edge of the umbrella and ducking his head to view her with one eyebrow flexed in amused enquiry.

'Manos. I was wondering.'

'Yyyees?'

'Ah. I was wondering if, being a postman, you know, if you know anyone called… called Nek… Nektarios. Nektarios Alexandrou.'

His expression sharpening into keen intrigue, Manos dropped into a crouch, resting his forearms on his thighs.

'Nektarios Alexandrou. Yes, I know Nektarios Alexandrou. Why do you ask?'

Charlene's eyebrows arched in surprise.

'Well. I… I know someone who used to know him, if it's the same one. The same Nektarios Alexandrou.'

'Well, I know only one Nektarios Alexandrou on this island. He is, how you say, well known. Especially when he was younger. He had a shop, a beautiful shop, the best shop. On the front, in the best position. It was there for a long time until he sold it. It is now the Belle Epoque bar and restaurant. You know?'

'Yes, we know it. It looks beautiful. We looked in but it was, well, it was a bit expensive.'

'Ah yes. It is expensive. The rich people go there. You know. They come off their boats and go there for a drink. Champagne, maybe cocktails and they eat there. The best food. Really expensive but really nice. Yes.'

Charlene drew her legs back again, pulling them against her chest and resting her chin on her knees.

'Yes. Oh well. That's good. I don't know about the shop but it could be him. The same man. It could be. Is he old? The man you know?'

'Old? Well, it depends. He's not so old. In his sixty years. My father knew him. He's older than my father, sure, but not so much. Five years maybe.'

'Mmmmn. He's a bit young then. Mrs Crawford was in her seventies.'

Manos dropped his knees onto the sand, straightening his back as he sat on his ankles.

'Mrs Crawford? Who's Mrs Crawford?'

'Oh. She's the lady I worked for. She lived here for a while. That's when she met Nektarios Alexandrou. That's why I'm here. She wanted me to come here. After she died. She… well, it's a bit difficult to explain…'

Cynthia interjected firmly as she pushed herself higher up her sunbed.

'Manos. Charlene worked as a carer for Mrs Crawford, an old lady, looking after her. Then, well, she died and left Charlene a letter in her, you know, in her will, asking her to come here. We don't know why really but that's why we're here. She didn't ask her to see this man but she'd had a fling, an affair, a love affair with this man and everyone thinks she should go and see him but, well, we've only got one more day so, well, I don't know what she's going to do. Do you, Charlene?'

Having watched Cynthia with placid resignation, Charlene lifted her face from her knees and stretched her legs out on the sunbed before replying.

'No. I don't know, Cynth. I really don't. I've left it too late, haven't I?'

Addressing the question to Manos, Charlene's face puckered into an expression between self-pity and feigned desperation. With his mouth stretching into a fond smile, Manos spread his arms wide.

'I can take you to see him. We can go now or soon. It will be a good time.'

Charlene's alarm at the easy generosity of his offer etched itself on her forehead.

'But what if it's not the same man? I mean, it's very kind of you, Manos, but, you know, it might be a different man with the same name.'

Manos emitted a guttural laugh as his smile broke into a grin.

'Oh, there's only one Nektarios Alexandrou. He must be your Mrs Crawford's lover. He had many girlfriends. Girls from many places. Not Greek ones. The women, they all loved Nektarios Alexandrou. Yes, I am sure it must be him. No problem. I take you to see him. He's there. I am sure he's there. It's no problem.'

Unable to fully process this information, Charlene hesitated before responding.

'… Well, I'm not sure. He doesn't, well, he doesn't sound like the kind of man Mrs Crawford would like and… and he didn't look like that kind of guy. I mean, she loved this man. For a long time. She never forgot him, in fact she left him money. She wouldn't have felt like that about a guy who fucked around. I mean…'

Losing momentum, Charlene turned weakly towards Cynthia who had rolled onto her side to face her friend supportively.

'Listen, Char, you can't make up your mind about him without seeing him. Talking to him. You need to check him out. You'll kick yourself if you don't, and how are you going to face Maria and the boys if you don't at least try? I mean, if it's not the same guy at least you've tried. Eh?'

Before Charlene could respond, Suzy spoke firmly without opening her eyes or moving.

'You got to do it, Charlene. I don't know how you can even think of not doing it. I would be dead keen to know what he's like. You'll kick yourself if you don't. You know you will.'

Charlene flopped back onto the sunbed, staring at the underside of the umbrella as she spoke.

'OK. OK. I'll give it a go. It's probably not the same guy but what the hell.'

Lifting her head, she looked at Manos.

'Manos. Thanks for the offer. I'll go see this guy if you're sure he won't mind.'

Manos bounced up into a crouching position, a smile breaking out on his face.

'No, he won't mind. I know him well. I helped him last year with his house putting new, what you call them, shutters, yes, new shutters on his windows. Anyway, he will be happy to see a pretty girl like you! So, yes, it's no problem. No problem at all.'

A gleeful laugh bubbling out of her, Cynthia leaned forward, glancing swiftly at Charlene before speaking to Manos.

'Look at you, Manos. The cat who got the cream! You can't wait to get her on the back of your bike, can you? Manos cruising through town with a pretty lady!'

Pushing up into a standing position, Manos batted his arm dismissively at Cynthia, before pointing in the direction of the promontory as he replied.

'Bah! Yes, she is a pretty lady. A very pretty lady but we go there. Not through town. We go over there for twenty minutes maybe. It's not far.'

Continuing to speak he bent over to dust the sand off his knees.

'Anyway. I go get the cokes. Then we go in maybe twenty minutes. OK, Charlene?'

Looking down at her, he cocked his head and smiled at her consensually, before walking off to the bar.

Chapter 40

With her tenuous trust evaporating, as Manos navigated the twists and turns in the road with increasing speed, Charlene abandoned her intention not to make close contact and pressed herself tightly against him. Feeling safer with her arms wrapped around his torso and trying to ignore the awkward intimacy, Charlene began to appreciate the sensations of this new experience. The flash of sights and smells seemed to fill her senses with an immediacy and intensity she had never felt before.

Her hair whipped wildly in the turbulent slipstream. She felt freshly cool in the rushing air, but was grateful for the flushes of warmth radiating from the rocks each time they sped through a cutting in the steep coastline. Rounding a corner, the view of another bay serenely still in the afternoon sunshine, flashed between the roadside parade of aromatic pine and eucalyptus trees. She felt a longing to be onboard one of the immaculate yachts peacefully secure on their moorings. The breezy, buffeting ride had become mostly bearable, sometimes thrilling, but the high-speed sections and the angle they dropped to when banking around corners were scarily unnerving. Her unease became acute when Manos released his hand to wave; firstly at an aproned woman standing on the terrace of a roadside taverna, and later at a smart-shirted man walking through the gates of an imposing sea-view villa. Sometimes it would lift completely for brief moments when her senses were consumed by fragrant smells, or by suddenly revealed views of a stately ship cutting a wake between hazy islands, or a cluster of buildings perched as they had for centuries on a jagged hilltop.

She was relieved when their rollercoaster ride slowed to a stop beside a small white-walled harbour, where Manos chatted to a man preparing his boat for night-time fishing. She breathed easily while he talked, and inhaled sharply when he revved the throttle before pulling away so quickly that she slid back on the seat. Feeling almost as though she had been forgotten about, Charlene tightened her hold around Manos and pulled herself into even closer contact. She groaned with a confusing mixture of fear and regret when he reached back to press his hand against her thigh.

Reaching a seafront settlement stretched along an empty beach, Manos changed down the gears, slowing to a throbbing crawl as they passed the quiet harbour at its heart. Jolting into first gear, he turned round a sharp corner between a taverna in mid-afternoon dormancy, and a small supermarket with racks full of fruit and vegetables stacked along its frontage. The noise of the engine growled loudly, reverberating between the buildings as they began to ascend the steep road out of town.

At first relieved to be travelling at a safer speed, Charlene then became disconcerted by the sensation of slipping back on the seat again. Determined not to resist this by tightening her arms around Manos, she pushed against the footrests and gripped her thighs more tightly on the seat cushioning. With the gradient easing, Charlene relaxed her legs and absorbed the new sights and smells as they wound past rustic houses and sheds amidst stone-walled olive groves, orchards, crop-filled fields and scrubby paddocks for goats and donkeys.

Bursts of bougainvillea, jasmine and clematis billowed along the walls of grander houses, grape-heavy vines sprawling on trellises. Small churches appeared and tavernas which exuded the promise of good hospitality. At some points along the way, vistas opened up of the sea stretching to the mountainous mainland, mythically mysterious in the distance. All of this was unfamiliarly foreign to her, yet she felt at ease as though she could inhabit this environment comfortably without being nagged by that unsettled feeling she experienced in other places. She continued to be absorbed in this unusual sense of thing,s as Manos brought the bike to a halt at a gate beneath the shade of a large fig tree.

Returning to the moment as Manos switched off the engine, Charlene became filled with a crippling apprehension about having to communicate meaningfully with this mysterious person who had been so significant in Mrs Crawford's life. She remained perched on the pillion until Manos's announcement of their arrival penetrated the fog of her anxiety.

'This is it. We are here.'

Charlene dismounted and looked around anxiously, while tugging down the hem of her shorts.

'OK. So the house is up there, I guess.'

'Yes. It is up there. You see? Behind the trees.'

'Yeah, I can see something.'

Manos pulled the bike onto its stand and looked up at the terraced garden.

'It's nice, eh? Like a, how you say, like a piece of paradise. No?'

Not responding to his enthusiasm, Charlene turned a full circle to survey the situation, her face remaining impassively neutral.

'Very nice. I like it.'

Manos moved to Charlene's side and, embracing her with his outstretched arm, turned her round to face the sea visible between the leggy pines on the other side of the road. Stooping down to her eye level, he swept his free arm across the view.

'Beautiful, eh? That is the mainland there behind the small islands and round there is the town. And there, there is the beach where we came from. Where Cynthia and Suzy are, maybe now with Spiros and Tassos. Yes, you see? It is beautiful. No?'

Charlene slipped out of his embrace, justifying her escape with an exaggerated spin of appreciation.

'It is, Manos. It's beautiful, but what do we do now?'

Ignoring her affectation of delight, Manos walked to the gate at the bottom of the garden pathway.

'Come on. We have to press the button for him to open the gate. We walk in before. The gate it was open but now people are careful. They are afraid strangers come. It is not so bad but it is not like before.'

Charlene reached him as he pressed the button.

'Will he come down or can he open it from the house? That's an intercom, isn't it?'

'This? Yes, we can speak there. We wait.'

Becoming agitated after a few seconds of waiting, Charlene inspected her fingernails, flicking out grains of sand as Manos leaned down to press the button again. After more waiting, Charlene scuffed the dirt with her foot and knocked the back of her hand lightly against his forearm.

'Come on, Manos. Let's go. He's not here.'

Turning away reluctantly, Manos addressed her back as he followed her to the bike.

'OK, but he should be here. It's a good time. Maybe one hour after sleeping it should be a good time. I am sorry. I like to see him.'

'Never mind, Manos. At least we tried. That's the main thing. No one can say we didn't try.'

Manos mounted the bike and, after kick-starting it, held it steady while Charlene manoeuvred herself into position.

'Can we go nice and easy on the way down, Manos? Nice and easy.'

Leaning back to shout a reply as they moved off, Manos's attention was caught by the sight of a figure moving in the high part of the garden. Bringing the bike to a halt, Manos pointed towards the person descending the pathway through the terraced garden.

'Look. That's him. Nektarios Alexandrou.'

Charlene pushed her sunglasses onto the top of her head and narrowed her eyes to focus on the man coming into view. She leaned forward to make herself heard above the engine noise as Manos turned the bike and drove up to the gate.

'That's not him, Manos. That's a different man.'

Manos turned the engine off and responded over his shoulder.

'What do you mean? That is Nektarios Alexandrou.'

'Well, it's not the one I'm looking for. It's not the one who came to Mrs Crawford's funeral. Definitely not, so we can go straight back after you've said hello.'

'Are you sure? I didn't know you have seen him already.'

'Yes, I have and it's definitely not him. I'm very sorry to have put you to all this trouble, but it's the wrong man.'

'OK. No problem but I need to speak to my father's friend.'

Dismissing Charlene's concerns, Manos turned his attention to the man who had the grey hair of an older person but was dressed with the casual confidence of a younger man in a vivid blue shirt, denim jeans and espadrilles. Manos waved at him as he made his way down the path in an easy stride and greeted him in Greek.

'Kalispera, Nektarios! Ti kanete!'

The man's face lit up with delight.

'Kalah spera, Manos, how good to see you! What brings you up here? Is your father well?'

'Yes, he's fine. Very well. We were just passing and I thought I should pass on his greetings.'

He opened the gate and walked over, raising his arms in a welcoming gesture before clasping Manos's hand with both of his.

'Manos, my boy. It must be over a year since I saw you. Is everything going well?'

'Yes. It's great thanks.'

Continuing to speak Greek, the man released Manos's hand and beamed benevolently at Charlene as he reached out to shake her hand.

'Excuse me. I didn't mean to ignore you. I'm Nektarios Alexandrou, an old friend of Manos's father.'

Manos interjected as their hands came together.

'Nektarios. This is Charlene. She's a friend. An English friend. She's here on holiday.'

Without hesitating, the man switched to speaking in English at the same time as increasing the vigour of their handshake.

'It's a pleasure to meet you, Charlene. I am always pleased to see English women on our beloved island. I am sure Manos is looking after you well.'

Charlene hesitated as he released her hand, dipping her eyes downwards before lifting her head to look at the man.

'Yes… yes, he is, thanks. He's very kind and… and…'

The man touched her arm lightly as he terminated the extending silence.

'He is a kind man just like his father, and he has been very helpful to me, but anyway, how are you enjoying the island? Are you having a good holiday?'

'Yes thanks. It's lovely. We're having a lovely time, thanks.'

Manos looked round to intervene.

'Charlene is here with friends. Two friends.'

The man continued to address Charlene as he stepped back.

'Oh good, so you were just going on a little trip with my friend here?'

'Yes... ah... we were just going for a ride.'

'Good. It's the best way to travel here, I think. You really get a better sense of the place on a bike. Much better than a car. Don't you think?'

'Yes. It's a bit, well, kind of scary sometimes but I know what you mean. It's more boring in a car.'

'Well, it can be dangerous, Charlene, that's for sure, but I do agree it's more boring in a car. Anyway, I'm about to go out on my own bike. I have an appointment in town.'

Manos extended his arm towards the man.

'It was very good to see you, Nektarios. My father will be pleased I saw you.'

Once again the man clasped Manos's hand with both of his.

'You take care, my boy, and tell your father I'll phone him to meet for a drink one evening.'

'I will, Nektarios. I will. He will be very happy to meet you.'

Manos flicked out the start pedal with his foot and just before kicking down on it raised his head, his brow creasing quizzically as he looked back at the man.

'Nektarios, do you know anyone on this island with the same name as you? Charlene has met a man in England with the same name. Nektarios Alexandrou. He lives on the island. Yes, Charlene? That is correct?'

Charlene pressed the tips of her fingers into Manos's waist.

'Yes, Manos. That's right, but it really doesn't matter. It's not important.'

The man's eyes widened and the lines on his forehead arched into deep furrows.

'No. I don't. That is very surprising. The name Alexandrou is not uncommon, but there is only one other Alexandrou family on the island over on the other side. You know, at Elenistiraki. He must be connected to them. Well, well. What an amazing coincidence. I must try and meet him.'

Manos kick-started the engine shouting his farewell in Greek.

'I'll let you know if we find him, Nektarios. We haven't much time. She leaves on Saturday. Never mind. It was very good to see you. The true Nektarios Alexandrou! Goodbye, sir!'

After revving the engine, Manos engaged gear and moved off, leaving the man waving and watching them disappear from view.

Arriving back at the apartment, Charlene dismounted and ran her fingers through her windblown hair. Manos remained on the bike as he switched off the engine and rested his forearms on the handlebars.

'Well. I am sorry that we did not find your Nektarios Alexandrou, but maybe we try to find him at Elenistiraki tomorrow. I can look at the addresses in the office.'

'Listen. It's OK, Manos. We tried and I don't want to spend my last day looking for him. It doesn't matter. Honestly.'

'OK, Charlene. Whatever you like, but anyway I need to go home now. I see you later at Island Nights. OK?'

'Sure. We should be there around nine o'clock. Are Spiros and Tassos coming out tonight?'

'I think so. Spiros will text me. Wait. I see.'

Reaching into the front pocket of his shorts, Manos withdrew his phone and opened his messages. Charlene observed him curiously as his expression transformed from surprise to amused delight.

'Hey. It's a text from Nektarios. Listen. I say it in English. *If Charlene is looking for the friend of Katherine Crawford, it is me. If she is, can we meet tomorrow? Prefer at mine.* Hey! It is him. What you think! Amazing!'

Confused by incomprehension, Charlene stuttered as she formed her response.

'But... but... how did he know I was looking for... how did he know about Mrs Crawford and... and the man at the funeral... it was a different man... and... and why would someone who wasn't Nektarios Alexandrou go to the funeral... and leave a lemon?'

'What you mean? I don't understand...'

Charlene pressed her hands to her temples and shook her head before replying.

'It doesn't matter, Manos, but there was a man at the funeral who looked Greek. He put a lemon on the end of the coffin and walked out of the chapel. I thought it must be Nektarios Alexandrou, we all did, but maybe it wasn't.'

Manos spoke slowly as he assimilated this new information.

'OK. So you do not know that the man you see in England is Nektarios, and he is not Nektarios for sure because Nektarios, the one we see, the friend of my father, is the friend of Mrs Crawford. So that is good. So you can go see him tomorrow. I take you, same as today. OK?'

'OK. I suppose I should. Yes, OK. Thanks, Manos, if that's OK with you.'

'Yes, it is OK. Sure. Only I have to play football tomorrow so I have to be quick. You know.'

'Yes. Sure, sure. That's no problem. I only need to say hello. It won't take long. So thanks, Manos, that's great. Anyway, look, I'll see you later. OK?'

'Yeah. See you later!'

A smile flickered across her face as she waved to Manos, before watching him ride down the quiet street, the roar of the engine fading as he disappeared out of sight.

Chapter 41

Nektarios stooped over to press his lips lightly against the yielding softness of her parted mouth. The intimate sensuality of this exploratory engagement initiated a powerful charge of raw desire, which surged with overwhelming strength from his groin through his heart to his head, filling it with a dizzying sense of unsurpassable excitement. He pulled back and looked at her upturned face, appreciating her beauty with a new recognition that made him gasp. With her eyes closed she appeared serenely submissive, an impression instantly belied when she reached her arm up to clasp the back of his head and pull it down towards hers with a gentle but insistent pressure.

As their mouths engaged, this time with passion-fuelled intensity, he felt his erection expand powerfully and irresistibly independent of his mind and the furtive fear of non-performance. The lush moistness of her mouth and the sensation of her breasts squashing against his torso, filled him with electrifying excitement. The end of his engorged penis, now pressed sidelong against her belly, tickled deliciously in anticipation of the possibility that this journey of sensual discovery might lead to the ecstacy of being received into the ultimate union.

Pulling his head back, the struggle of trying to reclaim his mind for rational thought etched itself on his face. He scanned her face in search of signals which might reveal her state of mind, but could see nothing to correspond with his anxious need to banish nagging doubt. Her face seemed to emanate a calm certainty that, having succumbed to all-consuming rapture, they should let this journey take its course. She confirmed this impression by snaking her arm downwards within the tightness of their embrace and slipping her hand inside his linen trousers to grasp his penis. Feeling confidently strong and thick in the grip of her slender hand, he felt again that giddying promise of fulfilment burst in his head with dazzling radiance.

Seeing that she had opened her eyes he mustered sufficient willpower to lock her into visual contact and launch the beginning of a question, the end of which he had not yet determined.

'Are you... are you...?'

Leaving the sentence unfinished, he watched in wonder as she looked down to focus on unbuttoning his shirt with resolute dexterity. After opening it down to his midriff, she pushed her splayed hand through the hairs on his chest, moving it in a circular motion so that one finger traced a circle around the areola of his nipple. Feeling him shiver in response to the sensations aroused by the lightness of her touch, she looked up at him, her expression now drawn in desperation to be freed of any reservations and to submit themselves to unleashed passion. Before articulating her desire, she pressed the tips of her fingers emphatically into the flesh of his chest to ensure that her message received his full attention.

'I want this, Nektarios. I need it. Badly.'

Instantly allowing his defences to be swamped by the overpowering urge to be complicit in fulfilling her desperate need, he cupped his hands around the fullness of her buttocks and lifted her off the floor.

Emitting a sharp gasp of excitement, she pulled her hand out from his trousers and clung to him with her arms and legs as he moved inside from the terrace. She nuzzled at his neck as he carried her across the large cream rug spread across the terracotta tiles. He headed towards the rear of the room, the intensity of the afternoon light diminishing as they moved away from the full-height windows overlooking the bay.

The final strands of confusion and doubt lost their grip and were cast adrift in the wake of his charging desire. How was this happening? Who had started it? Did it matter? She arrived and they just ended up in each other's arms. It just happened and nothing was going to stop it now. The age difference didn't matter. He had never experienced someone so desirable and he had never felt so strong, so potent.

Flexing his muscles, he hitched her up into a more secure position. She in turn tightened the grip of her legs around his waist and, hanging her arms around his neck, rested the side of her head on his shoulder as they passed through the shaded hallway into the dappled light of his bedroom.

He lowered her with a groan of relief onto the white linen bed cover, and falling alongside her, they intertwined, kissing unrestrainedly and feeling each other's bodies, their desire growing more desperate as the wildfires of passion raged hotly within them.

In the midst of their frenzy she pushed him away abruptly and, rolling onto her back, unbuckled her belt. Then, arching her back, she pulled her shorts and knickers off her legs and kicked them onto the floor.

Stunned into a stupor of sexual stirrings, his wide-eyed gaze moved from the triangle of hair at the nexus of her thighs and belly to the intoxicating sight of her breasts being revealed as she shrugged off her bra. Breaking out of his awestruck inertia, he unfastened the remainder of his shirt buttons with fumbling haste and pulled off his trousers and boxer shorts. Then after flinging them into the room, he ventured an inconspicuous tug at his penis, his chest filling with the exhilaration of finding it stretched to full-strength hardness.

Fortified and eager, he rolled against her and engaged hungrily in a tumbling clinch across the bed. Ending up with her flat on her back he started to nibble and kiss his way down her body. Reaching her chest he nuzzled against her breasts, pulling lightly at her nipples with his lips, and working his tongue delicately around her areolae. Then, following the contours of her belly, he descended to her groin. Parting her legs she reached down to massage his head with her fingertips while he delicately probed the moist folds of flesh with his tongue. Feeling her stiffen and, hearing a shuddering intake of breath, he knew through the craze of his desire that he had found the pathway to her orgasm. Refocusing, he raised the level of stimulation in response to the groaning affirmation that his creativity was generating a rising tide of sensations.

Now, gasping and crying out from the storm of her euphoria, she writhed in the ecstasy of reaching the crescendo to her climax.

Gathering resolve with the abatement of her convulsive heaving, she pulled him up and shoved him around onto his back. She then knelt astride him and grasping his penis guided it to her groin until it nudged against the slippery mouth of her vagina. The tantalising tickle at the tip of his erection, and the rushing fizz of sensation in his testes, almost made him accede to the impetus driving him towards complete penetration but, reining back, he reached out his flailing arm to withdraw a condom from the bedside table. After tearing the foil wrapper with fierce determination and unrolling the thin sheath over his penis, he gasped as the sensation of slipping into full connection with her sweat-sheened body caused a thrilling tremor to shiver through his prostrate form.

Gradually increasing the rhythm of his thrust and withdrawal, she leaned over him emitting soft squeals of delight and sliding her hands up his torso. With each hand on her bottom he looked up and down her arching body with incredulous awe, as her breasts transformed from their softly contoured roundness to ripe fruits of flesh hanging above him. He released a guttering groan as her nipples brushed ticklingly against his chest, and threw his head back to seek distraction from these sights and sensations, which were stoking the fire of his desire so brightly, he feared that exploding point would be reached too quickly. Sliding her hands around the back of his head, she slid down to kiss him with rapacious intensity. Responding with ravenous passion, fuelled by the feel of her naked form pressing hotly against his, he felt the unstoppable beginnings of an ejaculation of such unprecedented power, a frisson of fearful exhilaration shot through his spine. Rolling her over onto her back with urgent force, he pushed up with his arms holding his body above hers as she parted her legs to allow him to penetrate deep within her. They looked at each other with wide-eyed intensity, their faces contorted in mutual recognition that they had reached the moment of release, his final ascent to climax. He shuddered and gasped sharply as a surge of electrifying power burst from his groin, initiating an urgent rush of semen through the stem of his penis. Ramming his throbbing erection to the deepest point of penetration, he roared in an involuntary reaction to the shockwaves of extreme sensation pulsing through him, as the ejaculate shot out in three powerful spurts.

Emitting a ragged moan, he shivered in delight as the final aftershock swept through him. Then, with the sensations subsiding, he looked down at her in wonderment before withdrawing and rolling onto his side. After removing the condom and throwing it beyond the rug onto the tiles, he placed his hand gently on her waist and arched over to kiss her tenderly on the lips. An enraptured glow spread over his face as he pulled back to utter a single expression, quietly but with emphatic clarity.

'Wow!'

Looking at each other in the calm afterglow of passion, the corners of her eyes crinkled and a lazy smile played around her mouth as she responded in an oozing whisper.

'Yes. That was good. I needed that....thanks!'

Emitting a grunt of laughter he swooped down to plant a pronounced kiss on her mouth before reaching down to pull the cotton cover over them. He then rolled over onto his back and reached down to hold her hand.

'Oh my god, Katherine, thank you. That wasn't just good, it was... unbelievable.'

Then, after squeezing her hand, he gazed through the window at the foliage providing a dappled screen to the afternoon sun, before succumbing to the soothing lure of tiredness and closing his eyes.

Chapter 42

The repeated ringing of the doorbell penetrated his awakening consciousness. He opened his eyes, blinking slowly as they adjusted to the daylight. Stretching out in the soft comfort of his mattress, he sucked in a deep breath and summoned the strength to swing his legs off the bed and stand up. He then stretched his arms upwards before running fingers through his hair and going through the unsteady motions of retrieving his clothes and pulling them on. While buttoning up his shirt, he slipped into his espadrilles and shuffled drowsily towards the door. He stopped at the large wall mirror to brush his hair, flinging the brush back on the shelf as a prolonged ring of the doorbell resonated shrilly in his sleep-numbed brain.

At the door, he inhaled sharply through his nose and shook his head, before pulling it open and addressing the two people standing there.

'Hi, hi. Welcome. I'm sorry to keep you waiting. I was asleep. For a little longer than usual for some reason.'

'Hey. It's no problem, Nektarios, I thought you might be sleeping. No problem.'

'Well, I don't usually sleep this long but come in. Come in.'

Ushered forward by Manos, Charlene walked in first. She looked around, meekly inquisitive to take in the details of this significant place, before turning around to face Nektarios as he spoke while closing the door.

'I was just dreaming about Katherine, actually. It's not often I remember my dreams but this was a nice one.'

A wistful smile stretched warmly across his face.

'A very nice dream about nice times. A beautiful time. The first time she visited me here. She was some woman, Katherine. I still can't believe she's gone, passed away, that she can never visit here again. That's hard to accept.'

Looking from Charlene to Manos, his face brightened.

'Hey, look. Let me show you something.'

He re-opened the door.

'Do you see that tree? The lemon tree? Katherine planted that thirty years ago, shortly before she left the island. It's magnificent, don't you think?'

Without waiting for a response, he beckoned them to follow and stepped outside into the afternoon sunshine.

'It's not easy to grow lemon trees but Katherine's has thrived. I've looked after it, of course, but even so it's grown beautifully. The fruit looks a bit green at this time of year but actually they're OK to use.'

He reached out to slide a glossy leaf lightly between his thumb and forefinger.

'I sent a lemon from this tree to my cousin, so that he could take it to Katherine's funeral. Instead of flowers. Better than flowers. A fruit from her own tree. He said he put it on her coffin. I am so glad I found out in time and so glad he was able to do it. That he was prepared to do it. He couldn't introduce himself because, well, I didn't know if Katherine would have told anyone about me or about her time on the island, but I guess she did and, well, you obviously thought he was me. Eh? He is the same age and he's from here, this island, but he's lived in London since he was a young man. So I'm sorry, you must have thought Evangelos was me and you must have thought I was very rude, doing that without saying anything or introducing myself.'

Mesmerised by Nektarios and his home, the setting for his relationship with the most profoundly influential person she had ever known, Charlene stuttered as she tried to articulate a response.

'Y… yes… I… I… we did think it was you. We all did. But… but we didn't think you were rude, we were too surprised and, well, I guess we just thought you were, you know, shy.'

Smiling gratefully, Nektarios leaned towards her and placed his hand softly on her arm.

'Thanks, Charlene. That's reassuring, but I am sorry to have caused such confusion. It's just that I couldn't come. It wouldn't have been right. I hadn't ever visited her when she was alive. I couldn't. I'm not sure how much you know about us, our relationship, but, anyway, it was never possible to see her when she was alive and so I wasn't going to turn up after she had passed away… I couldn't. I could only send her a lemon but, for me, it was a symbol. Fruit from her tree, the memorial of our special relationship.'

Moving closer to Charlene, he held each of her hands in his and looked into her eyes.

'I am so glad you came, Charlene, and I am fascinated to know your connection with Katherine. I know she didn't have many relatives so I assume, well, there's lots I want to know about you and… and what Katherine told you about me, about us.'

'Well, ah, I was like a, like a carer or an assistant carer anyway and, well, Mrs Crawford wanted me to come here but… but, how did you know, how did you figure out I was, like, connected to Mrs Crawford?'

His eyes shining, he laughed warmly before replying.

'Oh, well, it just clicked after you left. It should really have occurred to me straight away, that a young English woman looking for Nektarios Alexandrou would be connected somehow with Katherine, although I wouldn't have guessed you were her carer, her assistant carer, helping to look after her. It's hard to imagine her needing a carer, although I realise she wasn't well. Not as strong as she used to be but, anyway, thank God I made the connection and thank you, Charlene, thank you so much for looking for me. Did she ask you to find me or… or, well, I don't know, I hope she wanted you to find me.'

'Well, she, ah, she didn't exactly ask me but, well, I'm sure she hoped I would see you, I think, but, well, we didn't know where you were exactly so… well…'

'Well, never mind, Charlene. You did find me eventually, thank goodness, so let's go inside and tell each other our stories. The lemon tree is the only living connection I've had with Katherine and, well, it's wonderful to have a human connection after all this time.'

Releasing her hands he gestured to Manos.

'Come on, my boy. Let me get you a drink. We can sit on the terrace.'

Excited to be spoken to amidst dialogue about a person he did not know, a flash of brightness lit Manos's face before dimming as he spoke.

'That would be good, Nektarios, sir, but I have football so I can stay only thirty minutes or maybe not so much. I have to be there in one hour.'

'OK, Manos, but, Charlene, you can stay longer I hope? I can give you a lift later.'

Charlene flushed as she looked back at Nektarios, her eyes widening with anxiety.

'Well… ah, the girls, my friends will be waiting for me so… so… maybe I should… maybe… but, but I could stay. For a bit.'

Nektarios stretched his arm out behind her and, pressing

gently against her back, ushered her through the house.

'Oh, I hope you can stay for more than a bit, Charlene. I can take you back. It's no problem. I am hoping we will have a lot to talk about. I'd like to tell you about the Katherine I knew, and I hope you can tell me about how she was when you knew her. It's such an opportunity. I don't want her passing to go silently, if you know what I mean?'

Charlene looked up at him as they walked side by side, her eyes softening as her apprehension eased.

'Yes… Yes, I think so.'

'Do you think your friends will be OK if you stay for a bit?'

'I… I think so. Yes. I'll send them a message to let them know I'll be back a bit later. It won't take me long to get ready, so… so… well, anyway.'

Nektarios looked down at her, his eyes glowing warmly.

'Great. Come on then. Let's enjoy the rest of the afternoon on the terrace. If you can stay a bit later I can give you one of the best sunset views on the island. Katherine and I spent many nights watching it go down.'

*

Charlene reclined on the sunlounger and looked up at the vine, its leafy spread of branches and tendrils rendered sharply against the brilliant blue of the sky. Screwing her eyes to protect them from the brightness, she lowered her gaze to focus on a densely packed bunch of grapes hanging heavily in the shade of the canopy. A fusion of disbelief and wonder effervesced in her heart.

She looked around, marvelling that she was present in the place Mrs Crawford had cherished with such longing, the place where she had reached the highpoint of her passion, passion for this man she had managed to find. This man who would return soon after saying goodbye to Manos. Two kind men who were delivering a successful outcome to her holiday. A soft smile of satisfaction stretched across her face. Maria and the boys would be delighted. Her sense of excitement surged at the prospect of telling them about this handsome man and his beautiful home. They would be as enthralled as she was that it looked as though nothing had changed much, not even him, she thought. Still so good looking. No wonder so many women fell for him.

After taking a drink from the glass of orange and soda, she placed it on the floor and lay back with a sigh while closing her eyes.

She speculated dreamily on how different Mrs Crawford must have been, living here all those years ago when she was strong and fit. She had begun in the drift of her thoughts, to transpose herself into these imagined scenarios when the sound of Nektarios's espadrilles slapping and scuffing on the tiles alerted her attention.

'Hi, Charlene. Listen. If you're OK there for ten minutes I'll go and freshen up. I like to have a quick shower after my siesta. Would you mind?'

Charlene squinted up at him as he appeared in front of her.

'No. No, that's fine. I'm fine. No problem.'

'Good. That's great but please feel free to have a look around. I'll show you around properly after, but please make yourself at home. OK, Charlene?'

'Yeah. Cool. Thanks.'

After taking one step towards the house, Nektarios rocked back to express an afterthought.

'This place. This is my place on earth, Charlene. This place and everything you can see from it.'

He then swept his arm around in an all-encompassing gesture, and turned towards the sea and the hazy mainland beyond. After a contemplative pause, gazing across the emerald tones of the shallow bay to the shimmering blues beyond, he looked back at Charlene, his brow compressed with the weight of memories.

'This is where I was born and where I will die, God willing, and it's where the most meaningful events in my life have happened.'

Realising from Charlene's strained expression that she was struggling to formulate a response, a crinkling smile emerged on his face.

'Hey. Sorry for getting so profound. So serious. Perhaps it's the effect of Katherine's… of Katherine passing away that's affected me. Made me reflect on things. On life.'

Walking off, he projected a parting comment over his shoulder.

'I'll try to lighten up. I promise. Don't worry.'

Charlene flopped back on the sunlounger as she listened to his footsteps fade to silence as he scuffed back to the house.

Relieved at this respite from dialogue that was becoming disconcertingly deep, she closed her eyes and submitted to the soothing warmth of the vine-filtered sunshine. Stretching out on the cushioned cover, her thought processes slowed to a halt as her empty mind became suffused with the amber glow of sunlight penetrating her eyelids.

A sudden whisper of shaken leaves above her, stirred Charlene back to full consciousness. She opened her eyes and looked up, her forehead creasing into a wary frown as she scanned the confusion of branches and leaves trembling in agitation. Her face flinched as she connected with a pair of feline eyes staring down at her.

Sitting up, she watched the glisteningly black cat disengage and pick its way along the branches to the gnarled trunk. The rustling of disturbed foliage belied the agility of the cat's descent. After dropping lightly onto the tiles, it walked past Charlene with high-tailed hauteur. She turned to watch its progress and, seeing it approach the French windows, she rose from the sunlounger and walked after it while trying to decide if she should discourage it from entering the house.

She stopped at the French windows and watched it continue through the main room into the inner hallway beyond. She flinched on seeing Nektarios appear from the bathroom, barechested with a white towel wrapped around his waist. After taking a step backwards she froze as he leaned down to stroke the cat under its chin with one hand, while gripping the towel at his hip with the other. Resisting the temptation to continue watching, she turned around discreetly and tiptoed away, stirred by the sight of Nektarios in a semi-naked state. She would not have believed a man of his age could have such an attractive body. This, along with his easy charm and good looks, would have made him very desirable. He had clearly made the most of these attributes. Had that been the reason for his relationship with Mrs Crawford coming to an end?

Swaying contemplatively out of the semi-shade to the front edge of the terrace, Charlene stretched her neck muscles as her body submitted to the relaxing heat of the late-afternoon sun. Drawing in a deep breath of contentment, her nose was filled with a fragrant mix of Mediterranean aromas from the clustered herb pots, the flowering plants and the more distant pines.

The contrast between the vivid pleasures of this place and the ordinariness of home, struck her more powerfully now than it had at any other moment. She began to grasp for the first time how this could be more than an island for holidays. How it could be a home, a home to cherish, a home to love fiercely.

Distracted from her reverie by the noise of Nektarios approaching, she wheeled round to face him.

'Hi, Charlene. I hope you like the view. I never tire of it. Ever. It sustains me. Looking out over my place in the world. This place without which I am nothing. Anyway, before I get too deep again, can I offer you a drink? It's that time of day, wouldn't you say, when we can indulge in a nice drink? I was thinking of a Metaxa mojito. Very refreshing. Would that be OK do you think?'

A diffident smile played at the corners of her mouth.

'Well. Yes. I haven't had one of those, I don't think, but it sounds nice.'

'OK. That's good. I think you'll like it. I only discovered it recently. It's got Metaxa, you know, Greek brandy, mixed with a bit of brown sugar, lemon juice, lots of mint and topped up with soda. Oh and lots of ice and a quarter lime. Very refreshing. A nice feel-good drink.'

'Sounds good.'

'Great. Come on then. I'll show you how to make it.'

Sweeping his arm through the air as an invitation to follow him, Nektarios smiled warmly as she moved forward to accompany him back to the house.

Sitting on one of the high stools arranged around the dining bar, Charlene alternated between watching Nektarios prepare the cocktail and looking around the kitchen. She ended up focusing on the photographs pinned to the noticeboard on the wall at the end of the bar. The other photographs stuck onto the fridge in the corner, were too far away to make out any details.

She looked for Mrs Crawford amongst the many photographs of different women, but could not discern a likeness in any of them. She wondered if they too had fallen in love with him, and if some were even now yearning for a long-lost relationship.

Her heart ached with regret that Mrs Crawford may have been just one of many women who had been intimate with Nektarios. Diverting herself from this hurtful thought, she transferred her attention to photographs of what she was sure was the same young male at different ages, from boyhood to somewhere in his twenties. She wondered if it might be Nektarios, but thought it unlikely that he would display photographs of himself and, anyway, the clothing and haircuts were probably too modern.

Hearing the rapid knocking of metal on wood, Charlene turned back to watch Nektarios, as he chopped the mint with practised dexterity. Scooping it up between the wide blade of the knife and his hand, he dropped it into the glass jug before mixing it with a long spoon. He spoke loudly to be heard above the crackling and clunking of the swirling ice cubes.

'There. Done.'

After removing two tall glasses from a wall unit, he poured in the cocktail regulating the number of ice cubes dropping with the knife blade. Smiling with satisfaction he handed a glass to Charlene.

'There you go. I hope you like it.'

Immediately raising the glass to her lips, Charlene sipped a small amount, continuing to look at Nektarios above the tipping rim. Lowering the glass she responded to his enquiring expression with a preliminary nod of pleasure before speaking.

'That's nice. Really nice. I like it… a lot.'

'Hey. That's great. I hoped you would. Well, let's drink it outside as a sun-downer. A slightly premature sun-downer.'

Holding the jug in one hand and his glass in the other, he waited while Charlene dismounted from the stool.

'Oh. By the way, these photographs. Did you notice the photos of the boy, or young man, I should say? That's my son. All of them. At different ages, although I don't have any recent ones up there. He's twenty-eight now. I don't suppose you knew I had a son?'

Charlene twisted round to look back at them.

'No, no, I didn't but, well, he looks nice. He… ah… he looks a bit like you. Yes. Definitely. He looks like you.'

With his eyes glowing warmly, Nektarios gazed fondly at the photographs while he spoke.

'The true love of my life. Constantinos. That's his name. Different from the other love I've felt, of course, but he's the most important person in my life.'

He turned to look at Charlene who was now facing him.

'Unfortunately I haven't been able to play a big part in what you might call his normal life as he grew up. He lives in the States with his mother. That's her there. Top right. She's a professor. A professor of classical studies at Harvard. A very intelligent woman, of course, and a good woman. A very good woman and although it could never have worked between us I am eternally grateful that our brief time together produced such a wonderful person.'

Unsure of how to respond, Charlene looked around in discomfort until fixing her focus on the surface of the bar in front of her.

'That's sad. I mean, it's great that he's wonderful but it's sad you don't see him so much. You must… you must miss him.'

Unnerved by the lack of response, Charlene glanced up at Nektarios. Seeing his features wrought in sadness and the sheen of moisture in his eyes, she continued to look at him as he finally vocalised his feelings.

'I do regret it, Charlene. That I couldn't be, you know, a regular dad for him. But, anyway, I have to be grateful for the contact I have had with him. And we are close. Very close. He comes here every summer. He always did. With his mother to begin with and then on his own. Thankfully, he feels a need to come here. Not just to see me but also to connect with this place. He feels a great connection to the island, to his home here. Thank God.'

Breathing in deeply, the melancholy lifted from his face and he smiled brightly.

'In fact, he's here right now. Living with me for the summer. He's working at the museum. That's his field. Archaeology. Gets that from his mother. He's not back until late tonight, so you probably won't get to meet him which is a shame. Another time! But, anyway, come on, let's go and drink our mojitos.'

Placing the jug in the fridge on the way out, Nektarios gestured towards the door after closing it.

'More photos. Friends mainly. Friends who've visited this island through the years. Reminders of happy times. None of Katherine here. I keep the photos of her elsewhere. I used to have some of her in the kitchen, but I've changed it since she was here. It's roughly the same as it was but everything is newer, smarter. Can't say the same of myself unfortunately. Life doesn't work that way. I'm roughly the same, I suppose, but older and not quite as fit as I was. Not quite.'

*

Having settled back onto the sunlounger closest to Charlene's, Nektarios lifted the glass off the small table beside him and raised it towards her. Lifting her own glass she reciprocated the gesture with a questioning smile.

'Cheers, Charlene. It's great to have you here.'

'Yes. Cheers, Nektarios. It's nice being here. Lovely. Thanks.'

His beaming smile widened with each word of her response. Without saying anything further, he continued to look into her eyes as he raised the glass to his lips. Following his lead, Charlene also sipped deeply from the cocktail. Without breaking visual contact, Nektarios returned his glass to the table.

'I really mean it, Charlene. I am so glad you came.'

'Well, I wouldn't have, you know, come all the way here without trying to get in touch. That wouldn't have… wouldn't have been right. It would have been a waste.'

His face clouding, Nektarios leaned back and looked out to the sea.

'Absolutely, we don't want any more wasted time, Charlene. Any more wasting of opportunity. Life's too short.'

Then, after sighing deeply, his eyes brightened.

'This is a favourite moment of the day for me, Charlene, when I get the opportunity. This moment of relaxation, looking out at the backdrop of my history. My history, my parents' history, their parents' history, and so on, through many generations. Always a wonderful moment. Deeply satisfying and reassuring.'

He rolled his head round to look at Charlene.

'Not very adventurous, I guess, to stay in one place and different, I suppose, to your situation, Charlene.'

Nestling the glass on her lap, Charlene looked back at Nektarios.

'Yes. It's different. Very different. But you think, well, that's home and this is holiday. I didn't really think that this place could be a home until I came here today. You know, a real home. It seems too nice for someone to live here all the time. Much too nice.'

A fond laugh burst softly from Nektarios's mouth.

'It is nice, Charlene. More than nice. But we have all the difficulties of life here as anywhere, and of course the joy. The joy and sometimes the pain. Of course we do.'

Charlene twisted round to face Nektarios in a flurry of confusion and concern.

'I'm sorry, Nektarios. I didn't mean, you know, I didn't mean that things weren't real here and that, that things didn't happen to you like other people.'

Nektarios's voice crooned reassuringly as he turned to look at her, his face crinkling with good humour.

'No need to apologise, Charlene. Many visitors have this impression of our island. It seems so benign and looks so beautiful. They know as you do that underneath lies the beating heart of a real place with all the ups and downs of life going on, but it's not so obvious.'

His smile fading, he lay back and looked out across the bay glistening under the sinking sun.

'Of course, Katherine came here with pain and found solace. It is a place that can heal and restore. Many people have found that. After experiencing the effect of this island they usually feel the need to come back. To get their fix. But not Katherine. It became too complicated for her, unfortunately. She didn't want to feel confused. Above all, she wanted to remain true to Amy. She said that being here had helped her a lot but that it had confused her emotionally... I missed her so much, especially when we lost contact. We spoke on the phone for a while but then, well, it kind of fizzled out. Life moved on, I guess. I did try phoning her after, but she had moved house and the number didn't work. No cell phones then, of course. She never let me know her new address, so I don't know much about her life after that... until now, I hope. Now that her messenger has arrived! Unbelievably, out of the blue!'

He glanced back at Charlene, smiling conspiratorially.

'Eh, Charlene? I know that wasn't the reason you came. To fill the gap, those lost years, but I would be so grateful for any information and insights you can give me into Katherine's life in her later years. I am eager to find out as much as you can tell me.'

Charlene looked down into her glass, swirling the ice cubes around slowly and carefully as she replied.

'Well, there are things I can tell you, Nektarios. Mrs Craw... Katherine didn't ask me to tell you anything, but I can tell you things. Things about Mrs Crawford. Things she told me. Things I learned.'

Ceasing to swirl her glass, she lifted her head to look into the haze of the far distance, her brow furrowing faintly as she thought about how to convey an impression of his former lover that would fulfil his need.

'She was amazing. I had never met anyone like her. She wasn't well. She couldn't get about easily because of the arthritis. Hardly at all but she was strong and sure, you know, in her mind. She knew about things, about life, about people and she was kind, so kind...'

Her hand trembled as she raised it to her nose, while sniffing sharply to suppress the surge of emotion which threatened to destabilise her voice. After expelling her deeply held breath, she continued, her vocal clarity restored.

'So kind, even though life had not been kind to her after losing her daughter, her only daughter, her lovely Amy. Oh and her husband... David, yes, that's right, David, although she didn't talk about him. Well, she never talked about him to me anyway, only once.'

She turned away from the distant view of mainland mountains to look intently at Nektarios.

'She didn't have many friends, you know, Nektarios, hardly any, in fact maybe no real friends at the end which is very strange for someone so... so lovely. She had Maria who came every day, well, every weekday, to look after her. I did the weekends when I was there and helped her other days. She was great and they were quite close but she didn't have many friends. Her best friends were probably these guys, you know, gay guys who lived next door. They were great. She had a laugh with them and they were great to her. Very caring but very funny as well. Other people came to visit her like the vicar and some people she used to work with, but she deserved better. She really did. I mean, I should have been, well, I should have been better as well but anyway...'

Nektarios continued to gaze at her as she sipped her drink. Recognising as she lowered the glass that she was not showing any signs of being able to restore her flow, Nektarios interjected sympathetically.

'We all think like that when someone dies, Charlene. Most of us, anyway. We usually feel or wish that we'd done more, said more. It's normal. Absolutely normal.'

A grateful smile flickered on Charlene's face as she glanced at Nektario,s while remaining silent.

'I feel the same, Charlene. I wish I could have done more to make her life better. At the time, she was all I wanted. I thought we could be good together, although I'm not sure I would have been good for her in reality. The truth is I've never been that good about relationships. Not good at sustaining them, at sticking with them. It's a weakness on my part, I guess, and now… now it's too late to start getting good at it. Much too late.'

Nektarios swung his legs off the sunlounger to sit on its edge as he looked across at Charlene.

'You, however, have most of your life ahead of you, Charlene. It would be great if you could learn from the regrets of older people to… to make your life better, as good as it can be. Of course it helps to be blessed with good fortune, Charlene, and not to suffer the tragic loss that Katherine did. The kind of loss that you never recover from. That was something we had in common in a way. She lost Amy, her beautiful daughter, and I lost my parents, my beloved parents. Ironically, if that's the right word for it, when my mum and dad died, I was the age Amy was when she died. The same age. It was one of the reasons we were drawn to each other. Why we bonded… Anyway, before we get too gloomy, I'm going to get more mojito. We could do with a top-up before the sun goes down. Won't be long.'

Accepting that Charlene was not going to respond, he flashed her a rueful smile and pushed himself up onto his feet. After waiting until he had walked out of earshot, Charlene emitted a groan of frustration and, loosening the tension in her body, allowed her head to fall back against the cushion.

The inflammation of anger at her inability to form some kind of meaningful response subsided, as she became consumed by sympathy for the six-year-old boy suddenly losing his parents. She guessed that they must have been involved in some kind of fatal accident. Should she enquire? Would it be insensitive to ask or appear uncaring not to? She would have to find a way of expressing her sympathy. Mrs Crawford would have been able to do it so elegantly. The searing ache of compassion became soothed by thoughts of how Mrs Crawford would have been able to provide solace and empathy better than anyone. But, she reflected, only for that summer. She withdrew after that to deal with her own loss. Perhaps they had given each other as much as they could in that short time. Perhaps they both knew, for different reasons, that neither could commit themselves to the other, and yet they never seemed to stop longing for each other. Longing for what they could not have. The truth, Charlene supposed, that Mrs Crawford would have faced was that Nektarios was probably what her mother described as a "womaniser". That must have played a part in her decision never to see him again.

Pushing herself into a more upright position, she took a slow, contemplative sip of her drink, narrowing her eyes as the blinding orb of the sun edged below the vine.

A smile stretched across her face as a rush of triumph spread through her. She had made it. She was actually sitting on his terrace. It had been a close-run thing, too close for comfort. Her smile faded. If only she had known how important it would be. If only Mrs Crawford had asked her to find him, her lover, the man she had held in her heart for so long. He may not be fully aware of the depth of Mrs Crawford's feeling for him. Should she tell him that she had loved him for all those years when he was with all those other women? Perhaps she should. If she didn't tell him, he would never know.

Charlene finished the drink and placed the glass on the table. She then relaxed back on the lounger, submitting again with a sigh of pleasure to the soothing warmth of the setting sun.

Her thoughts turned again to Nektarios and his solitary status. Orphaned at six and on his own, even now, so many years later. How many years? Her calculations faltered as images of him formed in her mind. She mused admiringly on his good looks and the fit condition of his body. The contrast between his vigour and Mrs Crawford's frailty was very stark. It was difficult enough for her to imagine them together thirty years ago but impossible to see them as a couple in these later years. It would never have lasted. Nice though he was, she felt increasingly sure he would have left Mrs Crawford to pursue younger women, and to be the willing quarry of their pursuit. Her growing conviction of this persuaded her that she should safeguard Mrs Crawford's dignity, by not telling him about the depth of feeling she had retained for Nektarios and this island, his cherished home.

Hearing his distant footsteps, she tried to lodge this resolve in her mind as it began to spin with nervous excitement about continuing their communication. She flinched at the sound of his voice.

'Hi. Sorry I took so long.'

Twisting round in her chair, Charlene looked up at him as he appeared from behind, carrying a tray laden with the jug and some small dishes filled with olives, cheese, pistachio nuts and crisps.

'Oh, no problem. I'm fine. It's, ah… it's lovely sitting here.'

Crouching down to place the tray on the ground, Nektarios transferred the small bowls onto the table next to Charlene.

'Help yourself to snacks, Charlene. I wouldn't want you to be drinking on an empty stomach. I'll top you up anyway, of course. Here we go. I hope you like it. A feel-good drink, I would say.'

'Yes, it is. I love it. I've never had it before. I mean, I've had a mojito but not with… with…'

'Metaxa. Yes. Finest Greek brandy. Seven stars for you. Nothing but the best!'

After filling up their glasses, Nektarios placed the jug in the shade behind the sunlounger and, flipping the espadrilles off his feet, fell back onto the cushions.

'Sorry to be so gloomy by the way, Charlene, although it occurred to me, before we change the subject, that I should have explained how I lost my mum and dad. If you want to know, which I guess…'

He looked across at Charlene inquiringly and seeing her nod affirmatively while eating crisps, he resumed his forward-facing gaze and continued.

'Well. They died in a road accident. They were on my dad's motorbike. My mum was on the back. It was a wet and windy day in winter. We get weather like that in winter and, well, a car was overtaking the local bus on a blind corner and crashed straight into them. They didn't stand a chance. The car driver was OK but, well, you can imagine.'

He paused, allowing a heavy silence to open up before continuing in the same flat tone.

'It was awful, of course, although it would have been much, much worse if it hadn't been for my grandparents, both sets. They were wonderful. I was brought up by them, mainly by my dad's parents here. We lived here. In my house where I was born, where I will die, as I said, God willing. I don't like to be away from here. I'm not sure about heaven, but this is my heaven on earth where I can be close to my parents somehow. They couldn't look after me but they left me this house. My shelter. My comfort.'

He rolled over in his seat to look at Charlene who, having eaten the crisps, was watching him with a steady gaze. His voice took on a brighter, apologetic tone.

'I'm sorry, Charlene. Here I go again. Getting all gloomy and, what's the word, maudlin. Yes, that's it, maudlin. Katherine taught me that word. Something she never was. She never liked to show grief or get sentimental. Not to me, anyway. So I'm sorry for being like this with you, Charlene.'

Charlene stretched her arm out towards him in an instinctive gesture of support, retracting it as she spoke.

'No. Don't apologise. I didn't realise. Mrs Crawford never mentioned it. It must have been awful. I'm so sorry.'

'Well, it was a long time ago and I've been lucky in life otherwise, so I can't complain. I'm not surprised Katherine didn't mention it. Her loss was much more difficult to bear. Much more. Not that you should compare these things. Anyway, I would be surprised if Katherine had mentioned me much, if ever. I am flattered that she remembered me at all. I didn't really deserve to be remembered by her.'

Trickling her handful of uneaten pistachios back into the bowl, Charlene sat forward trying to recall why she had resolved not to communicate the reassurance she now felt compelled to provide.

'No… no, Nektarios. It wasn't like that. She… she never forgot you. She definitely didn't. She… she… well, she never forgot you. I know. She told me. About you. She never said your name but she thought of you… a lot. I know.'

The sombre set of his face softening, Nektarios stretched his arm towards Charlene beckoning to indicate that she should do the same. She reached out hesitantly, until her hand was close enough for Nektarios to grasp it.

'Thanks, Charlene. It's kind of you to tell me that. It's good to know that she thought of me. I realised of course that she had remembered me when I received a letter from her with the lawyer's letter. That was sad. To receive a message from someone after they've died. Sad but amazing at the same time. That she could be so strong and powerful after she'd died. That she could have that effect on me. That she could influence my life when she's no longer here. No longer here for me to respond to. To say thank you. To tell her, well, to tell her how fondly I remembered her. Suddenly it was too late. All opportunity gone.'

After releasing her hand, they both settled back and looked out into the distance. Then, breaking the silence, Nektarios continued in a softly-reflective tone.

'It was a lovely letter. Of course I wanted it to say more and I've had to resist the temptation to read between the lines. It's pointless to do that. Read between the lines. You can look at it in different ways and reach different conclusions. None of them will be right, probably. I have just had to take it at face value. A kind letter expressing fond memories and explaining the bequest. Do you know about that, Charlene? The bequest? Her gift?'

Charlene glanced over while responding.

'No. I don't. I knew she'd left you something but that's all.'

'Well, Charlene, she gave me something very special. Incredibly thoughtful and incredibly… incredibly well timed. Actually, she gave me money. Now I don't need money, and I would not accept money from anyone or at least if, let's say, I couldn't refuse it, I would pass it on to a worthy cause or something, but this was different. This wasn't really a gift, it was money to be spent on something Katherine wanted. Something she wanted but I can use and, this may sound strange to you, Charlene, but she wanted to spend the money on buying a new boat, a fishing boat. Like the one I had when she was here. The one I still have, as a matter of fact. *Thalia*. My old boat and my father's before that. Named after my mother. *Thalia*. She's lasted a long time and could do with a rest. I wouldn't have replaced her, mind you. I would have carried on using her and would have begun to worry more and more about her condition, so Katherine's bequest was… was perfect. It felt like a shining ray of light beaming into my life and banishing a dark cloud that was beginning to form. She fulfilled a need that I myself was only beginning to come to terms with. Amazing. But she was an amazing woman. My god. She really was.'

Awed by a flood of memories, Nektarios shook his head before drinking deeply from his glass and glancing at Charlene, her face fixed in concentration as she absorbed the details of his revelation.

'She wrote that she hoped I would be able and willing to fulfil her wish of having a boat in her name, travelling the waters around this island. Of course, I am more than willing. I am delighted, thrilled that she had this wish. It showed to me that this place, these waters, did mean something to her. A lot to her. She loved the sea here. Swimming in it. Did she ever mention that?'

Excited to be able to corroborate this, Charlene broke out of her spellbound state.

'Yes. Yes, she did. She said how much she loved it. Swimming. It was difficult to imagine her swimming in the sea. But now I'm here I kind of get it. How she was different then. How she could swim then.'

'My god she could swim all right, Charlene. Strongly, gracefully, elegantly. She was elegant in everything she did and she loved the water. Being in it. She loved the idea that it connected everything across the planet. Water. It gave her a sense of freedom. A sense of release. Especially swimming naked. She always swam naked from her private spot on the rocks. Just down there below us. Over there. She loved it on her own in the water. Naked in the water. Like a nymph. A beautiful nymph. I guess you might find that hard to imagine, Charlene. Katherine swimming naked. For long periods. Swimming and diving down, twisting and tumbling.'

Looking away from Nektarios's enquiring gaze, Charlene responded with subdued uncertainty.

'No. She didn't really mention that bit. Not really. Well, never to me, anyway, and not to Maria I don't think. It is hard to imagine. Her being like that when, when, well, you know, she had to use a wheelchair most of the time.'

Frowning as he turned away from looking at her, Nektarios's voice trembled.

'Well, that's the bit that's difficult for me to accept. Katherine losing her mobility, her effortless grace, her elegant physicality. That's something I find difficult to imagine. She was so athletic and so... so much fun despite the tragedy she had to deal with. You wouldn't believe how much fun we had. Not all the time, of course, but a lot. So much fun.'

Suddenly swinging his legs off the sunlounger, Nektarios stood up and shoved his feet into the espadrilles.

'Excuse me, Charlene, but I need to go to the toilet or the loo as Katherine used to say. One effect of ageing, I can't deny. When you need to go, you need to go. And a bit more often than you used to. Or at least it seems that way. Anyway, I won't be long.'

Suddenly feeling tired, Charlene rolled her head to one side and closed her eyes as the sound of Nektarios's scuffed footsteps receded into the distance.

Her thoughts about catching up with the girls drifted off, her mind too tired to dwell on them. She felt the weight of drowsiness descend.

"*Ever and ever, forever and ever*
You'll be the one…"

Charlene opened her eyes, instantly awakening. She sat up electrified by the music, this song which connected two situations in a way she did not understand but guessed must be significant. She scanned her surroundings eagerly until she had identified the speakers fixed discreetly to the top of pergola posts. Filling up with excitement as the music and singing swelled expansively into the space around her and beyond, she stood up and turned towards the house. Seeing Nektarios approach with a joyful smile stretched across his face, Charlene called out to him, her voice ringing with the zeal of disclosure.

'Nektarios, this is amazing. This music. You'll never believe it, but…'

She stopped speaking as Nektarios grasped her hand and, wrapping his other arm around her waist, swirled her around and swept her across the terrace in extravagant revolutions. Both now laughing in dizzy hysteria as they spun around, at times with an unsteadiness which filled Charlene with thrilling alarm, she suspended her attempts to tell Nektarios about the connection until, sensing that he was slowing down, she blurted the beginnings of her story.

'Nektarios. This music! You'll never believe it. I've heard it before…'

Enveloping her in an embrace as they slowed to a stop, Nektarios interrupted.

'You know it?! But it was a hit a long time ago. When Katherine was here. This was our song. For dancing to. For having fun. Just like now...'

Spreading the palms of her hand against his chest Charlene pushed against him, looking up at him eagerly as she broke the embrace.

'I know, Nektarios. That's what I'm trying to tell you. I know or at least I knew it meant something. It was, it was in her CD player when I was in her apartment. The first time, the first time after she died, I went to her apartment. Maria was there but she went out and I was in the front room and saw this CD in the player and I switched it on and played it. I danced to it on my own. I mean, I didn't realise that it was your song but I thought it must be special... isn't that amazing? You know she must have been listening to it when, well, not long before... you know...'

Nektarios listened, gazing in wonder at Charlene's face glowing in the amber rays of the sinking sun. Taking his cue from her loss of momentum, he responded hesitantly in a hushed tone as he assimilated the significance of this revelation.

'My god. That is amazing. It's hard to believe. Wonderful but... but hard to believe that she would listen to this music. To Demis Roussos after all these years. This music which made us laugh but also moved us in a way although we didn't admit it. Pop music. Not serious music but great music. Great singing. And the words, we never really mentioned the words. We never really talked about their significance but secretly, secretly I felt they held a truth for me at the time but I never imagined they would mean anything to Katherine, not about us. And yet, and yet she listened to it, even at the end of her life... forever and ever... anyway, we shall never really know what it meant to her but it's nice to know that much, very nice, so thank you, Charlene. Thank you very much.'

Her eyes gleaming with excitement, Charlene released another wave of words.

'But, Nektarios, imagine that. That shows you, doesn't it? How much it meant to her. Greece, being here. Being here with you. It shows that... that she was thinking of you. I mean, she must have, well, she must have loved you. Mustn't she? She must have wished it... it could have worked out differently. That it hadn't... she hadn't let it end like that. Not keeping in touch. She must have wished it could have been different. That she could have come back here. Here, to this place. My god. This place, Nektarios. Don't you think? That proves it. Her listening to that CD. That proves what it meant to her. It must do... don't you think? My god, Nektarios. I'm so glad I came to see you. I didn't really, well, I didn't realise it would be so... so important.'

Smiling wistfully, Nektarios stepped forward to wrap his arms around her in a grateful embrace. Easing his hold on her as the music ended, he inhaled a jagged sigh and stepped back to look down at her upturned face.

'I am glad you came, Charlene. Very glad. To talk about Katherine. To remember her and to show you this place. This place that she loved... Come on. You haven't seen the garden. Let's walk around it before the sun goes down. Katherine loved it. She spent a lot of time in it. Sitting, reading and, well, anyway, come on. Let me show you.'

Taking her hand, he smiled brightly at her as they walked off the terrace and down the stepped path.

Descending to the level of the first terrace, he released her hand and, stepping off the paved pathway, led her through the trees and past the plants trailing down the stone wall. Identifying the different species as they walked, he stopped occasionally to invite her to smell a flower or to admire clusters of nuts or ripening fruit. Reaching the end of the terrace at the fenced boundary, he held her hand to negotiate the steps down to the next level. And so they progressed, winding down through the terraces, looking around them and outwards through the trees at the sun now seeming to increase its speed of descent towards the sharpening division between sea and sky. Halfway down they stopped in a clearing paved roughly with flat stones. A weathered wooden bench stood at the rear against the stone wall.

'This was a favourite spot for Katherine. She spent a lot of time here in the late afternoon. It gets the sun from after lunch to sunset. It's a nice spot. Come on, let's sit here and watch the sun go down. You'll feel the warmth radiating from the wall. Nice on cool evenings. We don't need it today, I guess.'

Responding to his gesture, Charlene walked to the bench, tugging at the hem of her shorts as she sat down. Nektarios lowered himself onto the other end of the bench, stretching his arm along the backrest as he settled.

'I would often find her here if I came back from work early. She used to bring cushions and towels down for lying on the ground or sometimes she would be sitting on the bench. Occasionally she would shower herself using that hose. The water coming out of that tap is warm, well, when the sun shines. In summer it gets very warm. After she went swimming she would usually stop here for a while. Rinse herself down and enjoy the late afternoon sun. Naked, of course. She liked to be naked. Not me, though. I wasn't comfortable being outside without any clothes on except when we, well… never mind. Anyway, it's very private here. We can see out but no one can see in unless they were in a boat… with binoculars. Not that Katherine would have been worried about that. She was relaxed about nudity. She wasn't the slightest bit vain or a show-off, although she did have a beautiful body. A body to be proud of… Those were wonderful times, Charlene. Memories to be cherished. Just one summer but such a special summer. Short but so significant. Brief but intense. In a good way. Intense in a very good way. Powerful. And when it ended. Well, that was hard but it had to end. It had to. It had to end just as the day has to end. Just like this day. With the setting of the sun.'

Mesmerised by the spectacle playing out before them, they sat rendered into a silence they knew could only be broken when the sun had cut into the dark sea and disappeared, leaving the fiery afterglow to fade against the night sky.

'There we go, Charlene. She's served us for another day. Gone to shine on other parts of the world. Of course we can carry on without her. Come on. Let's go back up while we've still got some light. I'll make you something to eat. It's about time we had something to eat. Don't you think?'

Sitting upright, Charlene looked sideways at Nektarios.

'Well, I don't know. I need to catch up with the girls. Perhaps I should be going now. They'll probably be out already. They'll be wondering where I am.'

Nektarios leaned forward resting his elbows on his knees and turning his head to engage her eye to eye.

'It would be a shame if you left now, Charlene. I mean, you should go if you feel you really need to, but it would be better if you could stay longer. Do you think your friends would mind? What do you think?'

A diffident smile tweaked at the corners of her mouth, as she cast her eyes downwards before looking away.

'Well, I guess. For a while. I'll text them to let them know. To stop them worrying. I mean, they'll be… they'll be disappointed with it being our last night and all, but anyway they'll understand, I guess. The only thing is my phone's in my bag so…'

She looked round abruptly as Nektarios stood up and, turning around with a flourish, positioned himself in front of her with each hand offered out for her to grasp. After a slight hesitation, she held onto his hands and allowed herself to be pulled to her feet.

'Come on then. Let's go back up. I'll make something to eat. It gets dark quickly and the moon won't appear until later.'

Keeping hold of her hand he pulled her gently towards the far end of the terrace.

'The terrace below is easier. Not so many trees. There are steps down to it at the end. Follow me.'

Releasing her hand, he smiled at her reassuringly before walking off slowly. After a few steps, he looked back to check that she was making safe progress as the seaward silhouettes darkened against the glowing sky.

'It'll be easier when we get down to that level, and the steps up to the house will be fine. The lights come on automatically when it gets dark.'

Charlene replied while looking down at the ground as she followed carefully behind.

'It's OK, Nektarios. I can still see everything quite well… it is amazing though. How quickly it gets dark.'

'Well, I guess. I suppose I would be amazed how slowly it gets dark where you live. It must be nice having long periods of twilight. I don't remember it being like that in Maine, you know, where Constantinos lives in the States, although we did see nice sunsets. Not over the sea, though. Not on the east coast. I'm lucky that way, living on this side of the island. But, anyway, look, we're at the steps. Let me help you down.'

Turning round, Nektarios looked back at Charlene, her form now smudging in the greyscales of the gloom, and reached out to grasp her hand as he began to descend the steep steps in a sideways motion. He proceeded slowly with Charlene following tentatively one step behind. Nearing the bottom, having lowered his foot with deliberate care to feel the next step, his espadrille slipped heavily off the crumbling front edge. Losing balance he tried to break his fall with his free arm while keeping the other held high in an attempt not to drag Charlene with him. Seeing that she had managed to remain upright he released his grip and, grunting with effort, pushed himself up into a standing position on the step below as she spoke.

'Oh my god, Nektarios, are you OK?'

'Yes. Yes. I'm fine. Sorry about that. I'm supposed to stop you from falling and then I go and do it myself.'

'Well, it is getting difficult to see now. Especially here. It seems darker here at this end.'

Nektarios wiped his hands together to brush off the dirt, and then reached down to pull his trousers up and inspect his shins.

'I guess the tree canopy is denser here but it'll be better down there. Much easier. We'll get a clear walk through to the path and then it's plain sailing from there.'

Skirting tentatively around him as he peered at the scrapes on his leg, Charlene continued her descent.

'Well, as long as you're all right. Aaaaah! Oh shit!'

Slipping on the same crumbled step, Charlene lost her balance and stumbled down the final few steps in an ungainly rush.

'Charlene! My god! Are you all right?'

Regaining her poise as she steadied herself, Charlene emitted a burst of laughter which seemed to resonate both with relief and nervous hysteria.

'Yes… yes, I think I'm OK.'

Stepping forward, she groaned as she felt a stab of pain in her ankle.

'Oh no. Oh f… f… flipping hell. Here we go. I think I've done it again. I think I've sprained my ankle.'

Nektarios spoke firmly as he moved to her side.

'Right. Wait there. Don't move… .OK, it's this one, is it? Your right ankle?'

Charlene placed her hand on his shoulder as he leaned over to look at her ankle.

'Yes. That's it. I did it before. I don't know. It should be OK by now. It should be stronger. Oh God. This is all I need. Oh well…'

'Never mind. I'll help you back up and then we can get an ice pack on it. Hopefully it won't be too bad. Come on. Let's go. Nice and slow. I'll get my arm around here, and you get yours around me and hang on to my shoulder. Really, you know, use me. I can take your weight no problem. OK.'

With his arm wrapped around her waist and her arm stretched across his back to grip his shoulder, they shuffled across the terrace to the illuminated pathway. After pausing briefly to readjust their coupling, they negotiated their way up the steps and across the platforms.

'How are you doing? Is it OK?'

The tension in her body and the exertion of hobbling and hopping up the steep pathway, caused her voice to tighten.

'Yes, it's… it's not too bad. It's hard work but… but I don't think it's so painful now.'

'Well that's good, although I do feel bad about it. I shouldn't have been taking you down there.'

'It's… it's no problem. It's happened before. I… I think it must be… must be weak… the ankle. And I haven't been doing… much exercise recently.'

'Well, hopefully it won't be too bad. We'll get an ice pack on it in a minute. That should help. Once we've got you settled down I'll make something to eat. I've got chicken pieces which I could roast with rosemary and garlic, and then we could have roast vegetables with it or this potato dish I do, in the oven with yoghurt. A bit like dauphinoise, you know?'

Reaching the top terrace and finding herself able to bear weight on her ankle, Charlene relaxed her posture as they headed back to the sunloungers. Her voice brightened with optimism that the injury was less serious than she feared.

'That sounds great, Nektarios. I like chicken and, you know what, Nektarios, my ankle doesn't feel so bad now.'

'Hey. That's great. But let's not take any chances. Easy does it.'

Gently increasing his grip to command her attention, Nektarios slowed to a stop and looked into her eyes as she gazed up at him in quizzical anticipation. He spoke urgently in a hushed tone.

'Charlene. Are you OK to stand for a minute?'

Her eyes widened in wonder and she whispered 'Yes'.

'OK. Let's turn round. I want to show you how still it is. I've just noticed it. It's very rare for it to be like this. Very rare. It's kind of ethereal. Like everything's stopped except you and me. Do you see? Do you feel it?'

Releasing their hold on each other, they stood side by side each becoming aware of their breathing and heartbeat with heightened awareness, as they absorbed the silence and looked out at the still nightscape. There was no discernable movement in their field of vision. The constant, unfaltering glow of the town lights reflected perfectly without distortion on the flat, calm sea. The trees in the foreground appeared drawn in statuesque outline against the deep lustre of the sky.

Nektarios turned to speak, his quiet voice imbued with awe.

'This is rare. For it to get so still. As though time has stopped. Do you get the feeling that we are the only living beings left?'

Charlene diverted her enraptured gaze to look up at him.

'Yes. Yes, I do. Oh wow! Yes, I do, Nektarios. It's so strange.'

A frisson of shared excitement flaring inside him, Nektarios continued to talk quietly but with eager intensity.

'It happened the last time a few months ago, except I was on my own. It was so unusual and the effect of it was… was so powerful and it was just before I received, Katherine's letter. It was almost as though it was, you know, what's the word… portentous. Yes, that's it and… and I even thought of her at the time. She came strongly to mind for some reason. So strange. Like now. Look, there's still nothing moving anywhere. It's… Ow! What the hell!'

Bending over to one side, Nektarios looked down at the black cat dragging itself along his legs while looking up and miaowing plaintively.

'Kitty Kat! My god! What a fright! What's up with you, Kitty Kat?'

Nektarios laughed as he looked back at Charlene.

'Well, Charlene, it looks like we are not the only living things around. Kitty Kat's come to remind us of her existence and to tell us she's hungry, I guess. She's an unusual cat but I've grown very fond of her. She's been with me for a while now. A few months. She adopted me. Didn't you?'

Nektarios crouched down to stroke the cat as she continued to slink sinuously around him, her tail held high.

'She's a real character and she chased all the cicadas off the vine. Katherine found them too noisy under the vine. They do get very loud. Anyway, they've all been chased off to other parts of the garden. Katherine would have loved that the terrace is quieter now. I actually call her Kat, you know, as a name, short for Katherine.'

Looking up round-eyed at Nektarios, the cat miaowed softly and walked off to lie down and clean itself.

Nektarios and Charlene glanced at each other smilingly as he stood up.

'Katherine liked the peace and quiet. You'd think she might want the distraction of other people, or at least I thought she would, but she liked her own company. On her own in nature. She found solace in that. She would have marvelled at this. The stillness of it. How surreal it is… how kind of… spiritually surreal. How it makes you consider your existence. That's what I think of, anyway. My existence. My place in the scheme of things. Do you see what I mean? It grounds me and uplifts me at the same time. I hope that makes sense to you, Charlene.'

Charlene nudged herself against Nektarios who responded by embracing her. She rested her head briefly against his chest before raising it to look out across the bay.

'It does, Nektarios. Yes, it does. And it's like time is standing still. It's amazing.'

Nektarios gently increased the grip of his embrace.

'That's it, Charlene. It's like time is standing still. Sometimes I wish it would stand still or even that we could reverse it. It's much too quick. The progress of time. Unfairly fast but, well, it just keeps going. It keeps marching on consigning good times, bad times, the whole pageant of time to history, sometimes with consequences, sometimes just with memories. But, hey! Too much talk, eh? I'll need to start concentrating on the here and now like making you comfortable and feeding you. Eh, Charlene? You and the cat.'

Nektarios looked back at the cat now lying on its side, its body relaxed but its head alert as it looked out into the distance.

'Look. She's sensed the stillness. Look.'

Charlene placed her hand on his chest as she leaned across to look at the cat.

'Yes. That's amazing. She's noticed it. Noticed how strange it is.'

Exchanging intimate smiles, Charlene pulled back into his gentle hold. Each knowing that they would move away in a moment but each also wishing to prolong the experience of being immersed in absolute tranquillity, they stood together in silence. Then, feeling a sudden freshness flutter in their faces, they glanced at each other before looking around as a bustling, pine-scented breeze blew in through the trees and rustled the vine behind them.

Her eyes gleaming with wonder, Charlene looked up at Nektarios as he spoke.

'Well. That's it I guess, Charlene. New life breathed into our world. Time to go. Kitty Kat certainly thinks so. Come on, let's get you settled.'

Lowering his arm into a more supportive position, Nektarios waited until Charlene had stretched across his back to grasp his shoulder, before turning around to follow the cat across the terrace.

'How's the ankle?'

'It doesn't feel too bad, thanks. I don't think it's as bad as I thought.'

'That's good. I could feel that you aren't needing so much support. You're moving a bit more freely.'

'Yes. Thank God. I was worried about getting home with a bad ankle.'

Charlene grunted quietly as Nektarios helped her to settle on the sunlounger. Releasing her arm, she lifted her legs onto the bed and stretched them out as she reclined with a grateful release of tension.

'Well, we'll do what we can to make it as good as we can. First off, I'll go and get an ice pack and, I think we should get some arnica on it to minimise any bruising. Have you used arnica before? Is it used in the UK?'

'Yes. I think so. Yes, I used it before. Maria put some on... you know, Mrs Crawford's carer. I'm sure that's what it was. When I sprained my ankle before. Yes, that's right. It was good. It worked, I think.'

'Good. Well, we can try it again. But really the best thing you can do is rest it just now. So just relax. I'll be back in a minute.'

The cat circled around Nektarios in a high-tailed, agitated canter as he moved away, all the time looking up at him with a green-eyed gaze.

'Hey, what's got into you, Kitty Kat? I'll feed you in a minute. Hey! Where are you going?'

Diverting from the direct route back into the house, Nektarios followed the cat around the side of the building towards the path leading down from the upper gate. He shouted back to Charlene before disappearing from view.

'Won't be long. Kitty Kat's taking me on a detour.'

Charlene closed her eyes and shivered as her body adjusted to the lower temperature of nightfall.

She recalled the previous time she had sprained her ankle, and how that had started the experiences which had led to her sitting here now. Life had become so different for her. She could not have envisaged ending up in this situation with this man, this kind man, this handsome man, this strong man, this man who smelled so nice. A glowing sense of appreciation flared within her as she became filled with an understanding of why Mrs Crawford had fallen in love with him.

The attributes which made him so attractive still shone brightly. It seemed that his enjoyment of life had continued unabated, while Mrs Crawford's strength and vibrancy had faded until life itself slipped away from her. As Nektarios had said, it was not fair that the effects of growing older were so cruel on some people.

Blanking out this distressing thought, Charlene began to feel uplifted by the surging recognition that she herself should feel fortunate to be alive. Lucky to be alive and lucky that fate had brought her here when she had so nearly left the island without finding Nektarios. So near to returning home without ever knowing about all of this.

Shivering in a confusion of self-reproachment and relief, she sat forward abruptly, galvanised by the need to let Cynthia and Suzy know about her situation and how it was likely to unfold.

She grabbed her phone from her bag but, pausing to reflect on where her friends would be at this stage of the evening, she became overwhelmed by a compulsion to send a message to Maria instead. A sense of excitement fizzed inside her as she imagined Maria's amazement and delight on reading that she had found Nektarios.

Hunching over her phone, she frowned as she thought through how to communicate her message. After a process of entering words, deleting them and rephrasing, she finally sat back to review the finished message.

Hi. Found Mrs Cs man! It wasnt him at the funeral! He sent his cousin. Will explain when I see you. At his house now. Fab place and he is cool. They wd have been great together. Shame it didnt work out. Hope ur well. Take care. Charlene xox

Hearing the distant scuff of his espadrilles, Charlene pressed the "send" button and shoved the phone back into her bag. She then lay back and looked across the bay in awe that she had occupied this position from when the sea below had been active under the afternoon sun until now, when the veil of darkness was bringing the day to a peaceful end. The ferry boat coming into view, its shadowy form illuminated by lights and glowing windows, filled her with a sense of coming home.

Turning her thoughts again to Cynthia and Suzy, she imagined the alcohol-fuelled activity and noise of Island Nights. She reluctantly conceded that she would find it difficult to raise the enthusiasm and energy to participate in their last-night revels. It would also be too difficult to join in with an injured ankle. Staying here longer was definitely the sensible option. It would be good, anyway, to find out more about Nektarios and to drink more mojito.

Hearing him return from behind, she hoped that he would be carrying the jug of mojito with him or a freshly filled glass.

'Hi, Charlene. Sorry about the wait but I think it'll be worth it. Kitty Kat went running off so I followed her round to the lemon tree, you know, the one Katherine planted. Well, she started stretching up the trunk and digging her claws into the bark, you know, the way cats do, when I remembered that lemons have very effective anti-inflammatory properties. So I picked a couple. You grate the skin and rub it in. But first, let's apply this ice pack. Oh and I brought some more mojito. You might not feel like drinking but, well, it's here if you do. Would you like some... now or later maybe?'

Charlene looked up as Nektarios appeared alongside and lowered the tray onto the ground next to her.

'Well. That sounds nice, Nektarios. Thanks.'

'What, you mean the lemons or, or...'

'No, I meant the drink, although... although the lemons sound great too, and the ice pack.'

After carefully pushing Charlene's flip flops to one side with his foot, Nektarios placed a cushion from another chair on the ground and knelt down. Amusement twitched at the corners of his mouth as he handed her the drink.

'Quite right, Charlene. You always get the anaesthetic first. Cheers! I'll make more later.'

Then, with measured movements and a tender touch, Nektarios lifted Charlene's leg gently into a more suitable position and, after wrapping a flannel cloth around her ankle, pressed the ice pack into position. He then transferred his attention to grating the lemon skin, while providing Charlene with a softly spoken commentary.

'Luckily your ankle isn't too swollen. I really should have got you settled and got it on sooner, however I think we've got away with it. It doesn't look too bad and I'll rub this lemon skin into your ankle, wrap it with a bandage and then put the ice pack back on, oh, and I guess I should rub some arnica in first. Yes, that's right. A triple treatment, that should do the trick. Right, that should be enough of Katherine's healing lemons. Funny the way the cat led me to the tree. Never come across a cat quite like her. Right, well, here we go.'

Nektarios looked up at Charlene, his eyes gleaming hopefully.

'How are you feeling? OK? Not too uncomfortable?'

Charlene placed her glass on the table beside her as she replied.

'No. I feel good, well, apart from the ankle which isn't too bad, I feel great, thanks.'

'Good. Well, this treatment should make a difference, although you shouldn't use the ankle for a while just to be sure. You need to relax. Let me look after you for a while. OK?'

Charlene closed her eyes as she succumbed again to the hypnotic effect of his voice. Its soothing tone, along with the sensation of her ankle being dried gently with a fresh towel, drained all the tension from her body leaving it limp and her mind pleasurably numb. She exhaled a deep sigh of satisfaction before whispering her response.

'Yes, Nektarios. I can do that. No problem.'

Nektarios proceeded to apply the arnica, his hands sweeping over and around the contours of her ankle to ensure complete coverage. He then pressed the grated lemon against her skin, massaging it in with gentle strokes.

Breathing in the fresh smell of lemon, her mind closed down to everything but the intoxicating sensation of his tingling touch.

After a few minutes, he wiped off the residue and wrapped a bandage securely around her ankle before replacing the ice pack in position. His low-pitched voice insinuated itself murmuringly into her consciousness, providing sufficient stimulus for her to open her reluctant eyelids with a slow flutter.

'You stay nice and relaxed, Charlene. Like I said, your ankle doesn't look too bad. You should really avoid using it too much, though. In fact, I don't think it would be good to go out with your friends tonight. That might not be wise especially when you're travelling tomorrow.'

Nektarios finished tidying up and leaned towards Charlene, his hands resting on his thighs.

'In fact, Charlene, you should stay here tonight. That would be the best thing, wouldn't it? I've got a nice guest bedroom and everything you would need more or less, except, I guess, except a change of clothes although I've got T-shirts. You could wear one at night and anything you wash would be dry in the morning. That way we don't need to worry about getting you back and we can just relax, eat and drink and carry on talking and… and you'd get to meet Constantinos! What do you think, Charlene? Would your friends understand?'

Her eyes widening, Charlene hesitated before stumbling into her response.

'Well… I don't know… I'm not sure… not sure what… well, maybe… it might, ah, it might…'

Then, hearing a message being received on her phone, she sat forward and reached down to grab her bag.

'Oh, sorry, excuse me. Do you mind if… it's just, well, that'll be from one of the girls. I'd better… I'd better…'

Lifting the phone out of her bag she frowned before her face lit up with delight as she read the message.

Wow! Well done Charlene! Can't wait to hear all about it. Find out as much as you can! I am very well. Everything is going well. Love. Maria xxx

A smile bursting brightly across her face, Charlene looked up at Nektarios.

'Yes, Nektarios. That would be great. Thanks very much. We worked out we could wait until the ferry at eight o'clock, you know, at night so there's no rush. I'll just, ah, I'd better just reply and let them know.'

Nektarios beamed with delight as he sat up.

'Fantastic! Well, I'll leave you to get in touch with your friends. I'll go and get the food ready, oh, and make more mojito. I don't need to worry about riding my bike now.'

Shifting into a crouched position, Nektarios took hold of the tray and rose to his feet.

'I want to find out about you, Charlene. I haven't found out anything yet. You are an intriguing mystery. Yes, I want to find out much more about the delightful Charlene, or at least as much as you are prepared to divulge. No pressure, I promise. Actually, there's nothing wrong with being enigmatic. It's a very tantalising quality. Especially in a beautiful woman such as yourself.'

He broke eye contact, to range his gaze down her outstretched body.

'Actually, Charlene, you have a very similar kind of beauty to Katherine. Physical beauty. You probably won't be aware of it but it's striking. Very striking. Different facially but your physicality is very similar. Long limbed elegance. Athletic in a very feminine way and, well, anyway, enough for now, I'll go and get food on the go. I won't be long. You just sit back and relax.'

Charlene rolled over to watch Nektarios walk away, her face straining with the agony of confused emotions. The words she would like to have spoken ran through her head.

'Oh my god. I don't want to sit back and relax. How can I? You've done something to me. It's crazy. It's not right but it feels so good…and so bad… Oh my god.'

She flopped back in the lounger, while emitting a faint howl of frustration.

Chapter 43

A slow, sensual wrestle of hot, slippery flesh and limbs entwining and straddling, as they rolled and stretched over every part of the expansive bed. Her mind consumed by ecstasy, she alternated between closing her eyes to relish the sensations and opening them to see the intimate contacts which were stimulating her to reach these dizzying heights of pleasure.

Combing his hands roughly through her wild hair, he grasped the back of her head to command face-to-face connection. She looked into his urgent, desire-crazed stare.

Emerging from her dream, she replayed her imaginings, her body gripped with a physical yearning for it all to happen in reality. It had been too long, much too long since she had been consumed by sexual passion.

Awakening fully, she opened her eyes wide and arched her back, pulling her feet up the bed to raise her knees and bend her legs. She then extended her arms above her head and stretched her body. Keeping her back arched, she pulled the T-shirt up to expose her body to the turbulent downdraught from the ceiling-mounted fan.

She felt uncomfortably hot. So hot she could not imagine being able to fall asleep again. She knew it was not just the heat that would keep her awake. It was also the excitement. The excitement of Nektarios's son turning out to be the coolest guy she had seen at Island Nights. The sexiest guy. Her confused craving for the attentions of his father had faded when he appeared. Her initial excitement had turned into a burning desire with his revelation that she had captured his attention when he saw her on the dance floor.

After pulling the T-shirt off, she tossed it onto the far side of the bed and caressed the contours of her body with increasing intensity. She started writhing as the sensations began to consume her and then, pressing her hands into the mattress, she stopped and lay still. Releasing herself to the temptation of going further would not be right with the door wide open, the door she had left wide open to possibilities which had not come about.

Resolving to try and relax, she pulled the cotton sheet over her body and wriggled into the soft mattress. Then, closing her eyes, she attempted to still her racing thoughts and achieve a state of restfulness.

After a short time lying prone, she flickered her eyes open and, at the same time as rising into an upright position, swung her legs off the bed. She sat on the edge for a few seconds before standing up and walking dreamily towards the door. Grasping a silk gown draped over the back of the chair, she slipped her arms into the sleeves and wrapped it round her body, tying a knot in the sash to secure it around her waist. She then walked across the hallway, through the sitting room, over the threshold of the open French windows and onto the terrace. She flexed her feet appreciatively on the surface of the terracotta tiles, still warm from the sunshine absorbed over the course of the day. Awed by the transformed appearance of the terrace under strong moonlight, she surveyed every part of it before moving to sit down on the same sunlounger she had occupied earlier. Lying back she looked through the tracery of vine branches and leaves at the star-crammed sky.

A frisson of excitement fizzed up from deep within her, stimulating an involuntary shiver through her body and galvanising her mind with a revelatory sense of comprehension. She reached a fuller understanding in that moment of what she had come close to grasping earlier. That sense of connection to nature Nektarios had talked about. That connection which Mrs Crawford had felt so strongly. That sense of being an intrinsic part of it. A very small part. Insignificantly small on this earth, even more so in relation to the vastness above her and all those stars, many more than she had ever seen. Many more than she knew existed. It was so big. Too big to contemplate. She needed to shift her focus. Turn her attention to the beauty of this place. This place which made the everyday concerns of home seem so remote and meaningless.

She sat forward, drawing her legs up and hugging them against her chest, as she looked out through the moon-silvered trees at the glinting ripples on the quiet sea.

She mused on the probability that Mrs Crawford would have occupied the same position all those years ago, looking out on a similar night at the same view. Charlene could not see anything which looked as though it would have changed much. Perhaps some of the trees, like her lemon tree, would have grown bigger, taller, but otherwise she was sure everything would look familiar and recognisable to her if she were here now. But she was not here. She could never return to this place which meant so much to her. That opportunity had gone. She had closed it down a long time ago and it was now fully and finally cut off by death.

It seemed important to Charlene that she was here now. A link between Nektarios and Mrs Crawford. Someone who could bring some comfort to Nektarios, some peace of mind, a sense of closure. Why hadn't Mrs Crawford insisted that she come?

Then, suddenly becoming aware of movement under the lounger, she gripped her legs tighter and cast apprehensive glances to each side. She exhaled a sigh of relief and stretched out her legs as the cat moved into view, slow-paced and low slung, its head turned back to look up at her with an implacable gaze. She spoke to it in a soft, lilting whisper.

'Hello, Kitty Kat. Can you not sleep either?... Eh? I'm not surprised. I'm wide awake too.'

After rubbing itself against the leg of the lounger, the cat moved off a short distance to lie down, its body forming a relaxed curve while it looked at Charlene with still intensity.

'What's up, Kitty Kat? Why are you looking at me? Eh?'

The cat rose, walked some way towards Charlene, before turning sleekly to trot off in the opposite direction until reaching a further point where it stood, looking back expectantly.

Charlene swivelled round, sweeping her legs off the lounger and planting her feet on the tiles.

'Strange cat, aren't you? There's something about you, though. Not like cats at home. You're a character. A smart cat.'

She rose to her feet and followed the cat as it danced off across the terrace and down the pathway in a high-tailed gambol.

'Where are you going, Kitty Kat? Taking me for a walk, are you?'

Charlene looked around dreamily, awed by her presence in this place and by her inexplicable sense of belonging. Being here thrilled her profoundly and she knew that it had already become a significant place in her life. Its appearance had changed so much since her arrival and now, in the ethereal moonlight, it transcended any scene within her experience.

She navigated the path with slow detachment while the cat weaved an erratic trail, bounding forward and taking off at tangents before returning to Charlene's feet.

Having descended to the level where she and Nektarios had joined the path on their laboured return to the house earlier, she knelt down to greet the cat as it returned from a foray ahead. She tickled it under its chin and then stroked its side while it pressed its purring body against her leg.

'Well, you're lively tonight, aren't you, Kitty Kat? And friendly. I'm surprised to get so much attention from you. You like me, do you? Well, that's nice but I think we should go back up now. Eh, Kitty Kat? We've gone far enough, don't you think?'

Charlene stood up and turned around carefully while the cat disengaged from its self-absorbed preening and walked off the pathway onto the adjoining terrace. Charlene continued to look back at the cat as she took one step towards the house.

'Come on, Kitty Kat. This way. Come on. It's time to go back up. That's a good cat. Come on.'

Her entreaty having had no effect, Charlene stepped towards the cat, beckoning her to follow.

'Come on, time to go. Come on.'

The cat looked up at Charlene in open-eyed defiance before twisting round and darting off along the terrace. Raising her voice, Charlene called after the cat as it raced away along the terrace.

'Oi, Kitty Kat. Where are you going? We can't go along there. Not now, Kitty Kat.'

After the cat had disappeared from view, she lingered briefly before stepping off the pathway onto the scrunchy layer of dried needles covering the dusty earth. Stooping warily, Charlene walked between the trees, looking out for low branches. Seeing that the trees were thinning out, she relaxed and looked in front of her. The clearing ahead was instantly recognisable.

Charlene looked around as she moved into Mrs Crawford's favourite part of the garden, her gaze fixing on the cat sitting Sphinx-like while staring out over the lustrous sea. She walked towards it, speaking softly again.

'There you are, you crazy cat. Well, maybe not so crazy. You've brought me to Mrs C's special place. It's amazing in this moonlight. Amazing. I don't know why I don't... don't... well, don't find it a bit freaky but I don't. It's cool. Magical.'

She crouched down and stroked the cat's back.

'We can't stay long, OK? Just for a while. I'm going to sit on the bench. Feel the warmth of the wall though, my god, it's still warm out here. Nicer than inside though. Much nicer.'

Charlene rose to her feet and, lifting her arms up and behind her head, stretched her body before moving towards the bench in a lazy sway.

Swirling around as she reached it, she sat down, clasping her hands behind her head. After a few moments of rest, she stood up, untied the sash around her waist and shimmied the gown off her shoulders and down her body before laying it along the length of the bench. Having positioned it to her satisfaction, she smoothed her hands down her waist and over her hips and spun round slowly. Looking out across the water to the night shades of the mainland, she pushed her fingers up through her hair and stretched her body again. She then reversed back and lowered herself to stretch out on top of the gown, her shoulders resting against the armrest.

Closing her eyes, she dropped her head back, her hair hanging down, raggedly unbrushed. Arching her back and bending her legs, she began a sensual exploration of her upper body until, hearing a man's voice, she froze into sculpural rigidity.

Remaining absolutely still, she strained to listen through the crackling blood-rush in her ears.

'Charlene? Are you there? Charlene?'

Looking back towards the pathway, she called out her reply while sweeping round and standing up.

'Yes. I'm here. At... at the bench.'

Her voice faded as she saw Constantinos appear. She

whipped the gown off the bench and put it on rapidly before continuing to speak.

'Ah, I, ah, was feeling restless. Restless and… and hot so I went outside and the cat, Kitty Kat, came up to me and then started going down the path so I followed her here and then I thought, well, I'd just lie down here and… and cool down a bit. It's nice here, really nice.'

After pulling the gown flaps tightly around her and tying the sash, Charlene looked sideways at Constantinos as he spoke while facing out to sea.

'Well, I'm glad I found you. Sorry to disturb you but I was worried. I went to the bathroom and noticed your door was open and you weren't in the room and then, well, I checked around the house and started to look around the garden. I was kind of panicking but anyway, I've found you so all's well that ends well and, hey, I guess your ankle's not so bad now.'

'Oh my god. I hadn't even thought about it. That's amazing. It's completely fine. Not sore at all!'

Constantinos turned to look at her, smiling benignly as she approached.

'That's good. I guess my dad did a good job with his lemons and everything.'

He turned back to look across the bay, as Charlene replied while moving alongside him.

'He did. A great job. So gentle. He made it feel better straight away. Like magic.'

His face glowing with pride and pleasure in her appreciation of his father, he glanced down at her.

'Yeah. He's a great guy and a great father. I just wish I could spend more time with him here in this amazing place.'

'It is amazing. It's like the most beautiful place I've ever seen.'

'Yeah, well, it's very special to me of course and, wow, on a night like this it's so beautiful. Magical. It's got a kind of unreal quality.'

'That's what I was thinking, Constantinos. It's magical. Like a scene from a fairy tale. Even the way Kitty Kat brought me here was kind of magical. She came straight here and... and, where is she, anyway? She was sitting there, just there, looking straight out like she was in a trance. Where's she gone?'

Constantinos turned his head to look down at her.

'Oh, don't worry about her. She comes and goes. Appears and disappears. Suddenly she's there and then suddenly she isn't.'

A low laugh burbled up from his chest.

'Like magic!'

Responding eagerly to his light-hearted tone, Charlene looked up at him, her face shining with relief.

'This whole place is like magic to me, Constantinos. I love it. I've never been anywhere like this. It's so different and it makes me feel different which is why, well, you know, I wouldn't normally take my clothes off but, well...'

His laugh now bursting out in a generous gush, Constantinos reached out to pull Charlene against him in a reassuring embrace.

'Don't worry. It has this effect on people, Charlene. They feel more connected to nature I guess, and they do natural things like take their clothes off. I'm glad you... you sense how special this place is and that, well, it inspired you to do something different.'

Responding to the tightening of his hold on her, she nuzzled her head against the soft cotton stretched across the firm expanse of his chest. Her senses stirring in excitement at the feel of their bodies pressed together, her voice trembled as a frisson of desire shivered through her.

'Yes. Well, I know it had that effect on Mrs Crawford or, well, Katherine, you know, the woman I used to work for. Your father was telling me about, well, about her being here. The things she did.'

Her head rose and fell against his chest as he sighed deeply.

'Ah, yes. Katherine. I do know about her. Actually, I found

out more about her recently, very recently, yesterday evening in fact and, well, there's stuff you might not know about her, but I guess I shouldn't say too much. Probably shouldn't even have said that come to think about it.'

Screwing round within his embrace, Charlene pressed her hand against his chest and looked up at him.

'Stuff I don't know? What do you mean? Are you sure? I know a lot about her, about when she was here. Your dad told me lots of things.'

'Yes, well, that's good but he told me when I came back tonight that there are some things he's going to tell you tomorrow so, well, I guess I shouldn't say much more. He wants to tell you in his own way.'

Lowering her hand and clasping her arms around his waist, Charlene leaned back, smiling excitedly as they looked at each other with bright-eyed anticipation of where these beginnings of physical intimacy might lead.

'Come on, Constantinos. You can't leave me hanging like this. What more is there to know?!'

'No, Charlene, I can't say except, well, I didn't realise until yesterday how much Katherine meant to Dad. How much he loved her. I had no idea. I mean, he really did.'

'Oh, he's already told me that or at least I guessed already. And she really loved him. I don't think he realised that. Not till she died anyway, and sent him a letter. That's what he told me, that she said how much she cared for him in the letter, but even then I don't think he realised how much she… she loved him. Such a shame, isn't it? Such a waste. All those years and they didn't know, you know, that the other person loved them. It seems crazy, although I get that it was too complicated and that Mrs Crawford couldn't get over Amy and, well, your dad, I guess she thought he wouldn't like the commitment.'

Freeing his hand he brushed strands of hair back from her face.

'Well, I guess you do know a lot and I guess you're right. It was all too difficult. Life should be simple, Charlene, shouldn't it? We should try to keep it simple. Not let it get complicated.'

The eagerness on her face fading, she slid her arm out from his embrace to run her fingers through his hair.

Seeing the desire in his eyes grow wilder, her features strained, and she sucked in a rapid rush of air as the anticipation of sexual fulfilment tingled through her body.

She rocked her belly slowly against his groin and caressed the back of his neck. Then closing her eyes to mask her growing desperation, she tilted her face upwards as he bowed his head.

She shivered as his lips came into contact with hers initiating a surge of sexual craving and intensifying her impulse to let these overwhelming urges propel them to a climactic conclusion. Then, just before submitting to the momentum of their desire, he halted and looked into her eyes with searching intensity. They remained momentarily frozen until he broke the silence with an awestruck whisper.

'Wow, Charlene! That was… wow!'

Wrapping his arms around her shoulders, he pulled her close. She pressed the side of her head against his chest and closed her eyes as he continued to speak in a husky murmur.

'You're some woman, Charlene. Beautiful and… sexy. I couldn't take my eyes off you the first time I saw you, and I can't believe you're here now. It's amazing. You're amazing.'

He loosened his hold and, reaching behind her, clasped her waist and turned her round to face the bench.

'Come on. Let's go sit on the bench and talk some more.'

Her face flinched with the anguish of unrealised desire, and the light in her eyes flared brightly before fading, as her urgent passion gave way to resignation. Perhaps, she reflected wryly, this was the way of things with intelligent men. They were driven as much by the need to vocalise their thoughts as by their sexual desire. Whatever the case, they certainly liked to talk, this father and son.

After stretching his arm across her shoulders, they sat down on the bench together and settled into a comfortable embrace. Remaining silent, they looked out across the land and sea serenely devoid of activity in the moonlit dead of night.

'This is my father's world. His place on this earth and his heaven I guess. He doesn't like to go away from here. He feels insecure when he's not here. So I have to come to him. That's just the way it is and I'm happy about that. Alexandrous have lived here for generations and he wants this to be my home one day.'

He paused before continuing, his chest heaving with a deep sigh.

'Actually, Charlene, he didn't intend to have a child. I wasn't planned. I was conceived in a moment of passion but I'm cool with that. Both my parents love me probably even more because I came into their lives unexpectedly. My father's so grateful to have a son, I know that, but he was scared to have children. Scared of commitment for sure, but scared to have children also. Scared to love too much. To love and to lose. Like he lost his parents and like Katherine lost her daughter.'

Charlene turned round to look up at him, wanting to respond supportively but unable to summon any words other than to name Katherine's daughter.

'Amy.'

'Yes. Amy.'

'I love that name. Amy. It's beautiful.'

'It is beautiful. It means beloved, did you know that?'

'No, I didn't but that's amazing and so true. Mrs Crawford loved her so much. All her life. She once told me that… that it's the biggest love you ever feel. Love for a child. That there's nothing like it. I could see that with her. A lot, like loads.'

Constantinos leaned forward to plant an affectionate kiss on her forehead.

'Well, I guess it'll be some time before we find that out, you know, before you and I have children but I reckon my parents would say the same. They have given me so much love. They don't love each other, don't even get on but they've always made me feel loved. I'm their only child. I mean, my mother's been married to another man for a long time, since I was three, but she was forty-two by then so I guess she was a bit old to have more children.'

'Wow. My mum's forty-one and I'm twenty-two.'

'Yeah, well my mum's sixty-eight now. She's in great shape mind you but, anyway, what about you, Charlene? How's it with you and your family?'

Turning away to look across the bay, Charlene folded her arms and, with a brief sensual writhe of her body, pressed herself into tighter contact with him.

'My family? Well, it's OK. I've got a sister and a brother. I'm the oldest and, well, I've got a mum and a dad.'

Constantinos lifted his outstretched arm from the top of the backrest to squeeze her with a gentle embrace.

'Wow. Do you get on well with your brother and sister? I mean, it must be cool to be part of a real family even though it's not always happy families, am I right?'

Charlene extracted her arm from his embrace and rested it along the length of his thigh.

'Yeah. You could say that. There's a lot of arguing. A lot of crap but, anyway, I'll be leaving soon. Moving out. When I get back from here.'

'Moving out? That sounds exciting. You're moving out and I've moved in. Well, only for another month but it's the first time I've really settled into life here. I love it and it makes my father happy to have another Alexandrou here. I won't be tied to it like he is, but I will always come back here. It will always be my spiritual home, if you know what I mean. The place where Alexandrous have lived for generations.'

She flopped her head against his chest.

'That's a nice thought. Your father said he was happy, very happy you want this place to be your home. So pleased, like you said, to have a son who can live here. An Alexandrou. Constantinos Alexandrou. It's a great name by the way. I like saying it. Constantinos Alexandrou.'

'Well, thanks, Charlene. I'm glad you like it. That's who I am, at least that's who I am when I'm here.'

Releasing his hold on her, Constantinos raised his arm and, recognising this as a signal that he wished to move, Charlene shifted over allowing him to stand up and walk forward to the front of the terrace. She sat poised, watching him keenly, her senses sharpened by his sudden disengagement.

He stood silhouetted against the cool luminescence of the sea and sky, his legs slightly parted and his hands pushed deep into his trouser pockets.

Mystified by his termination of their intimacy, she watched him in wonder, thoughts drifting through her mind as she waited for him to speak.

Intently absorbing the features of his thrilling beauty, her heart bubbled hotly. It was his eyes that drew her in, captivated her, but the form of his forehead and his nose, mouth and chin all inspired wonder and delight. His body too, those broad shoulders, those long limbs. She wanted to see him naked. Naked and active. Diving into the water and swimming. He must, she thought, be a good swimmer, a strong swimmer. He moved so elegantly and he was now moving back towards her. Back to her side.

Feeling another gush of heat burst out from her heart, she turned to look at him as he sat beside her and leaned back, stretching his arms behind and resting his head against the cupped support of his interlinked hands. He looked straight ahead as he spoke.

'Yes, Charlene. I am Constantinos Alexandrou. That's exactly who I am when I am in Greece. But, Charlene, that's not what it says in my passport. It's a different name written in my passport. My American passport.'

He leaned forward, bringing his arms down to rest on his knees, his hands remaining clasped together. Looking sideways, he smiled as he saw the tension in Charlene's face, his own expression softening with the rueful relief of imminent disclosure.

'The name in my passport is my American name. The name my mother gave me... James, my first name. The second name came from my father, he chose it and, yes, it is Constantinos but the last name, my surname, is my mother's family name, so in the States I am not Constantinos Alexandrou, I am James... James Crawford.'

The expression of attentive concentration on Charlene's face instantly lightened and she emitted a soft puff of laughter.

'Crawford? That's amazing. You've got the same name as, well, Mrs Crawford... Katherine. That's nice. Another name I like. Crawford! What are the chances of that!'

Sitting up straight, Constantinos swung round to face her, his expression serious.

Unnerved by his solemn demeanour, she blurted out other thoughts as they came into her head.

'James is nice, too. It's difficult to get used to it. To think that it's your name but it's a nice name. James.'

Benign amusement softened his expression as he leaned closer to her.

'Thanks, Charlene. I'm happy you like my names. All of them. I like them too, although I guess it's a bit weird having one set of names for here and another for home, well, I mean my regular home.'

'It must be weird, strange. Like you're two people and... and weird for your dad. Weird that your American name is the same as... as Mrs Crawford's.'

Constantinos leaned forward and took hold of Charlene's hands in each of his.

'Well. That's the thing, Charlene. It's not that weird. It's quite natural really. Well, depending how you look at it, anyway, but it has to be that way. My name has to be Crawford because, well, because Katherine, Mrs Crawford, is my mother's sister. My aunt, I guess. Yep, that's the size of it, Charlene. So it's no coincidence that my name's Crawford.'

Her eyebrows arched in amazement and her jaw slackened as she assimilated this revelation.

'Oh my god. That's… that's unbelievable. You're related to Mrs Crawford. I can't believe it.'

'Yes. It's true. I'm her nephew.'

'Wow. So does that mean… does that mean you're Lily's son? Maria told me about her. About Lily. Except she said she lives in Canada.'

'Yes, that's right. I am her son and Mum did go to Canada. To Toronto. That's where I was born, but then she got a job at Harvard, you know, the university. Ended up Professor of Classics and then we moved to Maine where we live now.'

Her expression transforming from wonderment to indignant incomprehension, she withdrew her hands and pressed each to her temples before throwing them forward in a gesture which added emphasis to her growing outrage.

'But… but, hey, wait a minute. Let me get this straight, you are the son of Mrs Crawford's sister and Nektarios. Nektarios, who was Mrs Crawford's lover… oh my god, how did that happen? How the hell did that happen?!'

Constantinos edged closer, pressing his knees against hers and recapturing her hands in his.

'Well, Charlene, this is what Dad was going to tell you tomorrow but, well, I need to tell you now so I'll try and explain, tell you it the way he told me. You see, Charlene, the way it happened is that my mum came here on holiday with Katherine. It was two years after Amy died and my mum arranged for them to come here. They hadn't got on well. Maria may have told you but Mum wanted to do something to help Katherine. To help her get over Amy, so she set it all up and they came here. Mum knew the place. She'd been to Greece often for her studies, so she thought it would be a good place for Katherine to get away from things and to… to come to terms with the loss of Amy. She hadn't had a break. She threw herself into work, you know, her pharmaceutical business and, well, Mum said she needed a break and she could afford to take time off so they came here, and then Mum went back to the States and Katherine stayed on. That's when she met Dad and you're right, they did love each other. I didn't know about it, that they had something going on but anyway Katherine had to go back to England and, well, I guess she discovered, like you said, that her grief hadn't subsided and she couldn't handle her feelings for Dad so it kind of cooled off. She didn't want to come back here and so Dad got a bit pissed with Katherine, a bit annoyed and then my mum came back the next summer and she met my dad and they had their moment of passion and, well, here I am twenty-eight years later.'

Calmed by the measured delivery of his explanation, Charlene looked down at her hands held gently in his supportive grip, her brow furrowing as she raised her head to seek a clearer understanding of these events and their consequences.

'But, but it's so confusing. I mean, Nektarios and your mum getting together, I guess these things happen although it's a shame for Mrs Crawford, such a shame because she loved him so much and never stopped loving him even though, well, even though all that happened and also… also, I don't get why she never said she had a nephew. Her own nephew. Not a word. In fact, she said she had no one to leave anything to. To pass things on to. That's what I don't understand. She was so kind and she must have loved you.'

The eagerness fading from his face, he sat up straighter.

'Well. It hurt her badly, I guess. They didn't get on anyway. My mother was a rebel, a black sheep, I guess. Not really in a bad way but she was a bit of a hippy, you know, free love, drugs, well, not much, weed mainly, but her parents, Grandma and Grandad, they didn't approve. It was difficult for them. Grandad, especially. He was religious. A lovely guy but he couldn't handle Mum and she couldn't handle them, so she went away to the States and started a new life. Changed her name. Well, she didn't use Lily, anyway. She's Amanda Lily Crawford so she just dropped the Lily. Her family still called her Lily. Grandad, Grandma and Katherine. Not that I would really know what Katherine called her. I never met her, my aunt, never. Never even talked about her, so it's kind of strange to me to find out she was such a big deal and such a good lady. That's strange and sad. Real sad.'

Charlene slipped her hands out of his grasp and took hold of his, as she sought to re-engage him in eye contact.

'My god. You never met Mrs Crawford. I can't believe it! She was amazing. You would have got on so well. It's crazy that you never met her.'

'Yeah, well, I do regret it now. Lots but I didn't think about it really. I just accepted that Mum and Katherine had fallen out, that they were very different and didn't get on. As Mum said, she was a free spirit with a passion for history and artistic things, and Katherine was a conservative and sensible businesswoman who had studied science. Also Mum was headstrong. I knew that and Grandma said Katherine was stubborn so I just accepted it was never going to happen. And, anyway, Mum never talked about her so I didn't really think about her. I know it seems crazy but that's the way it was and now, well, now of course I get why there was this big rift between them.'

He sighed deeply and looked away, his troubled eyes fixing on the horizon before turning back.

'Basically it's me. I'm the reason they fell out. The reason they never spoke to each other.'

Charlene reached out to squeeze his upper arm reassuringly.

'It's not you, Constantinos. You mustn't think like that. It was your mum and Nektarios. They shouldn't really have, you know, done it, not when Katherine was so in love with your dad.'

'Yeah, well. Like he said, he didn't really know how Katherine felt and he didn't really understand how much she was still grieving. He was kind of angry he couldn't have her, that she wasn't responding, so he thought, well, fuck it, I'll fuck her sister instead.'

'Constantinos! You mustn't think like that!'

'No, you're right, it wasn't like that but it was just a one-off thing, a night of sex. Unprotected sex, even though Dad said he was usually very careful. Obsessively careful about not taking any risks except for this one time. God knows why, but then, well, thank God, otherwise I wouldn't be here.'

Constantinos rose to his feet and, stretching his arms out high and wide, looked up and projected his gratitude towards the star-filled sky.

'Thank God for that moment of wild abandon. For trusting in fate that one time. Thank you. Thank you for allowing that moment to happen. That opportunity for me to be created. For me to be here now in this beautiful place.'

Lowering his arms, he turned and continued speaking to Charlene as he sat down beside her.

'It is amazing, isn't it? The miracle of life. How it only takes an instant, a moment to create each and every one of us. I mean, in my case that's all it was. There was no relationship. I mean, Mum said that they had a relationship and that they loved each other, except they knew it couldn't last. That's what she said and Dad never said anything different until yesterday when he said that they got carried away in a moment of passion. A beautiful moment, that's what he said, which turned out to be the most important moment in his life. That's cool and I believe him, of course I do, but it's kind of difficult as well, now that I know the full truth about Katherine. I mean, I knew there was something between them when she left him that money, but I didn't know everything until yesterday so, well, we've both learned something new, I guess.'

Charlene looked across the bay as she spoke, frowning as she focused on the guiding lights at the mouth of the harbour.

'I certainly have learned something new. My god. But the thing is, Constantinos, I wouldn't have known about any of this if I hadn't come here and I nearly didn't come here. Today's our last day and it wasn't until yesterday that Manos brought me here. I mean, it's lucky that he knows your dad and, well… it nearly didn't happen.'

'Well, I guess, Charlene, but it was meant to happen. That's the way things work here. It's a special place. Things kind of fall into place… most of the time, although I guess it didn't work out great for Katherine. Yeah, it could have been a lot better for her, that's for sure.'

Charlene's face as she turned back to look at Constantinos was strained with sorrow.

'I wish… I just wish I'd known. I wish she'd told us. Why did she keep it to herself? So secret? Imagine that. Living all that time with a secret. Losing Amy was bad enough and then, well, losing her man, her lover. Losing her lover because of her sister and… and her sister having a child after she'd lost her own child. Her lover's child. I mean, it's great that it happened, like your dad said, it's the best thing that's happened to him, having you, but I feel sad for Mrs Crawford. Having to live with all that. Really sad.'

Constantinos shifted his weight forward and rose again to his feet, this time pulling Charlene up with him.

'She did lose out. For sure. Big time, but she wouldn't want you to be sad. She wanted you to come here and have a good time. Didn't she? She must have wanted you to feel positive about it. Not to feel sorry for her. Don't you think?'

He looked down at her expectantly until, accepting that she

was not going to respond, he gripped her hand and pulled her behind him as he weaved his way between the trees. She allowed herself to be dragged along scuffing and tripping as she tried to match his accelerating pace. Becoming aware of the sash around her waist loosening she clasped the seams together at her chest.

'Constantinos! Stop!'

He continued undaunted and oblivious to her entreaty until, after lurching through a scratchy row of thyme bushes onto the path, he stood with his legs apart, tugged her towards him and, in a whirling flourish, cradled her in his arms, sweeping her off her feet and spinning her around with a triumphant burst of laughter.

Charlene gasped and then squealed with a mixture of excitement and alarm, as the flaps of her gown parted and fell away, except where her hand remained pinned to her chest.

'Constantinos! Put me down!… Help…'

Constantinos staggered giddily as he slowed down, turning one final heavy-footed revolution before lowering her onto her feet with a wild grin.

She hunched over, concealing her nakedness by overlapping the flaps of her gown, before looking up and laughing, her face bright with exhilaration.

'Constantinos! What was that all about? You're mad. Crazy.'

'Crazy? It must be the moon or maybe it's you. Maybe I'm crazy about you.'

A seductive smile teasing across her face, she straightened up to her full height and, with her arms folded, stepped towards him with a sensual roll of her hips. She pressed against him, releasing her right hand and raising it to stroke her fingers lightly down his cheek.

'I still can't believe it. You, the guy at the nightclub. The best-looking guy. You are related to Mrs Crawford. Her nephew. And… and I'm with you, in the middle of the night, here, in this amazing place. It's… it's unreal. Unbelievable.'

Her hand hovered below his chin before coming to rest against his chest as he wrapped his arms around her waist.

'But it is real. Even though we didn't know you existed, you are real and I am here in the place that Mrs Crawford loved so much, with the son of the man she loved all the rest of her life. The son of her sister, from the same flesh and blood. It's hard to get my head around it all. It's a lot to take in. My head's spinning, Constantinos. It really is.'

Constantinos pulled her against him with tender reassurance.

'I'm sorry to load you up with all this but I had to let you know who I am. I couldn't, you know, let things get intimate without you understanding who I am. I couldn't do that. It would have felt like false pretences, also, well, I just think it's best to know the full context… if that makes sense and doesn't sound, like, too pedantic.'

Charlene pulled her head away and, bending back as he lowered his arm to support her around the waist, she placed her hands on his shoulders to look at him full square, face to face.

'My god, Constantinos, don't apologise. I am so glad you told me. I mean, things were amazing anyway but now, well, it's gone off the scale. So…,so…'

Abandoning verbal communication, she stretched up onto the balls of her feet and, draping her arms around the back of his neck, engaged her lips with his, exploring his mouth with hungry passion. Leaning over he responded with equal intensity, running one hand up her spine to support her high between her shoulder blades, while slipping the other behind her naked hip as her gown fell away. She flexed back further against the strong support of his arms as their kissing ranged wildly around each other's face and neck. Slipping his hand under her buttocks he pressed her against him. Hanging her head back, she emitted a shuddering moan as a pre-orgasmic shockwave surged through her body. Her gown hung down from her shoulders as he lifted her higher. She wrapped her legs around his waist, gripping him tightly as they re-engaged in a ravenous mouth-to-mouth frenzy. Continuing to kiss, she dropped onto her feet and started to unbutton his trousers in fumbling desperation. Stumbling backwards as she released the final button, he looked down to see what had caused his loss of balance.

'Oh my god, it had to be!'

Charlene dipped sideways to look behind him.

'Bloody hell. Kitty Kat!... Again.'

They both watched the cat rub its purring body against Constantinos's leg, before moving away with feline grace and lying down on the next step where it started licking its underside with concentrated self-absorption.

Constantinos turned back to face Charlene and groaned with desire, as the sight of her naked body glistening between the parted gown reignited his all-consuming need to let their passion flow freely. Reaching out to grab her hand he turned round to pull her up the stepped pathway.

Hanging on tightly, she raced after him, the silk gown trailing in her wake. Reaching his side as he strode onto the terrace, she yanked his arm causing him to stop and turn around to face her. They stared into each other's eyes knowing without the need for articulation that they were reaching the point beyond which their unleashed desire would become insatiable until brought to a climax. Her chest heaved with the electrifying blood-rush of anticipation, as she pressed against him. His eyelids fluttered as he expelled a ragged moan. Then galvanised by urgent resolve, he stretched his arm out to hold her in a firm embrace before turning around and walking her towards the house. Taken aback by his purposeful actions, she pulled her hand free as she staggered to find her balance and match his pace.

The level tone of his voice conveyed an unstoppable determination.

'Come on, Charlene. We need to get to bed.'

Chapter 44

The sun appeared slowly above the forested ridge of the hillside, rendering the first touches of colour in the land below. Its low-angled rays cast the rippled surface of the sea into shimmering relief.

Stirred from stillness, the sheep followed each other up the hill, the bells around their necks clanking primitive notes in a random and discordant melody, as they found their way along narrow pathways through the rough terrain.

The butterflies spread their wings and fluttered noiselessly between the flowers of bougainvillea blossom, in the silence before it became warm enough for the cicadas to commence their daylong chorus.

At the lower reaches of the hillside before it steepened into the sea, the sheen of condensation on the roof terrace evaporated into an ephemeral mist.

Oblique shafts of sunlight penetrated the gaps and cracks around the shutters in the windows on the rear wall of the house. In one bedroom, the incompletely closed shutters admitted a blade of light which cut across the bed, searing a broad stripe on the sprawled legs of the sleeping couple.

The young woman stirred, opening her eyes and rolling her head over on the pillow to look at the man still deeply asleep on his side. Bending her neck, she looked down her naked body and disengaged from his embrace by lifting his limp forearm from her diaphragm. After resting it gently on the rumpled cotton sheet, she shifted in small movements to the edge of the bed where she pivoted on her bottom and lowered her feet onto the floor. She stood up slowly and, after looking back to check that he had remained undisturbed, moved with fleet-footed stealth to the chair where she grasped the gown, swirling it around her and slipping it on as she moved swiftly to the door.

Pausing at the threshold, she looked around the hall before stepping out of the bedroom and closing the door quietly behind her. She then flitted lightly across the hall and through the sitting room. After casting a wide-eyed glance back into the house, she opened the French windows and stepped out onto the terrace.

The terracotta tiles felt cool under her feet as she traversed the shaded terrace. No longer at risk of being discovered escaping from Constantinos's bedroom, Charlene slowed her progress to a pensive pace, as she made her way between the furniture to the slowly widening sunlit margin at the front edge. She stood looking out across the bay now sparkling with the nascent possibilities of a new day. The soothing sensation of the rising sun on her back caused a slow shiver of wellbeing to issue from the base of her spine. She turned her head in a circular motion to stretch her tightened neck muscles, while flexing her raised arms and pulling her shoulders back.

Luxuriating in the relief of eased muscles, she became awestruck by the recurring sense that she was walking in Mrs Crawford's footsteps. That Mrs Crawford would have stood here after waking and looked out across the sea feeling good to be alive. Alive and part of the miraculous matrix of life. A woman, agile and strong, filling herself with the freshness of a new day, while her lover continued to sleep, sprawled across the rumpled sheets.

The sweet thrill of drawing parallels between their experiences began to subside with the thought that she was walking in the footsteps of someone who could never return, who had become just a memory.

How strange for him, she mused. How sad. To have had her and then to have lost her, firstly because of all that grief and confusion and now finally, conclusively. And how awkward for her, Charlene, when he begins to tell her about it, not knowing that Constantinos has revealed so much of it already. And how much more awkward for her if he finds out they slept together.

Her clenched jaw slackened with puzzlement, when the sound of a slight creak followed by a muffled knock arrested her attention. Turning towards the source of the noises she saw the cat drop with sinuous ease from the nearby chair, before stalking up to her with stiff-backed hauteur. She crouched down to tickle under its chin and stroke its back, which began to vibrate with a rumbling purr of pleasure.

'Well, you are a one, aren't you? Always popping up out of nowhere. Part of the magic, eh? Is that right? You're just part of the magic of this place.'

She spoke in the hushed, sing-song tone she had used on her moonlit wander through the garden.

'That's it, Kitty Kat. You're part of the magic. Not like cats at home. You're special, aren't you? Like this place. Special. So special.'

She raised her head to look at the pines, glinting green against the emerald bay, and the graduated blues of the open sea and sky. Captivated by the morning view, she rose slowly to a standing position.

The realisation that she would never witness a scene like this at home disturbed her. The dead weight of grief began to pull at her heart, as she anticipated leaving the colour and beauty of this place behind; returning to the muted imperfection of her home environment and the difficulties and uncertainties of her everyday existence. Swamped by the sadness that she had left it so late to begin the discovery of all that had beguiled Mrs Crawford, she did not hear Nektarios's arrival behind her until he spoke.

'Charlene! I didn't notice you down there… How are you?'

She spun round in surprise, holding one hand against the knotted sash, the other clasping the edges of her gown together at her chest.

'Nektarios! Hi. I'm, I'm fine thanks. I was… I was just stroking the cat. Kitty Kat. So, so, anyway, how are you?'

Nektarios stood still, his face straining with distress. He blinked as moisture clouded his eyes.

Charlene's voice softened with concern.

'Nektarios, are you OK? Is anything the matter… Nektarios?'

Shaking his head he moved to straighten a chair at the table between them.

'No, I'm fine thanks. It's just that, well, the way you moved reminded me so much of Katherine and, like I said, you have the same physicality, you wear her gown just like she did so… so it hit me. The fact that it's been thirty years since she was here, although it doesn't seem like it. Thirty years. Long enough for life to pass and to end. It just hit me. You know, like a powerful aftershock. That the life that might have been will never happen. It's all beyond our reach.'

Placing each hand on the back of the chair, he leaned forward, his face crinkling into a smile.

'Anyway, it's a new day in our lives. You've seen the end of one day and the beginning of another. An end and a beginning. Perhaps we can take comfort from that. There's always a beginning after an end or, perhaps, an end is never reached.'

Charlene smiled shyly and shrugged as she replied.

'I don't know, Nektarios. I know what you're saying but I feel a bit confused right now.'

His smile widened.

'You're quite right, Charlene. It's too early in the day to be getting philosophical. We shouldn't be taxing our brains before breakfast. That's a golden rule so the only question I should be asking now is – would you like some breakfast? Perhaps a cup of coffee and some fruit juice to start with.'

Charlene dipped her head before looking up anxiously.

'Well, I'm OK right now and, well, I was wondering if, well, I feel a bit funny now wearing Mrs… I mean Katherine's gown and so I was thinking, maybe I should, you know, put my own clothes on.'

Nektarios's eyes widened as he opened his arms reassuringly.

'Please don't be sensitive about wearing Katherine's gown, besides, your clothes are hanging on the roof, and we should leave them there for a bit to let them dry out in the sun. They'll still be a bit damp from the morning moisture.'

'Well, OK, it's just that it's her gown and I'm not sure…'

'Look, don't worry about it, Charlene. You know she wouldn't mind. In fact, I'm sure she would have wanted you to wear it. She wanted you to come here. Only you. You were special to her so you shouldn't worry about it. Really.'

He pulled back the chair and sat down at the table. Following his gesture that she should do the same, Charlene lowered herself hesitantly onto a chair.

'Are you sure, Nektarios? I'm not so sure. I mean, she wanted me to come here to the island, to see what a beautiful place it is, but if she'd wanted me to come here, to your house, well… you see, the thing is, Nektarios, she didn't say I should come and see you and I nearly didn't. I mean, I didn't know where you lived and it was only at the last minute that, well, I found you thanks to Manos.'

'I know that, Charlene, but it was meant to happen. You coming here and everything before that. It all happened the way it had to happen. I'm sure Katherine knew that you would find your way here if it was meant to happen, and that if you'd come here under instruction it wouldn't have been such a meaningful or significant experience. She also knew of course that she could trust this place, this island to deliver an outcome. It's that kind of place. A small enough world.'

Charlene's expression brightened and she shifted onto the front edge of the chair.

'That's exactly what Constantinos said. He said that it's a special place. That things happen in a good way, well, usually they do...'

Realising that she had just revealed that she and Constantinos had talked after they had all gone to bed, she stopped speaking. Breaking eye contact she looked down, wrestling her hands nervously under the table as she waited for Nektarios to respond.

'Well, he was right of course. He's not only my son, my beloved son, but he is a child of this island as I guess he will have told you last night.'

She looked up, hope dawning on her face.

'Don't worry, Charlene. When I realised you were both out of your beds I worked out you would be together, down the garden, talking. I was pleased, very pleased and knew that Constantinos would have told you everything I was going to tell you today. He's my boy. I can rely on him to do the right thing.'

Unclasping her grip she sat upright, sliding her hands onto the edge of the table.

'You mean... you mean you don't, well...'

'Don't mind that Constantinos told you about his mother and that whole situation? No, I don't mind, Charlene. I was going to tell you today. I didn't want to go into all of that yesterday because I thought you should be introduced to this place with fresh eyes, without knowing about all the complications. I wanted you to appreciate those things about this place that Katherine cherished without being distracted by the events that occurred after she left. It became clear that you didn't know about them, so I decided to reveal them today, but Constantinos beat me to it and, anyway, I am sure he explained it well although, no matter how it's told, I don't come out of it looking very good or honourable but, well, there are things which Constantinos may not be fully aware, of which I would like to try and explain.'

Charlene pushed her hands across the table as she leaned forward to interrupt him.

'Nektarios, you shouldn't feel bad about it. Like Constantinos said, these things happen. He said it was a moment of passion, a beautiful moment, the best moment because, well, he wouldn't be here if it hadn't happened. So I know it was a good thing, a great thing although, well, you know, it was also a bit sad, I suppose.'

Nektarios stretched across to hold her hands.

'It was sad, Charlene, you're right. I felt so sad that Katherine never came back here. So sad. She was the one I wanted to come back. The only one. Others came back but never Katherine, the one I yearned for. I thought when she left her clothes that it was a sign she would return. We didn't speak about it at the time, but I took comfort from it. When I looked at them I dreamt about seeing them on her body again, brought back to life but, of course, that became an impossibility. Instead, you have come. It almost feels like you are, what's the word… a surrogate, yes, that's it, a kind of surrogate. Maybe that's going too far but, well, I am so glad you are here… In her dressing gown! Anyway, as I say, Charlene, I think she meant this to happen and I know you are sad for Katherine that we, her sister and I, people so close to her in different ways, could cause her such hurt when she had suffered so much. It was awful. Although I could rejoice in Constantinos, I was plagued by guilt and a sense of self-inflicted loss until, well, until I received her letter when she spoke to me with wonderful words and told me that it all happened the way it had to happen. I felt as though a great burden had been lifted from me. A burden I deserved to bear and one I had become used to living with, so that I wasn't wholly aware of it until it had been lifted. But my god, I am so grateful that she did that for me. She made my heart sing and fall in love with her all over again. So amazing that she could speak to me so strongly and have that effect on me when she's not here anymore. She let me know that she was approaching her death with hope and a belief, a firm belief, that it would bring a new beginning.'

He squeezed her hands gently but emphatically.

'She was an inspiration. *Is* an inspiration. And so strong and wise to make sense of it all with such clarity. I couldn't see it. Not completely. Her letter put everything into perspective… It was so powerful, Charlene, it was like life had been filled with a new light.'

Releasing his grip, he pulled his hands away, his eyes screwing as he looked into the brightness behind her, before re-engaging eye contact.

'I realise that it must be difficult to comprehend exactly what I'm trying to explain. I guess it's quite a lot to take in and not what you were expecting to discover.'

Charlene looked down at her hands, frowning as she started to formulate her response.

'It is, Nektarios. I wasn't sure why I came here. Why Mrs Crawford wanted me to come and then it seemed to make sense but now…'

Her expression was taut with vexation as she raised her head.

'… now I feel confused. I mean, I am really glad you feel better about everything, but I still don't understand why it was all OK for Mrs Crawford and also, the other thing is, why didn't she, like, clear things up sooner? Why did she leave it until, you know, until it was too late?'

Nektarios's mouth stretched into a compassionate smile.

'Charlene, I am not surprised you feel confused. So much of it had remained unresolved in my mind until I read Katherine's letter. You see, the thing is, what Katherine was saying was, she… she, oh, you know, you should read her letter. Yes, that would be the best thing. I'll go and make some breakfast and get the letter. She can explain it all much better than me. So, what can I get you? Coffee, orange juice, muesli, toast, bananas, figs… fresh figs… a boiled egg? What do you fancy?'

Charlene's voice sharpened with anxiety.

'But… but it's private, personal, Mrs Crawford's letter. I don't think she'd want me to read it.'

'Well, Charlene, I understand your concern, of course I do, but I don't think she'd mind, I really don't. After all, it brings resolution to a situation involving a number of people… including you. She wouldn't have gone to the effort of giving you the opportunity to come here if she hadn't wanted you to be part of the story and, anyway, I would tell you everything in my own way, my much clumsier way, so I really believe she would be very happy for you to read it. To learn from it. You know how she wanted to reveal things to you which might make your life better. I'll get it anyway. Constantinos should read it too. It can make sense of all of our lives in different ways. I feel sure about that. Suddenly very sure about it.'

Charlene watched Nektarios shove the chair back and rise to his feet. She felt her resistance wilt in the face of his resolve.

'I don't know, Nektarios, but if you think it's OK. If you really think she wouldn't mind.'

Nekatarios pushed the chair back in line with the others.

'Well, I will scan it quickly again to make absolutely sure although, well, actually, I have absorbed it so completely, in such detail that I am really confident there's nothing in it you shouldn't read… and Constantinos… when he wakes up which he will need to do quite soon. Not easy, I'm afraid. Waking him up. He sleeps so deeply as you will have discovered.'

She blinked rapidly as a flutter of panic tickled round her heart.

'Will I? I mean, have I? I… I'm not sure…'

'Well, perhaps you didn't notice particularly but he usually goes out like a light and sleeps deeply until he wakes up or I eventually manage to rouse him. Unlike his dad! I am a light sleeper especially now when it's a full moon. Anyway, let me get you some breakfast. What would you like? Muesli, toast, eggs… French toast, that's what Constantinos likes, at weekends, with maple syrup. What do you reckon?'

Consumed by confusion, she responded falteringly.

'Um, well, actually, that would be nice. French toast would be nice.'

'Great! I'll bring out the maple syrup so that you can add it if you want some. And what to drink? Coffee? I have a machine so I can do it all ways – Americano, cappuccino, latte… espresso?'

'Wow. Well, cappuccino would be great, thanks. Thanks very much.'

'Excellent. Well, I won't be long. Who knows, maybe Constantinos will wake up while I'm making it, although I wouldn't count on it. He doesn't start at the museum until later anyway, although he should join us for breakfast, shouldn't he? He really should. I'm sure he'd want to.'

Charlene slid her hand across the table as she leaned towards Nektarios.

'Oh, don't wake him. Let him sleep for a bit longer. I… I am sure he needs a bit longer.'

Nektarios smiled fondly.

'OK, Charlene, we'll give him a bit longer. I mean, you must feel tired yourself.'

She felt her cheeks and neck bloom hotly, and she knew that she would be reddening as she stuttered her reply.

'No… no, I'm fine. I… I don't feel tired. I slept well. We… we were in the garden talking, yes, talking and… and then we went to bed… we went to sleep. Quickly, so, so, no, I feel fine… thanks.'

Nektarios's smile brightened.

'Well, that's great. You're on holiday anyway so you can do

these things. In fact, you should do these things on holiday especially when you're young so, yes, I hope you had a special time. I really do.'

Her mind racing around in search of an acceptable presentation of their night together, Charlene stumbled through her response.

'Ah… yes… it was great. He's great, Constantinos, and it was great getting to… ah, talking to him, listening to him and… yes, it was special… very special… staying up talking on such a beautiful night. It was amazing… so beautiful, the moonlight and… and…'

'Well, I am really glad you had the opportunity to get to know each other better, and that Constantinos was able to tell you about everything, well, almost everything. Anyhow, I'd better get your breakfast so I'll leave you in peace for a bit. Give you a break from all this talking that we do! Eh!'

Nektarios chuckled generously as he looked at her with a knowing flex of his eyebrows, before turning and walking into the house.

She stared after him in despair that discretion had not been possible, and that Nektarios now knew that she had slept with his son. How bad was that? Bonding with him, the father, and then sleeping with his son just a few hours later.

She shuddered as her scramble to evaluate the morals of their night-time activities became mixed up in a turmoil of guilt and embarrassment.

Resting her elbows on the table, she propped her head on her hands as she tried to calm her mind by rationalising the situation.

Nektarios had not shown any signs of being concerned or disappointed. Why would he? A man who had enjoyed intimacy with many women. And, if he did think badly of her, he would not be suggesting she read Mrs Crawford's letter.

This final thought caused her anxiety to shift focus. Should she read the letter? She was torn between temptation and resistance; the fascination of what it would reveal versus the uncertainty that Mrs Crawford would want other people to read this communication with her onetime lover. Perhaps though it was not a deeply personal communication and, anyway, Mrs Crawford had always disclosed so much to her. Often more than she felt comfortable knowing. Yes, perhaps reading the letter would be no different to those many times she had listened to her life stories and worldly wisdom. Besides, she could not refuse in the face of Nektarios's insistence.

She sighed deeply while gazing through the gaps in the vine, and making her silent appeal into the clear blue of the morning sky.

'Would you mind, Mrs C? Would you mind me reading your letter? Reading it here in this amazing place? Your special place.'

She turned round on her chair to scan the bay shimmering quietly in the fresh light of the new day. Breathing in through her nose, she smelled the dew rich aromas of the herbs growing abundantly in the ceramic pots ranged along the edge of the terrace.

She understood that her visceral appreciation of these smells was linked to the heightened sense of connection to nature that she felt here. Nature and its eternal cycles. The environment on which humanity depended. Continuing season after season while people were born, lived their lives, short or long, and died.

She sat up straight, as the chilling fear of her own death at the end of an unknown future, shivered up her spine. Looking round to seek distraction from this unsettling thought, she saw the cat descend through the rustling foliage and trot towards her.

'Hello, Kitty Kat. Come to save the day again? That's it, come to say hello. Good girl. Oh, yes. You're a lovely cat, aren't you? How's that? Is that nice?'

She leaned over to stroke the cat with her fingertips, speaking quietly in a sing-song whisper as it settled at her feet.

'I wonder where you came from. Someone must be missing you, a beautiful cat like you. Still, it's great for Nektarios that you're here. He really likes you. Yes, he really does. You're a special cat. Yes, you are.'

Raising her head, she gazed wistfully around the terrace and its surroundings.

'You've certainly found a nice home. I wouldn't mind staying here.'

Surprised that she had said this without thinking about it, she began to challenge it. Could she actually live here? Was she special enough? Did she deserve to live in such a beautiful place? It was impossible to imagine. She would have to return to the dullness and difficulties of home.

She knew that leaving the island would be painful. Not just because its beauty and the sunshine made her feel good but, more so, because it would be a wrench to leave Nektarios and Constantinos. They made life seem much better, much bigger. She would miss them both and leaving Constantinos would also bring the pain of physical separation.

Sighing as her heart began to ache, she reached down to run her fingers along the cat's back.

She did not hear Nektarios return, until the sound of his voice made her jolt upright.

'Here we go… Are you all right, Charlene? Is everything OK?'

She screwed around to face him in an awkward flurry of embarrassment.

'Yes… yes, I'm fine. I was just talking to the… to Kitty Kat.'

'Oh yes. Of course. I talk to her a lot. Poor cat. She has heard it all. All my inner thoughts.'

He lowered the tray onto the table and placed a mug of cappuccino, a glass of freshly squeezed orange juice, a bowl of fresh figs, and a napkin next to her. He then lifted an envelope off the tray.

'I'll leave Katherine's letter for you to read while I prepare breakfast.'

He held it up in front of her.

'Of course, you should only read it if you feel comfortable about it, but I really think you should. It's the most powerful, the most wonderfully eloquent letter I have ever read. Of course it's written to me and provides me with a great sense of resolution, however, as I said, it will provide explanations and answers to your questions much better than I can and… and I'm sure it will help you find your place in this life, this world which Katherine wanted you to experience. Charlene, it is the voice, the vivid voice of someone you loved and respected and I want to share it with you, so please don't be afraid to read it. Anyway, I'll leave it here… just here… oh, and there's also a photo of Katherine in there. To let you see how she looked when she was here. The way I remember her. The way she lives in my mind and my heart. The way she will always be for me… until I die.'

He laid it down carefully in the middle of the table, safely removed from the food and drink.

'OK. I'll go and make your breakfast. Oh, and I'm going to wait a bit before waking Constantinos, just to give you peace and quiet to read the letter… OK? No pressure, of course… honestly.'

An innocent smile flashed playfully across his face as he turned and walked back to the house, swinging the tray by his side.

Charlene diverted her gaze from his retreating figure to watch the cat emerge from under the table and chase after him in a springy canter.

She was on her own now. Alone with no distractions. No excuses not to read the letter. No excuses, but she would need to drink the coffee first. Its rich aroma was intensifying her need for caffeine. For the energy and mental clarity it would provide.

She lifted the cup to her lips and closed her eyes, as the flavour of freshly brewed coffee and hot, creamy milk swamped her senses.

She smiled in gratitude to Nektarios for making such perfect coffee. All of the food and drink he had produced had been delicious. None of the men she knew had kitchen skills beyond heating up microwave meals or making cups of tea and instant coffee. They considered cooking to be women's work despite seeing all of the male chefs on television. To them it was a mark of masculinity that women catered for them. To Charlene it was clearer, now more than ever, that far from showing strength, their attitude was weak and pathetic.

She felt her contempt for them intensify until, recognising that these dark thoughts were at odds with the sun-washed tranquillity of her surroundings, she closed her mind to them and reached over to pick up the letter. Holding it up, her brow furrowed as her mind became besieged by doubts and concerns.

She felt engulfed by a sense of inadequacy, by the fear that she may not fully understand what Mrs Crawford had written. Nektarios seemed to assume she was intelligent and educated. So did Constantinos. It would be embarrassing if she was asked her opinion about something she did not understand.

She shook her head to banish this negative thought. She had not felt inferior for one moment in their company. It surprised her to recognise this. Apart from her discomfort about Nektarios knowing that she had spent the night with his son, she had felt confident in their company. They made her feel confident. They wanted her here. To be part of their world. The world which Mrs Crawford knew she would discover, even though she had not told her to find Nektarios. How could she have been so sure that these things would happen after her death? Could she have really been so calm about dying?

Agonised by these unanswerable questions, she once again

looked up through the vine to the brightening sky, this time vocalising her plea in a soft whisper.

'Why? Why did you have to die? I wish you were here now, Mrs Crawford. I need to talk to you. There's so much I need to ask you.'

Dropping her head sharply, she opened the envelope with a deft flick of her finger and pulled out the photograph.

Charlene stared at the face, radiant and beautiful, looking up at the photographer, her lover, Nektarios. Shifting her focus, she gasped as she recognised the setting. Katherine was sitting at the same table in front of the same bay shimmering in the fresh light of a new day. She looked into Katherine's eyes, seeing the joy sparkling against the steady gleam of deep emotion. Her heart glowed warmly as she marvelled at her beauty and delighted in her enigmatic smile, both coy and sultry. She looked so natural, so real, with her dark hair appearing as though it had remained unbrushed since rising from bed, tossed back and tied up loosely behind.

She slid the photograph back into the envelope and sat up, as an uplifting sense of resolve crystalised in her mind. Pulling out the letter, a thrilling sense of anticipation fizzed through her heart. She inhaled sharply, filling her lungs to quell her rising excitement. Her palms felt uncomfortably moist as she placed the envelope to one side on the table and carefully unfolded the letter. Holding it with the tips of her fingers, she moved the juice, figs and cappuccino away with the other hand before flattening the letter out on the table in front of her. She then reached for the cappuccino, leaned back in the chair and drank deeply. After carefully placing the mug back on the table, she leaned over the letter with her forearms resting on the table. She cast a final, fretful glance up through the vine, before breathing in deeply and exhaling slowly as she started to read.

My dear Nektarios
I must straight away let you know that I have written this letter to be read by you after my death. If this seems

strange and makes you feel sad, I can reassure you, my lovely man, that as I write it I am feeling warm and happy about the thought that you might be reading it on your terrace, and that if you lift your head you will be looking out across that beautiful bay. My favourite view.

Charlene gazed across the bay before turning around to look across the terrace at the quiet house. Her perception of everything about her situation seemed to have sharpened in clarity and heightened in significance. She looked down, a frown forming on her face as she resumed reading.

I am confident you will be reading this because Amanda tells me you are in good health, as you should be for someone so much younger – "my toy boy"!

I have not fared so well I'm afraid. I no longer have the physical strength I had when I was with you. I dream of the blissful experience of swimming in your sea. Oh Nektarios, those were the best days of my life after Amy. My life which has now ended.

Writing that I have died doesn't look right. It seems too absolute, too final. But the thing is that's not how I feel about it now. I actually feel positive about it. After years of angst and uncertainty about whether any form of after life could be possible, I have quite recently reached the clear conviction that we transition to some kind of transcendent state after death. Putting this down on paper feels uncomfortable, however I want to let you know about my certainty that I will be reunited with my beloved Amy and with Mum, Dad and all the other people I have loved and who have gone before me. I know this, Nektarios, because I have experienced things which have helped me reach this conviction and, hoping that you won't think me crazy, I would urge you to be open to metaphysical or transcendental possibilities becoming evident around you. If you are open to them I am sure you will have these experiences. You may already understand what I am saying. I hope so! I certainly felt closer to the essence of life on your magical island and to the unknowable states which go beyond life. So, watch out, Nektarios, I may realise the impossible dream of returning to your wonderful world in some metaphysical form! It's a thought which fills me with excitement, strange as that may seem. I could never return while I was alive, although I yearned, ached to do so. Nektarios, I loved your island so much, but it was falling in love with you which made it impossible for me to return. I can tell you this now with an open heart and without fearing the consequences. I feel an elated sense of liberation to finally communicate so frankly, although I am sorry if the inability to respond causes you frustration. I am sorry, my dear Nektarios, I had to have the last word, didn't I?! Too stubborn to the end! Please forgive me for this and for ending our relationship in accordance with my single-minded sense of how things should be. I don't know how much it will have mattered to you but, if it has upset you in any way, please believe me that I meant well. I was as sure as I could be that I was doing the right thing and later, with hindsight, I became certain that the decisions had been good and, more than that, that things have turned out as perfectly as they possibly could have done.

Of course, falling in love with you and then never being able to see you again or return to your beautiful island was devastating, however I was already broken-hearted and I didn't have the capacity or resilience to handle such strong feelings for another person or to engage in an active relationship. All I could do, deep down all I wanted to do, was focus on Amy and dedicate all of my love to her for the rest of my life. Should I have been stronger, tougher, made more of my life? Perhaps, but this is what I chose to do and this choice became easier to uphold after you and Amanda had your time together. Your miraculous union which brought about the conception of Constantinos, your beloved son.

It is one of my great regrets that I haven't told you that I am so happy your encounter with Amanda created such a wonderful outcome. I wasn't happy at the time or for some considerable time after, in fact I felt deeply hurt, unreasonably so, given that I had not responded to your communications for so many months. A hurt made worse because of my difficult relationship with Amanda. However, in time, I realised that there were good things, possibly very good things, about the way it turned out. I hope I am right to believe that the greatest of these was having a son unintentionally. I remember you telling me that you never wanted to start a family. That you could never make that kind of emotional investment in case you lost someone you love as you lost your mum and dad. Of course I understood that so well, too well, and felt such a powerful sense of love and compassion for you. At that moment you seemed once again to be a six-year-old boy. So lost, so vulnerable, so precious. And so it seemed to me that having a child you wouldn't dare to have had in conventional circumstances, and without risking your heart to a relationship, was a great blessing. Of course I know it must have been very difficult to live so far apart from Constantinos for so much of the time, and I hope this has become easier as he has grown older and able to spend more time with you in Greece.

As I said, I do regret not having found a way to communicate this, but I believed it was best to stay away from your life. I didn't want to be the spectre at the feast. I *couldn't have been an aunt to the son of the unattainable man who I have loved more than any other and, anyway I would not have been able to contribute anything of value to your lives. It has been better, I am sure, for my existence to be a memory to you and a non-event to Constantinos.*

I did in wavering moments harbour the vanity that perhaps I could have been the exception, the woman to capture you, the woman you could have loved, however I knew in truth that I could never have been that woman. Not just because of how you felt but also because destiny had determined that I could never live in love with a man again, and certainly could never have had another child. I did though come to be pleased that, I am connected to your son. I am grateful to Amanda for that although deep sibling rivalry and resentment has prevented me from telling her so far. I will overcome my stupid stubbornness and tell her soon! We are talking again after many years of not communicating. It's far too easy to let great lengths of time elapse without shifting from entrenched positions; however I have reached a stage when I have to do certain things before it's too late. One of these has been sorting out my will. I have made certain bequests, most of them in my usual deliberate way. I don't want my bequest to you to seem pedantically prescriptive, and I do hope it doesn't come across like this and, also, I hope that the need that it fulfils will be a serendipity in your life. Amanda seems to think it might. I do hope it will be. I have to admit it is also driven by the motivation to fulfil a romantic notion I have. Anyway, to get to the point, I would love it if you could accept the bequest and use it to build a new caique so that you can give Thalia a rest. I recall you saying that she should serve you well for another thirty years at most, so I expect that you will need a new caique for you and Constantinos to use into the future. I hope that she can

> be as beautifully built as Thalia, and that you would do me the honour of naming her 'Katherine'. I love the idea of you being borne across your beautiful sea in a boat bearing my name. It would be a symbol of my love for you and I hope you will be happy to make it happen.
>
> Nekatarios, I hope you are happy and healthy when you read this. Amanda has told me that you are well. She also tells me that you are still living on your own. I do hope that this is how you have chosen to live and that you are content with it. Who would have thought it, Nektarios? That we would spend the rest of our lives living on our own, protecting our hearts from further hurts.
>
> Nektarios, I have always had a big place in my heart for you. I cherish that and know that if we had tried to continue with some kind of relationship, it would have been difficult to sustain our love. It would probably have become tarnished or even, God forbid, destroyed. As it is, I have continued to love you as fully and as freshly as I did when I was with you on the island. I hope that you think fondly of me and that I will occupy your thoughts from time to time, until that far off point when we can meet again.
>
> With undying love
> Katherine
> xxxx

Charlene shook her head and closed her eyes, opening them as tears trailed down her cheeks. She sniffed sharply and dabbed her face with the napkin. She had been spellbound, absorbing every word. She was stunned by the immediacy of the writing. It felt as though Mrs Crawford had just spoken to her directly.

After taking in a deep breath, she stared across the bay at the harbour and the buildings facing out to sea between the side streets. The same view that Mrs Crawford would have seen; a long-standing tableau which would now be the backdrop to a scene of increasing activity, as life built up to its lunchtime crescendo.

Shifting her gaze, she watched a yacht emerge from the harbour and head for the open sea. Soon the winds would fill its sails and power its progress under the arcing sun, towards the respite of another harbour.

It seemed to signify the start of life in a new day. A new day after a long night. A day in which she would have to face the reality of returning home. A day which looked and felt so different to the night before. That ethereal night which seemed far removed from reality, like a dream. But it had not been a dream. Everything had happened and all the revelations had now been confirmed by Mrs Crawford. She understood now with a flash of clarity the truth of Mrs Crawford's belief that, despite the tragedy, everything had turned out for the best. The imperfections were hard to reconcile, but she knew with certainty that this was true.

Satisfied to have reached this understanding, her mind cleared and she became aware of a boat being propelled steadily by its outboard motor through the quiet water close to shore. The hypnotic drone of its engine soothed her mind, and she became captivated by the sight of the churning wake as it ploughed through the crystal clear sea.

'That's exactly like the boat Katherine wants me to build.'

The sound of Nektarios's voice broke her reverie and she spun around to look at him.

'Oh, ah... is it? Exactly like... well, it's nice, it's, well, not too big, just right, I should think.'

'Well, that's just the way they are, Charlene. They've been built like that for centuries. *Caiques*, that's what we call them. Fishing boats. Ideal for round here.'

He lowered the tray laden with her breakfast onto the table.

'So you've read the letter?'

Lifting the letter off the table, Charlene nodded affirmatively as she folded it and carefully reinserted it in the envelope.

'Yes, I have and seen the photograph... so beautiful. She was so beautiful.'

'Yes. Utterly beautiful. In all senses.'

'Yes. Yes, of course.'

Softly laying down the envelope in front of her, she stroked it reverentially before looking up at him.

'Nektarios, it was amazing. It was so alive. Like she was speaking. Speaking here and now. It really got to me and it made me really miss her and... and, well, it made me feel very sad, although I can see why it all had to happen like it did. It's not easy but I do get it.'

Nektarios pulled a chair back from the table and sat down.

'Yes, it's so moving, isn't it? It makes you feel such a mixture of emotions and really heightens the sense of loss, but I'm really glad you read it, Charlene, and that you get it. I knew it would help you to understand better than I could explain it; to understand why I found it so powerful. Why it made me feel so sad but at the same time why it provided such a release, although... although there is one thing, one great regret I still have, Charlene, the regret that, although her letter resolves so much and lets me know her feelings for me, she never knew my feelings for her. It was just one summer, one long summer and a holiday relationship, which she may have thought would become inconsequential to me like so many others, but it wasn't like that, not at all. There was something powerful about what we had. Powerful but natural. Passionate yet comfortable. It was a rare feeling and it felt so right that we should have found each other. I never stopped loving her, Charlene, and I always will. I wish I could have told her that. That she has been the only true love in my life. That... that I was worthy of her love.'

With the zeal in his voice fading, he shrugged his shoulders and raised his eyebrows while smiling ruefully. His eyes softened as she leaned forward to give him the letter.

'She did know, Nektarios. She did know how much you loved her.'

Looking puzzled he half opened his mouth as he searched to make sense of Charlene's firm reassurance. He took the letter from her and placed it down in front of him as he launched into a faltering response.

'Did she? But... but are you sure? I mean, did she say anything or, or... well, how can you be so sure?'

Charlene leaned forward, placing her forearms on the table. Laying one hand on top of the other, she looked into his eyes.

'No, she didn't say how much she loved you, not to me anyway, but she would not have written to you, not the way she has, if she didn't know you still loved her, and she would definitely not have asked you to build a boat with her name on it, if she didn't know that you loved her more than any other woman. It's so clear, Nektarios. It's so clear, so you mustn't worry about it. Really.'

Nektarios shifted forward and placed his hand over hers, his face now radiant.

'My god, Charlene, I love that way of looking at it and, well, I guess there's a lot of truth in it. A lot.'

He shook his head and emitted a burst of laughter before continuing in a brighter tone.

'Thank god you came, Charlene. In fact, that must have been one of the reasons Katherine wanted you to come here. Of course it was. To help me make complete sense of it all. Not that my peace of mind is particularly important, but I am grateful to have it. So grateful, so thank you, Charlene. Thank you.'

Charlene slipped her lower hand out and placed it gently on top of his as she replied.

'Nektarios, of course your peace of mind is important. Mrs Crawford, Katherine, somehow managed to find peace of mind.

Her letter shows that. Goodness knows how, after Amy and everything, but she did and she would have wanted you to find it as well, and, well, I'm glad if I've been able to help. Really glad.'

He raised himself up and leaned over to plant a kiss on her forehead.

'You're some woman, Charlene. It's no wonder Katherine wanted to help you make the most of your future. To open up opportunities for you. To live the kind of life she wasn't able to have. You were lucky to find each other, you really were.'

Leaning back in their seats, Charlene's face blanked as she gathered her thoughts.

'I was so lucky to meet her, that's for sure. I knew that anyway, but coming here has made me realise that even more. So lucky. More than I deserve. To have been given so much. Too much really especially when, well, you know... your own son, her nephew...'

'What? Constantinos? No, you mustn't worry about him, Charlene. Katherine looked after him. Not directly but through Amanda. She left money to Amanda for Constantinos to do something to make his own life better so, as it happens, Constantinos was saving up to do a doctorate in a specialised aspect of Hellenic archaeology and he's been able to do that sooner now. That's why he's here. Having a gap before starting it in a couple of months at UCL, you know, in London.'

'Wow! That's amazing. He didn't say anything about it.'

'Well. He may have thought you had more important things to talk about. He doesn't talk much about himself, anyway. He's actually quite reticent... unlike his dad! But, anyhow, that's what he's doing.'

Nektarios transferred Charlene's breakfast from the tray onto the table in front of her, removing the plate cover to reveal two pieces of French toast, soft in the middle, crisp at the edges. Charlene smiled with delight as she felt her appetite sharpen.

'Right. I'll go and wake up Constantinos. I expect there's a lot more you could talk about before he goes to work. Swap notes about the next stage of your lives and how Katherine's bequest has opened up possibilities for you. Funny that, isn't it? How it's happened when we've needed it the most. You two, especially.'

Charlene finished drizzling the French toast with maple syrup before speaking.

'It is weird, isn't it? The timing. Especially for us, Constantinos and me… and Maria. Like you say, how it's happened just when we want our lives to change, or just when they needed to change. Good things are coming out of a very sad thing.'

'Yes and I guess that's exactly what she wanted. She wanted to help all of you to make your lives as positive as possible and, pray God, not to suffer the misfortune she did.'

Charlene cut out a piece of toast while Nektarios stood up, lodging the tray under his arm and lifting up the letter. She looked up at him, her eyes narrowing in anxiety as she spoke with quavering uncertainty.

'Nektarios, you know, when you said "pray God", do you actually believe in God and everything?'

Looking nonplussed, Nektarios replaced the tray and the letter on the table and sat down. He then leaned forward resting his arms on his thighs and clasping his hands, while looking at her sidelong as he replied.

'Well, I don't know what your beliefs are, Charlene, but I have struggled with that question all my life. It's been difficult, very difficult to believe in a god who would take the parents away from a six-year-old boy and who would take a six-year-old girl away from her mother. The parents from an innocent child and the child from a good woman, and a good man, none of whom had done anything wrong. How could I believe in God after that?'

He sat up and stared across the sea in the brief silence before she ventured her response.

'I can see why it would be difficult, Nektarios. I can totally understand. I don't really get it anyway, but it's just that, in her letter, Mrs Crawford said that she believes in life after death. That she was so sure about it, she wasn't scared of dying.'

Nektarios turned round to face her, his voice now clear and fresh.

'It is amazing, isn't it? Amazing that after suffering such great loss in her life, she could be so certain about that. But then how can you deny the possibility that the miracle of this life, this nature, this experience, with so much of it unknowable, might be transcended somehow by a force and an existence which goes beyond our comprehension? I feel that possibility every day. I have never been comfortable with the popular concept of God and religion and all that, but I do feel a connection with something greater, more significant, something transcendental. A connection which feels stronger as I grow older.'

He shifted back in his seat as the cat crept out from under the table, stretched up to hook its claws on the cushion before leaping onto his lap. After laughing in surprise, he smiled fondly and started stroking its back as it settled into a comfortable position.

'Don't I, Kitty Kat? I get a sense of the transcendental every day now that life has slowed down. Eh, Kitty Kat? I do, don't I? Despite everything, despite all the injustices people suffer, I do get a sense that there is something greater than us. Something somehow benign.'

He looked up at Charlene, his eyes shining with a subversive glint.

'I mean, how could I account for an angel coming into my life and delivering truths which I hadn't recognised? Bringing me peace of mind.'

A broad smile stretched across Charlene's face as she glanced away, before hesitantly engaging eye contact.

'Well, I don't know, Nektarios, but I do like the thought that

Mrs Crawford might be reunited with Amy. That's a really nice thought. Really nice.'

Nektarios reached across to take hold of her hands.

'It's a lovely thought, isn't it? And we should believe that they are reunited. We have to believe that they are together now. United at last in their great love. We really do.'

Releasing his hold, he sat upright, grasping the tray with one hand and the letter with the other.

'Come on, Kitty Kat, let's go and wake my sleeping son and leave Charlene in peace to eat her breakfast, before it goes completely cold.'

After dropping softly onto the floor, the cat looked back to watch Nektarios rise to his feet.

'Right. Well, I'll be back shortly. Constantinos will probably have a shower while I get his breakfast ready, but that shouldn't take too long. Can I bring out another cappuccino for you?'

Charlene squinted up at him.

'No thanks, Nektarios. It was delicious but one's enough for me.'

'Me too. One coffee in the morning does me. Right. I'll be back in fifteen minutes but you know where I am if you need me.'

He stopped and turned round to face her as she spoke.

'Nektarios?'

'Yes.'

'It should be the same for you then.'

'The same?'

'Yes, if Mrs Crawford's reunited with Amy, you'll be reunited with your mum and dad.'

Nektarios's face tensed and his eyes sheened with moisture. His voice trembled as he spoke.

'Oh my god, I hope so, Charlene. I have always felt them here with me in this place, my heaven on earth, and I have a feeling that they will always be with me and, yes, perhaps even more so beyond death. I certainly hope so, Charlene. To be with my mama and papa again. That would be perfect.'

'It will happen, Nektarios. We have to believe it will. We have to.'

'You're so right, Charlene. We have to believe it will happen. That we are all reunited with our loved ones in the end. We have to believe it.'

A slow smile pushed the sadness away from his face as he turned around and walked back to the house with the cat trotting by his side.

Charlene exhaled a quivering sigh and blinked the tears out of her eyes as she watched them disappear through the French windows.

Chapter 45

She gripped the handrail and frowned as she tried to rationalise the cause of her unease. She knew that it was not just because she felt insecure standing exposed to the headwind on the shuddering deck of the ferry, as it battered its way through the rolling swell. She knew that it was bound up with leaving the island, that place of enrichment which was now reduced to a black shape diminishing in size beyond the increasing expanse of turbulent sea, as the ferry continued its unerring progress towards the mainland.

She had known that leaving would make her feel bereft, but had not anticipated that she would feel so deeply unsettled. She turned away from the island and looked down into the inky froth of the churning sea.

Raising her head, she looked across the waves glinting dangerously under the emerging stars. It was hard to believe that this was the same sea she had slipped into that morning from the soothing warmth of the rocks.

Her troubling concerns calmed as she closed her eyes, and recalled the delight of pushing off into the turquoise edge of the bay. Reaching Mrs Crawford's place on the rocks had required some awkward scrambling and clambering, but lying naked under the sun had felt sublimely natural, and swimming without a bikini had heightened her sense that she was at one with nature in that secluded haven.

Looking back again at the island, now reduced to a size on the horizon she could blank out with her hand, her sense of agitation returned as she struggled to relate this dark mass, dotted with faint pinpricks of light, to the place which had filled her senses so vividly. She felt a growing fear that the whole experience would become as ephemeral as a dream to be engulfed by the dark clouds of reality at home.

Desperate to assert control over her spiralling sense of panic, she released one hand from the handrail and, after combing her tousled hair back with her fingers, kept her hand pressed on top of her head to stop strands from whipping across her face. She then focused her gaze on the island, concentrating her mind on her experiences over the past two days in a determined attempt to pin them down and recapture their substance and significance.

Her sense of it all seemed to crystallise when, inhaling deeply through her nose, she caught a waft of coconut oil from her upheld arm, the oil Nektarios had given her to use that morning, the same kind Mrs Crawford had used. Holding her arm to her nose she delighted in this fragrant reassurance that it had all been very real and very significant. But how much meaning would it have had for Constantinos… and Nektarios? Would her time with them and everything that was said, slip away from their memories? Would they forget about it all as though it had never happened?

Her shoulders slumped as a dead weight of despair settled heavily in the pit of her stomach. She turned away to look across the deck, leaning back against the railings and allowing her hair to be blown wildly in the wind.

She became consumed by the conviction that Constantinos's passion would fade quickly, and that he would recede from her life. He would not look her up in London and she would be left on her own to sort her life out.

She lurched off disconsolately across the empty deck towards the doors into the lounge. Halfway across, a vibration at the top of her thigh caused her to stop. Spreading her feet apart to brace herself in the buffeting tail-stream, she reached into the pocket of her shorts and withdrew her phone. She held her hair back and blinked rapidly to relieve the rawness of her eyes before focusing on the message. Her heart flared hotly as she read the name of the sender. She scrolled down, her pulse racing as the message appeared.

Hi Charlene. I am watching you from the garden and wishing you were still here. It was amazing to meet you and I look forward to spending more time with you in London. It's so cool the way things are working out. Take care. Love Cxx

She pressed the phone against her chest, a smile lighting her face as she spun round and raced back to the railings.

Looking back at the island, her mind flooded with all the possibilities they had talked about. Visiting his apartment which they had worked out was only a few Tube stops away from her aunt's flat. Letting him show her around the British Museum and the Natural History Museum. Wandering through the parks. Going to the cinema and maybe the theatre. Finding a Greek restaurant.

Her heart brimming with an exhilarating mix of emotion, she rolled around on the railings to face into the deck, before crouching into a squat. Then holding the phone in front of her she typed her reply.

Hi Constantinos. I've been looking back at you! It's so sad to see the island disappear. I wish I wasn't leaving. It was magical. See you soon in London. Say hi to your dad. Love Charlene xx

She lowered the phone and looked across the deck, a slow

smile stretching her mouth as she imagined how things might be between them in London.

His passionate appeal that they should stop before progressing to sexual fulfilment had seemed both impossible and mystifyingly needless at first but then, when their rampant desire had stilled, she began to understand why he had been seized by this conviction. And now, as she reflected on it, his rationale appeared completely clear. It was not about avoiding the recklessness that had brought him into being, it was about the possibility that much more could be gained from taking more time, time to nurture the relationship, time to build an enduring love. When he had asked her if she too sensed an essential connection between them, she had said "yes", but it was only now that she could feel the full truth of this. It was only now that she could fully understand his suggestion that they should be building strong foundations and not burning bridges. Letting their relationship develop in a different environment, in the context of real lives rather than run the risk that it might explode and expire like another holiday romance. They should take it easy, unleash their passion gradually, not do anything which might complicate things or compromise Charlene's freedom to return. He said that was what Nektarios would want, and Mrs Crawford, that they should learn from their regrets.

He was certainly different. Unlike any other man she had come across. The girls would never believe it if she ever let them know. That she had been with the hottest guy on the island without having sex.

She twisted round and, after reaching up to grasp the handrail, pulled herself up onto her feet. Slipping her phone into the pocket of her shorts, she turned to look back at the island, now too small on the horizon to hold her attention. Her focus drifting, she watched an old fishing boat passing in the opposite direction. Apparently unconcerned by the hulking mass of the ferry powering its unstoppable course through the heavy sea, the lone fisherman stood at the stern looking ahead resolutely, his hand firm on the tiller. Propelled stutteringly by its outboard motor, the boat rose and thumped through the rolling swell. Despite appearing vulnerably insignificant, the fisherman seemed calm and free from any doubt that he would be borne safely to his fishing grounds, before returning to harbour at the dawn of a new day.

She thought of Nektarios soon to be left on his own when Constantinos returned to the States before moving to London. Alone without his beloved son. No more fishing trips together on *Thalia*. No more working together in the garden. No more hugs. She was fascinated that they hugged so freely and so lovingly. She had never seen her father hug anyone, and he never engaged in the kind of wide-ranging conversations which Nektarios and Constantinos embarked on so readily.

Her heart ached as she thought of how much they would miss each other. It would not be long though before they were together again and it would be much easier for Constantinos to travel to Greece from London than from Maine. It would be his mother, Amanda, who would see less of him. Parted intermittently from her son and permanently from her sister. For the first time since learning about Amanda, Charlene felt sympathy for her. She could recognise that although her relationship with Constantinos would probably be quite different to Nektarios's, it would be equally loving. Constantinos would always feel drawn to each parent, travelling across the world to be with them.

There was also the pull of the island. His connection with it was not so strong as his father's, but the need to return would be undeniable, irresistible.

With the fishing boat disappearing into the darkness, Charlene turned towards the barely perceptible form of the island. It seemed incomprehensible that somewhere on that smudge in the deepening dusk, Nektarios and Constantinos would be sitting on their terrace ingrained in their history and feeling content. She hoped that they would also be thinking of her. Not sadly, because they would see each other again. She would definitely return. She may not have the same genetic connection but she knew she would feel drawn to return. A need that she would be able to respond to with a freedom denied to Mrs Crawford.

Lowering her gaze to look at the sea now shining under the strengthening starlight, she mused on the tragedy that the one person Nektarios longed for, and desperately wished would return, never did. Worse, she had exiled herself without ever explaining why until writing the letter. She had remained resolute in protecting the memories of that precious summer and dedicating her love to Amy. Nektarios had also dedicated his love to his only child, but how fortunate for him that he could hug Constantinos and talk with him.

Turning to face the bow, she lowered her hand to hold onto the railing as her hair, blowing back from her face, streamed raggedly behind her. She closed her stinging eyes and then opened them abruptly as a surge of emotion flooded through her.

She felt overwhelmed by Mrs Crawford's loss. Not just Amy, but also losing the freedom to love another person, and to be in a place that had begun to restore her appreciation of life. Did it really have to be that way? She could see clearly now that these two strong people, so intelligent and knowing, had become incapable of bringing about more positive outcomes because of fear. Because they were scared of life, scared to love and, more than anything, scared to lose loved ones again. They used their strengths not to overcome their fears, but to accept them, and deal with the hurt. The hurt that had cut Mrs Crawford so deeply.

She looked up at the sky, now star strewn in the deepening night. Before learning about Amy, Mrs Crawford had appeared to be fortunate in everything except her health. So lucky to be rich and living in a beautiful apartment. To be looked after by Maria and to have no apparent stress or worry in her life. She realised now with blinding clarity that she, Charlene, was in a much more fortunate position, a position made more fortunate by Mrs Crawford. She, and Constantinos, were at a starting line in life with so much opportunity in front of them and so few complications. It was as clear to her now as the far-reaching space above.

Elated by this sudden revelation, an overpowering sense of excitement and extreme gratitude gushed up inside her. Her heart racing and her chest heaving, she tightened her grip on the railings, flexing her arm muscles to stop them shaking. Shining tear trails lined each side of her upturned face as she blinked to clear her blurring vision.

She wished she could proclaim her revelation to Mrs Crawford and express her gratitude. To reassure her that she would take the opportunity to make her life better. To work hard. To be bold and determined. To have Constantinos, Nektarios and the island as part of her life going forward. She wanted to be able to communicate her newfound conviction, to share in her excitement, her joy. To go to Marine Heights and tell her all about it. But the apartment was empty now. She was on her own now. It was all down to her.

Her euphoria subsiding, she bowed her head and relaxed her grip before turning around to face across the deck. She lifted her head to look at a young couple seated on the benches at the stern, drinking bottles of beer and making each other laugh. They appeared to be completely happy, filled with the unassailable, carefree confidence of youth.

Out of the corner of her eye, she became aware of the only other two people on deck. A mother and child hand-in-hand making their way towards the doors of the lounge area. The daughter was dragging at the mother's arm, forcing her to break into a reluctant trot. She was giggling, brimming with excitement. The mother's laugh was warm with maternal love. Charlene recognised them instantly.

She reached out her arm and stepped towards them, crying out loudly to be heard above the rumble of the engines behind.

'Mrs Crawford! Stop! It's me… Charlene!'

Turning back to look at Charlene, her face lit up with a warm smile of recognition. She then raised her trailing hand, palm upward in mock exasperation, before being pulled through the door as it closed behind them.

Charlene shook her head sharply to release herself from the shock and ran across the deck to shove the door open and enter the lounge area. She scanned the room with wild-eyed desperation. Not seeing them, she walked quickly over to Cynthia and Suzy sitting at a table alongside the central walkway.

Seeing Charlene approach, Cynthia trilled out a greeting.

'Hi, Char! We were just saying you really missed yourself last night. It was mega, the best night we had, wasn't it, Suze?… Mind you, we missed you… big time. It would have been loads better if you'd been there. Wouldn't it, Suze?'

'Yeah. But for Christ's sake, Cynth, she only scored the hottest guy on the island. Who could blame her? The only one of us to get any action the whole holiday. One minute she's nowhere and then she scores! You're some girl, Char…'

The brightness in their eyes dimmed as Charlene interrupted.

'Did you see a mother and child passing… just now… laughing… they were laughing and holding hands… they must have passed you just a minute ago, not even that… Did you?'

Taken aback by Charlene's urgency, Cynthia exchanged a perplexed glance with Suzy before replying.

'A mother and child? Maybe. Two people passed us a minute ago. We weren't paying attention, were we, Suze, but I think they headed over there… towards the bar. Anyway, why do you want to know?'

Charlene spoke over her shoulder while moving towards the bar.

'They... they dropped something. I need to find them. Won't be long.'

She looked keenly from side to side as she passed through, but could see no sign of them. Quickly establishing that they were not in the queue at the bar, she walked through to the toilet lobby. After finding the disabled toilet empty, she entered the women's toilet where she washed her hands while watching the movements in and out of the cubicles until she was sure that they were not there. Shaking the excess water off her hands she left the toilets and rapidly descended the stairs to the lower deck. The lounge at this level was brighter and, although busier, it did not take long to see that they were not there. Neither were they anywhere to be seen on the small deck behind or on the narrow decks to each side. She lingered at the top of the stairs to the car deck, but convinced herself that the red rope strung across the landing was a barrier that no one would breach.

After slowly climbing the stairs to the upper deck, she stood next to the bar and, shielding herself as much as she could from her friends' sightlines, ranged her gaze carefully across the lounge to ensure she had not missed them earlier. Certain that they were not there, she stepped out of the door to look down the empty side deck before crossing the lobby to walk down the other side to the rear deck now devoid of people.

Returning to the position she had occupied earlier, she rested her hands on the railing and looked out across the sea, now calming as they passed into the lee of the mainland peninsula. Feeling the tension dissipate, she sighed as thoughts formed in her head.

It was them. It was definitely them. It was definitely Mrs C. So beautiful... and young with her lovely little girl... with Amy... it was definitely them.

Flexing her arms, she pushed against the railing and looked up into the night sky. She focused her gaze on a pair of stars shining more strongly than the others.

Her eyes gleamed as she spoke softly but with clear conviction.

'It's OK, Mrs C, isn't it? It's all working out… for everyone… at last.'

Then, feeling a surge of elation burst dizzyingly in her head, she strengthened her grip on the handrail and, hanging her head back to survey the limitless depths of the sky, she laughed with wonder and joy and she smiled and she smiled and she smiled.

"You smile
You smile
And then the spell was cast
Now here we are in heaven
For you are mine at last."